D0862043

Operation Underworld

Paddy Kelly

SHAWN:
ENJOY THE READ!

P. Kelly

Legend Press

Independent Book Publisher

Legend Press Ltd, 3rd Floor, Unicorn House,
221-222 Shoreditch High Street, London E1 6PJ
info@legend-paperbooks.co.uk
www.legendpress.co.uk

Contents © Paddy Kelly 2007

The right of the above author to be identified as the author of
this work has be asserted in accordance with the
Copyright, Designs and Patent Act 1988.

British Library Cataloguing in Publication Data available.

ISBN 978-1-9065581-5-4

*All characters, other than those clearly in the public domain, and
place names, other than those well-established such as towns and
cities, are fictitious and any resemblance is purely coincidental.*

Set in Times

Printed by JF Print Ltd., Sparkford.

Cover designed by Gudrun Jobst
www.yotedesign.com

All rights reserved. No part of this publication may be
reproduced, stored in or introduced into a retrieval system, or
transmitted, in any form, or by any means electronic, mechanical,
photocopying, recording or otherwise, without the prior permission
of the publisher. Any person who commits any unauthorised act in
relation to this publication may be liable to criminal prosecution
and civil claims for damages.

Legend Press

Independent Book Publisher

For

Mary who tried to know me, but never could.
Kate, who I pray knows me
and
Erin, who will never know me but through the words of others.

Introduction

In the spring of 1972, there was little doubt in my mind that there was an organised, well-planned conspiracy between the Joint Chiefs of Staff in the Pentagon and my mother. I wanted to be a frogman, so in the last week of basic training in San Diego I filled out all six requests for billets, (duty stations), and all six were to go and join the little party LBJ was babysitting over in Southeast Asia, after a short stop over at the Underwater Demolition School in Coronado, California. When I opened my orders, they said I was going to the Naval Air Station in Lakehurst, New Jersey to learn how to be a weatherman. Couldn't get much further away from 'The Nam' than Lakehurst, New Jersey, or so I thought until I told the Navy I wasn't going to be a weatherman, I wanted to be a frogman. My next set of orders were to Reykjavik, Iceland.

My suspicions of a conspiracy were confirmed.

There wasn't a hell of a lot to do during the day in Lakehurst, New Jersey, much less in your off-duty time, so after hours I started asking around about the Hindenburg disaster and I was eventually steered towards a guy who was on the airfield the day the famous zeppelin burned. Human nature dictates that most people like to talk about their larger-than-life experiences (which is probably why some of us write books), and over a period of weeks he put me on to several other members of this exclusive club, which is no doubt a hell of a lot more exclusive today, and they were all very congenial about discussing their experiences that day in May of 1937.

The vividness of their descriptions was riveting. Although witnessed thirty-five years prior to our interview, the emotional fervour of their stories was infectious. In particular, the attention to detail, the variation of perspectives and the way they seemed to regress to that exact day and time, was enthralling.

The ability to pass on to another person, not just a story but the emotional intensity and mood of a given event, is fascinating and, although my emotional barometer is sometimes as reliable as a politician giving sworn testimony, I was hooked. Thereafter, anywhere I'd travel, world-wide, for the next thirty-seven years, the immediate priority became seeking out individuals who had witnessed or participated in some significant historical event. What happened around here and who saw it?

It's a strange feeling now that all you have to do is go to: **http://www.youtube.com/watch?v=YDU2MWJwJDc**, and you can actually watch it happen.

One of the more interesting of these stories was first told to me as a child by my mother and reiterated to me years later on Mott Street, in Little Italy.

It was the story of how, in February of 1942, a German U-Boat crept into New York Harbor and sank the world famous French luxury liner, Normandie. Later, I would find there was no U-Boat. There was, however, a great story about a ship that sank and, after extensive investigation, it appears to be a history-changing story that has never been told. The action takes place over a six-week period in early 1942 and should you wish to first appreciate this chain of events and the unique atmosphere of the time, I have offered a brief historical background in the Notes at the end.

I hope you enjoy this story.

'When we are dealing with the Caucasian race, we have methods that will determine loyalty. But when we deal with the Japanese, we are in an entirely different field.'
California State Attorney General, Earl Warren in 1942, commenting on the imprisonment of 150,000 Japanese-American citizens.

'Now they have created a Frank-in-steen monster and the chickens have come home to roost all over the country!'
Presidential candidate Governor George Wallace, 1968, commenting on the opposition.

'Doodle Doodle Dee, Wubba Wubba Wubba.'
MTV's Downtown Julie Brown, commenting on the current state of politics in America.

Chapter One

The New York City waterfront is an interesting place. Anything can happen at almost any time and in late January of 1942, despite its two and a half centuries of violent history, relative peace and calm prevailed, while half a world away free China was lost, the Battle of Britain had been fought, and Hitler was dining in Paris.

The majority of men have always, and will always, allow themselves to be caught up in world events larger than themselves, and hopelessly swim against the tide while praying to their respective gods for a favourable outcome. However, a select few have the wherewithal and foresight to keep their heads and turn such events to their advantage.

One such man was in his sixth year of a fifty year sentence, without parole, convicted on contrived evidence and told he would eventually be deported to a nation whose leader had already issued a death warrant against him.

Clinton State Penitentiary, Dannemora, New York. Groundhog Day, 1942

The weathered, olive complexion of the visitor's face made him look older than his mid-forties. Other than the guard, who now stood sentry against the wall in front of him, he was alone in the under-lit, painted brick room.

Sitting patiently at the far end of the long wooden table, hands on top in full view as the large, baked-enamel sign on the wall dictated, he was kitted out in a dark blue, handmade suit complete with silk tie. He glanced at the stone-faced guard, who stared back with his best tough guy face. After a fifteen minute wait, the rattling of locks on the dark green, steel doors progressively echoed louder and louder throughout the adjoining chambers, until the door leading into the visitors room creaked open, and two more men entered.

The pock-marked-faced prisoner with dark hair and drooping right eyelid was the first to enter and was escorted to a seat on the opposite side of the table by a second, older guard. The visitor reached over the twelve inch high partition which bisected the thick oak top to shake hands with the dungaree-clad man on the opposite side.

"Keep your hands away from the prisoner!" Tough Guy guard yelled. The visitor was unfazed and proceeded with his inquiry in a tone of genuine concern.

"How ya doin', Charlie?"

"Ah . . ." Charlie shrugged. "It's Dannemora, you know. Fuckin' Siberia."

"Ya need anything?" Both men were visibly relaxed.

"Yeah. Get me down state!"

"We're workin' on it, Charlie. Anything else?"

"How's it goin' downtown?" He changed to a near whisper, and immediately both guards drifted closer to the table. The men looked up from their seated positions, and then at each other. With feigned disregard they resumed their conversation, only now in Italian. The guards didn't back away.

"Things ain't lookin' so good. Especially with these two assholes standin' here."

"Ya think maybe they're queer for each other?" Neither of the men laughed at the comment, but the younger of the two guards became visibly annoyed, and started towards Lucky. The elder guard raised an arm to stop him and the men once again resumed their conversation, however this time in an obscure dialect of Sicilian.

"Why? What's goin' on?" The guards drifted back towards the wall as Tough Guy grew increasingly irritated.

"The Camardos are gettin' more independent, we're losin'

more of Jersey. Siegel says if they don't let him send somebody over there to put a hit on Goering and Goebbels, he's gonna do it himself."

"That crazy Jew bastard! Always with the gun! What's the story on working with the Navy people?" A downward glance introduced his reply.

"They nixed it!"

"What? Why? What's our guys in DC say?" Charlie was surprised.

"Too politically risky. They don't want no part of it."

"Shit! Did you remind them . . . ?"

"Yeah."

"I was countin' on that deal ta solidify our operations fer after the war."

"Maybe get you down state while we're at it."

"Maybe." Luciano looked down at the table top. "Maybe they can be persuaded," Charlie suggested. The young guard could stand it no longer. The senior sentry nodded at his younger colleague and both started towards the men.

"Times up! Let's go!" Halfway through the door, Lucky called back over his shoulder.

"Send Albert A. up here next week."

Chapter Two

Free China might have been lost, the Battle of Britain may have been fought, and perhaps Hitler was dining in Paris, but on the Manhattan side of the Big Pond, relative peace and calm prevailed. The February sunrise peacefully crept over Hudson Bay, illuminating the pristine, bluish-green water of New York Harbor. The golden sunlight sent moonbeam-like reflections dancing playfully across the serene river and helped chase the morning chill from the docks.

For the last forty-five minutes, methods of transport of every shape and description arrived, depositing denim clad workers onto the planks of Pier 88 along Luxury Liner Row, just off 49th Street. Few arrived by automobile as parking spaces were all but non-existent and the limited few were reserved for the most senior executives and high ranking naval officers. Besides, cars were for the rich. Instead bicycles, buses, subways, and most often the 'shoe leather express', were the tradesman's common modes of transport. The second Monday of the month saw the slow, but purposeful activity of nearly 5,000 workers about to ease into their daily routine of organised chaos. As 6:30 a.m. approached, the change of shift whistle was about to sound and 2,500 weary bodies would be replaced by 2,500 fresh workers ready to expend their energy into the project at hand.

Despite the fact they all seemed to have the same look about them, this army of welders, fitters and carpenters were not dressed in a cohesive uniform. As the sporadic conversation and occasional joking of the scattered clusters of men became progressively louder, the serenity which signalled the prelude to the daily routine was suddenly shattered by an unscheduled outburst.

Just outside the gate a young couple, the woman cuddling a small wailing bundle, were heard exchanging insults. After a brief stare-off, the man turned his head and noticed the cluster of workers propped against the chain-linked fence observing he and his wife's public displays of affection. Knowing better than to attempt the last word, he terminated the argument and stormed away in the direction of the workforce. Not far behind, a metal lunch pail sailed through the air after him and although these tin alloy containers were never designed as missiles, in the right hands their aerodynamics were appreciable.

Landing on the ground just behind the disillusioned young husband, the pail burst open and spilled its contents onto the asphalt. As he stooped to rescue the only food he would have for the next twelve hours, his co-workers seized the opportunity to offer their support.

"Ain't love grand?" one of them called out in a mock romantic voice and the floodgates opened.

"Hey Doll! Yankee try-outs next week!"

"You must be so proud being married to one of those new, modern women." As if to rescue him from further humiliation, the change of shift whistle blew and the horde of labourers and tradesmen slowly migrated towards the small gate leading to the dock. The narrowness of the gate was not an oversight on the part of the Third Naval District engineers. It was an intentional design to control pedestrian traffic in order to increase security on the strategically critical pier.

As the night shift filed out through an adjoining gate, spilling out onto the sidewalk under the West Side Highway, a glaringly evident look of fatigue on their faces, it was obvious that these men had begun to reach the point where it was no longer the hours or the physical output required of them which caused them to grow older than their years. It was instead the relentlessness of the work. Day after day, night after night, with nothing to break the tedium of the routine. All knew, without being told, that the shipbuilding would go on and on and on until, at some unknown point in time, in the distant future, the war was over. One way or the other.

Shuffling through the gate with an orderly sense of urgency, the off-going shift migrated out onto the streets and beyond. The on-going crew, which had now swelled to over 2,300 members, displayed a diversity not normally seen in times of peace.

Aside from civilians representing all walks of life, there were over 1,100 men in active duty Navy, Coast Guard and Reservist's uniforms.

As a means of proving who they were and foiling potential saboteurs, everyone was required to have some form of ID. The military men carried standard issue armed forces cards with photos and serial numbers. The civilian workers and tradesmen, however, had each been issued a small brass medallion, about the size of a silver dollar, as their means of ID. Stamped into each coin were a series of five numbers as well as the name of the shipping line each worked for. Some held their medallion in their hand and flashed it to the guard as they passed through the gate. Some pinned it to jacket lapels and still others had them attached to baseball caps bearing the logo of their favorite ball club, each member of the labour army attempting to express a measure of individuality in an ocean of sameness.

After about ten minutes, when a couple of hundred men had already passed through the checkpoint, the line suddenly stopped moving. Heads peeked right and left of the line to observe the short, slight man standing in the threshold of the gate, frantically frisking himself in an attempt to locate his medallion. Arms folded across his chest, the stocky Marine corporal stood glaring at the man.

"Hey Fitzy, take your time! Nobody's got nuthin' ta do here!" someone called out from down the line.

"Yeah, no rush. Hitler'll wait." Sporadic laughter added to Fitzy's consternation until, finally, he was able to locate the all-important item and was waved through. With the line once again flowing freely, the seemingly endless stream of work boots paraded past the guard and fanned out across the pier, making their way towards the behemoth-like luxury liner looming in the berth before them.

A large, rectangular wooden sign hung on a pair of thick, square timbers, adjacent to the main gangplank amidships. As an afterthought, a dirty grey tarpaulin had been lashed over the sign, but one end flapped loosely in the breeze revealing the words, New Troopship, and Lafayette. As if to reinforce the contradictory pattern which had thus far characterised the US war effort, high above the sign, prominently embossed across the bow of the ship, was the name, NORMANDIE.

By way of protesting her forced makeover and imposed new identity, the magnificent vessel had stubbornly sulked in harbour for nearly three years while argument after argument ping-ponged off commanders' desks as to what to do with her.

The Generals wanted a new troopship to ferry troops into the European Theatre, while the Admirals reasoned that, after Pearl Harbor, a new carrier fitted the bill.

Her official designation up until now was AP-53 and, despite the fact that politicians of the highest level were involved, no one could possibly guess that the events of the next few hours would result in her remaining in harbour for the rest of her life, after which she would emerge as a symbol of poor judgement and wasted effort.

As each of the men gravitated towards their respective work stations, no one seemed to notice the lone figure who carried no lunch pail, his unscuffed boots, peeking out from long-hemmed, crisp Levi denims, shuffling across the creosote-soaked timbers. He carried a small, grease-stained brown paper bag at his side. The lanky individual walked directly towards the gang plank amidships.

Focused on the sheaf of papers clutched tightly in his fist, the Site Foreman was far too angry to notice the new man as they crossed paths. Making his way to the Site Overseer who stood behind a partially sheltered podium, the irritated foreman stared at the man hunched over his work and was greeted with forced cordiality.

"Morning, boss. How's . . . Holy shit! What now?"

"'What now?' As if you're the only schmuck in the yard that doesn't know! Where are they?"

"You talkin' about the riggin' the fire hose, fake leak in the hull thing?"

"I'm in no mood, Eddie!" thundered the Foreman. "Do you know what this is? It's a report! And guess what's in it? Where are they?"

Eddie inadvertently glanced over his boss's shoulder and turning, the Foreman spotted his two victims. "Never mind!" He anaesthetised the Overseer's agony and re-directed his fury. "*YOU TWO, BUD AND LOU! HERE, NOW!*" The two workers were taken completely off guard and hesitated before slinking over to the gallows.

"I just spent twenty minutes explaining to ten people that we really don't have a leak in the forward hold!" By way of response, the shorter of the two was seized with a sudden urge to scratch his head.

"See this? This is our quarterly safety review which happened to occur exactly the same day you two morons *GAVE UP GOOD JUDGEMENT FOR LENT*!"

"But Boss, Lent ain't til' . . ."

"*STOW IT!*"

"Stowing it, boss."

"Boss, we have no idea what you're talkin' about," the tall worker responded with near sincerity.

"I told you it was a bad idea," prompted the co-accused.

"The Personnel Department says I'm to sack you two jerk-offs! Friday. But I, in my infinite generosity and benevolence, I told them there are no more fitters down the hall. *DON'T MAKE ME CALL 'EM BACK*!"

"Boss, we're sorry. It's just... the freakin' boredom!"

"It's not really so much the boredom as it is the tedium!"

"Just get your shit together, will ya?" he pleaded. "This big grey taxi has ta be ferryin' dog-faces by mid-March and my

Damage Control crew runnin' around playin' sophomoric pranks, disruptin' operations don't exactly help matters. Besides . . ."

"It's all fun 'n' games till somebody gets an eye poked out," Tall Man interjected.

"Then it's a sport." Shorty nodded in affirmation.

"Get the hell outta here! *Assholes!*"

The work on the vessel proceeded until the lunch break, when the loud cacophony normally present gave way to a relaxing silence. To avoid the long journey back down through the labyrinth of the vessel's passageways and onto the pier, everyone more or less sat and began eating where they had been working. The topics of conversation ranged from the usual war news, to the tragic death of Carol Lombard in a plane crash in Las Vegas. Then, shortly after work had resumed, the routine on the 49th Street Pier, as well as the American war effort, was irreversibly altered.

Insidiously, a narrow but widening plume of thick, black smoke slowly crept its way down the port-side passageway leading from the promenade deck. Ominously, the treacherous dark cloud rolled along the deck contained only by the freshly painted bulkheads as small red-orange flames crackled behind it, fighting to gather momentum. A minute later, the plume was a blanket covering the 50 or 60 square feet of the deck.

A welder's helper shuttling tools back and forth for the workers rounded the corner and came out onto the promenade, and a wall of flames exploded out into the open air and over the rail 100 feet over the dock.

To the crew members working on the pier, the trouble was not immediately apparent. However, as the yelling and the chaotic activity on the upper weather decks grew louder, an electrical sensation crackled through the air and was instantly recognised as something drastically out of sync. With animal-like instinct, each man of each crew throughout each successive deck level stopped what he was doing, raised his head and listened. Then, either smelling smoke or sensing the steadily mounting pandemonium, they ran for the exits. In less than ten minutes, the port-side promenade deck was completely engulfed.

The mild breeze which blew that afternoon fed the flames enough oxygen so that by half past two, all the weather decks were involved. To add to the rapidly mounting problems, the freshly applied coat of paint allowed the entire main deck to be consumed only minutes later. The resulting 1,000 degree temperatures were in stark contrast to the 33 degree levels of the ambient air of the harbour. To appalled observers, the involvement of the lower weather decks meant that anyone working above those levels, if they had not yet escaped, was suffering the most horrible death imaginable.

By now several things were occurring simultaneously. A number of men working at pier level began to realise what was happening, and three of them ran for the guard shack, which housed the only land line. As they burst through the door, they discovered that the alert young Marine had already notified the NYPD, the fire department, and was currently in the process of dialling the Harbor Master on his emergency line.

"Did you call for the docs?" one of the men asked in a frantic voice. The big guard held out his index finger while he finished dialling.

"Yeah! The police are going to notify the hospital to prepare a triage team."

Talking into the telephone the Marine continued. "Harbor Master, this is Lance Corporal Deuth, Pier 88, Luxury Row. We've got a code two emergency. Yes sir, yes sir. Already done both of those! Thank you, sir!" As he hung up the phone, the Marine instructed two of the men to return to the ship to help, and one of the men to stand by the main gate to prevent anyone from blocking access by parking in front of it. As they ran back to the ship, one of the men turned the other,

"Hey, Harry!"

"What?"

"What the hell's a triage?"

"I don't know, but they better get a shit load of them out here!"

With Normandie longer than the width of Central Park, the

2,000 foot long dock, plus the additional two to three hundred feet to the main gate, was a distance few of the men had given any thought to until that day. Running from the guard shack towards the ship was not only complicated by the bitter cold, but wading through the crowds of workers moving in the opposite direction while wearing heavy work boots and heavy winter coats made it a triple effort. Tools and gear and canvas fire hoses littered the dock, half of them covered in ice and men tripped and stumbled regularly.

Several workers, noticing that all four gang planks were clogged with fleeing workers, immediately set about erecting ladders against the hull at appropriate hatchways.

Through the unending stream of panic-stricken workers, the Foreman fought his way back up the starboard-side forward gangplank. Halfway to the Quarterdeck he recognised the exhausted face of his chief engineer. Taking the awestruck man by the shoulders, the Foreman looked straight into his eyes.

"Mac, what's our status?"

Gasping between phrases, the out of breath engineer stared through the Foreman as he responded. "Bilge to 'C' level is clear. But if it reaches the POL stores, everything from Jersey City over to Broadway's gonna be a fuckin' airfield!"

"You're sure there's no one else below?"

"Only those two lunatics."

"Which two lunatics?"

"How many lunatics you got working Damage Control?"

As the Foreman continued to struggle his way through the fleeing workers deeper into the ship, it occurred to him how easily a man could vanish into one of the thousands of human-sized pigeon holes the partially stripped down ship had become. Fighting through the passageways below decks, he spotted an OBA case on the port bulkhead. The Oxygen Breathing Apparatus would buy him at least fifteen minutes of breathable air while he searched for his two derelict ship fitters. Grasping at the latch handle, he stared in dismay as the case opened and in lieu of the life-saving device a large, pink inventory tag appeared.

"Fucking bean counters!"

After an eternity of choking through the ever thickening grey smoke, he reached the Paints, Oils and Lubricants cages and his attention was immediately diverted as he detected singing in the far corner of the large storage area.

Through a shroud of grey, he saw the two men he had chewed out earlier that morning, both with sledge hammers, alternately beating a four inch water spigot in unison to the *Anvil Chorus*. Over the roar of the encroaching flames, he cupped his hands around his mouth and yelled, "What the hell are you two assholes doin' here?!"

"Tryin' to rig a leak!" Both continued to pound away at the thick brass spigot. As if on cue, the fixture burst and the resulting torrent of water dowsed the flames just as they were about to reach the main POL stores. Breaking into a celebratory dance, both men dowsed themselves in the water.

"Never mind that shit! Get the hell outta here!" Smiling angrily and following the men out of the compartment, the Foreman muttered to himself. "Assholes!"

Back on the dock area, a few of the men who had initially fled were now returning to lend a hand and began to set up an area away from the ship to gather the casualties for the docs to assess.

One of the men was the man who earlier had asked what a triage was.

✦

Staring through the oversized binoculars, the young boy felt more like a man then he had ever done sitting in a classroom. Jimmy had quit school two months ago when the war broke out and, through some friends who were connected, got a job in the Harbor Master's shack. Next year, when he turned seventeen, he would sign up.

Although the building which housed the Harbor Master and his team was still referred to by its eighteenth century name, it was anything but a shack.

The red-enamelled, two storey, clapboard structure, which sat on what was essentially two sets of steel stilts, overlooked most of the harbour from its strategic position on the tip of Pier 62 just off West 23rd Street, and was equipped with the latest in modern advances. High definition FM radio, lamp-lit map boards and a dedicated direct telephone line to the fire tug outposts along Manhattan Island.

Due to the immensity of the New York Harbor, it was impossible to view the entire area at one time from any land or sea position, so Jimmy was unsure exactly where the smoke plume he now observed originated. In this instance, protocol dictated an emergency procedure be enacted whereby the area of the potential trouble was approximated, and a grid mapped out. Then all hands would man the radio and phone lines to pinpoint the location of the problem and notify the nearest tug team.

"Hey, Mr. Rorro. Mr. Rorro, sir. I think I see something way out there," Jimmy said, squinting through the ship's binoculars.

"You're supposed to see something way out there, Jimmy. That's what binos are for." The old HM was annoyed but tolerated his work being interrupted by the young boy's enthusiasm.

"Sir, can you have a look at this, please?"

"Son, I have got to get these tug escort reports done today! So stop buggin' me!" The old man remained at the desk and continued to write.

"Sir, it looks like something. A fire maybe." The old man's head came up from the paperwork. "Out near the tunnels."

The HM walked over and took the glasses from the boy. Even before he raised them, he knew. "That's a fire alright! Get on the grid! I'll notify the tugs!"

Just as he reached for the emergency line, it rang.

"Hello! HM shack, who is this?" It was Lance Corporal Deuth. "Yes, corporal! Have you notified the fire and police departments? Alright then, keep the main gate clear of traffic and continue to man your station. Report to the fire chief when he arrives. The tugs are on their way. Corporal Deuth, good job!"

"John! I got Harbor Side on the line. How many units?" The

21

Assistant HM spoke hurriedly but remained cognisant of his professionalism.

"Dispatch unit 52 Able and tell him to report as soon as he's in sight of the fire, then tell South Park Baker to standby and get South Park Able up there for back-up. Tell 'em to step on it. Those creosote-soaked piers get involved, there's gonna be one helluva lot of freight landin' in Jersey!"

"Why not dispatch 52 Baker with them?" Rorro didn't miss a beat.

"If the wind shifts north, we'll need somebody up there to intercept. Ronnie, get on Channel Nine, notify all vessels as of . . . 14:21 hours, unless associated with the fire, we are on radio blackout until further notice. Frank, get busy! Divert all traffic south of the G.W."

"I'm on it!" Frank shot back.

The HM notified the harbour-side fire brigade, and then proceeded to broadcast on the emergency band, Channel Nine, to divert all traffic away from the area. For a full twenty minutes the old HM showed why he was in charge, running back and forth across the shack directing personnel and issuing orders.

Through all the activity, Jimmy dutifully sat at the small corner table, struggling to plot the grid as he'd been trained. As the situation in the shack gradually came under control, the HM noticed the youngster still tucked away at the desk. Walking over to him, the man placed a hand on the boy's shoulder. Jimmy continued to plot.

"Hey, Jimmy," he said quietly.

Without looking up, Jimmy responded. "I've almost got it, sir. Just one more minute!"

"You can stop now. We're there. It's eighty-eight." Masked in a look of despair, the youngster turned towards the leathery-faced man. Rorro turned to walk away, then hesitated.

"Hey Jimmy, nice job. You done good. You'll get credit in my official report for spotting the fire." A dejected Jimmy slumped in his chair. Rorro crossed the room and without turning back added, "You may have saved a few lives today."

Jimmy hoped his parents would understand when he told them he wouldn't be joining the Navy. He was going to sign on to become a Harbor Master.

Back at the Normandie, events were mushrooming out of control as the number of men streaming out of the flaming vessel and onto the narrow pier steadily swelled. Realising that the entire dock may be engulfed, they began moving back towards the gate area carrying as many of the injured as possible with them, where they were met head-on by fire-fighters, dragging hoses, hard-pressed to reach the entire length of the berth.

As one of the men rushed back to the blazing vessel, for what was his third time in half an hour, he was forced to avert his eyes in horror. A body, its arms and legs flailing, fell through the hot air, over 100 feet from the main deck of the ship, and violently slammed into the hard wooden timbers of the pier.

Forty-five minutes into the blaze, the burning had progressed far enough that the fire was declared out of control. Smoke and flames were visible across the Hudson River in New Jersey, and several fire units from that state had been mistakenly alerted.

Ripping spectacular wakes through the river as they sped northward, a dozen fire tugs were under full throttle, their sirens heard all across the West Side.

They arrived only seconds behind the smaller, swifter police boats, and immediately entered into their life-saving ballet from the outboard side of the vessel. In an effort to coax the flames back into the ship, the small boats furiously pumped icy sea water onto Normandie. The resulting black plumes of smoke floated into the grey of the afternoon Manhattan sky and were carried by the winter breeze out over the island, meandering through the tall buildings. The upper levels of most of the garment district skyscrapers were obscured and traffic was at a standstill as the smoke filtered down and settled at street level.

The cloud had not quite reached the office of the city's highest official as of yet, however City Hall parking lot was full and the mayor's office was crammed with reporters.

Fiorello LaGuardia sat at his desk, his large form nearly invisible from the neck down for the forest of microphones fanned out in front of him, his flabby chin wagging. The big man spoke to his constituency in one of his regular radio broadcasts. Just as he was building up steam, telling everyone how well he and his party had done so far this political season, not to mention how many of his campaign promises he had fulfilled, an aide entered from the sidelines and handed him a message. LaGuardia read it and asked if it had been confirmed. When the aide nodded, the politician stood and, with an alarmed look on his face, apologised to the press and excused himself.

Ten minutes later, with a police escort screaming around them LaGuardia and two men selected from his army of aides were in their official limo plotting strategy.

"I want an update on traffic problems ASAP. And prep for additional manpower in police, fire and road works," The Mayor ordered to the senior of the two aides.

"It's taken care of, sir." There was a brief pause and the two aides exchanged glances.

"Your Honor, there's something more important we need to consider."

LaGuardia looked back from the window.

"Depending on how this thing happened – sabotage, accident – we could get hurt."

"How bad?"

"Depends on the death toll. With an event this size, a few bodies would be acceptable . . . " the junior aide chimed in.

"Depending on who they are."

"Of course. But dozens, god forbid, *hundreds* . . . "

"Do we know who the scene commander is?" LaGuardia inquired.

"Chief Patrick J. Walsh"

"Democrat or republican?" The junior man began flipping through a notepad.

"Irish. Hell's Kitchen."

Arriving at the scene, LaGuardia had to struggle through the crowd. He was escorted past the medical triage center on the south side of the pier which had been established by medical support personnel, and it was at that moment that the gravity of the situation hit home.

Over the encroaching dusk, a 1,000 foot wide fog of smoke rose over the ship, painting half the grey sky black, then leaned south and floated towards the Atlantic. In gut-wrenching contrast to the misleading serenity above Luxury Liner Row, over a dozen fire tugs danced around the vacant adjoining slip, deciding how to keep the largest ship in the world from listing any further and becoming swamped. Suddenly, the chaotic cacophony of the casualties flooding in at an unmanageable rate, snapped him back to reality as he watched the woefully outnumbered doctors and nurses, hard-pressed in their heroic efforts to keep up.

The mayor dispatched an aide to seek out the fire chief, and fifteen minutes later Chief Walsh, his face smeared in soot, was briefing LaGuardia as to the current situation. The chief spoke in a controlled, professional tone, but was compelled to raise his voice above the clamber of the rescue efforts.

"Your Honor, at this point we have every fire tug on the West Side involved, as well as all of the shore-based apparatus we can effectively manoeuvre on this narrow pier."

"Chief, why is she leaning so far to the side?"

"From all the water we've pumped into her, sir. There's no way for it to drain out," he explained above the din.

"What happens if she flips over?"

"In that event, Mayor, we have a crew standing by to cut the mooring lines. But we've secured permission from Admiral Andrews to cut holes in her hull to drain the water and try and balance her out."

"Why not just stop pumping all that water into her? Or at least slow it down a little?" The mayor's inexperience in disaster management was obvious.

"Mayor, we have reports of over two hundred men still trapped below decks. If those men were able to secure themselves in the various compartments and we stop pumping water onto the flames… sir, they're as good as dead." LaGuardia folded his arms and looked down. If two hundred lives were lost in this tragedy, and the decision for the action causing those deaths could be traced to him in any way…

"I understand, Chief. How long before it's under control?"

"Your Honor, we may not be able to get her under control."

As the Chief excused himself, the mayor realised he had no choice but to accept the senior fire-fighter's expert opinion.

As night fell, the ever darkening backdrop highlighted the spectacular display of top-side flames and dancing shadows. Glancing up at the burning hulk, the mayor's thoughts turned to the potential affects on his political career now that German saboteurs had brought the war to America.

Suddenly, a small swarm of reporters appeared around him, and began the traditional feeding frenzy of questions. Nearly surrounded, LaGuardia held his hand up, messiah-like, and began to speak. The press listened.

"Gentlemen! I've just finished speaking with Fire Chief Walsh. He assures me the blaze is under control and that the Normandie can be salvaged. There'll be a press conference in the morning. No more questions. Thank you."

Swiftly walking away from the mob, amidst a barrage of questions, LaGuardia nodded to his junior aide. The well-groomed young man stepped between the press sharks and their intended chum and, paying particular attention to detail, began to speak at length about nothing, and then pretended to answer questions as the politician vanished through the gate and into his limo.

Now, with the fire nearly extinguished, and very little available light remaining, not much else could be done for Normandie that day. Walsh's men had cut the mooring lines as well as making several holes in her hull, but it didn't help. Sometime during the night, the eloquent lady nearly twice the size of Titanic who had twice held the trans-Atlantic record, gently rolled over and came to rest in her berth at 90 degrees port.

✦

The battleship grey and pumpkin orange, ice-encrusted hull glimmered in the morning sunlight, and it was impossible to resist the visual images it projected. Only a couple of hundred yards across the river, on the Jersey shore, some high school kids had gathered on the rail road tracks which ran parallel to the river. They stood and watched a lone fireboat continue to coat the sleeping beauty with sea water.

"Jeez-o-Pete-o-man! Look how big them propellers are!" It was the younger of the three boys who spoke first.

"They ain't propellers, dummy! They're called screws!"

"Says who, know-it-all?"

"Says my brother!"

"Aw, lay off, Jerry! Just 'cause your brother's in the Navy, that don't make you in the Navy!"

"Yeah? Well, it will next year! Whatta you civilians know, anyways?" He waved a hand in disgust and, the lesson in marine engineering concluded, the three boys moved on to more mundane things such as class work and teachers.

✦

The noise and confusion of the previous day on the 49th Street pier had subsided during the night. However, early next morning it was resurrected into an organised rhythm of work. The long, tedious task of clean-up had commenced.

A small wooden building sat on the north-east end of the dock. Originally built in the 1920s as a ticket office, it had only last month been transformed into a supervisor's office for management of the Normandie refit project. This Tuesday morning, however, the tiny structure was once again transformed into something it had not been intended for, a press room.

The single sheet of paper taped to the front door, the only door, was hardly discernable through the winter dark and read, *Press Conference 0700 hours*. The interior had been made into a makeshift facility by shifting the chairs around, classroom style, on either side of the room. At the front stood a small podium, behind which was a large blackboard. The board bore an outline, in chalk, of the Normandie in profile. In one corner of the board, someone had scribbled a laundry list of statistics down the right-hand side; *83,000 tons, 1,029 ft long*, etc.

The throng of reporters, far outnumbering the amount of available seats, were dressed in heavy winter clothing, sipping coffee from blue and white paper cups and trying to keep warm in the unheated shack. As they spoke, their breath formed puffs of steam in the air, adding to the atmosphere of drama which hung in the room.

They were verbally bombarding a junior Naval officer trapped between the podium and the blackboard. With his greatcoat open and his tie undone, the beleaguered Lieutenant, Junior Grade heroically fought off the questions, but was hampered by his inability to control the crowd.

He was sent in from the Public Relations office to buy time for the Admiral who was now twenty minutes late. Their press deadline approaching, the reporters wanted a statement, and they wanted it now. Particularly about certain rumours no one would comment on.

"Come on, Lieutenant! Give us a break! What's the dope on this sabotage thing? Who actually spotted the submarine?"

"Hey, L.T.! We heard two hundred guys were burned alive below decks! When can we get pictures of the bodies?" It was the representative of the *Enquirer*.

"Now that she's sunk, do we got a Pearl Harbor East?" In exasperation, the officer held up a hand, but to no avail.

"Sir, could this be a co-ordinated plan by the Germans to sink ships up and down the Eastern Seaboard?"

From behind the mob, the sound of the door closing was heard and a voice rang out. "Where do you aspiring Walter Winchells get these questions?"

Everyone quietened down and turned to see who had entered. A visible expression of relief came over the Junior Grade's face. The Admiral, flanked by two officers, strode up the aisle while removing his overcoat.

As he was replaced from behind the podium by the Admiral, the JG sat down, and became aware of the state of his uniform. The other two officers stood off to one side, the JG began to collect himself and the Admiral waited until all of the pressmen were completely silent. He didn't have to wait long. Like a fourth grade class about to be given crucial answers to their next exam, they poised, pens and pads in hands.

"Now why the hell couldn't I do that?" the young Lieutenant whispered to one of the officers on his flank.

"Because you're not a god-damned admiral."

"Gentlemen, I am Rear Admiral Adolphos Andrews, Commandant of the Third Naval District. Apologies for being late. Let me start by asking you to hold your questions until I finish my statement.

"First, in response to the rumour that two hundred men were trapped below decks, everyone got out. Sorry, Dave." The Admiral looked at the reporter from the *Enquirer* and the rest of the room broke into a ripple of laughter which quickly subsided.

"There is a casualty list which will be released to you pending notification of next of kin. I can tell you, however, that at this time we have seventy-two hospitalised, ninety-three treated on the scene and one known dead." The Admiral knew what they wanted to hear. He made the decision to skip the rest of the details of the prepared briefing, and get to the point.

"About the sabotage rumour. It was a fire. An accidental fire. Nothing more. There was no U-Boat. There were no spies in the yard. Just an accidental fire."

"Sir?" One of the pressmen ignored the request to hold questions. "How can you definitely rule out sabotage when there's been no investigation?"

"Because we know where and how the fire started," the Admiral replied, careful not to reveal his annoyance.

"But sir . . . " the reporter pushed, knowing he had the support of the entire press corps present. "It's not even been eighteen hours! She's still smouldering out there, fer cryin' out loud!"

Andrews realised he had to be more assertive.

"Gentlemen! From the best information I have available at this time, the fire started on the port-side promenade deck. A spark from an acetylene torch ignited a life jacket. Exactly like this one." Holding up an orange, thick-collared Mae West, he produced a knife from his hip pocket and sliced deeply into the vest.

"This material . . ." he explained to his audience, reaching into the hole and producing a handful of dark, straw-like substance, ". . . is Kapok. Very good flotation properties, but highly flammable. One of the welders got careless. A spark from his torch set off a pile of Mae Wests, and it got out of control." Andrews hoped that by using a more familiar lexicon, he might get through to them more effectively.

"Sir, we understand there's gonna be a DA's investigation. If it's a clear-cut accident, why are the cops in on it?"

"Just covering all the bases, Phil. We don't want anything coming back on us later. Know what I mean?"

"CIA, hey sir?" There was another bout of sporadic laughter, but Andrews wasn't off the hook yet.

"Sir, can you honestly tell us that with thousands of people milling in and out of here all day long, a saboteur couldn't sneak in and start a fire?"

"I'm not telling you that couldn't happen. However, under the circumstances I'm telling you that it would have been impossible due to our unbreachable security."

Maintaining his professional attitude was becoming more difficult; however, he sought to get the briefing back on track and asked if there were any other topics they would like to discuss.

"Sir, can she be salvaged?"

"We are confident that the AP-53 can be salvaged. However, that's an engineering question, and I'm a ship driver." Nodding to one of the other officers, he continued as the officer stood up. "Lieutenant Commander Scott is Chief of Naval Repairs for the Third Naval District. He'll field all of your questions concerning the salvage operation. And then wow you with his technical knowledge," Andrews explained. "I have to leave. However, when the engineer is finished, he'll give you back to our PR man. Be gentle with him, fellas, it's his first time. Thank you." The Admiral stepped down and took his coat, while the Lieutenant Commander stepped up and prepared to speak.

The JG, still in his seat, buried his face in his hands and shook his head.

Outside in the street the Admiral's Adjutant did his job. In the Admiral's interest, he asked the unthinkable.

"Sir, what if a subsequent investigation reveals the possibility of enemy agents? Are we prepared for that?"

Andrews donned his gloves as he gazed out at the hazy sunrise colourfully tinting the vast harbour.

"Gene, do you remember all the anti-war sentiment before Pearl?" Andrews spoke in a low, but firm tone.

"Yes, sir."

"A good part of that argument was because a helluva lot of people in this country were sick of war, but thought we were invulnerable. Nobody could touch us, nobody *would* touch us! Nobody would touch America! So let the Europeans fight their own war, we're safe way over here. And then came Pearl. All of a sudden, the US of A is not only in the war, we're in it without a Pacific fleet. Now, how do you suppose the general population of this country would react if they knew that we were losing upwards of fifty ships a month in the Atlantic, let alone that there might be enemy agents in New York City?"

Disarmed, the Adjutant stared out across the harbor.

"With our delusions of invulnerability gone, Gene, all we got left right now to hold the people together . . . is patriotism."

Chapter Three

Pan Am flight No. 47 from Tampa was about twenty minutes outside New York. The trip had taken nearly seven hours and the suits in the corporate office would be very pleased. There were no empty seats on the maiden flight of the new wider body DC-3 and the 257% desired profit margin would be achieved.

With two seats on either side of the aisle, it was the first sleeper transport, and boasted an in-flight bar service as well as in-flight meals, which was something no other airline offered. No more lugging picnic baskets on the flight with you.

Mrs Kaminski was grateful for the new state of the art, double-paned, safety glass windows Pan Am had installed specifically for the enhancement of her travel pleasure, and as the slender, dark-haired beauty sat gazing out her window, mesmerised by the heavenly scenery, her excitement mounted when the New York skyline came into view. In her excitement, she did exactly what the man sitting next to her hoped she wouldn't do. She struck up a conversation. As she spoke, she continued to marvel at how a single, dark, low cloud which seemed to emanate from the waterfront, hovered over lower Manhattan.

"I yust love to fly! Don jew?" The young women spoke with a heavy Cuban accent, but was very proud of her command of the English language.

"Excuse me?" came the terse response. Her soft, perfectly tanned facial skin beamed with a broad smile. This time the young woman spoke slowly and distinctly.

"I say, I-yust-love-to-fly! Don-jew?"

"Ah, yeah. Can't think of nuthin' else I'd rather be doin', lady," the man dressed in the brown leather bomber jacket and baseball cap answered, facing straight forward, hardly acknowledging her presence.

"Dew-jew-no-speak-inglesh?"

"Yeah, yeah lady, I speak English. Don jew?" he replied sarcastically. The aircraft jolted for a second time with turbulence as it entered the warm airspace over the city. The stranger clung more tightly to his seat, and tried not to look scared.

"Oh, I see! Jew have afraid! Dat's okay, jew have afraid!" The young woman sat casually, seatbelt undone and legs crossed over. She made no attempt to ignore his white knuckles, welded to the armrests of his seat.

"I'm not afraid!" The man became conscious of his loud speech and lowered his tone. "I just don't like the air bumps!" he exclaimed as he slowly released his death grip on the seat handles.

"Air bimps?"

"Jess! De air bimps!" he replied with increased sarcasm, no longer making any attempt to conceal his irritation at the women's intrusion on his misery.

"Oh! Jew meen disturbulance!"

"What?"

"Disturbulance!" The women turned her body to face him and began to demonstrate with broad, sweeping gesticulations. "Iz when atmoosferic disturbulance comes from cold air mass and warm air mass crash together and make unstable, dense air mass. So jew have disturbulance! No air bimp!"

He stared, open-mouthed. "Who the hell are you lady, Charles A. Lindbergh?"

"No! Jew silly boy! Lindbergh, he a man! I Martina, Martina Kaminski. Are jew in dee Army?"

After a brief hesitation, the man relented. "Doc. Doc McKeowen." He gave a cursory nod. "No. 4-F, perforated ear drum. Not supposed to fly."

"Oh! Jew are a Doktor? How nice?" Her sweet, coy voice dripped through her broad smile and all over the seats and she slowly snuggled up to him. Doc moved over in his seat to maintain the distance.

"No lady, I'm not a Doctor. I'm a private investigator."

She pulled back from him with a noticeable change in attitude. "Jew a cop! Jew dun look like no cop!" she said suspiciously.

"I'm not a cop. I'm a PI." She looked at him quizzically. "Private Investigator." He caught sight of her oversized handbag on the floor. "You know, like when a guy thinks maybe his wife is cheating on him, say with a younger guy or something." He slid a little closer and propped himself up on the arm rest. "Like maybe she came back from a vacation, in Havana, say, and she's very pretty, and her husband is a little older, and they haven't been married that long." He leaned into her. "And he's worried that she might go puttin' the make on every guy she meets because maybe, just maybe she married this guy to get her citizenship. You know, stuff like that."

The young girl was now sitting with both legs pulled up to her chest, feet on the seat, a look of extreme worry on her face. Doc noticed her concern had turned to fear, and felt a short tinge of remorse. He smiled and sat back to allay her fears.

"Look, lady, I'm sorry. Really, I didn't mean anything by it." She didn't respond, but continued to glare at Doc.

"Honest! Lady, I'm sorry."

"How jew know dees dings?! My husband, he send jew?"

"Look, Mrs Kaminski . . . Martina. Your first name is Hispanic, I can see your passport in your handbag, it's American." Doc pointed to the small black carry-on, poking out from under the seat in front of Martina. She allowed her eyes to dart briefly to her bag and then back again. "If you were coming from Florida, you wouldn't need your passport. And your wedding ring is brand new. Plus, I doubt I would find too many Kaminskis in the Havana phone book."

The women began to relax a little. Doc wanted to stay her fears a little more.

"How did you know about that warm air mass and cold air mass stuff? That's pretty interesting."

Martina was still trying to make up her mind who he was, and so remained in the foetal position on her seat. Without turning away from Doc, she reached into the seat back in front of her and removed a trifold brochure. Like a dagger from a scabbard, she pulled it and thrust it at Doc.

"I read about the disturbulance in dees!" Taking it from her, Doc glanced at the latest issue of *Captain Carl's Tips*, an informational brochure published by the airline.

"They many good dings in dare. Maybe someday jew read. Den jew don be so scared and den jew don drink so much," Mrs Kaminski explained to her involuntary travel partner, nodding at the seven or eight empty drink glasses stuffed in the seat back, in front of McKeowen.

"Tell ya what, lady, my mother dies, you got the job!" As he spoke, he jammed the pamphlet back into the seat packet.

She was slapped by his irritation but didn't want any more tension between them. "I sorry! I Dun mean to criticalise jew! My father? He used to drink also. All dee time!"

Doc smiled and nodded, reminiscing about happier times when the woman was being quietly entertained by the clouds.

"All dee time, he drink, drink, drink, drink, drink." She was again very animated in her behaviour. Doc wished he had a drink.

"Are you anything like your mother?"

"Why jes! Sometimes people dink dat we are seesters. Why do jew ask?"

"Just wonderin' why your father drank." Doc was back on form.

"I dunnno . . ." Martina seriously contemplated the question.

After the plane taxied to the appropriate tarmac, McKeowen reached under his seat and produced a small, navy blue gym bag. The initials *YMCA* were stencilled across one side of it and it was easy to see there wasn't much in it.

Doc always travelled light for two reasons. One, he hated carting luggage around, and two, he didn't own any. He didn't need it. The fact was that he had never been out of New York State before. Except to New Jersey, and what the hell, that didn't really count now, did it?

Standing around the base of the roll-up stairs, out on the tarmac, were several skycaps in their mandatory dark blue uniforms. The sky blue Pan Am logo on the breast pocket and brim of the cap showed they had paid their mandatory fees to work for free. These men, all of them black, made their livings solely on tips. One of them approached Doc with an oversized metal cart, and asked if he needed a grip. Doc looked at the enormity of the cart, then to his diminutive bag, shrugged and said, "Why not?"

Doc passed him the bag which he placed on the cart, tilted it back and they headed across the tarmac towards the terminal.

"Mr McKeowen! Mr McKeown!" Doc turned to see Mrs Kaminski running after him, her black, slide-on heels clopping on the asphalt while struggling to keep her overstuffed black bag on her shoulder.

"Go on. I'll catch up," Doc instructed the cap. "Mrs Kaminski. What a pleasure to see you again."

She came alongside and dropped anchor, then removed her oversized sunglasses before she spoke. "How do jew know my husbent he's older?"

Doc sighed. "I figure there's plenty of young guys in Cuba, but no money, so you come here where there's money. But not many guys your age have that much money. If they do, they're probably connected, in which case you probably wouldn't be screwing around."

She didn't know whether to be pissed off, indignant or just clop away.

"Anyding else, whise guy?"

"Yeah. If my wife had a body like that she wouldn't have time to go to Cuba."

Her anger began to leak away. "Are all jew Irish so smart?"

"I'm not Irish. I'm Scottish."

Outside the terminal, taxis snaked in a never-ending line along the curbside. A black Checkered pulled up immediately and the operator hopped out. While the driver went around to open the trunk for his passenger's luggage, Doc tipped the cap.

"What happen, Mac? Bastards lose your luggage?" asked the cabby, eyeing the cart.

"Yeah, second time this month," Doc answered, as he threw the gym bag into the trunk and got into the cab.

"Where to?"

"1929 Christopher Street. Don't wake me till we get there, and don't go by way of Brooklyn Bridge," Doc instructed.

Nearly an hour later, the taxi pulled up outside *Harry's Front Page News*. Doc got out and, with the last of the bills and change in his pocket, paid the driver.

Despite the early hour of half past five, the dark of winter had set in. Traffic was flowing freely now in The Village, and the evening chill could no longer be ignored.

Harry's Front Page, which everyone called The News Stand, occupied the entire ground level of 1929 Christopher Street. The corner entrance and small display window were capped by a hand-lettered, green enamel sign which hadn't seen a fresh coat of paint since Lindy had seen Paris.

Packed with black wire, twirly racks, stacked with postcards that never sold, (come to think of it, nothing ever really sold except newspapers and an occasional stale candy bar), you'd be hard pressed to squeeze four people in there at any one time. That included Harry.

Harry's claim to fame was the time Mel Blanc came into his candy store and said it was so small you had to go outside to change your mind. Harry was a Bugs Bunny fan forever after.

Harry's life had long ago settled into sitting on a high-backed stool all day, framed by racks of candy bars and potato chips, and he was rarely seen to venture out from behind the counter. An unseen radio constantly played in the background and he read all day long. To his credit, he read only the classics. Captain Marvel, The Shadow and The Phantom. These were by far the best, for it was common sense that they were the most realistic. Every time Superman or Batman got in a fix, they would come up with some wild gizmo they just happened to have nearby or hanging on a belt, and escape certain death. Ridiculous. Who ever heard of yellow kryptonite, anyway?

Harry had lost a leg in the last war, and in between warm sodas and cold coffees, the old man would give Doc tips on horse-racing, despite the fact Doc had never been to the track in his life.

Doc respected Harry because he was one of those old people who could tell you what he had for breakfast on any given day, six months ago, and he seldom ate the same thing every day. This made Harry the perfect lobby watch-dog.

The ground floor of the five storey building was never intended as any sort of a shop, so when the owners remodelled it, just before World War I, access to the upper floors had to be rerouted. The ground floor conversion was an attempt to keep up with the flood of businesses which swept the Greenwich Village neighborhoods just before the war broke out. Doc walked in through the glass door which opened into Harry's.

"Doc! Where the hell you been for a week?"

"Vacation, Harry. I figure I earned it. Anybody hangin' around I should know about?"

"Not a bad guy in sight, Doc."

"Gimme a late edition, will ya."

"Didja hear the news? The Krauts sent a sub into the harbour! Sunk some big boat!"

"You sober?"

"Honest 'ta Christ, Doc! They did!"

Doc took the half-folded newspaper and tucked it under his arm while he headed for the door to the upstairs offices.

"Thanks, Harry. See ya later."

"I'm tellin' ya, Doc, this war ain't like the last one. We could lose!"

"We ain't gonna lose, Harry. We're the good guys. Hell, Lamont Cranston lives here!" Doc called over his shoulder, passing through the single door to Harry's left.

The sixty-year-old structure was immaculately cleaned and maintained but the elevator seemed perpetually out of order, so visitors and residents had to climb the ornate metal staircase to reach their destinations.

At the third floor, Doc turned left down the hall towards his office. He took the paper from under his arm and, just as he began to open it, a voice called out.

"Hey, Doc!" The voice startled him, making him jump, but as he looked to the right of the corridor, a smile slowly crept over his face.

"Hey, Redbone!" Tucking the paper back under his arm, he continued walking towards his office. The elderly black man, bent on one knee, was repairing a lock, and as he passed by, Doc patted him on the shoulder.

Redbone spoke in a slightly diluted Cajun' accent. "Sorry if I startled you, man. Just surprised to see ya," he said, reaching into his tool box.

Doc noticed the mop and bucket propped against the wall on the man's left.

"Still on double duty, eh, Redbone?"

"Goin' on six months now. But I don't mind. Keeps me busy since Saddie went to sleep." Doc smiled and nodded in acknowledgement of Redbone's stoicism. He continued down the hall and stopped in front of a door on the left.

"Hey, Redbone!"

"Yeah, Doc?"

Doc was staring at the glass pane on the office door as he unlocked it. "You get time, take this damn name off the door, will ya? It's stinkin' up the joint."

"Sure, Doc. First thing tomorrow."

McKeowen unlocked the door and went in, thought for a moment, stuck his head back out, and called down the hall.

"Redbone, there's probably gonna be a baptism tonight, so if you hear anything, it's okay."

"Don't be goin' doin' nuthin' stupid, Doc!"

The door shut and the glass panel was back-lit when Doc turned on the office light inside. *Sammon and McKeowen. Private Investigations Agency. We Peep While Others Sleep*, was the only office occupied at this late hour. The unremarkable office was only about 400 sq ft, and was partitioned to the right as you walked in the door. The partition was wood halfway up, then iced glass and stood just over six foot tall. There was a pair of opaque, deco globes suspended by chain from the ceiling around the lights. An army cot, half-sized ice-box and hot plate on the other side were home. They were semi-stashed out of sight. Just in case a client accidentally showed up.

Doc peered into the letterbox screwed to the back of the door, but didn't bother to remove the three or four envelopes it contained. He locked the door, dropped his bag and moved over to his desk in the corner of the room and, exhausted, removed his coat and flopped into his chair. Staring into space, he suddenly jumped up and violently kicked the chair, knocking it to the floor. He stared at it for a while to make sure it wasn't breathing, then sighed and reached into his jacket pocket and produced an airline ticket stub. Staring at it, he shook his head.

"Chump!" he mumbled as he tore the useless document into small pieces and threw them in the air.

Standing still for another moment, he righted the overturned chair. He decided he didn't feel any better and so he went over to the sink and washed his face for longer than necessary, and as he dried himself, the reason for his inability to focus dawned on him. He was fighting something that he had never felt before.

After all the physical and emotional strain encountered during thirteen years on the job, and seven years of marriage, something was different. Something made him feel like nothing mattered anymore. It was depression. Doc was smothered by it.

Throwing the towel in the basket under the sink, he walked back over to his desk and opened a wall cabinet behind him marked *Classified Files*. He withdrew a rocks glass and a bottle of Irish Whiskey. Pouring a full measure into the glass, he adjusted the chair and sat down.

Glancing around the room, which he realised contained the sum total of his life, he sank deeper into his depression. He saw the steely simplicity with which he used to approach life methodically eroding away and became lost in the resulting mist of confusion called apathy.

His lifted his drink and his eyes drifted off to the right, settling on a picture of a middle-aged man in a policeman's uniform sitting on a shelf next to some shooting trophies. The policeman's photo had a black ribbon tied around the upper left hand corner of the frame. A gold NYPD badge was mounted on a dark wooden plaque, and stood next to the photo. Doc stared at the picture and after a minute he smiled.

"Alright! You were right. I shoulda stayed on the force." He threw back his shot. "But ya gotta admit, it ain't nuthin' like the god-damn movies!"

Reaching underneath the desk and into a specially constructed compartment under the drawer, Doc removed a snub nosed .38 and a .45 Colt. After a functions check on both weapons, he loaded them and placed them in separate desk drawers.

He sat forward, leaned on the desk and slowly let his gaze drift until it fell on a picture of a woman, sitting on the shelf below the policeman's photo. She was a semi-attractive brunette, late twenties and wore some sort of graduation gown. The handwritten inscription read, *To Hubby, Love Forever, Mary*.

Doc downed his second drink and shook his head in the direction of the photo. He leaned back, put his feet up and turned off the desk lamp, leaving himself and the room bathed in the alternating shadows of Jimmy O'Sullivan's neon sign.

Like in those god-damned movies.

Chapter Four

The syncopated rhythm of the Smith-Corona keys reminded Shirley of the Morse code radio messages she had heard in an Alan Ladd war movie last week. Alan Ladd! Now there's a man! The engaging, eccentric black girl indulged her fantasies as she trudged through her work day. With instinctual dexterity, her well-manicured fingers floated in mid air, coercing the keys to perform.

Perhaps without the weight of a wedding ring to encumber the fingers, they moved faster, Shirley mused. Although attractive by any standard, she was, by her own reckoning, an old maid at twenty-six.

"Ouch! God-damn it!" Shirley cried out, quickly putting her index finger to her mouth.

"What's wrong?" It was Nikki Cole, the receptionist stationed with Shirley at the oversized reception desk.

"I busted a freakin' nail!"

"Do you kiss your mother with that mouth?"

"Maybe I got potty mouth, but there are worse problems to have!"

"Like what?" Nikki challenged.

"Like gettin' the hiccups when you're horny!" Shirley giggled.

"I told you that in confidence, damn it!"

"Don't worry, I won't tell nobody. Besides, I kinda think it's cute." Shirley smirked as she turned back to her typewriter. "This way he always knows when you're ready."

Nikki reached under the desk and produced a large pickle jar, nearly filled with nickels, and held it out to her workmate.

"About another week and we can have lunch at Grauman's,"

Nikki commented, as the five cent piece Shirley retrieved from her purse clinked into the jar.

"Grauman's Chinese Theater? That's in Hollywood!"

"I know." The sounds of laughter echoed through the empty, marble-plated lobby.

The curved, Art Deco reception desk was surrounded by a chest-high counter, covered in Carrera marble. It was a large, D-shaped island floating in the center of a lobby, set back from the elevators, which appeared much too expansive for the two slender women it housed.

The dual elevators, a few scattered ashtrays and the reception desk gave the distinct impression they were put into the lobby as an afterthought. There was no indication whatever that this was a headquarters for the intelligence service of the US Navy.

Although no sentries were visible, a tap on one of the buzzers installed underneath the desktop where the girls were working, would summon Marine guards to assist with any unwanted intruders.

As the conservatively dressed Nikki offered her help to Shirley, the switchboard buzzed. Donning the cumbersome headset, the attractive auburn-haired, blue-eyed twenty-something answered the incoming line.

"Good morning, Third Naval District, may I help you?" Nikki Cole and her switchboard, nick-named Cary, were the primary means of communication for 90 Church Street and the outside world.

"That would be Captain McFall's office, sir. Just one second and I'll connect you. Thank you, Major, your voice sounds lovely in the morning, too." Rolling her eyes towards Shirley, Nikki connected the cloth-covered cable to one of the dozens of brass plugs sprawled before her.

Upstairs, at the other end of the line, lay a new desktop model, black rotary Bell telephone. These latest models were much more of a pleasure to use than the old 'licorice stick' phones which were awkward, difficult to dial and required both hands to manipulate.

In stark contrast to the desolation of the lobby, the large upstairs office sprawled out to cover the entire floor, and was a cacophony of typewriters and telephones. Unabated activity was in full swing despite the fact the work day was only fifteen minutes old.

"Good morning, Captain McFall's office, may I help you?"

"I'm sorry, Major, but the Captain is in a meeting. May I take your number, sir? Uh-huh . . . yes sir, I have it." There was a pause as the secretary smirked into the phone. "And your voice sounds like Ethel Merman after a half pint of bathtub gin. Goodbye, Major."

Behind the secretary's desk stood a wooden frame door with an opaque glass panel. Lettering on the glass stated that it was the office of the Branch Chief of Naval Intelligence, Captain Roscoe C. MacFall, which explained why the door was closed for the better part of the day and, more often then not, locked.

A pair of thick fingers separated two slats of the metal Venetian blinds, allowing a pair of steel-grey eyes to peer out across the sprawling office. Like a headmaster staring at an oversized classroom, he observed the impressive collection of pre-war FBI agents, detectives, District as well as Federal Attorneys and Treasury Department operators at work in the office before him. Still facing the glass, Captain MacFall began to speak.

"Two months into the war and we're losing a hundred ships a month. We won't be up to full production capacity for six to eight months. And now a raving lunatic who is too stupid to get into art school has got saboteurs in our backyard!" He made his way back to the head of the conference table and flopped into his high backed chair. "Hell, I thought it was bad when Dewey lost!" MacFall's bad mood was interrupted by one of the men dressed in civilian attire sitting near the other end of the table.

"Sir, we don't know it was sabotage. The official investigation doesn't even start until today."

"You want to proceed on the premise that it wasn't and wait for them to hit us again?" the Captain responded, to no one in particular.

44

The agent had only stated what most of the half dozen operatives in the small conference room were thinking. Which didn't make it any easier when the CO pointed out the obvious to him. MacFall now stood facing the men in the sparsely furnished office. An awkward silence filled the room.

Gathered in this conference room were some of the most powerful military men in the country with, what they believed to be, the most powerful government in the world backing them. They were unaccustomed to defeat. However, now it appeared that not only had the enemy won the war in Europe and were winning the fight in the Atlantic, but he was knocking on America's front door.

The primary goal of the intelligence group, which up until this meeting had been the security of the Atlantic convoys, had now been shifted to the security of the New York harbour, and it was to this end that MacFall sought ideas and suggestions. The Tuesday morning meeting continued.

"Sir!" It was Lieutenant James O'Malley. "Seems to me what we really need is inside information about what's really going on, down on the waterfront I mean."

"Thank you for your blinding insight, Lieutenant." The Captain rarely employed sarcasm, but he was genuinely in the dark and didn't like it.

"DC has tripled our allocations, broadened our legal powers beyond our wildest dreams and we've even stooped to hiring girls."

The tension was broken and laughter circulated the room when the lone female agent present smiled at MacFall and slowly gave him the finger. Just then the door opened, and a burly, late middle-aged man made his way to a seat.

"Has anyone considered the idea of using . . . uh . . . snitches?" O'Malley continued.

"Glad you could join us, Agent Johnson." McFall was in no mood for lack of punctuality.

"Late at the range," Johnson grunted back as he perused the room. "What's all this about snitches?"

"Don't tell us. Another three hundred," the civilian agent seated next to Johnson quipped.

"Maybe I shot a two-nine-nine."

"Maybe I'm doin' Veronica Lake."

"We're battin' around ideas to upgrade intel on the docks," McFall interrupted.

"So somebody suggests stoolies? Who's the FNG?" Treasury Agent Johnson often regarded himself as the only one in the room with any level of expertise.

The OIC attempted to answer.

"It was . . ."

"I'm the FNG," O'Malley shot back.

"You think for a New York City second the Pentagon's gonna give you money to pay snitches?"

"We used paid informants all the time at the DA's office."

Looking around the office, Johnson continued in his vein of antagonism. "Will all the DA's please raise their hands?" Noting the lack of response, he added, "Gee, kid, I don't see no hands. How 'bout that!"

"I realise you're a lawyer, Lieutenant O'Malley but . . . sounds a bit thin," McFall prompted.

"You don't pay them in cash, sir. You barter with them. Sort of like using military script in a theatre of war."

"The United States Treasury is not about to print anything that can be counterfeited. You can take that to the bank."

"You're missing the point. You don't actually have to give them anything. Just tell them you're going to give them something. Or better yet, just make them *think* you're going to give them something!"

"Like what?"

"Like . . . you'll get the local cops off their back for a while. Or like, you want to know who the dirty cops are so you can get them off the take and save the crooks money. You just gotta use your imagination." O'Malley was a lawyer and made a persuasive argument.

With her heavy South Boston dialect, the lone female agent

joined the fray. "I say hear him out."

"You would," Johnson shot back. After an exaggerated glance around the room, the woman smiled.

"Somebody fart?" she loudly asked.

"Fuck off!"

"Snappy come-back, J. J.! Wonder why you're always striking out with the girls?"

Johnson glared at her.

"People!" It was McFall, once again trying to keep the train on the tracks. "Carry on, Lieutenant."

"Sir, most of us still have a lot of our old contacts. If we could somehow organise and enhance that information, we could pool it and draw up a plan of action. Theoretically, we could develop one helluva network."

"Theoretically!" Now it was one of the civilians joining in. "I was on DA Hogan's staff and I don't know about this stoolie idea. I can tell you from experience that the Mob has no sense of humour about songbirds. And the Mob controls the waterfront. Period! Nobody was allowed to even think that at the DA's office, but that don't change the facts. Nothing goes on down there without their say-so or them knowing about it."

Johnson saw his chance to euthanise the idea. "Gentlemen! You too, Betsy Ross. Do we honestly believe that stoolies, the most untrustworthy of criminals, the scum of the scum, are about to risk gettin' their heads ventilated just to help the people who are being paid to put them away? It's a stupid idea!"

"Hell! They could be bumpin' off Germans and dumpin' their bodies in the East River right now and we'd be none the wiser!"

"Yeah! Can you see some poor dumb Kraut bastard caught down on the West Side Drive by a couple of union guys?" The civilian agent mocked a German accent as he held his hands in the air, in mock surrender. "Nein, nein. I am nut a polleece man! I am only a shpie!" There was a ripple of laughter.

"As that may be our dream scenario, gentleman, we can't bank on it. I would also remind you that our infiltrators are not necessarily German. They may just as well be Italian Facists or

Spanish Anarchists." MacFall interjected the sobering thought to the assembled group, and everyone was involuntarily reminded that the overwhelming majority of the people they would have to deal with on the waterfront would be Italians or Sicilians.

"'Stupid' is a little strong, don't you think, Mr Johnson?" O'Malley was careful not to use Johnson's title. O'Malley folded his hands on the table in front of him and looked across at the bureaucratic treasury agent.

It took a couple of beats to soak through to the rubber-stamp-orientated agent, but he eventually came to the realisation that he was being challenged. The older man continued the volley.

"Sorry I hurt your feelin's, Junior. But we have a serious situation here. We have a lot of things to do and no time to do them. This is no time to be grasping at straws." Although the row had essentially been reduced to the two men, civilian against military, everyone else paid close attention to where it was going.

MacFall sat in his chair at the head of the table and observed with more attention then the others exactly how O'Malley defended his argument.

"Has it been tried?"

"As a matter of fact, yes it has! And as soon as it was sent up for approval, it came right back down again. Disapproved!"

"On what grounds?" The Lieutenant knew he was losing ground but refused to yield.

"On the grounds it was stupid. Worse yet, politically risky."

"With all due respect to the Treasury Department, your people aren't exactly trained for wartime counter-intel."

"If you have a better suggestion, I'm willing to listen," offered the Lieutenant.

The fat, balding man lost what little composure he had left. "You know what, sonny? I've been in government service since before the last war! Since before you were born, god-damn it! I made my bones on the Palmer raids, fer fuck's sake! And, besides having no respect, you haven't got the faintest idea what the hell ballpark you're playin' in!"

"At the very least we could kick it around and see if anything comes out of it. Wouldn't you agree, sir?" O'Malley's calm demeanor kept pace with Johnson's growing anger.

The pent-up tension of the room became even more restrictive, and some of the men were embarrassed that their weekly meetings had come to heated exchanges. Everyone remained silent. Johnson felt he had no choice. The federal employee slammed his briefing folder shut, stuffed it into his bag and headed for the door.

"Sir, I have a full agenda, and no time for childish ideas. I'll read a copy of the mimeo on the rest of the meeting. Good day, gentlemen." Johnson made a grandstand exit.

O'Malley remained sitting with his hands folded in front of him on the conference table. A second civilian, sitting at the far end of the table, broke the silence.

"Sir, I know Frank Hogan's office as well as anyone. I don't know that they're going to be in a big hurry to reveal their mob sources. Stoolies are their primary source of success in the courtroom. That's how Dewey got to Dutch Schultz and it's the only way he could nail Luciano."

"Jim, do you think the prosecutor's office will work with us?" MacFall had already come to the conclusion that it was worth a shot.

"Sir, they are very protective of their sources of information. It gives them tremendous leeway in the court room. But, given how critical our situation is . . ." O'Malley left his sentence hanging as he realised the direction it was taking.

"Very well. Are there any other suggestions, gentlemen? Lady?" MacFall asked, as the meeting pressed on.

"Yes, sir." It was the Commander. "I've drawn up a plan, along with a rotating schedule for a surveillance operation, that I'd like you to look at, sir."

"What is it?" asked the Captain, as he was handed the folder containing the details of the proposed operation.

"It's a plan to place agents on some of the strategically located skyscrapers overlooking the waterfront. They'll be issued binos and a hand radio, and pull six-hour shifts. They can watch for any suspicious activity and radio it in."

"What happens at night when it's too dark to see, Commander?" asked MacFall, as he flipped through the plan outline.

"Uh . . . they, er, pack up and go home, sir," came the resigned answer. Nobody laughed.

"Sounds like a good stop-gap measure, Commander." He handed back the folder. "See that it's put into action."

"Yes, sir."

"Anything else?"

The agents sensed the end of the meeting was at hand, and began to pack up. The Captain called one last time for input and then reminded various members of the group of different details requiring attention, before adjourning.

"Tomorrow, zero seven, sharp. O'Malley, need to talk to you."

As the men filed through the door, MacFall came up behind O'Malley, who was last in line, and spoke to him. "Lieutenant, I'm heading across town, walk with me to the elevators. I want to talk to you."

The puzzled young officer complied, and when the duo were clear of the office and out of earshot of the secretaries, O'Malley spoke first.

"Sir, I apologise. I know I was out of line, but that dumpy bastard really gets my goat with his bureaucratic attitude. I don't mean to ruffle feathers, it's just . . ."

He was cut off in mid-sentence as the CO raised his hand, displaying the same smile he had worn half an hour ago. "I'm glad you ruffled his feathers, Jim. Johnson doesn't make much of a contribution, but we're stuck with him until he retires next January. Just don't make it a habit."

"Thank you, sir, I won't."

"Anyway, that's not why we're talking."

"What is it, sir?"

"If we're going to do this thing, we need to approach Hogan's office in the right light. At all costs, they must not know how grave the situation is. Someone from here will have to contact someone from there. We'll have to do it fairly soon, and I'd like that someone to be you."

O'Malley was surprised that Captain MacFall had made these decisions so soon. He was also pleased and surprised at having been asked to make first contact.

"Thank you, sir. I really feel there's potential here. If we can tap into the information pool already in place . . ."

Once again he was cut off. "Save it for the Admiral, Lieutenant. He'll need the convincing, not me. He's the one that's going to have to sell it to Washington."

"Yes, sir."

The elevator arrived and MacFall got on. "Meet me at Hogan's office at eleven hundred hours. You'll liaise with Murray Gurfein."

After the doors closed, Lieutenant O'Malley hung his head and rubbed his eyes, mumbling to himself. "Gurfein! Great! A lounge singer sired by a used car salesman! Only not as sincere."

+

The elevator doors opened into the lobby and as he crossed the hall behind the reception desk, Lieutenant O'Malley checked his watch: 10:35 a.m.. It's only a fifteen minute walk to the DA's office, he thought to himself. Save cab fare as well.

"Goodbye, Lieutenant O'Malley." The echo of a female voice filled the lobby. O'Malley turned his head as he made his way to the exit.

"Goodbye, Shirley." He waved and gave a cursory smile, putting on his gloves.

"You're incorrigible!" Nikki said to Shirley.

"If that means I think he's cute, you're right. I'm . . . what you said!"

Exiting through the brass-plated double doors, O'Malley was temporarily overwhelmed by the bright winter sunlight. The noise of the traffic combined with the cool air to remind him of how much time he spent cooped up in an office.

Walking through the streets of the city, he was distracted by the faces of the passers-by. He could not help but notice for the first time since America had entered the war a few short weeks ago, that there were no real changes in the expressions on the faces of the people as compared to before the war. Not like the film footage coming back from Europe. Those were people who had not only seen the face of war, but had lived through it, too. There was one similarity, though. The shortage of working-aged men. Fortunately, in America it wasn't due to casualty rates or slave labour camps. But things were already getting tight. There was even talk about suspending the major league ball clubs for the duration. That was ridiculous! What would they do? Get women to play baseball?

Well, the men may be away fighting and dying, but at least they're not hanging around some soup line waiting for a hand-out, he concluded.

O'Malley shook the cold off as he entered the City Building. The fat, red-faced security guard at the reception window asked him who he was there to see.

"Lieutenant James O'Malley. I'm here to see the DA."

"Yes, sir. You just take the elevator to the – "

"To the fourth floor and turn left." He finished the security guard's sentence. "Thank you very much, officer." While riding in the elevator, he was struck by a powerful sensation of déjà-vu, as if it was just another pre-war work day.

In the office, he was greeted by a secretary who had a man sitting on her desk.

"I'm here to see Mr Hogan."

"Jim!" It was Murray Gurfein, one of Hogan's prosecutors. He hopped down off the desk and made his way over to O'Malley. "Welcome back, sailor boy. Good to see you!"

Gurfein hadn't changed, he thought. Worse yet, he still acted as if he and O'Malley were old drinking buddies, despite the fact they had hardly ever worked together before. O'Malley noticed that Gurfein still wore civilian clothes.

"Come on in, Jimmy boy, Captain MacFall is in with DA Hogan. Ah, Nancy, sweetheart, could we have some coffee?" The

DA's secretary didn't even give him the courtesy of an annoyed glance. She just kept typing.

The two men moved into the inner office where Hogan took a seat behind his desk. O'Malley and Gurfein arranged chairs next to MacFall in front of Hogan, and the pow-wow began.

"So, how can we help the United States Navy?" Hogan asked.

"Jim, I haven't told the District Attorney about your proposal yet. So why don't you give him the Reader's Digest version, and we'll take it from there."

Over the next ten minutes, the chief prosecutor was made familiar with the assumed potential for saboteurs to infiltrate New York Harbor, and how the Navy proposed to deal with the problem using stoolies. O'Malley couldn't help but notice that both times he mentioned the word 'sources', Gurfein and Hogan shifted positions.

When he had finished, both civilian lawyers sat in silence for a moment, and Hogan finally asked, "What exactly is it you would like us to do?"

"Well, first off, tell us if you think they'll work with us. I mean, do you think they're patriotic enough?" asked the Lieutenant.

"I think you'll find that most of the hoods here, despite the fact that they're liars, cheats, thieves and murderers, are good loyal Americans," volunteered Gurfein.

"Mussolini not only made the trains run on time, but when he first began his rise to power, he didn't want any competition in the country, so he kicked the Mafiosi out of Italy."

As was usually the case, with the exception of the loyal American part, the DA's office was about twenty years behind on the accuracy of its information.

What Hogan said concerning the Mafioso was true. His point, however, was moot. The Mafioso no longer controlled crime in New York, or in most of the rest of the country, for that matter. Although names like the Black Hand, La Cosa Nostra and Mafia would last well into the twenty-first century, the organisation now in control was the The Syndicate, run by The Commission.

The third year of the Great Depression was the only profitable year for Universal Studios between 1929 and 1936, thanks to one film, *Dracula*. Coincidentally, it was a profitable year for men like Buggsy Siegal and Meyer Lansky, as they began to organise crime nationwide. They were not alone. They worked under the direction of the man who would become 'The Boss of Bosses', Lucky Luciano. When Lucky finished implementing his national plan for organised crime, there were only three basic differences between the Unione and any other American corporation.

The Unione could account for all of their assets all of the time, it was crystal clear who was in charge and The Commission didn't have a seat on the New York Stock Exchange. They didn't need one, they controlled or influenced most everyone else's to one degree or another.

"In that case, Mr Hogan," MacFall said, "we'd like to have some names we could approach." Hogan immediately realised he would ultimately have no choice but to co-operate. But with a little bit of the old stall game, he might be able to manipulate the ground rules.

"Well, Captain, that's probably not the best way to go about it. Let me work on it. Give us a couple of days to go through the files, and we can get back to you." Co-operate or not, he was not about to let his territory be trampled on by anyone, least of all some Washington bureaucrat.

"Well, now that that's settled, welcome home, Jim!" Gurfein extended his hand towards the Lieutenant. O'Malley did not reciprocate.

"The Lieutenant won't be running our side of the show, Mr Gurfein. I've selected another officer," MacFall explained.

"Oh? Who would that be, sir?"

"Haffenden, Lieutenant Commander Haffenden. Lieutenant O'Malley will act as liaison between our two offices."

"I'll appoint a man to work with you as well, Captain, and get back to you with details of who it is," Hogan pitched in.

"Good enough." MacFall stood up, signalling that the meeting was over. "Lieutenant O'Malley will contact you at the end of the week."

"Look forward to working with your men, Captain," Hogan said.

After everyone shook hands, the officers left. There was a brief interval, then Gurfein turned to Hogan. "How do you want to handle this?"

"We'd better go slow with them. Go through the files." Hogan thought very intently as he came around from behind his desk.

"You do it. Don't give it to anybody else. When you go through the records, see who we've fingered on the docks. Let's give them only one. And for God's sake, let's keep this under our hats, huh?"

"Right-o, chief. I'll start on it right after lunch."

Gurfein began to leave. As he had the door halfway open, Hogan called to him.

"And Murray. Make sure whoever you pick out of the files has an indictment. I mean an airtight indictment. One we're going to win no matter what. I don't want to screw up any opportunities for convictions."

Gurfein nodded, then, as he stepped through the door, he hesitated. Coming back into the room, he closed the door behind him, leaned back on it and folded his arms, displaying a mischievous smile.

Hogan looked up from his desk. "What?"

"What about the wire taps?" Gurfein grinned.

After a short pause, Hogan instructed, "Leave them in place. This could get interesting."

As he passed the secretary's desk on the way out, Gurfein asked what had happened to the coffee. With no discernible movement whatsoever, the secretary kept typing while she issued her reply. "I forgot."

Meanwhile, outside the DA's office, in the hallway, a separate assessment of the meeting was under way as the two officers walked towards the elevators.

"Are you okay with this liaison position, Lieutenant?"

"Ah . . . yes, sir."

"You don't sound very sure of yourself," remarked MacFall, as both men reached the elevator.

After considering his words carefully, O'Malley spoke again. "Sir, we need to tread lightly with these people."

"Rest assured, Lieutenant, we'll only tell them what they need to know."

The elevator arrived and they boarded. They were alone. O'Malley continued. "I don't mean just that, sir."

"What *do* you mean?"

"They do business a lot different than we do, sir." The bell rang, and as the doors opened, both men stepped into the lobby. "I know. I used to work in that office."

"You have my ear, Jim." MacFall listened more closely.

"Sir, Dewey, Gurfein and that crowd have built a career on the fact that they got a conviction against Lucky Luciano."

"Well, from what I understand, he needed to be put away."

"No doubt sir, but . . ." O'Malley was clearly not comfortable discussing the inner workings of the DA's office and their Mob-like code of silence.

"Go on," MacFall coaxed.

"The trial evidence wasn't as they portrayed in the papers. There were some serious procedural questions. Most of those girls testified under what they believed to be the threat of physical violence."

"Well, gangsters are brutal people. That's why they belong in jail."

"I'm not talking about the Mob, sir. I'm talking about the prosecutor's office, particularly Dewey." Both men had now moved off to one side of the lobby, out of common earshot.

"What?"

"The threat of prison, sir. They wave it around like a magic wand. Testify or go to prison. The girls were threatened with unusually long prison terms if they didn't testify against Luciano. Some of them were even coached in what to say. Section 399 of the State Criminal Code says you can't get a conviction on one person's testimony. You're supposed to have corroborating evidence. They had no evidence, so they got hookers and people who wanted him out of the way to testify. No one can ever say the witnesses lied. The DA's office is the only one who can prosecute for perjury, so anyone who said what the DA wanted was safe. Later, half of them recanted and it wasn't all due to Mob threats. Perjured testimony alone is what got Luciano convicted. Political ruthlessness is what got him such an unusually long sentence."

"Well, what do you know, a lawyer with ethics!" MacFall said.

"Sir, don't get me wrong. I think all those bastards belong in jail. It's just that I don't consider that my brand of law. We play games like that with the rules, and we're no better than them. Or the people we're supposed to be fighting over in Europe, for that matter."

"So, what I'm hearing, Lieutenant, is that people like Hogan and Dewey have their own agendas, and are not adverse to going outside the rules to achieve their aims?"

"Yes, sir."

"Well, isn't that just good, red-blooded American politics?"

"Sir, my point is that if push came to shove and the potential for a scandal arose, someone in that office would see it as a stepping stone to their career, and the Navy would be the loser. Not to mention the world-wide propaganda value of the fact that the United States Navy is turning to gangsters for help," continued the Lieutenant.

"Having second thoughts about your own plan, Jim?"

"Not at all, sir. Just that after working both sides of the fence, there's a reason why most of those guys up there are not in uniform."

"I appreciate your candour. Your point is well taken, Lieutenant. "

"Thank you, sir."

The two officers exited the building, and as they pushed through the bustling lunch hour crowd, Captain MacFall nodded in the direction of a nearby hot dog cart.

"New York tube steak?"

"Why not? I've been eating too healthy, anyway."

Chapter Five

The New York City waterfront is an impressive sight when viewed for the first time. It is unique in the world of waterfronts. The convoluted structure of the docks allows them to encompass all five boroughs, as well as border seven cities along the New Jersey shore, just across the Hudson River. The sheer vastness of these structures can only be appreciated from the air, and their true splendour is best experienced during sunrise or the change of seasons. In addition, it is unlikely that any other waterfront in the world is marred by such a long and consistent history of violence.

It is here, amid the bitter sweet aromas of hemp and creosote, that nearly every King, Queen or Head of State has arrived, then embarked for some far corner of the globe, while on these same timbers someone's father, brother, uncle or son has became an unwanted coroner's statistic.

However, these docks are composed of more than timber decks and pitch-coated pilings. There are the men and women who live and work in this city within a city. Along with these temporary caretakers of the waterfront, are the terminals and warehouses which sustain life through the blistering heat of summer and the sub-zero temperatures of winter. The long, narrow buildings are large enough to house entire populations of small countries, and it is within these structures that the majority of longshoremen, stevedores or dockworkers, depending on your cultural orientation, work out their days, sacrificing their feet, knees, backs and sometimes their lives, to make ends meet.

The typical terminal had a thirty to forty foot high ceiling mostly composed of heavy glass in order to take full advantage of the sunlight. At night, the work was carried on under the blinding glare of mercury vapour lamps. The rectangular footprint of the building was divided into three parts. The shoreward end of the building, furthest from the water, was usually partitioned off for office space, while the remainder of the sparse floor area was divided through the long axis into equal halves. One side of the terminal was designated for arriving freight while the opposite side was usually designated for outgoing freight. In addition to this arrangement dictated by practicality, there was a special corner bin designated OS & D, as it was in terminal 16A.

"Hey, Danny! What's OS & D?" asked the newest member of the Longshoremen's Union who everyone called 'Kid'.

"You got that kid broken in yet? God-damn it!" The heavy-set foreman scowled as he walked by the two workers, who were standing next to a 1,500lb crate of loose M & M's.

"Not yet, Bennie. Just showin' him around," Danny yelled back.

"Well, get a foot under it! You ain't bein' paid to be a wet nurse!"

"How come he's always yellin'?" asked the sixteen-year-old dockworker.

Danny answered as he continued to shift freight. "'Cos, kid, he got ulcers. And he gets a bonus if he can get us to move extra freight. And he just got some bad news this mornin'."

"Like what?" the kid asked, not really interested, but making conversation as he helped Danny.

"Like Joey Morretti is doin' his wife."

"Joey Morretti from here?"

"Yeah."

"Shit!"

"Yeah."

"Whata ya think's gonna happen?"

"Don't know. He only found out a half hour ago, and Morretti ain't come to work yet." Danny updated the kid while they continued to move some boxes to give the illusion of working.

"Anyways, what wuz you askin' me?"

"What's OS & D?"

Danny looked around the floor and located a small wooden crate with a red metal tag wired to it. He motioned the kid over and began to explain.

"Okay, ya see dis here Spanish wine?" His apprentice nodded. Danny pulled back his right leg and one of his US Army issue paratrooper boots crashed into and through the pine crate. Rich coloured amontillado spilled out through the broken glass, staining the broken crate and concrete a dark red. The smell of alcohol permeated the air.

"Now," said Danny as he continued the lesson. "Ya see that red tag?" The kid nodded. "That means this piece of freight is insured for ten thousand dollars or more. But one of them bottles is busted. Which means now we gotta put this in OS & D. Over, Short and Damaged. Why?"

"Because it's damaged?" the kid responded in disbelief.

"Very good." Gesturing to the bin, Danny said, "Gimme a hand." And off they went with ten thousand dollars' worth of cracked timber and broken glass.

"When we're done here, we gotta load a flat bed with some oil ta go over ta the fish market."

About ten or twelve yards from the bin, Danny looked up as he heard screaming coming from the office area which was just adjacent to OS & D. The screams were punctuated by the sounds of breaking furniture and through the window the pair could see that the stocky foreman had just thrown someone to the floor by way of a desk, and was viciously attempting to rip the time clock off the wall. Danny, with twelve years on the wharf, understood instantly.

"Shit! Kid, drop the crate!"

"What is it?"

"Looks like Morretti came to work!"

Just then, Joey's battered body came crashing through the plate glass office window and hit the concrete floor of the dock with a sickening smack.

"No matter what happens, don't interfere!" Danny cautioned at the unexpected extension of the lesson. The kid suddenly noticed colours were a little brighter, and the harbour smelled stronger than usual.

There was surprisingly little blood surrounding the body that was lying there amongst the broken shards of glass. As Joey began to roll over, his supervisor broke out the remnants of the office window with a metal chair, threw it at Morretti, and stepped through the broken frame and out onto the platform. The burly foreman, completely consumed by rage, steam rising from his sweaty face in the cold morning air, looked around for another weapon.

By this time, most of the workers had gathered at that end of the dock to watch the latest show. Joey, now up on all fours, blood dripping from his nose, watched as his opponent spotted a bailing hook stuck into a nearby crate, and slowly moved towards the vicious tool. Joey seemed paralysed.

An eerie silence befell the terminal, accentuating the screaming of the gulls circling outside as they fought over a piece of meat.

"Morretti don't look so good," one of the men behind Danny and the kid whispered. The kid looked at Danny.

"Joey's connected on the Jersey side," the former paratrooper narrated, without turning away from the action. "He's took some real beatin's in his life. His father was on the docks during the depression when all dem blacks come down from Harlem with weapons, wanting to take over the waterfront."

"What happened?" the kid asked as Danny gave the history lesson.

"Game ended Mott Street 50, Harlem 0," Danny answered.

Watching his own blood dripping onto the concrete floor, Joey thought about his father's description of the bloody battle when the two factions met in Greenwich Village, and how the blacks were beaten back in an all-day battle with bailing hooks and Johnson bars. That was why he hadn't gone for the hook, even though he had seen it first. He knew better. With over a dozen witnesses, Morretti knew he was home free.

Having taken the bait, the infuriated foreman held the ten inch iron hook menacingly at his side as he walked towards his intended victim. Morretti, now up on one knee, fragments of glass embedded in the side of his baby face and blood flowing from his forehead, smiled as he watched the big man hesitate.

Three rounds in rapid succession fired from Morretti's .38 buried themselves in the foreman's chest, and it was his turn to lie face down in the broken glass and blood.

The kid jumped at the sharp crack of the weapon, and instinctively started towards the ex-foreman. Danny threw out an arm and blocked him. "Forget it! You wuz in the back wit' me. All you heard was some shots. Got it?" The kid couldn't avert his stare. "Come on, we got a flatbed to load."

An hour and a half later, the last of the police squad cars drove through the terminal gate, and right behind it was a flat-bed loaded with olive oil. The squad car turned south towards the Battery, but the truck headed straight across town to Fulton Street.

The overweight truck driver finished his coffee and threw the paper cup out of the window, but left the cherry cheese Danish hanging from his mouth as he manoeuvered his vehicle up to the loading docks, in front of the Fulton Street Fish Market. After turning off the engine, he lifted his hat to wipe the sweat from his forehead, and his dirty hair stood straight up, matted together from grease and dirt.

Theoretically, this huge complex of bins and stalls, stocked with every species of fish imaginable, was municipally owned. However, like the adjoining retail outlets, the cannery and nearly the entire distribution network, it was controlled by one man: Joseph 'Socks' Lanza.

Socks Lanza was the undisputed number one power in the American fishing industry. Period. He had gained and maintained control of this empire with a very logical technique. A stranglehold on union labour. Socks simply established his own unions, extorted funds for membership, and after filing some papers with the AFL, was in business.

For example, the Sea Food Workers Union, which was only

one of a handful of unions run by Socks, dominated the Fulton Street Fish Market. In classic mob fashion, he covered all the bases with a separate union for each labour force. It was a trick learned from the DA's office, where they would file up to half a dozen charges for one alleged offence, and try to get one to stick. A charge to cover all the bases, so to speak.

The market, which supplied seafood from Maine to the Carolinas and as far west as the Mississippi, was teeming with activity that Wednesday morning. Unlike the bitter-sweet aromas of the wharfs across town, there was only one smell here. The smell of fish. Acrid, pungent and overwhelming. The smell of fish which engulfed and permeated everything and everybody, from the workers in their blood-stained aprons, to the handful of clerks and typists encased in glass boxes which appeared to be stuck to the ceilings as they overlooked the masses of workers gutting, shifting and selling their loads sixteen hours a day.

The unsavoury truck driver waddled his way across the slippery floor, and weaved his way in and out of the numerous stalls of flounder, eel and shellfish. As he chewed his cherry cheese Danish with his mouth open, he considered himself lucky that he didn't have to work under these unhygienic conditions. Making his way to the staircase leading to the office, he ascended and, when he reached the top, ignored the paper sign on the door telling him to wipe his feet before he entered.

The heated air of the glass-encased room was a welcome relief from the bitter February chill flowing through the lower level of the open market. Stepping up to the chest-high counter, the middle-aged driver removed his gloves and reached into his coat pocket to remove the invoice for his delivery.

"Hello, Emily!" He addressed the receptionist, who although the same age as the driver, had weathered her years behind a typewriter far better than he had his years behind a mother-of-pearl steering wheel. His syrupy voice held no sway with her, and she showed her affection for him openly.

"What the hell you want, fat ass?"

He was undeterred. "How was your Christmas, Emily?"

"Let me tell ya, Burt. I remember three things about my Christmas. One, it was in Hot Springs. Two, it was too short. And tree, I didn't have ta conversate with no delivery boys!" Her last comment was in synchronised harmony with the strokes of her pen as she endorsed the document in front of her, pulled the pink copy and curtly shoved it back across to Burt.

Giggling circulated the office as Burt bid Emily a fond goodbye and wished her a happy Valentine's Day. The receptionist didn't answer, but instead made her way over to a door with a wooden letterbox fixed to the inside of it. Through a slot in the cross-piece of the door, she inserted the rubber-stamped, endorsed invoice. Above the slot, lettered on the frosted glass panel of the door, was the inscription, *J. Lanza, President Amalgamated Sea Food Workers Unions*.

On the other side of the door five men sat at a dark mahogany conference table, and it was a large, jowly man who was conducting the meeting.

"So what's the story in Queens?"

"Well, Mr Lanza, as far as we can tell, some guy named Dimitri has a coupla trucks and is deliverin' around Astoria for twenty per cent under the rate."

"How many trucks he got?"

Shuffling through some papers, a third man reported. "Five, Boss."

"Okay, you tree." Pointing to the three largest of the four men, "Get over to Queens." He spoke as he made his way around the table to his desk. "Find this prick! Work him over, good! But don't cripple the fuck! We still need him ta pay."

Two of the men standing in front of the desk smirked at one another. Lanza continued. "Wreck one, maybe two'a his trucks. Let him know who done this."

"Who should we say is callin', Mr Lanza?"

"Tell him you're from the Fulton Watchman's Protective Association."

Reaching into a bottom drawer of the desk, Lanza produced three strange-looking items. Homemade devices made from empty wine bottles filled with a yellowish substance and corked with a primitive fuse system, they were too large to fit into a conventional pocket, but small enough to conceal inside a coat.

"Take these stink bombs. Find three of the markets he's been deliverin' to and pop one in each of them. This way they'll get the picture, too. That'll be the day some God-damned Ruski son-of-a-bitch moves into New York!"

As the three men filed out the door, the phone rang, but before answering it, Lanza spoke to the remaining man in the room.

"Anything else?"

"No, Boss. That's about it." This man was smaller and better dressed than the other three. In addition, he carried a double-strapped satchel.

"Alright then. Make the rounds, check the numbers and get back to me this afternoon." As the man opened the door to leave, there was one additional instruction.

"And stay the hell away from Easy Emily!" Both men smiled.

Lanza picked up the phone. "Hello . . .? Yeah, speakin'."

"Joseph K. Guerin's office, please hold for Mr Guerin." A look of surprise registered on Lanza's face when he heard his lawyer's voice on the other end of the line.

"Lanza?"

"Yeah! What's up, Guerin? I thought we didn't need to meet 'til Monday."

"Something's come up. The DA wants to talk."

"Talk about what? If that prick wants to talk, tell him ta come here."

"He wants a meet." The lawyer tried to maintain his patience.

"What the hell for? What does he want, to cut a deal?" Lanza became slightly more enthusiastic about talking to the DA.

"No! No deal!" The difficulty in maintaining his patience was that Guerin knew, although he had not told his client this, that Lanza had two chances of beating his current indictment. Slim, and none, and Slim had just left town. Lawyers don't like to lose cases, regardless of the guilt or innocence of their clients. Of course, the Mob paid as well as any corporate entity, better than most, so he would stick with the case as long as possible.

"No deal? Then fuck him!"

"Joey! I think you should meet him. It's important!"

There was a momentary pause on the mobster's end of the line. Finally he spoke.

"This better not be a set-up. And it better be important, God-damn it."

"It is important, and it isn't a set-up."

"Awright then. What's the plan?"

"You tell me what time you want to go up to the courthouse, and I'll meet you."

"Whatta you kiddin' me or what? I go waltzin' up to the courthouse in the middle of the day and every punk from the Bronx ta Hoboken is gonna think I'm cuttin' a deal, and that fuckin' DA'll, do everything he can ta get the word out that I am."

"Lanza! It's not a trick, trust me!"

"Trust you? What? You stopped bein' a lawyer yesterday?"

"Very funny, prick! When and where?"

Guerin had no stake in whether or not Lanza met with the DA. He was not being paid by anyone for this, and it was not going to affect the outcome of Socks' trial.

"Tell him you'll call him. Tonight, at eight." Lanza had already worked out all the details in his mind in the last few seconds of conversation.

"When will you call me?"

"Tonight, at seven fifty-nine. I gotta go!"

"What's the rush?"

"The sea food workers and some retailers are havin' a dispute. I called a meeting to straighten it out."

"Straighten it out? You own the unions and the retailers!"

"Yeah, they're like little kids, always fightin'. Time for Daddy to have a talk. After all, the only thing that matters is the bottom line, right?" Joey checkmated the lawyer.

"Call me!"

"Guerin, one more thing!"

"What?"

"Ask the DA if he knows who's buried in Grant's Tomb," Socks asked laughingly.

"What?"

Lanza hung up, pleased with his forthcoming plan.

Chapter Six

Louie shook his head as he knocked firmly on the door of suite number 32. The glass panel read, *We Peep While Others Sleep*. That Sammon was an asshole. Louie elicited no response from inside so he tried again.

"Come on, Doc, open up, it's not a process server."

Pasquale Louige Mancino not only disliked the sacred sense of tradition his family tried to shackle him with, he despised it. He hated the tortuously long Sunday linguine suppers. He hated the language that Americans did not speak, and he hated that all the gangsters in the movies were Italian. But most of all he hated his name. Why couldn't he be Wayne or Lamont or Kent? Or some other dashing name. Why was he burdened with the name of some dead uncle he never met?

Growing up, he didn't understand why the other kids called him wop, meatball or spaghetti bender, but he knew it wasn't complimentary. So after three or four black eyes and a twice broken nose, the kids at St. Matthew's got the idea that he wanted to be called Louie.

He hated the gangsters. He hated the punks who acted like gangsters. He hated that everyone thought he was connected because he had an Italian name. He was careful never to actually say he was connected. Of course, he was just as careful to never deny it, either. All he wanted was to be a PI and to be called Louie. Louie the PI. Another month of night classes and he could take his state exam.

Louie Mancino, Private Investigator.

That's why he liked Doc. Doc treated him as an equal and

68

made a deal with him. As soon as he finished his courses at City College in March, he could work out of the office, on his own cases, and out of all the rotten things people said about Doc, not one of them could ever say he broke his word. Not unless they wanted to look stupid.

"Come on, Doc, open up. I got some good news. I know you're in there, I can smell you through . . . the . . . *SHIT*!"

The words were not yet out of Mancino's mouth when he saw them. Three bullet holes in the hall wall to the left of the door. Not a tight little shot pattern, either, but spread out as if there had been a struggle. A cold chill ran up his spine, and he banged harder on the door with no luck. Then he remembered.

Louie raced down the hall as fast as his green and orange bowling shoes would let him and slid to a halt in front of the fire hose cabinet. He ripped the door open and the glass shattered with the impact of hitting the wall. He was horrified to see the outline in dust of where the spare key used to be.

"Must be how the bastards got in," he surmised.

Sliding back to the office door, Louie The PI fought down a feeling of panic as he tried to think clearly. The glass! Removing his coat to reveal his white and blue bowling shirt, he wrapped it around his fist. Closing his eyes, Louie punched through the glass panel on the office door. As the shards of glass fell to the floor, he opened his eyes one at a time to see if there was any bleeding. However, his sense of satisfaction at not seeing blood seeped away as the unlocked door slowly swung open. Halfway, it hit a piece of overturned furniture.

He was aghast at the condition of the office. The floor was completely covered in broken furniture and debris. Doc's left foot peering out from under the desk reignited Louie's sense of urgency and he fought his way to the corner of the room to where Doc was lying, face down. Reaching Doc's body, he slowly rolled the limp form over.

"Tell me you're breathin', buddy! Tell me you're breathin'!

"Come on, Doc wake up . . . wake up! You can't check out yet . . . I ain't solved my first case!" Louie searched the body for wounds.

Doc moaned, and his eyes opened gingerly as he watched the ceiling slowly come into focus. "Where the hell . . . ? Shit! My head! Louie? What the hell you doing here?"

Doc breathed onto his friend. Louie gagged and recoiled with a wince.

"Jesus Christ, Doc! You smell like the Jersey Meadowlands in July!"

Doc sat up, holding his head with one hand and looked around the room.

"You okay?"

"You mean except for this god-damned excavation crew drilling through my brain?"

"Doc, I'm serious! You okay?"

Doc shrugged off Louie's help. "Of course I'm okay! Why wouldn't I be okay?"

"I mean like, you got any extra holes?"

Doc smirked. "Nah! I'm okay." Righting his chair, he eased himself into it, gingerly holding his head with both hands.

"Louie! Why the hell'd ja break the glass? I left the door open for ya!"

"Uhh . . . It was stuck. Doc, what the hell happened here last night?"

"Ahhh. I just had to talk things out with Mary. Sorta get it off my chest, ya know." Louie noticed the bullet holes were roughly in line with Mary's photograph and began to lose his patience.

"Jesus Christ, Doc! Didn't that letter from the landlord sink in? You had a baptism last night, didn't you?"

"Those courses are paying off already," Doc said, as he rose from the desk and made his way through the carnage to the sink. "How the hell can you be so thirsty the morning after the night you drank so much?" Doc asked to no one in particular.

"You got hammered last night and shot holes in the damn wall!" Louie pressed his point.

"I told you. I had to get it out of my system." Doc maintained his patience. After the preceding week, it was reassuring to be back amongst friends. Even if they were beginning to sound like his ex-wife.

Now Louie had to get it out of his system.

"Ya know, Doc, you're not the first guy to get shit on by some broad over money. And I ain't Nostradamus, but I think you probably ain't gonna be the last!"

Doc, now at the sink, listened to his friend as he drank three glasses of water and ate a handful of aspirin.

Louie continued as he paced around the office. "Life is how you want to see it, Doc. It's either a burden or an opportunity. It's what you make of it. Time to pick up the pieces and move on. No sense cryin' over spilt milk. Water under the bridge, ya know? To quote Shakespeare, 'There's other fish in the sea'."

"*Louie!*"

"What?"

"What's your point?"

"Don't be condensatin', Doc! This ain't funny. It's a good thing those offices across the hall are empty!"

"Thanks for caring, man." Doc continued to try and lighten the tone as he dried his face.

"I'm serious! There's enough local cops got it in fer you as it is, fer Christ's sake. The only reason they keep givin' you breaks is 'cause'a your old man." Louie nodded to the picture of the policeman on the shelf.

"Seriously, Louie, I appreciate your friendship, I really do. Just lighten up on the bitchin', will ya?" Louie appeared to calm down, and Doc continued to wash up.

"Doc, it ain't like I got an anterior motive or somethin'. I'm just worried about gettin' you through this shit!" Louie's client reports were always fun to read.

"Next thing you know, you'll be doin' something really stupid like hoppin' a plane to Miami and tryin' ta get her ta come back to New York." Mancino sat down at the desk and put his feet up. Doc put his towel down and, without looking at Louie, went into the back to change his clothes. Louie immediately understood.

"Tell me you didn't do something really stupid, Doc!" There

was no response from behind the partition. Looking down at the floor, Louie saw the pieces of torn ticket.

"You did! Didn't you? You hopped a plane, you went to Florida and . . ." Louie was cut off in mid sentence as Doc burst through the partition door in a half-buttoned shirt.

"I told you, god-damn it! I had to get it outta my system! And I did! So let's drop it, Louie! You made your god-damned point!"

"But Doc! Shootin' holes in the freakin' wall…" he pleaded.

"I said *DROP IT*! *I'M OVER IT*! She's history. Yesterday's news, a footnote in the archives. End of subject! Savvy?"

Louie was taken off guard by the intensity of Doc's anger, and wasn't sure how to react. So he sat in silence behind the desk.

Doc continued to dress in front of the mirror. Louie continued to sit, and the awkwardness of the silence intensified. Doc finished tying his cravat and slumped over the sink holding his head in a hand in a vain attempt to reduce it to normal size. Louie spoke first.

"Hey Doc?"

"What?" He turned to face Louie without lifting his head. Louie held up the empty whiskey bottle.

"Ya wanna go get a drink?"

"You're a sick son-of-a-bitch, Mancino! Ya know that?"

The tension gone out of the room, they both laughed.

"So is this why you came up here at the ungodly hour of noon? You felt sorry for me because I didn't have a wife anymore, so you decided to take over as the pain in the ass in my life?"

Louie didn't speak, but rose from the desk and, as he made his way to the door, produced a folded sheet of paper from his breast pocket and handed it to Doc. He continued across the room to the letterbox on the inside of the front door.

Doc unfolded the paper and read aloud.

"Ira and Norma Birnbaum, apartment 2B, 127 East 64th. What the hell is this?"

"What the hell's it look like? It's a client," Louie said, with a smug look on his face, knowing nothing had come into the office for over two weeks. Doc welcomed the work with guarded optimism.

"Who are they? What's the skinny?"

"She's Doris's hairdresser, she's a nice girl, you'll get a kick out of her."

"If she's so nice, why does she need us?"

"She thinks maybe her husband is screwin' around on her, and she wants to know for sure." Although he had no choice, Louie was tentative about giving this information to Doc. He knew how Doc felt about that alimony, divorce shit.

Louie was facing the door, so Doc didn't see him mouth the words as he spoke.

"Oh Jesus, Louie! You know I hate this alimony, divorce shit!"

Again Louie didn't answer. He reached into the same pocket and produced five $50 bills and laid them neatly on the desk. Doc stared wide-eyed at the money.

"On the other hand, work is work. Where'd this come from?"

"I had her make the cheque out in my name. I didn't know where the hell you were or when you'd be back. So I took a down payment and signed the case. I told her you'd call early next week."

Doc picked up the money. "Ya did good, Louie."

"Ten per cent of that's mine!"

Doc handed him a fifty. "Here. Go buy Doris a chocolate layer cake."

Louie's eyes lit up.

"Shit, Doc! Thanks! You okay with this?"

"Shut up before I change my mind."

"No problem!"

"This ain't no gimme. You're gonna work this case with me."

"You serious?" Louie was thrilled. "But I ain't got my licence!"

"You won't need one. We follow the guy, find out who the girl is, take a few snaps, and show up for court. Clean and simple. What could happen?"

Doc was pleased to see Louie so excited. He would make a good PI. There was an unspoken agreement that Louie would one day take over the agency.

"Louie . . . ah, sorry about flyin' off the handle. I just want some peace and quiet, and ta get back to work."

"Well, there you are, partner. A nice, simple client to ease you back into the saddle." Louie was still holding the mail in his hand and Doc asked what was in it.

Shuffling through the four pieces, Louie recited, "A subpoena, the electric bill, another subpoena and an invite to join the Ancient Order Of Hibernians." Louie couldn't repress his smile as Doc shook his head.

"Give me that."

Doc took the envelope from Louie and made his way around behind his desk. From a drawer he took a large rubber stamp and stamped the post in several places with the words, *Scottish! Not Irish!*

Louie laughed as Doc handed him the solicitation and told him to put it back in the box.

"Louie?" Doc flopped into his chair.

"Yeah?"

"How do you do it? I mean, spend so much time away from Doris and still have such a healthy relationship after twelve years?"

"I dunno. I guess it's . . . true love," Louie said in a mocking voice.

"Bullshit! It's 'cause she's horny all the time. That's why you married her in the first place."

"Yep. Body of a woman, sex drive of a man. Hell, only way it could be any better was if she was a rich mute and owned a liquor store."

"Come on, shit head! I'm tryin' to be serious here! Emotionally, what makes it work?"

"Jesus, Doc. You're startin' ta sound like those phony letters in *True Romance* magazine."

"Go to hell!"

"The truth?"

"Yeah, the truth."

Louie took in a deep breath and let it out slowly. Than he sat down next to the desk and spoke in a serious tone. "Doc, I love her so much that... that when I'm away from her, I'm so miserable I feel like she's here."

"I asked for it."

The brass letters, 2B, were neatly polished and contrasted aesthetically against the black enamelled door of the apartment. Doc knocked, and to his surprise the door opened immediately, as far as the safety chain would allow, as if someone had been standing there waiting for him. An elderly woman, maybe early seventies but spry, very short, undid the chain and opened the door. She was visibly upset. Doc rechecked the sheet of paper.

"Yes?" she enquired.

"I'm looking for Mrs Birnbaum?"

"Yes?"

"Mrs Norma Birnbaum?"

"Yes, that's me." The elderly woman held a tissue in one hand and spoke with a Jewish accent.

"I'm Mr McKeowen. The detective."

Opening the door wider, she gestured for Doc to come in, then locked up behind him.

The modestly decorated rooms were immaculate, and Doc thought about his office. Contributing to the feeling that he was visiting his grandmother's house, was the fact that the air was saturated with the delicious aroma of some food which Doc did not recognise, simmering on the stove.

"Ah . . . Mrs Birnbaum. You have a daughter, that wants to hire a private investigator?"

"No, I half no daughter." *If Louie screwed this up, I'll brain him!*

"I was told someone wishes me to investigate the possibility of . . . infidelity. That their husband may be having an extra-marital affair. Is there a woman in this building in that situation that you know of, Mrs Birnbaum? Perhaps with another name?"

"Did your muther half a difficult delivery? I am Norma Birnbaum! I am da voman! Andt my husbant is cheatingt on me! Mit a rich, younger bimbo no less!" she declared, making her way to the kitchen.

Doc was taken off guard. *If this guy is anywhere near her age and is foolin' around, I gotta meet him*, he thought.

"What makes you think Ira has been seeing someone else, Mrs Birnbaum?"

"Dink? *DINK*? I don't dink. I know! A voman knows dees dings. Since the war started! Maybe he wants to sow some vild oats, who knows? In case we're invaded, maybe. Come, sit!" They both took seats in the kitchen.

"What did you notice, since the war started? That made you suspicious, I mean?"

Mrs Birnbaum explained as she stirred pots and made tea.

"The usual. Stayingt out late. Goink to verk at odd hours. Dinks like dat."

"Has there been any money missing, say from his pay, or anything like that?"

She shook her finger vigorously as she spoke. "No! Dat's how I know da little hussy is rich. He still gives me all his money, and den some! But he still has money to play mit da hoochie-coochie." Norma embellished the words with pelvic gyrations.

"What does your husband do, Norma?"

"He is postal clerk. You know, for dee postal office."

"So, he works at the 42nd Street Station?" Doc asked as he kept notes.

"No. Two years ago they give him promotion and easier job, downtown. Soon, he retires. He is seventy-nine, you know! Andt still vorkingt! We promise each other he only vork until he is eighty. You know, that way we can spend last twenty years or so together."

Doc's eyes involuntarily widened. "Well, it's important to be optimistic. Your plans may still work out, Norma. How long have you and Ira been married?"

Mrs Birnbaum stood up straight, and allowed her slight

shoulders to set back ever so gently. "Today is our anniversary! Fifty-seven years, two months, and seventeen days! Today!"

Jesus! I should live so long, thought Doc.

"Well Norma, here's what we'll do. Why don't you give me his work address. I'll have a look around, and we'll see if we can't work this thing out."

"I yust don't vant I should lose my Ira, Mr MackQuen."

"I don't think that's going to happen, Norma."

"He vas in da films, you know. Da real films! Not dis talkies nonsense! He vas an actor! He vas friends mit Joelson!"

She began to sob, and Doc got edgy. He was useless around crying women.

"Norma, I really need you to act as normal as possible, keep up your daily routines, and wait for me to get back to you. Okay?" He handed her a tissue from the box on the table. "Now what's the address?"

"It's on Church Street. Number ninety, Church Street." He couldn't place it, but Doc recognised the address. "Here, eat some soup."

"No thanks, Norma. I really need to . . . "

"Eat! Eat!"

Doc realised he was out-gunned and gave in.

Chapter Seven

In 1936, Murray Gurfein was instrumental in the conviction of the Boss of Bosses, Charlie 'Lucky' Luciano. This conviction, which resulted in a sentence roughly five times greater than any 'normal' criminal would receive, was intended to put Luciano away for the rest of his life. It didn't.

Some of the tactics employed by DA Thomas Dewey compelled many people working with him to ask questions. In particular, why the majority of the dozen or so witnesses they called said nearly the same exact thing. Or why the three key witnesses had recanted their statements almost immediately after testifying and had then signed sworn statements to that effect. Lastly, there was the issue of perjury on the part of some of the witnesses for the prosecution, along with the DA threatening those very same witnesses with imprisonment if they did not testify as directed.

Of course, there can be little doubt that the mobsters probably made some threats as well. But apparently Dewey's boys threatened harder, and his political ambitions, of which he made no secret, were eventually fulfilled. He was able to buy the Governorship of New York.

Although Dewey's shady victory had taken place three years previously, Gurfein, as head of the rackets division, had gotten nearly as much mileage out of Luciano's conviction. And now it was time to meet another one of these hoodlums. Only this time Gurfein would not have the safety of a courtroom. He would meet him face to face, alone on his own turf. At midnight.

To complicate matters, he was going to ask this gangster for help. Even if he hadn't been 'asked' by the DA to do this, as head of the NYC Rackets Division it was his responsibility.

Murray had a problem. If he came back empty-handed, it wouldn't go well for his career. If he came back with something, he would probably have to make a deal. A deal he had no authorisation to make.

Standing outside the City Hall, Gurfein held his watch towards a lamp post so the faint glow would allow him to read the dial in the winter darkness.

Eleven forty-seven. Shit! he thought to himself. Desperate to find a taxi to take him uptown, Gurfein stepped out into the street and peered downtown into the gloom of the night. As if on cue, a cab pulled out from around the corner, and came to a stop in front of him.

Getting in through the back door, he didn't notice the 'off duty' roof light was lit and, before he could get himself seated, he felt the cab pull away.

"103rd and Broadway," he instructed the driver.

"I know," came the response. The lawyer wanted to ask questions, but thought better of it.

It was at least a twenty minute ride uptown, even without traffic, which gave Gurfein time to think. He nervously shifted his position several times before settling down and gazing out the window into the desolation of the Manhattan night. *Ah, what the hell?* he reasoned to himself. *If the hoods co-operate, the DA looks good. If not, they look like what they are, a bunch of scumbags. If it all goes to shit somewhere down the line, I can always say I was ordered by Hogan to do it, in spite of the fact I was repulsed by being told to do business with known criminals.* He practised how to say 'repulsed', and make it sound believable.

Despite all of his self-posturing, the thing he had the most difficulty dealing with was the possibility that anyone even remotely associated with the Mob may be shown, by their helping the War Department, to have any redeemable values.

As the taxi cruised up a deserted Central Park West past the Museum of Natural History, Gurfein couldn't help but think how the shadowy images of the park seemed appropriate for the mood. His mind drifted further, noting how the picturesque peacefulness engulfed the entire scene and how it would look in just a few hours as the morning sun broke over the treeline, soon to be shattered by the brutality of rush hour traffic.

As they passed into the 90s, one last chilling thought occurred to his active, worried imagination. Was there any chance the Navy intelligence people could have underestimated the current state of German technology? What if the U-Boats had a longer range and extended sea life than the government knew about? Unlikely, he reassured himself. America had the greatest scientific and military minds in the world. That's how we'd beaten them in the last war. Besides, the Krauts were essentially neutralised at Versailles.

These were the thoughts that raced through Gurfein's mind as the cab rounded the corner and pulled to a halt at Broadway and 103rd. It was shortly after midnight when he attempted to exit the vehicle but was blocked by two men getting in. It was Guerin and Lanza. Socks sat facing the two lawyers who in turn were sitting with their backs towards the rear of the taxi.

"Where're we going?" asked Gurfein nervously.

"Somewhere else," Lanza quipped. Continuing on for another few blocks, the driver altered his northerly direction and turned west until they came to Riverside Park. Another right-hand turn meant they were again heading uptown, and Guerin noticed a sign in the park as they drove by: *Grant's Tomb Next Left.*

"You're a regular Bob Fuckin' Hope, Lanza," Guerin cracked. Socks smiled. Gurfein looked puzzled.

After pulling into the park just south of the memorial, the three men got out. Lanza paid a twenty, and deliberately waited until the two lawyers were out of earshot before telling the driver to go over to Amsterdam Avenue and wait.

Lanza walked past the others and across the narrow stretch of park to the wrought iron fence overlooking the Hudson River. The lawyers followed and when they reached Lanza, Guerin stepped off to one side to allow his client and the DA's representative to talk. Gurfein immediately began to paint the picture for Socks.

"Here's the story, Socks . . ."

"It's Mr Lanza." *Off to a good start*, thought Guerin, standing on the sidelines, lighting a smoke.

"The Navy needs our help. They been losing supply ships left, right and centre to the U-Boats. They don't think the subs can stay out that long, or that the Krauts have enough of them to keep rotating their Wolf Packs."

Socks glanced at Guerin, then back at Gurfein. It was too hard to swallow. The US Navy looking for Socks Lanza to come to the rescue? Even with a war on, there wasn't a chance in hell they would want to get Mob guys mixed up in a legitimate operation, he thought. The DA was up to something.

"So?"

"So, they think the Krauts are being supplied from here. By a network or something."

"You tryin' ta tell me you think some'a my guys are supplyin' Nazis!"

"No. But such an operation would take an organised network and a fair amount of logistics. These guys would need fresh water, food, fuel, medicine and God knows what else. This wouldn't be any nickel and dime operation."

"So whatta ya want from me?"

"They can't find any leads."

"So why don't you guys do what you always do? Frame somebody? Or are you askin' me ta play spy?"

"Not exactly. The Navy wants to place agents on the boats, trucks and in the markets."

"Fuck you!" Lanza backed away as he exploded with anger. Guerin was startled. "I was born durin' the fuckin' day, but it wasn't fuckin' yesterday!" He turned to a startled Guerin. "Can you believe this shit? This prick wants to put Feds inside my operation!"

"Socks, calm down!" Guerin threw down his cigarette and walked over to his client. "Calm down, damn it!"

"This bastard wants to put cops in my market! Can you believe the cahoons on this guy?"

"Don't be stupid! He's got nothing to do with it. If you agree to help, you'll deal straight with the Navy. No one else," Guerin reasoned with Lanza. Socks looked at both of them and then again at Guerin. He began to settle down. As much as any man could, he trusted his lawyer.

"How do I know they won't be Feds?" he asked.

"If they are, or if the DA tries to sneak a Fed in, anything they obtain, or try to obtain, will be inadmissible. Besides, if you want I can have them checked out." The two lawyers exchanged glances. "But I'm telling you, I met the Navy guy you're going to be dealing with. He's on the square."

"Is he ex-cop?" He wanted as clear a picture as possible.

"No. Strictly intelligence work," Guerin reassured him.

Socks walked around a little in small, irregular circles and lit a cigarette.

"You'd be doing your country a great service," prodded Gurfein.

"Yeah, wouldn't hurt your career either, would it, councillor?"

Socks was told that not only would he not be given any consideration for his help, but that it would probably not even be permitted to be brought up at his upcoming trial. There was nothing that Gurfein or Hogan were going to do to jeopardise a conviction. His lawyer made one last plea.

"Socks, I'm tellin' ya. It's on the level."

Socks stood, hands in pockets assessing the two lawyers. "I'll call you in a day or so. I'll see what I can do." With the sparkling lights of the Jersey shoreline at his back, Lanza slowly walked away. He was headed in the direction of Amsterdam Avenue when he stopped and turned. "Hey, Guerin! You comin'?"

Turning to Gurfein as he walked away, Guerin said, "Don't worry, he'll do it. He's got no choice." The lawyer caught up with Lanza.

"Look, I don't want to call that prick. I want to deal with this Navy guy, what's his name?"

"Haffenden, Commander Haffenden."

"Hey!" It was Gurfein calling after the other two men, who were by now across the street. "How am I supposed to get back downtown?"

"Call a cab!" Socks suggested, and then continued walking.

"You know, he could lean on you pretty heavy at the trial," counselled Guerin.

"You think for a second he's gonna play Mr Nice Guy? Let me tell you somethin'. When guys like that develop political ambitions, they find ways to bend the law and then go around tellin' people it's ta fight crime. Then, after they get away with it a'nuff times, comes the delusions of grandeur and invincibility! Then it's only a small step to ignoring the law altogether."

"Voice of experience talking, Joey?"

"*Basta conoscerne uno, per conoscerli tuti*. Ya seen one, ya seen 'em all! *Capito*?"

The two figures faded into the dark mist.

Next morning, the two figures of Socks Lanza and Guerin emerged from the bright sunlight and passed through the large, revolving brass doors into the palatial lobby of the Hotel Astor. Outside, the New York winter air was crisp and cold, but inside the elaborate lobby it was a warm, comfortable and lush. An atmosphere neither man was a stranger to.

The immaculate detail and spaciousness of the vestibule was impeccable. Plush, intricately woven, red and gold carpet was bordered with black rope and ran snugly into the richly stained and varnished mahogany baseboard. The walls were a combination of paper and paint, coloured in soft maroon and eggshell. The ceilings of heavily moulded plaster reliefs, were ornamented with massive, gold-plated chandeliers large enough to require a crew of ten men to install. Once on the inner borders of the huge, rotating, brass plated doors, save for the attire of the guests scattered about the lobby, one would think it was still 1870.

The two men made their way to the staircase on the left and

ascended to the mezzanine level. Although this was not Lanza's first time in the Astor, he was forced to think to himself as he looked around for sentries, "If this is a set-up, they're sure goin' the whole hog!"

Owing to the sizes of the suites on the mezzanine level, there were a limited number of them. Guerin knew the suite number, and despite the growing irritation he felt for all this cloak and dagger stuff he wasn't making a penny on, he was curious as to how the third reel was going to play out. He gave two short knocks and a voice yelled to come in.

Each room was large enough to permanently house a family of four, and was just as plushly decorated as the lobby.

"And they call us crooks!" Lanza said in a low voice to Guerin as he closed the door behind them. Straight ahead, down the long hall, was some sort of sitting room, and off to either side of the hall were four other rooms, two on each side.

Socks and his lawyer walked down the hall poking their heads into each room until they found the one which was occupied.

"What the hell's he doin' here?" Socks blurted out. He was standing in the doorway of the last room on the left, pointing as Guerin caught up with him.

"I'm just here to baby-sit, Socks." Gurfein, seated in the corner, was basking blissfully in Lanza's surprise.

Lanza recalled how easy it was to bait and evade the cops when they chased him as a teen and quickly composed himself. "Your tax dollars at work, eh, Murray?"

"At least we pay taxes, Lanza!" Gurfein was easily goaded.

"We pay taxes too, councillor," Socks retorted in a matter-of-fact tone. "The taxes you haul in from the people we employ alone, more than pays the salary of everyone in City Hall, with some left over to help the war effort. Of course that's only a rough estimate. It's very difficult to know exactly how much is extorted from us in graft."

"Gentlemen! We're not here to play cops and robbers." It was the man seated behind the broad wooden desk, an impressive figure dressed in civilian clothes. He looked to be late forties, early fifties, but well built. Socks was impressed with the man's presence and shook his hand with respect as the man introduced himself.

"Mr Lanza, Lieutenant Commander Charles Haffenden, thanks for coming."

Gurfein smirked silently as he thought to himself, *Mr Lanza! Gimme a break!* Socks sat down in the chair facing the desk. Guerin stood, as there were no more chairs in the room. The lawyer, in his sixties, was visibly uncomfortable.

"Mr Lanza, I'm told you can help us."

"Please, Commander, call me Socks," Lanza said, pretending not to notice Gurfein's glance. "What is it I can do for youse?"

Commander Haffenden had been briefed about Lanza's legal situation, and so understood fully the relationship between Gurfein and Socks. He also knew why the DA's representative was there. It had very little to do with Lanza. He would no doubt be tripping over himself to report back to Hogan the instant the meeting was over. Little did he realise he was out of his league.

Charles Haffenden had not only been in service since 1917, he was considered a founding father of Naval Intelligence. He played in the same playground as Aaron Banks and 'Wild Bill' Donovan. While people like Hogan and Gurfein were paying for tips and blackmailing petty criminals, men like Haffenden were spying on heads of state and collecting data as field operatives behind the lines in enemy territory.

"Well, I believe your lawyer has already filled you in on the details of the difficulties we're having with our shipping?"

Guerin had no idea what Haffenden was talking about, but kept quiet. Lanza caught on right away.

"Yeah, all the details," he responded. Gurfein sat up straight and looked at Haffenden.

"Good. What can we do?" Haffenden continued. Socks reached into his pocket and produced a pen. He wrote two phone numbers on a piece of notepaper he took from the desk and slid them across to the Commander.

"Call me at either one of those numbers in a day or so, sir."

Lanza stood along with Haffenden, and they shook hands.

"Nice to have met you, sir."

"Likewise, Socks." Gurfein remained seated.

Lanza left first and as Guerin was putting his hat on, he turned to Gurfein and quipped, "Told ya he'd do it."

Commander Haffenden put on his coat as well and indicated to Gurfein that it was time to leave. Gurfein tried to get a look at the piece of paper on the desk, but Haffenden scooped it up and put it in his pocket.

"Commander, I have a right to know what's on that paper!" They started down the hall towards the exit.

"Ya know, Murray, I get the impression you're the kinda guy likes ordering secretaries around." Haffenden stopped to open the front door to the suite. He reached in his pocket and produced a piece of paper. Outside in the hall, he addressed Gurfein again.

"I'm told you're an expert in Sicilian?"

"Yeah, So?" Haffenden handed him the piece of paper and proceeded to walk down the corridor towards the stairs.

"Get back to me with a translation on that, will ya?" Haffenden was about to set the ground rules for the NYCDA's relationship with his intelligence network.

Gurfein stood in the middle of the hallway and unfolded the paper.

In bold, block, hand written letters, was a single word in Sicilian: *FANCULO*!

Chapter Eight

Louie stood against the granite wall of Central Park pretending to read the early edition of the *Daily News* in the morning cold, as he shelled his breakfast of salted peanuts. Columbus Circle was buzzing with activity by 8:00 a.m., and Mancino had his work cut out for him. Mrs Birnbaum had told Doc that Ira always walked to the Circle in the morning on his way to work. Louie's assignment was to spot Birnbaum, follow him to whatever mode of transportation he would utilise to get downtown, and then call Doc, who was waiting in a phone booth in the Woolworth Building, around the corner from the Church Street office. Doc really didn't need Louie to do this, but he needed him even less hanging around Downtown bugging him. He didn't mind teaching Louie, but he wasn't a babysitter.

Strategically positioning himself behind the line of cabs parked along Central Park South, where he was able to see the subway kitchen on the corner of Broadway and 59th, Louie's eyes darted back and forth across the pack of pedestrians.

Louie took the photo Mrs Birnbuam had given Doc out of his jacket pocket and studied it for the tenth time. It was taken at a family function of some sort, and showed Ira and Norma sitting at a table alone while dozens of others around them danced and ate, almost as if the old couple weren't there. Louie was still puzzled by the age of the subject he and Doc were to investigate. *If this guy has got something going on the side it's gotta be one for the record books!* he thought.

Louie looked up with an unshelled peanut still in his mouth. Five foot two, balding, glasses, dark suit and bow tie. Bingo! As

Ira was descending into the subway, Mancino had to fight his way across The Circle, leaving a trail of peanut shells and dodging traffic to reach his subject in time.

The fresh smell of ozone greeted Louie as he took the steps two at a time leading down to the subway platforms and rounded the bend, past the crowded news kiosk to the turnstiles. Reaching into his pocket, he produced a handful of change, and mixed among the hodge-podge of coins were two ten cent tokens. He selected one and inserted it into the slot and pushed through the clicking ratchets of the wooden turnstile and walked onto the platform pretending to read the paper. But something was wrong.

He looked up and down the platform. No Ira!

There were less than a dozen people milling about. *Jesus! Was this guy that good? How could he have known he was being tailed?* The space between the edge of the platform and the wall was too narrow for him to step back and peer behind the only place to hide, the wide steel girders supporting the ceiling. To compound his problems, Louie could hear the screeching of steel wheels growing louder as the Downtown express approached the 59th Street station. Walking rapidly to one end of the platform he saw no sign of the old man. *Shit! Doc won't let this one go! Bad enough he has to pay forty-seven dollars for a new office window, now I drop the tail!* Louie ran back up to the turnstiles. He heard the train squeal into the station, and had a brain-storm. He double-timed back downstairs and as the passengers began to board, he ran over to the centre car, stood in front of the door and sighted straight down either side of the train, to observe who was boarding. He peered left, and as he turned to look down the other side of the train, a group of five or six commuters pushed into him.

"Excuse me, sir, you're blocking the door." Louie looked down, and gasped. He'd found Ira.

Meanwhile, around the corner from Church Street, over on Broadway, Doc was milling about in the elaborate mosaics in the cruciform lobby of the Woolworth Building, near a bank of phones. A security guard looked up for the fourth time in the last quarter of an hour, suspicion etched a little deeper into his grizzled face. Doc did the only thing he could, he smiled, waved and cursed Louie.

The subject of Doc's anger was now making his way to the back of the crowded car to put some distance between himself and Mr Birnbaum. When he reached the rear of the car, he remained standing, carefully hiding behind his *New York Daily News*. Ira was opening a pack of Wrigley's, and Louie tried to note the stations from the blur of signposts in the windows.

Finally, the train began to slow and eventually came to a stop at the Wall Street station. Birnbaum stepped off, Louie was right behind him, and as they ascended to street level, Louie checked his watch.

Looking up from his watch, Doc noted Louie was twenty minutes late with his call. McKeowen made a decision to walk around the corner to Church Street and chance an intercept with Birnbaum.

Doc was annoyed, but not really angry with Louie. He had long since taught himself to control his anger where friends and family were concerned. He thought about his father telling him not to join the force, and how the discussions about medical school gradually deteriorated into shouting matches.

Turning the corner onto Church Street, Doc was struck by a strong, cool breeze. Glancing across the street, he shook his head and fought back a smile. There was Louie, standing in a phone booth, stamping his feet to keep warm, and dialling the phone. As Doc crossed the street and walked up to the phone booth, he could hear Louie giving someone on the other end a physical description and asking for Mr McKeowen.

Doc rapped on the glass and Louie half turned, covering the receiver with his hand, while yelling to the intruder.

"Sorry, pal! Find another phone. This one's – hi, Doc."

"Hello, Mr Tracy." Louie slowly hung up and stumbled out of the booth. "Where's Birnbaum?"

"He's in there." Louie pointed to the marble-façaded Art

Deco building across the street. A large double glass door served as the entrance to the multi-story structure and the lobby could be seen through the glass. The number 90 was smartly lettered in gold leaf above, on the transom.

"How long ago did he go in?"

"Exactly one minute and seventeen seconds." Louie held his sleeve pulled up over his watch and hoped the precise time he tried to bullshit Doc with would carry some weight.

"Alright, I'll go check on Birnbaum. You go back to the office and see what you can find out about 90 Church Street, start with who owns the property. Call down to the city engineer's office and ask for the grid and plot number on the city plan for the Federal Building. When you get that info, cross-reference the owners in the City Property Guide and the phone book. Maybe we can find this guy's department. You got all that?"

"Doc, I'm sorry about mucking up the tail."

"Don't sweat it. You remembered the first two rules of a successful tail. Find out where he's going, and never let them see you up close." Louie looked down at the ground. "Now go back to the shop, get that info and wait for my call."

To be sure Birnbaum was clear of the lobby Doc took his time crossing the street. Once on the other side, he turned down the fur collar of his brown leather bomber jacket and stuffed his ball cap into his back pocket. Approaching the entrance at an angle, he looked up and down the street, then swung through the glass doors.

He was immediately surprised by the size of the lobby and how sparsely decorated it was. However, he was more surprised to see Birnbaum being fussed over by a beautiful, well-dressed, auburn-haired woman who easily stood eight or nine inches above the old man. Doc pretended to ring for the elevator, as he continued to keep tabs on the couple standing beside the large, marbled reception desk. The lift hit the ground floor, the doors opened and Doc stepped off to the side to tie his already tied shoelace. After about a minute of fussing over his tie and jacket, the women kissed Birnbaum on his balding head and bade him goodbye.

"Son-of-a-bitch! At least the old guy's got taste," Doc mumbled to himself. Watching the woman walk around and take a seat behind the reception desk, he saw Birnbaum disappear through a pair of doors at the end of the hall. Doc decided to roll the dice.

Approaching the desk, he could hear the auburn-haired woman, who was obviously the receptionist, having trouble with some of the plugs on the switchboard, occasionally jiggling them to get a clearer connection. Shirley noticed Doc first, and nudged Nikki.

"Having trouble with your connections, Miss?" She gave him an annoyed look as she answered another call, still having to jiggle the cable and hold it to hear clearly.

When she finished, he spoke again.

"We have the same type of switchboard in my office. Usually it's just a loose jack plug," Doc said, eyeing the board and cables over the counter top. Shirley stopped typing, and swung around in her chair to face Doc and Nikki. Using both arms, Doc leaned forward on the marble top.

"Funny, I wouldn't have pegged you for the type who knew a lot about equipment," Nikki responded.

Leaning over the desk, Doc took one of the plugs and held it up, pretending to study it.

"You'd better be careful. Some of this equipment is pretty old." Nikki addressed Doc in a condescending tone.

"Just because it's old doesn't mean it don't work good. Besides, once something's aged a bit, it usually . . . fits in better." Shirley grabbed her mouth and pinched her nose to suppress a laugh. "With its job, I mean." He fiddled with the end of the phone cable.

"I'm told the newer models function better." Nikki folded her arms across her chest as she spoke. Doc continued to inspect the cable.

"Maybe, but they usually don't stand up as long." Twisting

the brass jack plug and the cable in opposite directions, he tightened the brass jacket clamp around the cable.

"There you are, Miss. Good as new." Doc returned the cable to its position, purposely leaning too far over the desk, and making direct eye contact with Nikki. "All they need is to be handled every once in a while. Like it says in the instructions."

"You want me to buzz him?" Shirley asked, moving closer to the secret red button.

"Not yet, Shirl." She spoke to the typist without breaking eye contact with Doc. "Why do I get the feeling you're the kinda guy who doesn't follow instructions very well?"

"Rarely need them. Always know where all the parts go."

"Lemme buzz his ass!" Shirley chomped at the bit with her finger on the button. Nikki raised a hand.

"What exactly is it I can do for you? Mr. . . ?"

"McKeowen, Mike McKeowen. My friends call me Doc."

"What exactly is it I can do for you, Mr McKeowen?"

"That little fella that just came in?"

"Ira Birnbaum?"

"Yeah, Birnbaum. Does he work here?"

"He's our mail clerk. Who wants to know?"

"Just curious."

"Yeah, and I was born during the day. But it wasn't yesterday. What's the story? You a cop?" Nikki was genuinely curious. Doc just became a little more interesting.

"No, I'm not a cop. Does he always work odd hours?"

"No more than the rest of us since the war started."

Since Pearl Harbor, Doc realised.

"Well, if you're not a cop, and you're not investigatin' for the DA, who are you?"

"Who says I'm not with the DA?"

"Because if you were, first thing you woulda done was flash your badge to show me what a big man you were. Then you woulda tried pressuring me into answering your questions after I told ya ta take a flyin' leap fer hittin' on me. And for a grand finale, you'd threaten me with some arcane law like you were some kinda bey or something."

Doc was unprepared for the barrage, but found it entertaining.

"Sorry, just thought I knew the little guy. My mistake. I was looking for the Woolworth Building."

"So you're a private investigator."

"I'm impressed." And he was.

"You're a PI, and you're following Ira ta see if he's fooling around on his wife." This girl was a little too cocky, she knew something.

"Well?"

"Well what?"

"Well, is he?" Doc persisted.

"You're pullin' my leg!"

"No. But it would be a nice start."

"Da's it! Buzz time!" Shirley was growing anxious to see the two Marine guards escort Doc out.

"Relax, Shirl. He's harmless. Just a little confused."

"So I can't buzz 'im?"

"Not yet. But keep your finger ready." Shirley raised her hand and started repeating a finger exercise while glaring at Doc. Nikki leaned forward and put both arms on her desk to get a running start at Doc before she pounced.

"Go back and tell that ungrateful old bat that that man was offered retirement two years before the war broke out. But because he's the only one with a Top Secret clearance, he volunteered to stay on until they could get someone else in there."

"Easy, sister! Don't go breathing fire at me. That old bat, as you called her, sits at home all day cryin' her eyes out wondering what the hell he's doing. Just because these two people have been around since Christ was a corporal doesn't mean they're made of stone, you know!"

Nikki sat back in her chair. Shirley was impressed and lowered her finger.

"You got a point, I guess. I never really thought about her end of it." Nikki was touched by Doc's defence of Ira's wife.

"Look, I'm sure they're both good eggs. But there's no way they could have been prepared for this. How's about I go back and tell Norma that he's not foolin' around and, if you feel you know him well enough, maybe you could mention that he oughta let the wife in on the scoop down here. Fair deal?"

"Is that her name? Norma?" Nikki was subdued as she realised in all the time she'd known Ira, she'd never asked his wife's name.

"Yes. Fair deal, Miss . . . ?" Doc held his hand out across the counter top.

"Fair deal, Mr McKeowen. Miss Cole, my name is Miss Cole." She shook his hand.

"Her name is Nikki. And she's here Monday to Friday, eight to six and Saturday till noon every other week," Shirley blurted out as she suddenly lost her enthusiasm to buzz Doc.

"Sounds like you got a great agent there." Doc nodded at Shirley as he backed away from the reception desk. "You'll be playin' Radio City before you know it."

"Yeah! Shirley the agent." Nikki was embarrassed and made a mental note to give Shirley a good balling out later. Someone entered through the front door as Doc was preparing to leave.

"Thank you for your help, ladies. It was a pleasure to meet you, Miss Cole. And you too, Shirley The Agent. Careful with that finger." Doc turned to leave. Nikki watched him turn up his collar and don his ball cap as he passed through the door.

"Girl! You should'a got his number!" Shirley said, slapping Nikki on the arm.

"I got his number when he walked in here!" Nikki held up the swear jar and Shirley dug through her purse.

"He ain't no Alan Ladd but he got potential!" Shirley dropped the nickel in through the slot cut in the cap.

The man who had entered the building was now standing at the elevators when Doc passed him. It was Treasury Agent Johnson, and after watching Doc leave, he walked over to the two girls who were once again engaged in their work, or at least tried hard to look like they were.

"Who was that?" He asked in his best casual manner, dripping with suspicion.

"A guy," Nikki replied to Johnson, without looking up.

"What guy? What'd he want?"

"He was looking for the Woolworth Building." Both girls, as did all of the girls before them, found Johnson repulsive. Nikki once reckoned, during a girls' night out, that if John Merrick were a woman he still wouldn't have dated Agent Johnson.

"A little late for Christmas shopping, wouldn't you say?"

"Look, agent Johnson. I ain't baby-sittin' the guy, just givin' him directions. Ya know?" Nikki's tone was clear, even to Johnson, that the conversation was over. Her switchboard buzzed and she took the call. Johnson was looking at Shirley, and continued to impose himself.

"Speaking of dating, when are we gonna get together, sweetheart?"

Shirley refused to call him by his official title. "Mr Johnson, we've had this conversation before. I don't date married men. Especially ugly married men."

Johnson got the hint and meandered back towards the elevators. As soon he was out of earshot, Shirley spoke to Nikki.

"He's got to be the only guy on the planet sufferin' from penis envy!"

"Jeez, Shirl, how do you really feel?"

Back around the corner, in the ornate lobby of the Woolworth Building, Doc called Louie and relayed what he had found out. Louie in turn informed Doc that the location was a Federal building, filled with civilian offices, except for a few which were Navy. Louie said he had a complete list of all the departments, but Doc didn't have the heart to tell him that his efforts were wasted. It looked like Ira was on the level. He told Louie he would see him back at the office after lunch, and that he would call Mrs Birnbaum himself.

"Oh, and Louie one more thing."

"What is it Doc?"

"Go downstairs to 2C, guy in there's a lawyer. They got an unabridged Webster's. Find out what the hell a 'bey' is, will ya?"

Chapter Nine

Commander Haffenden wasted no time in launching *Operation Underworld*. Lanza's tentative consent to co-operate was more than enough to draw up plans, requisition agents and supplies, and to establish a base of operations along with a channel of covert communications. So by the time things appeared to have cleared the DA's office, and Lanza gave the Navy his okay, the ball was rolling within 24 hours.

In the beginning, there would be three basic areas of operations. The fishing boats, over which Lanza had virtual control, the retail and shipping, that is the lifeline from the boats to the markets, over which he had a large measure of control, and the docks and warehouses, over which he had a little control, providing they were related to the fishing industry.

Socks would handle all the field operations on his side, Haffenden would control all his agents, and the only two who would know about the operation as a whole would be Lanza and Haffenden. At least that's what Lanza was told. However, for the moment, both parties had a vested interest in excluding the DA to as great an extent as possible.

Lanza had to conceal his involvement in order to avoid exposing the extent of his operation if he were to stay in business. A valuable lesson he learned from the Boss.

One of the cornerstones of Luciano's success was the code of silence. Not the 'keep your mouth shut while sitting under a hot police lamp and being slapped around' code of silence, although that went without saying. Instead, it was the ability to isolate information from everyone except those with the absolute need to know. Combine this with the uncanny ability to keep locations and extents of specific operations secret, and the results spoke for themselves.

For example, a quarter of a century after Luciano's deportation in 1945, local state and federal officials, in one investigation after another as well as in sworn testimony, continued to give vastly conflicting stories concerning him and his operations. These incongruities even exist as a matter of Congressional record.

Luciano shared a hotel suite with the Head of the Democratic Committee at the National Convention in Chicago in 1932, the year FDR won. The same FDR who earlier, as governor of New York, pardoned over sixty of Luciano's associates from Federal prison, most of whom were drug trafficking offenders.

Haffenden had as much at stake as Lanza. Although he was internationally renowned for his work in intelligence, having been the subject of numerous books and articles, he was in a new ballpark concerning domestic saboteurs. The world of international espionage had changed drastically since his first tour of duty in 1917, back when, incredibly enough, few of the Naval Staff and none of the Army Staff Officers put any credence whatsoever in the burgeoning area of military intelligence. It wasn't even mentioned in an official capacity at the war colleges.

The prevailing attitude towards the subject was amply demonstrated by the story of a British Colonel who, in the First World War, was presented with intercepted German dispatches. The officer ordered them promptly returned, unopened, commenting, "Gentlemen don't read other gentlemen's post."

However, that was a quarter of a century ago, and things had changed. Virtually every major operation of the Second World War, on both sides, depended on available intelligence prior to launch. In addition, as the war dragged on, an even more valuable strategy was adopted. Namely, that of supplying the other side with false intelligence. It was a much more complicated game now, and as a consequence, Haffenden intended to isolate information from everyone except those who had an absolute need to know.

The first order of business was for Socks to meet with the Commander and get a list of his needs. This happened the next day, and the meet was brief, as initially needs were simple. Get as many eyes and ears as were available on station, as soon as possible.

The next step was for Socks to get a list of contacts together to allow him to begin placing operatives into key positions, in as much as the primary concern was to nab the enemy agents and potential saboteurs who were resupplying the U-Boats, the docks and the fishing boats had priority.

Naval Intelligence agents were scattered around on the fishing vessels, being passed off as a friend of a friend, or somebody's cousin on his mother's side. Naturally, preference was given to personnel who had fishing experience and/or grew up in the local New York districts, "On accounta dey could tawk da right way".

Stationing agents with the fishing fleet had at least two unexpected side effects. One good, and one that would eventually counteract all their efforts at keeping the operation secret.

Prior to the onset of the project, it was not inconceivable for the shipping agents, civilian authorities or the US Navy to have to wait weeks or even months to find out if a ship had been lost at sea. Whether lost to severe sailing conditions or, as was more often the case, the Wolf Packs, this delay in information was a serious hindrance to the flow of supplies.

With trained agents out on the water armed with radios, bad news of the loss of a vessel could be relayed much sooner. Wreckage could be identified, or in rare cases survivors rescued. In the even more remote instances, if discovered soon enough, 'alert aircraft' could be launched and the offending U-Boat sought out.

The negative effect was both inevitable and unforeseen. Fishing boats, like all small sea-going craft, can only accommodate a given number of individuals. One agent goes on, one fisherman comes off.

In time of war, with money tight, rationing and the seasonal nature of fishing, being put off the boat made for some unhappy people. This, combined with the bulky radio gear required on board, made it nearly impossible to keep the Top Secret operation covert. Within a couple of weeks, everyone on the docks knew something was going on.

After the first month, the operation was going well, in terms of logistics. In terms of effectiveness, though . . . well, that was an interesting question. Were the designers of *Operation Underworld* not catching any saboteurs because they were scaring them away, or were they not catching any because the secret was out?

Haffenden and his men, for the most part, were in uncharted waters. American intelligence-gathering capability lagged far behind that of the warring nations and many elements in the Federal government were very slow to understand the significance of it.

Despite intelligence gathered in the pre-war years indicating that the Japanese were amassing a hostile naval force, the American politicians still went so far as to prosecute and punish visionaries such as Billy Mitchell. To compound Haffenden's problems, none of the allies were sharing information.

For example, later in the war, when the Allies realised that the first nation with an atomic bomb would win, heavy water became the priority. So, one moonlit night, in a French harbour, a team of OSS (Office of Strategic Services) operatives paddled their rubber boats toward a freighter anchored in a slip. On board the freighter was Hitler's last significant supply of tritium. As they made final preparations to mine and sink the ship, it exploded, burned and sank right before their eyes. In the sullen moonlight, the OSS operatives sat dumbfounded as they watched three canoes paddling away from the burning hulk. Klapper canoes, the hallmark vessels of the British Special Operations Executive, the SOE.

Whatever the reasons, the early stages of the operation were not very successful. At the same time, expanding out into the shipping branches of the fishing trade, such as the trucking industry, the project demanded more contacts and consumed more territory and resources. Socks complied and set it up by helping extend the net starting with trucking company owners, dispatchers and in some cases enlisting the help of small independents whom he would normally attempt to put out of business, promising to lay off if they helped out.

Riding trucks all day helped the operatives to learn their way around, but did little to put them in close touch with any potential enemy agents. Unknown to any of the players, involvement with the trucking unions would also initiate a development in the operation which would have an unforeseen impact.

Infiltration of the docks was a much more complicated affair. Lanza's influence was limited to those areas where the fishing industry flourished. With such a complicated network of waterfronts as exists in New York Harbor, no one person or entity could control it all. With five boroughs on the New York side, plus Long Island and seven cities on the Jersey side, the linear area alone was mind-boggling. This did not take into account the New England states, or the states further south such as Delaware and Maryland, and, at the time, the Fulton Street Market shipped as far south as the Carolinas.

All the same, agents were placed on the accessible piers and adjoining areas, and for a short time, a routine developed. Communication was carried out primarily by phone, and operatives checked in with Haffenden on a rotational basis. They were assigned and reassigned as needed and information was recorded.

The primary record of the secret codes, contact locations and most importantly, the names of those involved, was Commander Haffenden's 'little black book'. This book was supposed to stay on his person at all times. At least that was the standard operating procedure for classified materials at the time. It was officially known as 'chain of custody'. In other words, who had it last?

However, like a McGuffin in a Hitchcock film, the little black book was destined to impose a significant emotional event on the lives of more than one player in *Operation Underworld*. It wouldn't turn out to be the stuff dreams were made of.

Codes for the members of Lanza's crew were really not

required. At least not new ones. They all had their passwords, known locations and contacts in place long before the war. In fact, these men had effectively been at war since 1931. A ten year jump on the Navy.

One interesting code that did evolve, however, was the password used when one Mob member wanted another Mob member to know he was in on the operation.

"I'm working for the Commander," became the verbal high sign between them.

Not long into the operation, the load began to show on Lanza. In addition to his indictment, and the time he was devoting to the Navy's business instead of his own, a third factor began to compound his life which he had not banked on.

It first hit him one afternoon at Morrelli's Restaurant on the corner of Mott and Hester Streets. He was having lunch with a couple of representatives from the Brooklyn docks, one of the locations where he had no influence. Haffenden wanted to get some men over there to snoop around the shipping piers. Lanza told the Commander he would see what he could do, and instead of contacting the Camardo brothers directly, Socks thought it wiser to use intermediaries.

The winter air was frigid but the crystal clear Manhattan sky allowed the sun to impose a comfortable greenhouse effect on the area just inside the restaurant window. The intoxicating aromas of sauces and pastries floated gently throughout the small room, and a thin veil of cigarette smoke, highlighted by the sun's rays, lingered in the corner to give a Hopper-esque quality to the three men sitting at the four seat table.

Under the cloud of spent tobacco, the larger of the three men ate as if it were his last meal and, increasingly agitated by the shrill scraping of the knife and fork on the big man's plate, Lanza snubbed out his cigarette and broke the silence.

"So whata ya tellin' me, Jimmy? I'm no good no more?" Socks looked Jimmy square in the eye, who twirled his empty cup of demitasse.

"I ain't sayin' you're no good, Socks! It's just that a lotta the guys are a little edgy right now, that's all." Jimmy's words were compelled to escape in between mouthfuls of *primavera*. He hoped that Lanza would get the picture without him having to spell it out.

"This guy's straight up, I'm tellin' ya. You can talk to him yerself. He's got guys all over the place. The docks, on trucks, on the boats."

"That's exactly the problem, Socks. Feds all over the place. A lotta people don't think that's such a good idea, ya know?"

A waiter approached the table from the side just as Socks let go on Jimmy.

"They ain't Feds! They're Navy!" Lanza kept his voice down, but let his growing irritation seep through. The young boy detoured to the other side of the room.

Jimmy looked at the other man at the table who had been sitting in silence since the start of the meal. It was tradition to politely avoid talk of business until after the meal, and so up until now he had only engaged in chit-chat. He accepted the signal from Jimmy, and took over the conversation.

"Socks, I gotta give it to ya straight. There's talk'a you makin' deals."

"Deals wit who?" He was coming to a slow boil. Not because of the accusation, it really wasn't an accusation. If the Camardos said they heard rumours, then there were rumours. And Lanza was pretty sure he knew the source.

"The DA. Some guys got it figured that you cut a deal ta let the Feds in on some of the operations, so they'd go lighter on ya."

"They ain't fuckin' Feds! They're United States fuckin' Navy!"

"Navy, DA, Treasury, they're all the Law, Socks." Frankie spoke in a controlled tone, and Socks began to see the futility of his argument. It was a tactic as old as the frontal assault, but a lot less risky for the accuser. Once you were put on the defensive with a simple accusation, no matter what you said, you sounded guilty by virtue of the fact you were defending yourself. No substantiation or real evidence was needed.

"Does the DA know about this little party?" Lanza certainly

couldn't lie about that. Frankie would never have asked if he didn't already know the answer.

"Dem DA's are only there for one thing, Socks. Ta become politicians. We got Soldiers, Lieutenants, Captains, and a Boss, they got Assistant DA's, DA's, Attorney Generals and Governors. Look at Roosevelt. Sure, he helped us out when he was Gov'ner, but what the hell? Was mostly our money got him elected." His partner was moved to chime in.

"Better than that little worm Dewey. Frames Lucky, buys the judge and Charlie goes up for fifty years fer a crime ain't worth ten! Am I right, Socks or am I right? Tell me. You agree or not?"

"Yeah, I get yer point. Now, you look me in the eye and tell me you think I'm a fink." Lanza knew he risked Frankie's friendship with this challenge, but he was too frustrated to care.

"Socks, it don't matter what I think . . ."

"Look me in the fuckin' eye and tell me you think I'm a fuckin' fink!" Lanza was leaning over the table now, only inches from Frankie's face and staring him straight in the eyes.

Jimmy instinctively reached under the left breast of his jacket. Frankie reached over to lay his hand on Jimmy's forearm. Frankie kept eye contact with Socks, and pointing his index finger, replied, "I don't think you're sellin' out Joey. I wouldn't never peg you for a fink. Never. But lettin' this DA in on operations is bad business."

Lanza at last felt some relief and fell back in his chair. He took a deep breath, let it out and peered across the table at Jimmy. "What the fuck was you doin'? Scratchin' ya tit?" he asked with half a smile.

"Socks, look here. You want the Camardos involved, you know whose okay you gotta get? Right?" Lanza didn't answer right away. "Are we okay? Socks! Are we okay or what?" Frankie prodded.

"Charlie would never deal with these bastards. Not after what they done ta him in court," Socks replied, reaching for the check. "Yeah, we're okay. But do me a favour, will ya?"

Frankie nodded a 'What?'

"Next time leave this big prick at home, will ya? He eats like a fuckin' horse!"

Chapter Ten

For the first time since the turn of the century the overall labour situation in America was stable. The violent union wars of the twenties were replaced by the violent labour wars of the thirties and the Depression, which in turn gave way to the retooling and re-employment required by the war effort. There was an unwritten 'no strike' agreement for the duration of the war amongst the waterfront labour force, and virtually every individual or entity involved in labour utilised this time to posture and jockey for political position in preparation for the day when things would return to normal.

A significant piece of the union pie was being sought after by the American Communist Party, represented by the Industrial Workers of the World labour union. In 1942, the CPA were a legitimate political party and, in contrast to any other party, stood on a platform composed almost entirely of labour issues. They held sway with large segments of the labor population of America owing to their earlier victories against vicious factory owners in New England and New York, and until the witch hunts of the Late Forties there were no widespread fears of Communists taking over the country and eating all the babies.

The labour union leaders of other factions, however, were very afraid. The Communists offered members of the labour force something the other parties would not even talk about, a share in the pie. However unsuccessful this would prove to be in later years, at the time it was a difficult enticement to ignore.

The party had gained considerable momentum on the West Coast and the man out there doing all the talk about pie sharing was a man named Harry Bridges.

Harry made the mistake late that February, of coming to New York. He compounded this error in judgement by letting his intentions be known, before leaving the West Coast, that the goal of his pilgrimage would be to organise labour in New York.

Officially, he was functioning completely within the law, as a duly elected representative of a legitimate political party and an international labour union.

But that was in California. Seems way out there on the sunny West Coast, Harry hadn't gotten the word that New York labour was already organised. By some Italians.

From LaGuardia Field, Bridges took a taxi into mid-town and arrived at the Hollywood Hotel about mid-morning, across from one of Luciano's former favorite night spots, the Paradise. Although the Hollywood did not boast the elaborate floor shows of the Paradise, the service was good, the rooms spacious and it suited Harry's love of comfortable surroundings. After all, if one were to battle the bourgeois, one had to understand its ways.

The effeminate desk clerk saw nothing unusual in the dark-haired, medium-built man in the dark grey suit and as Mr Bridges registered, the desk clerk rang for a Front, and then handed the new guest his metal tagged room key. The bell boy, who had been leaning against the wall reading a comic book, took his time getting to the desk and Harry headed for the elevators. Waiting for the guest to be out of earshot, the desk clerk, in his lispy dialect, addressed the Front.

"Franklin! I've told you time and again about that gum! Take it out of your mouth this instant or I'll report you to Mr. Carlson!"

The bellhop made an exaggerated gesture of swallowing the offending confectionary.

The frail little desk clerk, about half the size of Frankie the bellhop, did not think it a good idea to push his luck, so when Frankie approached, the clerk turned and occupied himself at the back desk.

As Frankie watched the new guest walk towards the elevator, he squinted his eyes in a gesture of faint recognition. Turning the register around, he read the name and smiled. He carried the two suitcases to the elevator, which had already taken Mr Bridges up to his room. Setting them aside by the large fern, he went across the lobby to a bank of phone booths.

"Lemme talk to Mr Lanza." Frankie felt like a kid at Christmas when he pulled the door shut.

"Who the hell is this?"

"Frankie. I need to talk to him."

"Frankie who?"

"Frankie, over at the Hollywood. Tell him I got something for him."

"Hold on." The bellhop knew he had a chance to start establishing his reputation in The Unione. Frankie reckoned that if his guess was right, he would no longer have to wait for his piece of shit brother-in-law to get him connected.

"Yeah, who am I talking to?" Lanza asked impatiently.

"Mr Lanza! This is Frankie. Frankie the bellhop, uptown at the Hollywood Hotel.

"Frankie the bellhop?"

"Yes sir. I think I got somethin' for ya."

"Yeah, like what, Frankie the bellhop?"

"You know that Commie Pinko labour guy from California?" He had trouble containing himself.

"Harry Bridges the Commie? What about him?"

"Guess who just checked into room 1017?" By now, the diminutive desk clerk had swished across the lobby and was heading towards the phone booth.

Lanza asked in a low, slow controlled voice, registering increasing satisfaction as he spoke. "He's there, at the Hollywood?" There was a momentary pause on Lanza's end of the line. "Room 1017, is dat right?" Lanza reconfirmed.

"Yes sir. I'm supposed ta take his bags up right now."

"Well, nice job, Frankie the bellhop. You still want in at the union?"

"Hedy Lamarr got nice tits?"

"Go down to Fulton Street on Monday morning. See Joey

DiTorrio. Tell him I sent ya. Hey kid, what the hell is that bangin' sound?" Lanza held the receiver away from his head and looked at it. The desk clerk had found Frankie.

"Nuthin', Mr Lanza. I'll take care of it, thanks." Frankie hung up and slid open the bi-fold door. The clerk stopped his banging, and took a step back from the phone booth.

"Did you put Mr Bridges' bags in the elevator?" Frankie the used-to-be bellhop gave no verbal response. Instead, he walked back over to the fern, lifted the two suitcases and threw them into the open elevator. He reached in and pushed several buttons, and the cases disappeared behind the closing doors.

Removing his small, round, blue and gold cap, he walked over to the reception desk, and after tossing the cap over the desk, Frankie magically produced the gum from his mouth he was supposed to have swallowed, and spat the wad on the open register book. Giving a broad smile to the clerk, who prudently remained across the lobby, he slammed the book closed and pressed firmly, being sure to smash the gum flat.

Bravely, from his safe position by the phone booths, the clerk called out that Frankie had better find another job because he was never going to work at the Hollywood again.

Oh yeah. He was going to report him to Mr Carlson, too.

Lanza's luck that morning ran thin after Frankie's phone call. Although he immediately dispatched a reception committee, by the time they arrived uptown, Bridges had left his room. Next, he called Commander Haffenden's suite at the Astor, but there was no answer.

Lanza instructed the three men to hang around the hotel and call when Bridges returned. Their wait was short. About an hour later, Harry walked across the lobby and took the elevator up to his room. Socks picked up the phone on the first ring.

"Yeah, who's talking?"

"It's me."

"Commander! I was just tryin' ta call you!"

"Have you got something for me on the other dock situation?"

"No. But we got an out of town visitor."

"Who?" Haffenden's anticipation quickly peeked as he harbored hope that someone had finally caught a saboteur.

"Harry Bridges."

"The labour organiser?" Haffenden was seriously surprised.

"Yeah!"

"So?" He did not attach the same significance to this development as did Lanza. Then again, Haffenden was not involved in illicit labour manipulation. Not technically.

"*So*? He's a Commie!"

"Socks, being a Communist isn't illegal." It never occurred to Lanza that Haffenden would give him any opposition on this.

"What if he starts talking some of that Commie shit out here? What if he came out here to disrupt the unions? What about if he's in cahoots with some German spies or somethin'? Then it would be illegal! Right?" Haffenden knew what Lanza was driving at. He wanted Haffenden's okay to take care of Bridges.

If he gave the nod, and anyone ever found out he sanctioned violence against an elected representative, the operation, as well as his career, may be over. On the other hand, if he told Lanza to lay off, he might not have as much co-operation as he was presently enjoying. Haffenden's long silence ended.

"Do what you gotta do. Only, I don't need to know how. Just let me know when it's done." There was nothing more to say. He hung up.

Socks called the hotel and gave his men their instructions. Then he placed a second call and arranged for a flight.

Harry didn't know it yet, but his pilgrimage was over.

✦

A block away from the Fulton Street Fish Market, there stood a three storey brick warehouse, circa nineteen twenties. The two hobos standing at the side door were surprised when they saw the bright yellow sign nailed to the door: *CLOSED BY ORDER OF NEW YORK CITY BOARD OF HEALTH. INFECTED RATS*

FOUND ON PREMISES.

"What's it say?"

"What'sa matter? Can't you read? It says, 'Closed . . . for . . . remodlin'."

"Damn! I really liked that place, too. Spacious, nice gentle ambience."

The two disappointed men turned and walked away in search of other accommodation, and a place to share their bottle of vintage Thunderbird wine.

Originally used to store large shipments of dry goods, the warehouse was abandoned in the late thirties when temperature-controlled storage and the advent of more efficient trucking came to lower Manhattan. With most of the windows broken out and literally every single fixture, removable or not, having been removed, the building was of little use to anyone except some of the less desirable hobos who had been banned from the doorways, streets and sewers of the Lower Bowery.

Of course, New York being New York, the building might have been abandoned but that didn't mean it wasn't occupied. Voices could be heard emanating from the basement. They were the voices of Lanza and Haffenden. The words, however, had a Marconian crackle to them.

In a small room, in the basement, were two men. The room they were in was in the extreme corner of the lower level, and its door had a crooked sign hanging by one nail which read: *JANITOR*. The two men wore bulky headsets and were staring intently at the RCA eight inch reel-to-reel tape recorder, while listening to the play-back of *Operation Underworld*'s two prime players.

"What the hell do you make of that?" one of the agents asked, sliding his bulky headset down around his neck.

"Got me by the short ones! I figure the guys at the Hollywood belong to Lanza. But this other guy he's reportin' to has to be somebody pretty god-damned big."

"Well, it sure as hell ain't Luciano. Must be some new boss, moved in to take over."

"The Commander?"

"Where the hell do they come up with these ridiculous names?"

✦

That night, Harry Bridges remembered coming around the corner onto Broadway, and then the stars were swirling in front of his eyes, and his vision blurred to a haze. Now he sat in the back of a car with a huge man sitting on either side of him, and his arms were pinned behind his back.

A short time later, he was in the back room of a restaurant, lying on the floor, still blindfolded, beaten and bruised, while sounds of banging pots and crashing dishes surrounded him. A car pulled up outside, and he was man-handled into the back seat. At LaGuardia Field he was escorted onto a plane, shortly before take-off, and he understood that, except for in the movies, he had no reason ever see New York again.

✦

The next morning, even before he had eaten his eggs, Socks was back on the phone with The Commander.

"We don't anticipate any more trouble concerning that Brooklyn Bridge deal. He got on a plane last night."

"Alright. What about Brooklyn?"

Lanza hesitated before answering. "No, nuthin' yet."

"We need a meet after the weekend. Monday, the usual place, alone. If you get there first, don't order the fish."

"I won't."

Lanza had a nervous feeling as he hung up. Not only was this operation taking away from his own business time and making no contribution to his impending case, it appeared to be rapidly gaining in intensity and scope. Worst of all, what if Jimmy The Bull was right? No one anywhere had discovered any saboteurs.

Times for meetings were on a rotational basis per day. In other words, if a day was given over the phone, it actually meant the day after, and depending on which day the meeting was actually

112

on, the times were previously set. For example, Mondays were always three o'clock, Tuesdays were always four o'clock and so on. If a special, unscheduled meeting was necessary, a code word was used in the conversation and special couriers were utilised. Late that afternoon Socks got a special courier.

✦

Lucky Luciano had a close partner, Frank Costello. Frank Costello had a top-notch bookie, Eddie Erickson. Eddie would regularly meet with Walter Winchell. Every so often, in order to get the inside scoop on 'bigtime' crime stories, Winchell would pass information on winning horses to a very highly placed law enforcement official. The same official who now stood at window number three of the betting cages.

The elderly man in the cashier's cage read the ticket the gambler had just slid across the counter.

"Belmont. Albany Eddie to show in the third." He looked up at the small man in the dark suit with the oval, baby face. The cashier recognised him instantly, even without the two bodyguards standing on either side of him. Double-checking the clipboard hanging next to him to confirm the results, the cashier filed the ticket and counted out the man's $250.

The man stepped off to one side and faced into the wall to put the money away, and one of the short, pugnacious men with him commented as he removed his wallet from his breast pocket.

"You don't bet too often, Chief, but when you do, you sure can pick 'em."

"You just have to know how to study the ponies, agent. That, and a little luck."

The opened bill fold showed an ID card with a red stamp across it which read, *DIRECTOR* and a picture of the little man, as well as a small, toy-like gold badge. The name under the photo read: J. Edgar Hoover.

Belmont Park was the third leg of The Triple Crown and one of the oldest and largest racetracks in the country. Although races were normally restricted or suspended in the winter months, the combination of the mild weather and the wartime atmosphere persuaded the owners to extend the season.

Saturday was always the best day to be there. There were specials at the restaurant, happy hour started earlier, and there were more races to bet on. Whenever someone brought a friend to the track for the first time, they were careful to bring them in through the main arcade. For it was here that the excitement flowed over the lucky losers at its strongest, and the absolute sensation of privilege at being allowed to donate your money to such a fine establishment was most appreciated. It is highly probable that this is the very atmosphere that first inspired Buggsy Siegel to claim to have conceived the idea of a casino in the middle of the desert, to his compatriots a few years later.

The awful stench of the food and cigar smoke permeated the arcade and flowed out onto the first few tiers of stadium seating, where they collided with the pleasant aromas of horse shit and damp turf.

"What time is it?"

Looking at his watch, short agent number one answered, "Half past five, Mr Hoover." All three men wore identical dark suits, white shirts, Fedoras and shiny black shoes so you couldn't tell they were FBI.

"Alright, you two go and watch the races. Meet me by concession stand three, at six o'clock."

"But Mr Hoover, we're supposed to stay with you at – " short agent number two began to protest, but was cut short.

"*I SAID GO, GOD-DAMN IT*!"

They went.

Hoover was the most successful bureaucrat in the history of Washington DC. From the time his father got him his first job at the Department of Justice, in June of 1917, his borderline fanaticism, which he mistakenly believed to be loyalty, grew ever stronger and increasingly self-perpetuating.

In no time at all, J. Edgar's ability to manipulate knowledge and information before it reached the people had grown to legendary proportions.

During the Deportation Hysteria of the early 1920s, Hoover worked at the Enemy Alien Registration Section, appropriately abbreviated EARS, of the Bureau of Investigation. It is from the 'reports' of the misguided scientists who testified with 'scientific proof' that aliens, especially Eastern European Jews, were by-and-large undesirable, (due to everything from crime and disease to an increased tendency to display feeble-mindedness), that he first learned how easy it was to dupe the American public.

Performing centre stage with a backdrop of anti-immigrant fever suited Hoover's purist mentality, as well as taught him that oldest of government bureaucrat's tricks. Find something or someone to label a dangerous common enemy, and after shining the spotlight on them, rally supporters to mould into a power base on the premise that you are the man to defeat that enemy. Before the First War it was the Eastern Europeans, mostly Jews, during the Second War it was 'The Hun' and later it became the communists.

Appropriating money wherever he could, Hoover began to build his empire within The Empire. However, money was not the only ingredient in the Hooverville recipe.

From his early days in the Twenties, Hoover learned that money and political influence bought access to the broadsheets, accompanied by sympathetic stories which would go a long way towards helping him achieve his dream of becoming a national hero.

He sensationalised his police stories through the media with consummate skill. His personally approved police dramas for the *Lucky Strike Hour*, a popular radio show, were by 1932 specifically designed to establish his bureau, and by default himself, as pop culture icons. The children's episodes of *Junior G-Men*, broadcast nationwide, told youngsters how to recognise and report suspicious persons to the local authorities, as well as teaching them how they should think and behave if they were going to grow up to be good little agents. Follow-up shows such as *Gangbusters* and *This Is Your FBI* continued his unending quest for popularity.

Ironically, even though it was from his hatred of aliens that Hoover built a career, it was an alien that would help him establish it once and for all in the public eye by giving him Public Enemy Number One, John Dillinger. From the first time 'Baby Face' Nelson called them "G-men" and John Dillinger's body was splashed across the front page, J. Edgar knew he would be a star.

His big break came in 1924 when the Bureau reached an unprecedented level of corruption. He seized the chance when it was offered and accepted the directorship of the Bureau, and took the post on the condition he be allowed to isolate it from politics, effectively transforming it into an autonomous entity.

By 1941, Hoover had been in service for twenty-five years, twenty-one of those years as Assistant Director or Director, and although most career individuals would consider themselves prime candidates for retirement, J. Edgar wasn't even halfway through his dictatorship.

How was a multi-million dollar government organisation, which was later able to enact law allowing a file to be compiled containing the details of every one of its citizens' personal lives, held at bay by a criminal syndicate which Hoover claimed did not exist?

The answer is very basic. Hoover was bought.

Lucky Luciano understood two principles regarding the approach towards the American way of doing business when he established The Commission: every man has his price, and when attempting to buy someone, always start at the top.

J. Edgar's inane fear of bad press had kept him away from open confrontations with organised crime, and his policies regarding this behaviour are well documented. Through his consistent and unwavering public denial of the existence of organised crime, Hoover did more to help the criminal syndicates than any other single entity up until the circus known as the 'War On Drugs', (which seems to have replaced the 'War On Poverty' but has recently taken a back seat to the 'War On Terror').

David Marston, a retired FBI agent, in his much acclaimed

book, *Inside Hoover's FBI*, commenting on the relationship of organised crime and the FBI under Hoover, stated that, ". . . although they, [the FBI and organised crime], were presumptive enemies, in the first four decades they competed primarily for newspaper space."

This may have been an understatement. Marston, in the same publication, comments that, "J. Edgar Hoover was the best FBI Director Organised Crime ever had."

This attitude set the ground work for The Unione at a time when they already had controlling influence in New York's City Hall through Albert C. Marinelli, the well known Tammany boss with whom Lucky shared a suite at the 1932 Democratic National Convention, at the Drake Hotel in Chicago. Marinelli's rival, Jimmy Hines, another New York top political leader, shared a suite with Frank Costello, Lucky's partner in the Unione. Both of these rival delegations were there to elect the Presidential candidate for the 1932 elections. If this sounds a little convoluted, let's simplify it.

The American Presidency is basically a popularity contest with little or nothing to do with leadership ability or competency. Whoever has the most money to maintain the highest profile wins the contest. So in 1932, between the Great Depression and Prohibition, (only in America would someone attempt to make alcohol illegal in an effort to better society), the general public were not happy with the existing leadership, which was Republican. Ironically, this opinion was arrived at largely due to political corruption. As a result, it was pretty certain the Democrats would take the election. The question was, which Democratic candidate would get the nod?

This being the case, Luciano and Costello each escorted a delegation leader to the convention, along with appropriate financial donations, so that regardless of which Presidential candidate won, Al Smith or Franklin D. Roosevelt, The Unione were assured of being in the right camp.

FDR who, only a short time before the convention, as Governor of New York, set free from prison approximately sixty members of The Commission, was the front runner. In January of the following year FDR was sworn in as the thirty-second President of the United States.

Start at the top.

The FBI were no exception. J. Edgar, a man who, given the chance, would impose the death penalty on anyone who opposed capital punishment, loved horse-racing. Eddy Erickson was a top-notch bookie who worked for Frank Costello. Walter Winchell was, well, Walter Winchell, anything for a story.

Costello would give Erickson the expected winner of a given race, Erickson would contact Winchell who in turn would get it to Hoover.

Ever wonder how Winchell got the scoop on so many top crime stories?

Every man has his price.

So, in the space of a few short years, Lucky's organisation held considerable influence in all the upper echelons of authority, and in turn established contacts, patterns and techniques which are considered to be standard operating procedures to this day when dealing with or within the Federal Government or any large corporation.

Hoover headed over to the concession stand and ordered a hot dog. A race had just begun, so the stand was nearly abandoned. There was a man standing in the far corner, nursing a cup of coffee, and Hoover walked over to him while he ate.

"Hello, Socks, how's the fish business?"

"Stinks!" Lanza wore a hat, and was visibly uncomfortable. "Let's drop the names, huh? Whatta you want from me?"

"You want a hot dog, Socks? They're really good here. Not like that shit they pawn off on ya over at Yankee Stadium."

"No, I don't want a fuckin' hot dog! What's this about?!"

"What, the dog? I just like to treat my guests right, Socks." J. Edgar spoke while he chewed, and allowed his words to drip with arrogance. "I hear you had a guest a coupl'a nights ago."

"What the hell you talkin' about?"

Hoover finished his frankfurter, wiped his hands with a napkin, threw it on the floor and reached into the side pocket of his jacket. Reading from the notepad he produced, he began to give Lanza an education.

"I want complete details concerning the Brooklyn Bridge deal. And its association with the Hollywood Hotel on Broadway. What exactly, if any, is their significance to one Harry Bridges?"

Lanza, initially expressionless, slowly smiled. "Lemme ask you a question. How come you guys always talk like you got a rod up your ass or something?"

Hoover began to boil. Spectators could be heard behind him cheering the race on.

"Besides, you ain't got it all," Lanza informed him.

Hoover looked at him quizzically.

"You forgot the Manhattan, the Williamsburg and the Queensboro," Lanza baited.

"I'm warning you, Lanza, you ain't as immune as you think! I could shut you down tomorrow!"

"Yeah, and if Frank Costello and a coupl'a others testified, we could shut you down today! So don't give me that strong arm of the law, holier-than-thou bullshit. You're just another crooked cop."

Hoover looked around nervously. Lanza clearly had the upper hand now.

"I want to know who the hell all these new guys on the docks are, and where they're coming from!" Hoover demanded.

"They're just new workers. Friends, relatives. We need the help. There's a war on if you ain't heard."

"Yeah, I heard! And soon there's gonna be another war on, wise guy!" Hoover threw a newspaper on the counter. It was folded open to page four. Lanza picked it up and read the short story with the 'X' next to it. The story reported a California labour leader who was irate at the treatment he received while visiting New York, and that he intended to ask his state representative to launch an investigation.

Lanza was taken off guard, but not shocked, he had already read the paper.

Turning to page two, Lanza began, slowly and neatly, to tear out a second article which ran for nearly an entire column. He spoke as he worked. Then he slid the article over to Hoover.

"You know, with all the tax money you take from the people you pretend you're supposed ta be defendin', maybe you could spend a few bucks on a pair of elevated shoes."

Livid at the insult, Hoover's expression registered extreme anger as he eyed the lead line on the article: *FBI DIRECTOR ADAMANT; ORGANISED CRIME NON-EXISTENT!*

The public address system announced the last race of the day was about to begin.

Chapter Eleven

Just south of the Fish Market, on the corner of Peck Street and Franklin D. Roosevelt Drive, was a small fish restaurant frequented by local workers. The Italians had their pick of restaurants, the Jews usually brought their meals with them, but the Irish and the British workers were blessed with The Chinaman. The Chinaman, no one could pronounce his name, owned and ran Chanze Chinese Chippy, which served the most authentic fish and chips in Ireland's westernmost county, New York.

Lanza approached Chanze just before the late rush hour, which started about 11 p.m., and shook his head and smiled as he glanced at the six stove pipes Chan had installed at different points on the roof and exterior walls. The pipes served no structural purpose, but instead vented the smell of the fried fish dishes in various directions, and could be opened or shut individually so as to allow the aromas to waft in any given direction. The strategy of course, to this venting conspiracy, was to entice patrons who might otherwise waste their time eating more healthy lunches and suppers, or whatever the after-pub meal might be called. *I wish I had that guy working for me*, Lanza thought to himself.

He entered the eatery and took one of the red-enamelled booths in the back. As always, he sat facing the door; after all, this was a popular time for his co-workers to kill each other in restaurants. An attractive Chinese girl with long, silky black hair and green eyes, one of Chan's sixteen offspring, approached the booth the minute Lanza sat down. She looked to be in her late teens.

"You want I should bring you a menu, Mac?" She was born and raised in New York, and so spoke perfect English.

"No, I'm waitin' on someone." She left Lanza looking at his watch. He was ten minutes early for the special meeting.

How the hell did Hoover know about the Hollywood? And worse yet, the god-damned Bridges job! It just didn't make sense! *Nice future, Socks. A contract on me for working with the Feds, FBI on my ass, and some big shot Navy Intelligence guy givin' me grief! Prison's startin' ta look pretty good!*

There was no easy way out and just as Socks began to regret his patriotic feelings, Commander Haffenden came through the door.

Socks waved, but it didn't matter, Chanze was so small it rivalled Harry's.

"Socks, what's the story on Brooklyn?" Haffenden wasted no time.

"Commander, the hell with Brooklyn! We got bigger problems than Brooklyn!"

"Socks, you okay?" Haffenden was unprepared for the change of schedule. He had called the meeting to increase the load on Lanza. Now it looked as if someone had beaten him to the punch.

"Sir, I haven't got a god-damned clue how or when it happened, but Hoover is on to us!"

"Hoover?"

"Hoover. J. Edgar Fucking Hoover. Mr FBI!"

"How do you know?" Hoover wasn't necessarily a serious problem as far as Haffenden was concerned. He would likely be able to deal with him through normal channels.

However, his maniacal devotion to his bureau, and the fact that there was a government operation he wasn't in on, had the potential to make things messy.

"Well, maybe it was the meeting I had with him at Belmont Park this afternoon. Or then again, maybe it was the fact that the little sawed-off son-of-a-bitch knew all about The Hollywood and the Bridges job, I'm not sure. But what I know for sure is that you got a serious god-damned leak in your operation!!" Lanza had a hard time containing himself as he spoke. He kept looking at the door.

"Socks, nobody on my side had access to any of that information. When you called me, that was the end of it. There was no reason for me to tell anybody about that."

"Yeah? Well, somebody told somebody! Either that or we got fairies in the god-damned phone lines!" Haffenden looked at Lanza, hesitated, and then sat back in his seat. The Commander had an epiphany.

"Maybe we do."

"What the hell are you talkin' about?"

"I think the only other people who know about our little merger might have a leak."

"Fuckin' Gurfein!" Lanza had a delayed epiphany. "Whatta we do?"

"We do what all good operatives do when they think they're compromised. We use them!" Haffenden hadn't felt this mischievous since he was a teenager. He was making Lanza edgy.

"You call me tomorrow at half past ten. Talk in the open. Don't use any code. Tell me we have to meet immediately. Something's gone drastically wrong since last night. Act panicky." *That shouldn't be hard*, thought Lanza.

"Tell me you'll have the microfilm from the FBI job ready to hand over. Got it?"

"What FBI job?" Lanza was feeling he was definitely in over his head.

"Just do it! Okay?"

Chanze daughter returned to the table. "Youse ready ta order, or what?"

✦

The next morning, as prearranged, Lanza rang Haffenden and set the meeting for that afternoon at half past twelve. An hour and a half before meeting time, a jazzed-up, cherry-bomb red pick-up truck pulled up outside the fish market on Fulton Street. The chrome-garnished vehicle sounded its horn twice and Lanza came out of the market carrying a brown paper bag. He had no way of seeing the agent on the top floor of the warehouse a block away, but Haffenden warned him he would be watched.

As the agent in the warehouse checked his watch and went to make the call, Lanza and the driver of the pick-up pulled away from the market.

"So, Frankie the bellhop! You got the routine straight?"

"Forget about it, Mr Lanza! Just sit back and enjoy da ride like you wuz at Uncle Milty's!" Frankie had been pleasantly surprised at being called into work a day early to do a special favour for Mr Lanza.

The pair had no sooner looped around the Battery and were heading north onto West Side Drive when Frankie saw the dark blue sedan in his rear view mirror.

"Our friends are here, Mr Lanza. Ya want I should start now?"

"Just north of the tunnel. Around Pier 40."

The pre-lunch hour traffic was yet to hit, so the run north of the Holland Tunnel took about five minutes. However, right at the Christopher Street cross-over Lanza braced both feet against the dashboard, sat back and gave a nod. Frankie the bellhop smiled and the two agents in the sedan watched in disbelief as the ten-year-old truck grew smaller and smaller, until by the time they reached the 12th Street cut-off it vanished altogether.

"God-damn it! Go red! Right now, god-damn it! Go red!!" The senior agent knew first-hand how much J. Edgar appreciated failure. The driver floored the pedal and the sedan raced around several cars until reaching a point on the highway where they had an unobstructed view for half a mile.

"They couldn't have just vanished!" The driver spoke to his preoccupied passenger who was consulting the neatly folded map he held in his lap.

"Pull off on Tenth Avenue! If they're leavin' The City, it'll be the Lincoln or the GW! If not, we'll get them by West 57th." At the exit, the sedan unit called in by telephone and alerted the 69th Street office of the likely intercept locations and then drove north along tenth.

The old pick-up, which was now approaching River Side Park, was used extensively during Prohibition. After refitting her with a larger, six cylinder engine, a four-barrelled carburettor and the new experimental tubeless tires, slightly under inflated, she was better suited to "runs" now than in the days of running rum over the Canadian border.

"You still wanna take the bridge, Mr Lanza?"

"No, they'll have it covered. What time is it?"

"Twenty afta aleven."

"Get off on 96th, cut across the park. Go to Central Park South. A little birdie told me we could probably find our friends there." Twenty minutes later, as predicted, they found the dark blue sedan parked on Central Park South and Sixth Avenue.

Both agents were outside their parked vehicle and while the driver was half way through a hot dog, the senior agent stood by a telephone booth, impatiently waiting for a location check, smoking a cigarette in the cold midday air.

Lanza and Frankie had driven past them, turned around at Columbus Circle and were half a block away, approaching from the west end of the park.

The corner pay phone finally rang and before he had the receiver to his ear the senior agent heard his partner yelling, "There they are! The bastards are back!"

Pointing at them, he threw the remainder of his lunch into the street and drew his service revolver. His partner yelled into the phone. "We got them! East on Central Park South! We're rolling!"

Slamming the phone down, he ran to the car as his partner fired three rounds at the passing truck. The first two shots buried themselves in the wooden bed of the vehicle, but the third shattered the small rear windshield, spraying glass all over Lanza and Frankie. Lanza went straight to boiling.

"Dem crazy bastards! Shootin' wild in the streets like that! Did you see that shit?" Without waiting for an answer, he put the bag on the floor and reached into his shoulder holster. Frankie gradually accelerated after turning south onto Fifth Avenue and slowly smiled as he watched Socks do a quick functions check on the .45 Colt.

He gradually reduced his speed to allow the FBI agents to close the gap between vehicles.

"Hold her steady, kid. Don't make no sudden moves." Breaking out some residual glass in the rear window and bracing himself against the frame, Lanza fired two rounds into the grill of the sedan, which by now was only two car lengths behind, and one into the windshield between the two agents.

Radiator fluid gushed from the grill and the fan could be heard whacking the engine.

As steam hissed out of the grill through the bullet holes, the two agents, panicked by the shots, lost control of the car, which snaked back and forth across first three, then all six lanes of Fifth Avenue traffic. A Canadian tour bus swerved to miss the sedan and climbed halfway up a Sunshine taxi parked on the north bound side, before coming to a halt.

The agent driving the sedan struggled against the uncontrollable momentum of the huge vehicle, but managed to regain steering long enough to avoid hitting the parked cars on his right. However, the serpentine pattern continued and they quickly ran out of road. Only a few seconds later, they slammed through the wrought-iron fence surrounding the public library at 42nd Street.

Pedestrians, as well as visitors walking to and from the busy building, were thrown into pandemonium as the momentum of the large vehicle sent it careening up the granite stairs and crashing violently into one of the Corinthian columns adorning the entrance.

Socks turned back around in his seat and replaced his weapon as they continued down the avenue.

"Dopy bastards!" He turned back and yelled out the window. "This ain't Chicago, ya know!!"

"Where to, Socks?"

"What time is it?"

"Twelve-twenty"

"Go to Tompkins."

Tompkins Square Park was a small park which occupied about three square blocks. The centre of the park was dominated by a large grassy field surrounded by a paved walk and benches spread out around the footpath and other areas. Tompkins provided visitors with a refuge from the urban landscape by virtue of the tall trees and assorted foliage dominating the entire perimeter. Due to its small size, only four gates were available to enter or leave the park, one at each corner.

Socks had Frankie drop him off at East Houston and Essex and told him to wait at the Tenth Street entrance. He then began to stroll slowly north on Avenue A with the bag tucked under his arm. Within one block of the park, he noticed a man following him.

At exactly twelve-thirty the party started.

Socks appeared and made his way across the brown grass towards the north west corner of the park, waving in an exaggerated manner to an old man sitting on a bench, feeding the pigeons. Lanza sat down next to him and slipped him a small container which he removed from the brown bag.

Three of Hoover's men, inconspicuous in their gray suits, and black shiny shoes, worked their way past the crippled beggar in the grass, the old lady on the bench and four old men sitting at a table playing chess

The three agents had slipped around behind Lanza and the man, and remained out of sight in their imaginary stealth. Fedoras cocked at just the right angle, arms outstretched with snub-nosed .38's pointed at the ready, they sprang forth precisely as Lanza was helping the old man loosen the lid on the jar of heart medicine he had removed from the brown paper bag.

"Get your hands up and drop your weapons!" The crippled beggar stood behind one of the agents and held a pistol to the nape of his neck as he spoke. Turning slowly towards the right to look at his assailant, the agent saw the four chess players now had their military issue .45's aimed straight at his two partners.

"I suggest you comply, gentlemen." It was the old man sitting on the bench, who had a remarkably young voice. As the revolvers were being collected, Lanza saw his cue and immediately stood and walked towards the exit in the north east corner of the park.

Two unmarked sedans pulled up to the gate, to a position just behind the assorted collection of Government agents and, as the last of the FBI agents was handcuffed and escorted into the back of the first car, they were driven away by the old woman. The Naval Intelligence Operatives piled into the second car and both vehicles U-turned and drove away from the park.

✦

"Excuse me. I have a delivery for a Mr. D. A. Hogan." The young Parcel Post driver consulted his clipboard as he spoke to the fat, red faced guard at the city court house behind the window.

"That's DA Hogan, numbskull! You know, as in District Attorney of New York City DA!" the obese guard corrected.

"I'm impressed. You can spell." The driver leaned forward and eyed the rotund stomach of the guard. "Guess I don't have to ask why you're not on active duty. Meanwhile, I still have a package for this guy Hogan. Where is he?"

"Some place you ain't goin'. It's restricted." The guard smiled at being able to exercise what little power he didn't have.

"Fine by me, lumpy. I get paid either way," the driver said as he turned to walk away. "Tell him it's a priority shipment from the Department of Naval Intelligence, and it's marked Classified Delivery." He was nearly out of the door. "He can pick it up between nine and five at the uptown . . . er . . . the North Bronx station."

The guard had a noticeable change in attitude when he heard the classified part, and forcing himself out of the booth, which he normally did only twice a day, he waddled out to the street to the driver, who was already in his truck.

"You said there was a classified ticket on that package?" Trying to be humble while attempting to project authority was difficult.

"Yep."

"Maybe you better get that upstairs. Ta the fourth floor."

By now it was nearly three o'clock and after the DA's secretary had signed for the package and the DA got around to opening it, it was four-fifteen. The three FBI agents had been in their cell at the Federal Holding Facility on Governor's Island for nearly four hours.

The DA stood alone in his office behind his desk, hands on hips, staring down at the three badges, empty service revolvers and ID cards which lay in a neat stack on his desk, and his secretary was attempting to contact the New York office of the FBI.

Hogan knew the taps were now essentially useless, but could not bring himself to give the order to disconnect them. When a judge grants special permission to install a wire tap, he is very unhappy when he finds out it has been in place for several months, and nothing came of it. Most judges believe it reflects on the competency of the police work. Hogan had asked for two bugs, one for each of Lanza's phones. The judges were justified in their beliefs.

✢

"Which one's Moe? Huh? Just tell me that. I want to know which one's Moe?" It was now seven-thirty, and although it had only been an hour and a half since their release, the three FBI agents already missed the serenity of their cell, on Governor's Island.

"Somebody's got to be Moe because I know *I'M LOOKING AT THE THREE FUCKING STOOGES!*"

The three agents stood motionless in front of the desk. Hoover's New York office at 69th Street and Third Avenue was only used by him on rare occasions. It was situated in a good part of town only three blocks off the FDR Drive and not far from Roosevelt Island. He hated New York. Mabel, the middle-aged secretary, could hear him through the sound-proofed door and decided it was a good time to call it a night. She quickly gathered her things and left.

"How in God's name did you three ever get selected for New York branch? Did you know somebody? Did you have connections? Better yet, how the *HELL DID YOU EVEN GET SELECTED FOR AGENT TRAINING?*" Hoover paced behind the big desk while the New York Bureau chief sat quietly in the corner, hands folded in front of his face. He didn't respond when Hoover addressed him.

"I hope ta hell this isn't the best you've got up here!" He finally took his seat. The oversized desk made his small stature look clownish as he spoke again.

"Okay, ladies. Here's what we're gonna do. Have the secretary . . . what's her name?"

"Mabel, sir. Her name is Mabel" the agent, answered quickly and mechanically.

"Have Mabel contact the DA's office in the morning and your three . . . agents, will go over there and collect their government issue service revolvers. You know. The ones you swore an oath *NEVER TO RELINQUISH*! And then you will camp out on top of Socks Lanza. Not in the same neighborhood, not in the vicinity, *ON TOP*! He stops short, I want you up his ass! Somethin' is goin' on down on the waterfront and I intend to get to the bottom of it! Are we clear?"

No one was in a hurry to speak. Finally, the tallest of the three agents mustered the courage.

"Ahh, Director, we can't go over in the morning."

"And why the hell not, Moe?"

"Sir, the city offices are closed on Saturday."

Hoover was heating up again. He yelled through the soundproofed door for the secretary.

"Mabel! *MABEL*! Find out how to get a hold of the DA on a Saturday morning and book me a flight to Washington, for first thing Monday!"

Mabel didn't answer.

Chapter Twelve

Doc was different from the average working class individual. Other than being willing to take a risk, a contributing factor to the financial mess in which he now found himself, he liked Monday mornings. It's not that it was any easier for him to get out of bed at the irritating sound of the alarm clock, but he always looked on Mondays as a time to start over. Another opportunity to keep that promise to himself he'd been breaking since New Year's Day. Or to do some little thing he put off all last week.

Louie, on the other hand, had a much more practical view towards these things. Every year Louie made the same New Year's resolution, which was not to make a New Year's resolution. And he never broke his resolution. Not once. This way, he significantly reduced the amount of personal anguish he would put himself through in the following 364 days.

Now, with the new glass panel on the front door, the office cleaned up, and a new table in the right hand corner of the room for Louie to work at, Doc felt a sense of renewal as he entered the office on this peaceful Monday morning. Adding to his sense of satisfaction was another case closed. Better than that, a potentially ugly divorce case with a happy ending. Very rare. Doc felt good about it, he liked the Birnbaums.

It was nine thirty-five and Louie was late. He was always late on Monday mornings, but there wasn't that much to do. Doc played a game of mental darts with Louie's good excuse calendar. The subway was late, the alarm didn't go off, or Doris was sick and he had to drop the kids off at school.

Doc sat down at his desk after setting the coffee pot on the hot plate, and opened the folder someone had placed squarely in the middle of the blotter so he wouldn't miss it. He opened it and saw it was the client report on the Birnbaum job. Louie must have done it to impress, and maybe to make up for losing track of Birnbaum last week. Just as he began to read it, the door opened and Louie came in.

"Hey, Doc! Got the new window in, huh? When are we gonna get it lettered?" Louie sounded extra chipper. He offered no excuse. Zero points on the dart board.

"I got Redbone working on it. Hey, Louie?"

"Yeah, Doc?" Louie hung his coat up and was making his way over to his table when Doc held up the report with two fingers like a used handkerchief.

"What's this?"

"Pretty good, huh? That's the Birnbaum case. Makes ya proud, don't it?"

"Louie, that's not a report. I've seen reports, they don't look like this."

Louie was impervious to insults. He took a magazine out of his back pocket, sat at his table, put his feet up and began to read.

"Come on, Doc. That's a completely usable report."

"Yeah. For the bottom of a bird cage."

"Tell me one thing that's wrong with it?"

"'Followed subject as he disembowelled himself from the station'."

"That's right! Disembowelled! It means to remove. I looked it up! Hey, Doc, look at this! Five acres of land for only 500 bucks! What a deal!"

"Yeah? Where? Siberia?" Doc crumpled the report and threw it in the trash.

"No, better, Southern Florida," Louie related. "Some place called Coconut Grove." He circled the article with his pencil.

"You ever been to Southern Florida, Louie?"

"No. But you have. Just recently, too, haven't ya?" Louie laughed. Doc didn't.

"You better get on the ball, Bonehead. If I'm not mistaken, you got about three weeks to your State Board exam. You screw it up because you're trying to describe the 'ambulance of a room' on your final test report, and you're gonna be back haulin' garbage with ya cousin Guido!"

"Come on, Doc! Don't I always pull through?" Louie opened the manual and started to idly flip through the pages. "Hey! Speakin' of screwin' up, you called that broad down on Church Street yet?"

"She's not a broad, Louie. She's a good kid that's had a tough break." Doc removed a blank Client Report form from the files and began to fill out a new Birnbaum report.

"Sorry, Doc. You called that nice broad that's had a tough break down on Church Street yet?" Louie lowered his magazine. "How the hell you know she's had a tough break? She spill her guts to you already?"

"Louie, what do private detectives do?"

"Well, in this town one of two things. They pay the cops or the judges to get work or . . . they starve. Which is probably why that prick Sammon is doin' so good uptown."

"They detect. That's what they do. Now get your head outta yer ass, Louie, 'cause you're *PISSIN' ME OFF*!"

Louie never saw it coming. Doc blindsided him by flinging a copy of the New York State Private Investigators' Regulations at him and nearly knocked him off his chair.

"Jesus, Doc! What the hell was that for?" He sat up straight and started to pay attention. Exactly the intended effect.

"Louie, you got a lotta potential. But you piss me off with your nonchalant attitude. You better start payin' attention! Because someday, when your ass is draggin' in the dirt and you least expect it, some asshole cop, some irate husband, or just some punk off the street is gonna put one in your back! Doris and the kids ain't gonna make it on what their handin' out downtown, god-damn it!" The part about Louie's family was unexpected, by Doc as well as Louie. Doc realised he had recently developed an uncontrollable gut reaction to images of kids and family.

Louie looked down at the manual. It was impossible to find

the right words. "Jesus, Doc, I'm sorry. I didn't realise you cared. I'll . . ."

"Don't say it! Just do it! Be a detective, god-damn it!"

"Christ Doc! Don't you think I wanna be? I try my ass off to figure stuff out. Get clues, find traces. Nuthin'! And then there's you! You look at a god-damned piece of dust and give me the history of the room! I can't do that. Honest ta Christ, Doc, I don't know how you're not rich! You should'a stayed on the force. You'd'a made Chief by now."

Louie's retort was disarming, but Doc wouldn't be thrown off the track of trying to focus his best friend.

"I couldn't stay on the force because most of those guys are in it for the steady pay check and the pension. Half the shit they solve gets solved because some guy rolled over for them, the other half gets solved because the crook screws up. Look, Louie, you gotta feel it. Here, in your gut. You gotta eat it, sleep it, breathe it and shit it. You gotta want it! It's not about the money. It's about doin' somethin' you love. Somethin' you're good at. Somethin' you're passionate about!"

"Yeah, but Doc. I ain't no good at nuthin'! Hell, I nearly lost that old Birnbaum guy last week and he's older then Methuselah!" Louie looked down at the desk. Doc guessed what was coming. "And there's something I gotta tell ya. I broke a rule. A rule of tailing."

"Yeah, I know. He saw you." Louie's head snapped to the upright position, and he looked at Doc like a dog seeing its own image in a mirror for the first time.

"Now see, damn it! How the hell did you know that?"

"I pay attention." Louie continued to stare. Doc felt compelled to explain. "You told me you and Birnbaum came downtown on the same train, that means you got off the train at the same time, at Wall Street. I saw you were in the phone booth before Birnbaum was through the door. And, since the phone is further up the street than the door, that means at some point you had to cross in front of or by him. So I had to assume that you were made." Louie was relieved Doc hadn't deduced the screw-up on the platform.

"The important thing is, that he didn't see you in two separate locations during the tail. That's a dead giveaway." Louie was exasperated. He threw the book on the desk and himself back in his chair, looked up at the ceiling and closed his eyes.

"Look, I'll help you. Teach you everything I can. But you gotta work with me here, Louie. Louie!" He looked back at Doc. "Focus, will ya?"

"I will, Doc."

"I'm serious!"

"I will!"

Doc had no way to know if he had really got through. If he hadn't, he would try again.

"Good. Now, where were we?"

"You were just about to tell me why you're so chicken to call that girl, what'd you say her name was?"

"I didn't. Her name is Nikki. Nikki Cole."

"Well?"

"Well what?"

"You gonna call her? Or you gonna wear your heart on your sleeve the rest of your life?"

"I don't know. I gotta think about it."

"Think about it? What the hell is there to think about? Ya pick up the phone, ya dial the number, she answers, ya pop the question!"

Doc winced.

"Sorry, bad choice of words!"

"I don't wanna seem too anxious. Besides I don't even have her number." Louie reached into his pocket and removed a small piece of paper from his wallet. He got up and laid it neatly on the corner of Doc's desk, smoothing it out a little for effect.

"What the hell's that?"

"Delancy 5 9000. Number to the switchboard at the Federal Building. You know, down on Church Street."

"What? You think I wasn't gonna look it up?"

"Yeah, Doc McKeowen. The original Romeo. Like the last day

before Prom Night when you were tryin' ta get up the guts ta ask Charlene Meeny ta go with ya."

"What's your point?"

"Jesus, Doc! The day before?"

"I like suspense. Besides, I already knew she didn't have a date." Doc tried to remain casual.

"Then, during third period break, you came around the corner like a bat outta hell 'cause you were late for gym and *slam*! There goes Charlene Meany bouncing down the hall on her bony ass like a little blonde basketball."

"Hey, I got the date, didn't I?"

"Yeah, but you were shittin' like a dog in a Chinese restaurant when you asked her!"

"So, I asked her!"

"Then the poor little thing had to limp into the dance from the size of the bruise she had."

"I suppose you saw pictures?"

"Jesus, ya asked her while she was still sittin' on the floor! What were you doin'? Waitin' ta see if she refused before you'd help her up?"

"Prom night? Isn't that the same night Doris slapped the hell outta you for gettin' so – "

"Don't change the subject, councillor! From what you told me and what I saw through that door, Nikki looked pretty good to me. And you know me, I'm no judge of women." Louie walked over to the hot plate and poured two cups of coffee. "Besides, Doris thinks it would be . . ."

"Doris? Christ, Mancino! Now I'm in the gossip columns?"

"Then give them somethin' ta gossip about, damn it! Call her!" Louie coaxed.

Doc picked up the piece of paper and put it in his wallet. "I'll call her!" Louie continued to stare. "I said I'll call! Later! I gotta be uptown at eleven. I have to go convince Mrs Birnbaum her husband is a patriot, not a playboy."

Doc went over to the rack and put on his coat. "Meanwhile, you stay here till I get back. With your nose in that Reg. Book."

As he was halfway out of the door, Doc turned back to Louie.

"Yeah, Doc?"

"She didn't tell me anything about her personal life. She was defensive, but pretended she didn't know how to fix the jack plugs on her switchboard. She had pat answers to my questions, and was middle to late twenties." As he spoke, Doc counted out the points he was making by extending the fingers of his right hand. "And she wore a charm bracelet with the name 'Katie' on it and a wedding ring on a chain around her neck. How did I know she had a rough break? Figure it out. See ya in a couple of hours." Doc left.

Louie hung his head as the door slammed shut and muttered, "I hate it when he does that shit!"

Chapter Thirteen

The gargantuan sundial of the milky white Washington Monument towered over the tree-lined Reflecting Pool, casting its long, late afternoon shadow across Jefferson Drive. The Potomac appeared bluer than he remembered it, roughly flowing in stark contrast to the well groomed, motionless, green landscape of Arlington and its endless speckle of white headstones. Hoover felt a comfortable wave of familiarity wash over him. He was home; Washington, where he had the connections, knew the system and had the operatives positioned to find out whatever it was he wanted to know.

And the thing that he wanted to know right now was who had the audacity to order the arrest of three of his agents? It couldn't have been locals, the disguises his agents described were too professional and, after their arrests, they were taken to a military installation. It could only be interpreted one way. Somebody was flexing their muscle.

Never having been a field man, Hoover was always uncomfortable away from his desk. His state of mind was greatly exacerbated by having been in New York a little too long for his liking. It wasn't his territory, people didn't intimidate easily enough. To add to his sense of aggravation about New York, his mind once again turned to the fact that he had not been consulted on the investigation of the Normandie. Even though they said it was a clear-cut accident, the FBI should've been called in. We should be called in on all large-scale accidents, he reasoned. Why the hell didn't the White House understand that? And what the hell was that Alien Registration Bill Roosevelt vetoed, on the same exact day of the fire? What the hell was wrong with him? How could he not see that America was being attacked from all sides and that the FBI were Her only hope? Twisting around in his seat, peering out the airplane window, his thoughts continued to flow.

Maybe we should try and appropriate funding for our own air force? He thought of the stiff opposition he was likely to get, based on the grounds that the war effort took priority for men and materials. However, he reasoned, if the American people were told it was needed to enhance the war effort, they would get behind it. He made a mental note to bring it up at a later date.

His most haunting thought, though, was that in any other circumstance, Hoover had his entire bureau at his disposal. Through a combination of field work and the process of elimination, he could find out who the culprits were. However, now he wasn't dealing with criminals. He was dealing with someone who knew the game at least as well as he did. His bureau was of little use to him now because the authority obviously came from someone higher up, but who? There weren't that many higher up. At least not in his mind.

He did not like being on the outside looking in.

A 1942 black Plymouth sedan was waiting on the tarmac and Hoover went straight for it, walking as fast as he could. His two bodyguards and official aide walked at a moderate pace so as not to pass him.

Even the most ruthless crime bosses had an occasional drink or meal with their men. Hoover, on the other hand, never made the mistake of appearing approachable.

Once inside the car, no one spoke until Hoover started the conversation, and then they addressed only the subject he choose.

"Rollins, what time is it?"

"Half past four, Mr Hoover."

"Driver, head straight for the Bureau building!"

"Yes, sir."

"Sir, you have a meeting with some of the Chicago agents this evening at – "

"Reschedule it for tomorrow."

Hoover was in a position that was unfamiliar to him, and he had been taken completely off guard by the chain of events in New York. As a consequence, he was still unsure of what to do next.

"Rollins!" Rollins removed a pad of paper from his satchel and prepared to write.

"Sir?" Hoover had already begun speaking.

"Call the New York DA's office and ask them for their status on the Normandie investigation."

"The luxury liner?"

"Yeah. Tell them you're from the Department of Transportation." The other three men in the car gave a quick glance in Hoover's direction and then at each other.

If he were going to do something classified, especially some type of investigation, it was uncharacteristic of him to talk about it in front of anyone not involved.

"No, on second thought don't tell them you're DOT. Find somebody. Who do we have over there?"

"We have someone in records and also – "

"Records, good. Go to them, get them to make the call. You be there, on another line when he makes the call."

"Sir, I'll need a memo or – "

"No, no paper trail. Just do it." Rollins was suddenly very uncomfortable. Tracking down known or even suspected subversives or enemy aliens was one thing, but investigating another legal branch? In The President's own home turf? That was frightening.

"Next, I want a meeting with the Attorney General, tonight!"

"Sir, the Attorney General is in Baltimore until day after tomorrow."

"What the hell is he doin' in Baltimore?"

"Some kind of personal business I believe, sir." Rollins shrugged in the direction of the other agents as Hoover looked around the car for an answer.

"Well, get a hold of his office as soon as we get in and tell me when and how he's coming back." Hoover looked out the window and saw they were approaching the Channel Lagoon.

"Take Memorial Bridge," he ordered.

"Yes, sir."

"Find out who the Representative is for the Frisco area and call his office. Ask him if he's received a formal complaint yet from that Commie bastard Harry Bridges and ask him for a copy. Tell him we'd like to help. No, wait. Say, 'offer our services to assist in the investigation'. Got it?"

"Yes, sir."

"Speak only with the Rep, not the aides or secretaries."

"Sir, we're here," the driver informed Hoover as they turned left and came off Constitution Avenue onto 9th Street. The car pulled up outside FBI Headquarters. Rollins fumbled to pack up his note taking material and get out of the car. He was the last one through the front door, having to struggle to get his foot in first and kick the heavy door open, as his hands were full of satchel, pad and overcoat.

Although Hoover had a secret entrance installed in back of the building, he seldom used it. It was much more appropriate for a man of his importance to make a grand entrance. And he did, whenever possible.

He ignored all the staff's greetings which followed him and his entourage as they made their way to the elevator. On the fifth floor he dismissed the two agents who were with him and nodded for the aide to come into his office. J. Edgar continued dictating as they entered the inner sanctum . Rollins had to drop everything and fumble his pad open to catch up with his boss's orders.

"Call the New York office in the morning and see what the subject is doing. Just ask them about the guy I told them to . . . No, wait. Get them on the line, then let me talk to them. Do that exactly at nine o'clock, got it?"

"Yes, sir. Anything else?"

"Yeah, those reports come back yet from the lab on the new wire tap devices?"

"No sir, not yet. But we have an indication there may be some problems from the phone company."

"What kind of problems?"

"Some of the higher up executives aren't too happy with us developing bugging equipment to place directly into their phones. They say it creates a bad image for their product."

"Get a hold of the lab. Tell that god-damned overpaid Professor I want a definite date for that bug by tomorrow! Tell him it better be no later than next week! Then call those pricks at the phone company and tell them we've decided to delay research until next year. No, till after the war."

"Yes, sir." Rollins held his breath, hoping that was finally it.

"Okay. That's it. Get outta here."

"I'll call the Attorney General's office and find out when he's due back. Will you be here, sir?"

"Yeah, call me here."

For the remainder of the evening, Hoover laid out a flimsy strategy based on what he thought he knew about the New York scenario. He did this in between phone calls to lobbyists, reporters who had in the past shown to be reliable informants and the few acquaintances he had who travelled in union circles.

The thinnest connections had always been in the union areas. His hatred towards labour organisation was well known.

Half an hour after he had left the office, Rollins rang Hoover and informed him that Attorney General Jackson was due in on the 10:45 train from Baltimore, Tuesday morning.

This planning went on late into the evening, when Hoover finally gave up and went to a place few civilian employees and none of the agents believed existed. His home.

✦

Nikki said goodnight to Shirley and thanked her for wrapping things up at the reception station as she climbed into her heavy overcoat. Although Nikki was tall, 5'10", she was slender and didn't function well in the cold.

However, when she passed through the brass framed glass door into the dark winter evening and turned right to walk up Church

Street, she was pleasantly surprised. It was very mild, not cold, and there was not a hint of a breeze. So, she decided to walk the twelve blocks to her apartment on Mercer.

Nikki, along with everyone else in New York, was disappointed at not having a white Christmas. 'The White Stuff' invoked an air of magic and beauty when it blanketed the trees in the parks and the turn-of-the-century Brownstones.

That disappointment was replaced with gratitude on January 3rd, however, when everyone went back to work and New York City still hadn't seen its first snowfall. Sloshing through the freezing, black-and-cinnamon-coloured slush was no way to start the work week, let alone with some jerk turning a corner and spraying a rooster tail of partially melted snow, ice and muck all over your new outfit.

Of course Katie and her little friends prayed every day for snow. Not only to play in, but if it snowed enough, most of the teachers had trouble getting in from Queens where they lived, and so school would be cancelled.

Nikki's meandering thoughts were interrupted when she had a strange sensation she was being followed as she crossed Franklin. Stepping up onto the curb, she turned to look behind her. Just the usual six o'clock crowd. She turned around and crossed back over Franklin to the produce market on the corner. Paying the clerk for the small bag of tomatoes, she resumed her journey back towards her apartment in SoHo.

Canal Street was still bustling with vendors, hawking away with every attempt to lure buyers into their stalls and through the arcades. The crowds jay-walking and playing cat and mouse with the cars in the streets were considerable, but after only one more block of wading through them, Nikki was at the corner of Mercer.

As a child, the Brownstone walk-ups with their imposing granite and red brick porches cascading down onto the side walk, reminded Nikki of gangplanks on gigantic luxury liners which would carry you away to exotic places like Coney Island, the Catskills or even the Jersey shore.

Walking up the steps, she could see through the frosted glass that there was a man in the vestibule searching the mail boxes. He held the front door open for her as she approached.

"Can I help you?" she asked in a friendly tone.

"Perhaps. I'm looking for Mr Murray's mail box. I have to leave him something."

"I'm sorry, there's no Murray in this building."

"This is 317, isn't it?"

"No, it's 86. 317 is two blocks north."

"Oh, thank you very much."

He tipped his hat made his way down the stairs and turned south.

Must be takin' the long way around, Nikki thought to herself, as she unlocked the inside door, went upstairs and knocked on 2C.

"Hello, Nikki!" Mrs Poluso always spoke to anyone at the door as if they had just come back from Poland specifically to visit her.

If refusing to come into Mrs Poluso's after knocking on the front door was a venial sin, then refusing to eat something after you had entered was a mortal sin. The fact that it was less than a half an hour to supper was no excuse.

Anyone who knew anything about eating knew it was important to eat something before every meal to stretch the stomach. Mrs Poluso, of course, was expert in this domain and as a consequence was compelled to happily walk around all day with her apron strings dangling unfastened at her flanks and the worn apron draped over her bulging stomach.

Nikki knew the routine, entered and accepted a small plate of sausage and boiled potatoes, while Kate and Mrs Poluso's two kids kissed goodbye. Watching them, she thought of the day she would tell the blonde-haired five-year-old about her Polish heritage.

✦

The janitorial staff were allowed into the building at half past seven, and about an hour into the daily tasks of mopping and sweeping, one of the older men let himself into the office of the Director to execute his chores. The career janitor was puzzled at the door not being locked; however, when he entered the office he was startled to find Mr Hoover sitting at his desk working away.

"Sorry, sir. I didn't know you were here."

"What time is it?"

"Ah . . . it's eight thirty-five, sir. You want me to clean up?"

"No, leave it until tomorrow." The old man left, and Hoover buzzed Rollins' office but there was no answer. Calling for a long distance operator, he was put through to the New York field office.

"FBI headquarters, New York field office."

"Who is this?"

"Who the hell is this?"

"This is J. Edgar Hoover! Who the hell is this?"

"Uh . . . Meyer, sir. Special Agent Meyer."

"Well, Special Agent Meyer, unless you want to be records clerk Meyer, I suggest you move your ass and get me the latest update on the Lanza file. Specifically, the latest surveillance reports. Got it?"

"Yes, sir!"

"Questions? Comments? Snide remarks?"

"No, sir! I've got them right here sir. Ah . . . ah . . . Lanza, Joseph, alias Socks, alias . . ."

"I know his god-damned aliases, Meyer! I want to know what he's doing!"

"Well, sir, ah . . . according to this report dated last night at midnight sir. . . ah . . . subject has not left the Fulton Street Fish Market in three days, sir."

"Three days?"

"According to the field report, Mr Hoover."

"You make a note that I called. You tell those field agents to stay on it and call me the minute he leaves that building. You got that, Meyer?"

"Absolutely, sir!"

Hoover buzzed Rollins again and this time he was in, and five minutes later he was briefing Hoover on the day's schedule of events.

"Sir, the Chicago agents will be in at ten o'clock, the lab says bugs are to be tested Monday and the Attorney General will see you in his office at three this afternoon." Rollins read from his carefully prepared notes.

"Change in plan. Have my car ready at ten, I'm going to meet the AG at the station. Get back to the lab and tell them I want a preliminary report on those bugs by five o'clock Monday afternoon. I'll speak to the Chicago agents at nine-thirty in the briefing room. What am I forgetting?"

"I have the info on the representative for San Francisco, but we won't get anybody on the coast until eight o'clock Western Pacific. About another two hours." Rollins began to pack up his notebook as Hoover came out from behind the desk and walked towards the door.

"You stay here and get them on the phone. I'll call you from the train station. Also call Sacramento, see if anything came across Warren's desk."

"Yes, sir. Anything else, sir?"

Hoover was opening the door as he asked, "Did you call the New York office yet?"

"No, sir. I'll go and do it now."

"Forget it. I already called them." Rollins could not understand why his boss frequently did that. It made him feel undermined and annoyed.

At ten o'clock sharp Hoover was boarding his car to go to the station in back of the building. This time he did use the secret entrance, and since Rollins was not making the twenty minute trip, and no one else was in on this, Hoover was alone in the vehicle with his driver.

"Where to, sir?"

"Union Station."

About five minutes into the ride, Hoover's attention was caught by the interview in progress on the car radio. He asked the driver to turn it up and listened as they drove.

The speaker spoke slowly and passionately to his audience, and with great conviction.

". . . and, when dealing with the Caucasian race, we have methods that will determine loyalty. But when we deal with the Japanese, we are in an entirely different field!" Applause followed the sign-off.

"You have just heard from the California State Attorney General, Earl Warren, his comments defending the relocation camps where thousands of Japanese-Americans . . ." The radio announcer's voice slowly faded as the driver lowered the volume at Hoover's order.

The Afro-Caribbean driver was careful, however, to leave the volume just high enough to allow himself to hear the rest of the broadcast as he manoeuvred the vehicle onto Louisiana Avenue and headed straight for the train station.

"John, pull it around on Second Street and wait for me there. And don't forget to change the sticker."

"Yes, sir, Mr Hoover.

After parking, John opened the glove box, removed an 'E' ration sticker, for emergency, and changed it with the 'B' sticker sitting in the special slot in the windshield.

A time-tested tactic to foster people's faith in their governments is to instill a sense of permanence. Which fosters confidence in the leadership. Anyone entering Union Station immediately felt that sense of stability and permanence its architects clearly intended.

The Neo-Classical/Art Deco building was a unique architectural hybrid, peculiar to America. In the heyday of the Work Projects Administration and the other assorted federal aid projects, LOC's, or lines of communication, such as roads and rail lines, held the highest priority. The largest, enduring benefit of this prioritisation, were the beautiful edifices which were either built or renovated as a result of these initiatives. Union Station, Penn Station and Central Station all stood as tributes to an era of craftsmanship which was now quietly fading into history.

Hoover made his way into the great hall past the marble, granite and bronze accoutrements, and stopped under the big black schedule board and saw that the 10:45 from Baltimore was arriving on time on track 29. He was early, so he went for a shoe-shine.

Afterwards, Hoover found his way to the bank of phone booths on the west wall and called Rollins. The assistant informed him that he still had no luck contacting anyone in California. Hoover then made for the platform.

There were some oak wooden benches in front of a rank of billboards, and Hoover sat facing the exit turnstile of the track. The train was already unloading, and as the dark-haired, well-groomed Robert H. Jackson, former Nuremberg prosecutor and now the highest law enforcement authority in the country, came through the gate, he spotted his unexpected one man welcoming party standing in front of a Big Ben advertisement.

That week was his birthday, he would turn 59, and he was feeling pretty good about himself and the general direction of the way things were going. Until he looked at the benches by the billboards.

Jackson was anything but pleased to see J. Edgar.

"What the hell are you doing here?" Jackson walked over to the benches and stood in front of Hoover.

"We have something to talk about."

"We have a couple of things to talk about," Jackson retorted.

"You want to go back to my office? My car is outside," enquired Hoover. The last place any politician in DC would ever feel comfortable discussing business was in J. Edgar Hoover's office. Jackson resigned himself to conducting their meeting in the station. He dropped his suitcase and sat down on the bench.

"No. What's so important you had to come all the way the hell over here to talk about?"

Hoover sat down. "There's something going on with the unions."

"Fer Christ's sake, Edgar! Not this union shit again!"

"There's something going on, and there's some higher-ups in on it."

"What the hell are you talking about? What are the unions doing?"

"It's the New York crowd. They're cookin' somethin' up on the waterfront. There's dozens of new faces all over the place and Lanza hasn't left Fulton Street for three days."

"You got people on him?"

"Of course!" Hoover couldn't believe Jackson would consider him to be so unprofessional.

"Well, then maybe that's why he's not coming out. He knows you're there."

"That's bullshit! How the hell could he know we're there?"

"Because they own New York, Edgar! Every time a rat farts they know about it. They know about your surveillance, they know about your tails and they know about your wire taps. The guy is under indictment, fer cryin' out loud. You think he ain't got his antennae up?"

Hoover was becoming less patient and more frustrated. He saw this as the perfect opportunity to infiltrate the illegal and immoral world of the unions.

"Look, if we don't keep our finger on the pulse of crime in this country, especially now that there's a war on, they'll be linin' up to take advantage. And when it's all over and the dust settles, we'll wake up one mornin' to find this country is bein' run by all those Commie politicians who are comin' up through the ranks right now in those god-damned unions!"

"Hoover, why in God's name do you have such a hard-on for the unions?" Jackson twisted around in his seat so he could watch Hoover's expression, straight on, as he answered the question. Hoover hated theses smart-assed college guys. Even though Jackson had never gone to college.

He leaned forward and made direct eye contact with the AG.

"Because they're hotbeds of Communist activity, god-damn it! That's why we need files on every person in this country!"

Jackson looked back into Hoover's eyes and understood why most of Washington was scared shitless of the little man.

"Every man and woman, J. Edgar?"

"Absolutely!"

"And child too, I suppose?"

Hoover sat back against the message on the billboard for Big Ben Clocks. It read, *Time won't wait for the nation that's late!*

"From the day they're born! Best time to start. Hell, we could use this Social Security thing. Everybody has a number, and it's tied to their money. We'll always know where they are and what they're doin'!"

Jackson gazed at Hoover in wonderment. He realised there was not a chance in hell of deterring him from this union obsession. On the other hand, if he were tied up with it, perhaps it would keep him out of the way for a while so that the rest of Washington could get on with fighting the war.

"I haven't heard anything about it here, but I'll put out some feelers and ask around. I could send out a memo to the state AG's to keep us informed. Meanwhile, I want to know about anything you come across." Technically, the Attorney General was Hoover's boss. However, after twenty-five years of entrenchment in the job, and the transient nature of the elected offices, Hoover never really considered himself to have a boss since his father gave the appointment back before WWI.

"I'll keep you on top of everything I find out." Jackson fought back a smirk.

"Edgar, there's something else we need to discuss."

"What's that, Bob?"

"This business about Joe Kennedy's kid."

Hoover's change of expression did not go unnoticed. He resented Kennedy for more than one reason. "What business?"

"This Inga Arvad stuff."

"Refresh my memory."

Nice move, thought Jackson. *He pretends he's ignorant, and I have to tell him what I know.*

"These charges of espionage. They're unfounded."

"She's a spy for the Krauts, with a DC cover and she's probably reportin' to the Commies on the side! You know it, I know it and everybody and his God-damned brother knows it!" Hoover's face was slowly turning red.

"She's not a spy, she's not workin' for the Axis powers and she is, as far as we can tell, a legitimate reporter for the *Times-Herald*. She's not even German, for cryin' out loud. She's a Dane."

"Dane, German, Swede, all the same!" His face was now gradually transitioning from beet red to a light purple as he spoke, trying not to shout.

"She's gonna walk."

"*WHAT*?" Hoover shouted.

"I'm dropping the charges. Lack of evidence. She's gonna walk."

"You want evidence? I'll get you evidence!"

"Drop it! So what if JP's kid had a roll in the sack with her? That doesn't make her a spy. I'm sorry about the bad blood between you and Joe Kennedy, but every freakin' editorial board in the country is on my ass for suppressing free speech. And we don't have any evidence. Besides, the kid has already paid for the scandal. They're talkin' about drummin' him out."

"Good! He could've leaked sensitive information to the enemy and cost American lives."

"Knock it off, will ya? Jack Kennedy is no more involved in espionage than Eleanor Roosevelt's fucking dog! He was hand-picked to work at Naval Intelligence, fer cryin' out loud!" Jackson decided to try the slim possibility of reason. "Look, J. Edgar, Joe Kennedy says he considers you a friend. Now, whatever it is you've got on Jack, photos, tapes, why don't you do us all a favour and get rid of them?"

"What makes you think I have anything?" Hoover was fishing again.

"Whatever you have won't be of any use. You know we got our tit in a wringer with the shipping issue. The Maritime Commission says the Germans are sinkin' them almost as fast as we can build them. And that Normandie thing in New York scared the hell out of everybody. FDR wants Joe Kennedy's help building more ships, and because of that Frank Knox is probably gonna get involved to see that the kid doesn't go down too hard."

Hoover was shocked at the fire power behind Kennedy. He had forgotten about Kennedy's influence in the industrial sector, and was compelled to resign himself to the obvious fact he was not going to hold any leverage against the kid. At least not now.

"All right. I'll see if there is anything and see what I can do about it," Hoover told him.

"Thank you. You'll make life lot easier for all of us."

✦

"Miss Tully, could you please come in? And bring your stenographer's pad with you, thank you." The President slowly reclined in his high-backed chair, dramatically backlit with the mid-afternoon sun of a clear winter's day flooding in through the picture window behind his desk in the Oval Office.

"I don't know what I would do without her, John." Franklin Delano Roosevelt, now in his ninth year as president, spoke to long time friend and confidant, Captain John L. McCrea.

McCrea was selected special Naval Aide-de-Camp by FDR above many other senior officers. In the natural political pecking order, a Captain would, at best, be aide to an Admiral. However, with his selection McCrea skipped all the Admirals, as well as all the other Washington posts including the Joint Chiefs and went straight to the top. There were no shortage of sore toes at his appointment.

FDR held up a two page report he had received that morning from Secretary of the Navy, Frank Knox.

"I'm impressed by this action, John. You have to give it to those Italians, they can certainly think outside the box. What's your assessment?"

"Damned impressive, sir. But scary as hell, too! If those little bastards start turning themselves into . . . human torpedoes, they're gonna be mighty hard to keep track of!"

"Is it accurate that they disabled both HMS Valiant and the Queen Elizabeth?" FDR spoke with a blend of concern and curiosity.

"Although we're not releasing it for security reasons, sir, best case scenario is they're both out of action until the mid to late spring." McCrea, sitting on the sofa to FDR's right, spoke with a combination of resignation and embarrassment.

Miss Tully, a middle-aged, grey-haired woman ever professional in appearance, entered the Oval Office. Captain McCrea stood as she entered.

"Yes, sir?" FDR gestured and Miss Tully took a seat to his right.

"Is there anyone outside for me, Miss Tully?"

"Yes, sir. The Attorney General is due for two o'clock."

"Very well, as soon as we're finished here please show him in."

He began to dictate as he casually swivelled around in his chair. "The White House, February seventeenth, nineteen hundred and forty-two. Memorandum for Admiral Stark. The action by those little Italian boats in the Eastern Mediterranean on . . . December twenty-second was pretty good. I would say damned good. If they can do it, why can't we do it? I wish you would turn loose your most imaginative people in War Plans to tell me how you think the Italian Navy can be effectively immobilised by some tactics similar to, or as daring as, those utilised by the Italians. I can't believe we must always use the classical offensive against an enemy who seems never to have heard of it. FDR."

McCrea smiled at the last line in the memo.

"Send that to Admiral Stark post-haste, will you please Miss Tully?"

"Yes, sir. Would you like me to send in the Attorney General?"

"Do we have a hint as to Mr Jackson's problem, Miss Tully?"

"No, sir. He said it was a matter of national security."

"Isn't everything these days? Show him in please. Thank you." FDR called after her, "Oh, and Miss Tully, you'd better give us some time."

Jackson came in through the west entrance as the secretary exited.

"Good morning, Robert." FDR always spoke to everyone in the Oval Office as if they were old friends on a social visit. "I believe you know John McCrea. John, Robert Jackson, my top cop."

They shook hands and Jackson was a little surprised. He had assumed that since he had labelled his visit 'a matter of national security', he would be alone with the President.

"Sir, we might want to discuss this in private." McCrea smiled behind Jackson.

"Is this of a political nature or of a military nature, Robert?"

"Well, sir, to be perfectly frank, I don't know."

"Okay, Robert, you have the floor." The Attorney General, although rarely lost for words, found it difficult to find a starting point.

"Sir, I realise I'm not privy to all the goings on of the war effort, or the White House. Nor do I expect to be." FDR knitted his brow as Jackson continued. "But, if you have something going on with the unions, maybe you should let me in on it."

"What in blazes are you talking about, Robert?" FDR was genuinely lost.

"Sir, any type of activity or operation to do with the war? Maybe something that most people might not consider to be completely above board?"

"Robert, I think you need to come to the point."

"Sir, when I arrived from Baltimore this morning, J. Edgar Hoover was waiting for me at the station."

"Is J. Edgar driving a taxi now?" FDR and McCrea chuckled, but Jackson maintained his serious tone.

"Sir, he's on to something."

"Such as what?"

"I don't know, sir, but whatever it is it has something to do with the unions in New York and he's pretty upset about something that happened up there." FDR sat back in his chair and turned towards McCrea.

"John, any of this make any sense to you?"

"No, sir. Nothing the Navy is in on, as far as I know." Like a child determined to relay something but hindered by a limited vocabulary, Jackson became increasingly frustrated as he spoke.

"He kept on about higher-ups being in on 'it', whatever 'it' is." Jackson juggled his Fedora in his hands as he spoke while looking down. "And something about the waterfront." McCrea looked at the President who quickly returned his glance.

"Yes John, go on."

"That's all I got out of it, sir. My concern is that he'll get my office mixed up in something that's potentially embarrassing for us all. That damned guy sees Communists in his sleep! And he's convinced that all unions are Communist strongholds."

"J. Edgar never did have much respect for the American working man. I believe he never will."

"Well, whatever it is, he's bound and determined to root it out," Jackson insisted.

"Where did you leave it?" the President coaxed.

"I didn't try to deter him on two counts. First, I figured he was off on another paranoid delusional wild goose chase. The second was to keep him out of my hair for a while."

"Did he give you anything in writing, a report, a memo?" FDR wanted to know. McCrea sat forward.

"No, sir. All verbal. He was rattling on at the station until I changed the subject."

"To what, Robert?" Jackson looked at the President and then at McCrea.

"It's alright, Robert. I don't keep anything from Captain McCrea."

"I confronted him with the Inga Arvad situation." As soon as he spoke, Jackson realised he was in over his head. That no one else knew that Hoover had something on Joe Kennedy's kid.

"Why confront him?"

"He wants to go ahead with the spy trial." FDR and McCrea instantly realised the negative implications of that course of action. Jackson was inadvertently dealt a new hand of cards by FDR.

"What is the status on Miss Arvad's case, Robert?"

"She's being released for lack of evidence. We don't have anything." Jackson monitored their reactions carefully.

FDR's intercom buzzed and he immediately responded.

"Miss Tully, I indicated that we were not to be disturbed," he said calmly. FDR always maintained an even keel except in the direst of circumstances.

"I'm sorry, sir but there's an urgent message for you, just arrived by special courier."

"What class message is it, Miss Tully?"

"It's a 'Flash', sir." McCrea and Jackson looked at the President. In the present day atmosphere of daily surprises on a global scale, everyone remained prepared for the worst.

"Have him wait, Miss Tully. I'll see him directly." FDR turned back towards Jackson. "Make sure you patch things up with the press, Robert. Let me know if I can say anything to them to help."

"Thank you, sir."

"I appreciate you coming to me on this. Sorry we couldn't be of more help. I really don't think anything is going to come of it, but keep an eye on J. Edgar for me. If anything evolves let me know." The Attorney General stood to leave, and shook the President's hand. McCrea remained seated.

The President waited a brief interval after Jackson was gone before he spoke. Then he turned his chair 180 degrees to face the picture window. Gazing out onto the winter lawn, he directed, "I want that little shit shut down, John! Keep it contained, but get him the hell out of that back yard. He'll muck things up on the Third District people just as sure as Hitler's a mad man. This thing leaks and we'll all be tap-dancing to blazes!" He turned back to face the Captain. "How are they doing up there, anyway? Any results?"

"I'm afraid not, sir. Progress has been slow. The DA's office has improved their batting record ever since '36 . . ."

"The Luciano case."

"Yes, sir. And as a result Third District reports having trouble recruiting operatives."

"Well, we need to catch some bad guys or shut this thing down."

"I'll pass the word, sir."

FDR clicked the intercom and spoke to his secretary.

"Miss Tully, will you send in the courier, please?"

"Right away, sir."

"John, what's Jack Kennedy's status?"

"He's been relieved at the Office of Naval Intelligence and is awaiting a hearing to determine fitness for duty."

"Don't kick him out. I believe Joe said he wanted PT boats?"

"Yes, sir."

The courier entered. He was a Navy Lieutenant and saluted smartly as he reached across the desk and handed the message to the President. FDR dismissed the officer and ripped open the red seal on the envelope. He sat there for an inordinate period of time, transfixed by the message. He slowly put a hand to his mouth and then suddenly and forcefully slammed the desk while continuing to stare at the piece of paper.

"*HOT DAMN IT*!" FDR's raised voice startled McCrea, who slid to the edge of his seat and was unsure how to respond to the President's reaction.

"Sir, is everything all right?"

FDR sat up straight and once again turned back to face the window. From behind the high-backed chair, McCrea heard FDR's voice as he spoke slowly and distinctly. FDR held the message up as if to emphasise its magnitude.

"The Italian navigator has entered the New World."

McCrea slowly rose to his feet. "That little genius son-of-bitch! He's done it!"

Enrico Fermi, from his laboratories hidden in Soldier's Field, Chicago, had just informed FDR that he had discovered the secret of nuclear fission. The gate had just gone up on the nuclear arms race.

Without turning his chair from the window, FDR again addressed his aide.

"John, contact ONI. See that young Jack is stationed in the Pacific. Put him with the PT's. The only thing he can get into a scandal with out there is palm trees."

Chapter Fourteen

One positive side effect of the war was the upturn in the wartime economy. Another was the technological advances everyone saw slowly creeping into their daily lives. Automats were a good example. Although Horn and Hardart's automats had been around since before the war, now more than ever they appealed to the new mass production mentality. The massive walls of small, glassed-door, coin-operated slots which allowed the customer to view, select and pay for the desired food items in one easy step, ensured that White Castle hamburger stands no longer had the corner on the fast food market.

The attractive woman with the two small children had her hands full. While trying to push her tray along the serving line, she was forced to wrestle with her young son who insisted on putting all the nickels into the slots himself and attempting to remove the plates of food from their pigeon holes. The two men in dress suits smiled as they watched the little girl, who was standing ahead of her mother, occasionally sneak a spoonful of pudding from her own tray. For one final time Mom lifted the feisty youngster, and allowed him to deposit the money into the tiny slot and open the small glass door. He refused to take the plate out. It was piled with vegetables.

The two men approached the register at the end of the self-service food line and handed the girl in the white and blue uniform their money to pay for their fountain drinks.

Ten minutes later the two men, seated at a table in the corner of the large banquet room, had finished their meal and were both nursing cups of coffee. Commander Haffenden opened the conversation.

"Ya know, I remember the Saturday morning my dad told me we were gonna have a talk about the birds and the bees. Late that afternoon, after the movies, hot dogs and ice cream, we were back in the house and I still knew as much about the birds and the bees as I did that morning before we left."

"That obvious, Charlie?" Captain MacFall asked with trepidation.

"Look, bad news is like removing a bandage that's been on for a week. Ya just gotta get a good grip on it and yank." MacFall rarely had lunch with his staff members, especially at three in the afternoon. Haffenden thought he was prepared for what was coming.

The lack of a crowd in the automat not only meant that it was quiet and conducive to the meeting, but magnified the silence Haffenden endured before McFall could bring himself to speak.

"I was in the skipper's office this morning. We talked for an hour and a half."

"That's a big chunk of the Old Man's schedule."

"Washington wants you to expand the operation." Haffenden sat back in his chair. The bandage was ripped off but it felt good. Something was wrong. The key phrase which got by Haffenden was the "Washington wants you", in lieu of "Washington wants us".

"They're worried about our results, aren't they?"

"Don't worry about what they're worried about. Just do your job." MacFall tried to speak in a reassuring tone.

"What about resource allocation?"

"Get me a list by tonight. I'll have authorisation from DC by tomorrow." *That's too fast*, thought Haffenden.

"Look, sir . . ."

"Roscoe." That didn't make Haffenden any more comfortable.

"Captain, it takes time to build an operation like this and still keep it under wraps."

"Believe me, that subject was brought up this morning. Everyone understands your position and what you're trying to do.

Trust me, Charlie, I sure as hell wouldn't want this damn mission!"

"Sir, I should think they were happy the threat isn't what they thought it was!"

"They're politicians, Charlie, not military strategists. Which is why, when this is over, I'm hanging it up."

Haffenden was surprised. "How does Meriam feel about that?"

"Are you kiddin'? She's already got the Florida condo picked out."

It occurred to Haffenden that he never really considered retirement. "Level with me, sir," he requested.

"Fair enough. They're worried. They're worried that you haven't produced any bad guys. They're worried that word of the op might leak and fowl up their precious plans for office after the war and, worst of all, they're scared shitless of losing any more ships."

"Jesus! Are we that far behind?" Haffenden was not privy to ship production statistics.

"No, not really. The boys upstairs figure this time next year we'll have the Krauts down from forty to ten per cent of total production. But that's not the point. It's the morale thing. Nobody in the greater tri-state area believes for a New York City second that the Normandie was an accident. Besides, the boys upstairs are still gun-shy from the Hindenburgh thing."

"What do you think?"

"What's important is if the general public thinks there's bad guys in every neighbourhood, we're liable to lose control."

"Speakin' about bad guys in the closets, what about Hoover and his mob?"

"Unofficial orders are they're to be shut down."

"Did I get your ass in a sling for that Tompkins Park manoeuvre?"

"Not really. But next time maybe you don't need to send the cuffs and badges to the DA."

"Honest ta God, sir, I already had that set up on the premise they were Hogan's goons. It wasn't till after the fact that we found out they belonged to Hoover." Both men stood and slowly walked towards the door.

"It's not an issue. But what will be an issue is if we lose another vessel in port. We'll all be in the shit locker. No pressure, mind you."

"Gee, thanks." The two officers were out on the street and preparing to go their separate ways.

"Anything else you need from me, Charlie?"

"Yeah, if it comes up, I'd rather not have to deal with that DA again."

"Don't worry. It's not likely."

Socks stepped off the pilings and into the six man motor launch and took a seat in the front. When he was comfortable, he signalled his coxswain and they started south towards Pier 14, a quarter of a mile away. Just far enough so the FBI agents on stake-out could eat their cold sandwiches and drink their lukewarm coffee undisturbed while Socks was in one of his favorite restaurants enjoying a hot steak, some pasta and glass of wine.

After exiting the launch, he made for a pay-phone on Exchange Street. This increased inconvenience was one of the topics he was discussing with his lawyer only minutes later.

"Please hold for Mr Guerin." It was cold inside the phone booth.

"Socks? What is it? They run ya in?"

"No, I'm okay. But I need your help."

Guerin was puzzled but had his suspicions. "I'm listening."

"Look, this Navy shit's gettin' pretty thick, I want out."

"Yeah? Congratulations! Me too!"

"What the hell you talkin' about?"

"I been on the phone six times with that god-damned DA so far. And that's just this week. Every time I bump into a lawyer at the courthouse who represents one'a you guys, he wants to know if you're makin' a deal, fer Christ's sake! Then he's worried his client is gonna wanna make a deal."

"So what?"

"So what? I'll tell ya so what! Guys in my game aren't crazy about spendin' two weeks preparing for court and then havin' the client cop a plea!"

"Look, that's their problem! I ain't makin' no deals with them pricks, and anything you hear is strictly grapevine! Now, help me get the hell outta this Navy deal, will ya!?"

"No can do, Socks!"

"What the hell you mean, 'no can do'?" Lanza was offended at Guerin's attitude. "I'm your lawyer, Socks, not your career counsellor. This secret shit is over and above the call of duty. I got other clients, ya know."

"Are you tellin' me you can't do nuthin', or you don't *wanna* do nuthin'?"

"What's the difference? Look, it's your game. I work in the courtroom, not on the streets and back alleys."

"You're tellin' me you won't call the Commander for me?"

Guerin was getting tired of playing footsie. "What am I? Fucking Mata Hari? You work for Haffenden. Talk to him! I'm busy!" Guerin hung up.

Lanza stared at the receiver, thinking, *what the hell am I gonna' tell him?*

Stepping out onto the street, he felt the dip in temperature as he noticed the sun silhouetting the Bayonne Bridge as it set in the distance. He turned and walked back to the launch.

✦

The next morning found Lanza a long way from the stench of fish. He was standing in front of a bank of ornate elevators. The magnificent gilded Art Deco reliefs and the lobby which occupied an entire city block meant he could only be in one place, the Empire State Building.

The evening before, Socks had paced nervously in front of his phone for an hour and a half debating whether or not to call the Commander. At about half past seven, the debate was settled when his phone rang. It was the Commander, he wanted a meet. When he mentioned Fay Wray in the conversation and the prearranged code for the time, Lanza knew where to be.

The familiar *ding* of the elevator bell signalled one of the two express elevators had arrived and Lanza put his cigarette out and boarded. As the four passengers quickly climbed to the eighty-sixth floor where they would be required to change cars, Socks smiled at the three foreign girls holding their stomachs and probably remarking, in some language he was unfamiliar with, about the speed of the elevator. He thought about the sumptuous meals he enjoyed on this very spot, 103 storeys lower, when the Waldorf-Astoria stood here less than a decade ago.

Out on the observation deck he lit another cigarette and surveyed the landscape. You could almost see the entire waterfront, he thought to himself. The whole piece of the pie.

The three foreign girls were now holding tightly onto the guard rail and babbling away at each other when the building increased the momentum of its sway as the wind picked up. Socks found it soothing.

"They say on a clear day you can see four states." Lanza slowly turned to his left to see a man in a grey suit leaning on the rail next to him. It was Haffenden.

"Be a shame if they have ta tear it down fer lack'a tenants," Lanza answered.

"Lack of people, Socks. That's why we're here." The wind began to pick up. "Let's go inside." Taking seats at the back of the Tippy Top Coffee Shop, Haffenden continued.

"The people in Washington are real grateful for what you've been doin' for us, Socks."

"Yeah? How grateful?"

"Sorry, we're still not authorised to offer anybody a deal."

"Look Commander, about Brooklyn . . ."

"Yes?"

"I can't do nuthin' over there."

"What are you telling me?"

"Sir, I'll lay my cards on the table. I want out."

"Out like outta the Brooklyn part?" Haffenden knew he was

kidding himself, but it was worth a try.

"Out like in-out out. The whole shootin' match. I can't do nuthin' else for ya." Lanza respected the officer and felt remorse at letting him down, but he was tired of not sleeping at night through worry about his reputation in the community.

"Socks, I just got word that they're so happy with us, they want us to expand the operation!"

"Expand the operation?!" Socks was shocked. Whatever residual doubts the veteran mobster might have had about pulling out instantly evaporated.

". . . and the building was completed ten months ahead of schedule and one million dollars under budget just nine years ago!" The voice of the female tour guide faded out onto the observation deck along with the clatter of the first tour group of the morning, as the meeting was momentarily interrupted.

"Sir, I've got my own problems piling up faster than I can keep up with 'em. But the reality of the situation is, I just ain't got the juice you need. I can't approach the Comardos directly, I don't know shit about Bayonne and hell, halfa them Jersey piers are military!"

Haffenden knew that the military piers were no more immune from Mob infiltration and corruption than the fish piers. However, it was clear his best source was already a lost cause.

"Socks, we can't just let you walk away."

"What? I know too much? You gonna whack me, Commander?"

"We don't operate like that."

"Sure ya don't. You just put people away somewhere, real cosy like, for national security's sake. In detention camps."

Haffenden was doing what he didn't ever want to do with one of his sources. Getting pissed off. "Third Naval District has nothing to do with those camps!" he retorted.

"You think I ain't thought ahead? There's a dozen guys with inside info on what I been doin' fer you. And there's a certain lawyer with a sealed letter and instructions to go public if there's any monkey business, should I go to trial." *This guy's not as dumb as as I thought.* "Now, I played it straight with you right down the line. And I'll keep playin' straight with you, Commander. But I gotta be here long after this war is over and you go home and retire. And them guys in the DA's office don't give two shits about me, you or the man on the moon, so long as they get up the next rung of the ladder and get a shot at makin' governor."

In light of recent events, Haffenden could find no flaw in Lanza's argument. "Does that mean you'll still help me out where you can?"

Lanza felt the sincerity in the request. "I'll do better than that. I'll tell you who'll get you access to the whole fuckin' shootin' match."

"I'm all ears."

"Charlie Lucky."

"Luciano? Lucky Luciano?"

Lanza smiled.

"But he's outta circulation, in prison somewhere. For life, according to our information."

Lanza stood and slowly stepped away from the table. "Yeah, hold onto that dream, brother. Sorry I can't be of any more help, but I won't do you or your project much good if they throw me in jail."

The Commander remained seated to digest what he had just been told, and Lanza patted him on the shoulder as he walked past, heading for the elevator back down to street level.

Haffenden considered his next course of action, then left to locate a phone.

"Captain MacFall, please."

"I'm sorry, sir, Captain MacFall has left the building. May I put you through to someone else?" Nikki's pleasant voice responded on the other end of the line.

Haffenden thought for a moment. "Yes. Put me through to Commander Marsloe's office."

"One moment, sir." The Commander could hear the buzz of the line, and after it rang three times, a voice answered.

"Yeah?"

"Tony?"

"No, wait a minute. I'll get him." He heard the receiver being laid down and a short time later Marsloe was on the line.

"Hello, who is this, please?"

"Tony, it's me, Haffenden."

"Charlie! What can I do for you?"

"Who answered your phone?"

"Ah, just one of the treasury guys. What can I help you with?"

"You worked on the Mafia stuff in Hogan's office, didn't ya?"

"I was the resident expert on Sicilian affairs, yeah, why?"

"I need an organisational flow chart. A sort of an order of battle if you will, and – "

"Charlie, that's gonna be kinda hard."

"Why?"

"Because we don't have one."

"You telling me the best intel service in the world doesn't have the skinny on a bunch of gangsters?"

"Ah . . . that's about it, Haff."

"Well, who does?"

"Only one person that we know of."

"Well, who the hell is that?"

"The head of the Mafia."

"Christ, Marsloe, give me a break! Who the hell is the head of the Mafia?"

"Well . . . we're not exactly sure."

"Sicilian expert, huh? In the largest prosecutor's office in the world? What the hell did you do? Swap lasagne recipes?"

"Hey, don't take it out on me! We could take a page, ya know"

"Shit, sorry, Tony. I been running into a coupl'a walls lately, that's all. Thanks anyway."

An hour later, Commander Haffenden was back on the line to MacFall explaining the situation with Lanza. He couldn't mention names on the phone but he made it clear that the DA would have to be consulted for some background information to kick-start the new phase of the operation. Haffenden tried, unsuccessfully, to convince MacFall to approach Hogan on his behalf.

"Sir, we go back to those guys with hat in hand and they'll use that leverage for every mile it's worth!" Haffenden pointed out.

"We'll have to do something to preclude that, I suppose."

"Sir, I'm certain if we both go over there together . . ."

"What's this 'we' jazz? You got worms? Charlie, I told you this is your show. You'll have to handle it. That's that. Now I'll call around and grease the skids, but I highly suggest you plan on being over at the DA's office in the a.m., Commander. Clear?"

There was a pause before Haffenden answered. "Aye-aye, sir."

"And Haffenden, whatever you do don't bring up the wires. Those people have no appreciation for flamboyance!"

"No sense of humour, huh?" Haffenden couldn't fight off the grin involuntarily creeping over his face.

To the Commander's pleasant surprise, when he rang Hogan's office a short time later, the secretary informed him she was to give him an appointment at his convenience; that the District Attorney instructed her to leave the schedule open. They agreed on two o'clock that afternoon and Haffenden hung up suspicious and bewildered. Grease the skids? He must have sent over a fifty dollar hooker with a lobster dinner!

Commander Haffenden was not a politician. He'd never had the slightest interest in politics. He was a sailor, first, last and always. Consequently, he would not deduce that Captain MacFall never spoke to Hogan. That he never had to. Instead, the DA's motivation came from a phone conversation designed to employ a different angle of attack. In fact, the skid-greasing was by way of Fiorrello LaGuardia's office. The mayor's secretary conveyed the message, and Hogan's schedule parted like the Red Sea.

When Haffenden entered Hogan's office that afternoon, he found it would be a three-way meeting. He wasn't comfortable with that so he asked to speak to Hogan alone. Gurfein, with a hurt puppy look on his face, stepped through the door into the reception area.

"Big boys only, huh?" The secretary didn't bother to turn around as she made her remark to Gurfein, who flopped down onto one of the over-stuffed sofas and picked up a magazine.

"Shut up!"

"Snappy comeback," replied the secretary, as she continued to type.

After explaining what he needed from the DA, Hogan asked

who the mystery man was. Haffenden cocked himself back in his chair and was amused at the expression, which bordered on shock, on Hogan's face.

"Luciano! That may not be doable, Commander."

"Let's start with where he is. Where do we find him?"

"He's a lifelong guest of the Gray Bar Hotel."

"Which branch?"

"Clinton State Penitentiary, up in Dannemora." The Commander began taking notes.

"We'll use the Lanza strategy. Who's his lawyer?"

"He had a whole team of them. I can have somebody look them up for you later. But they won't do you any good. You're wasting your time."

Haffenden ignored the advice. "What's the procedure?"

"That's what I'm trying to tell you. There isn't one. With Lanza, we were dealing with a free man. Luciano will never see the light of day again. You're dealin' with a crook of a different colour!" Hogan smirked at his own joke but Haffenden was in no mood to shadow-box.

"Look, Hogan, I'm gonna make this thing happen with or without you. So skip the bad jokes and give me the chain of command."

Hogan was irritated but running out of excuses to stall. "Commander Haffenden, understand what you're up against. Since you have to go through his lawyer, or lawyers, you'll have to let them in on your little op. Then, convince them to lend a hand. They're no doubt gonna bitch about money, and when you tell them they gotta do it outta the goodness of their hearts, they're gonna disappear like a bunch of drunk sailors on payday. Next, if you somehow miraculously convert them into believers and they see the light, they gotta convince Luciano, who can neither be believed, depended on, or trusted in any way shape or form." Hogan began to pace the floor as he spoke.

"Don't pull any punches, Hogan. Tell me what you really think."

"The best is yet to come! At this stage of your little safari, you've got to convert Commissioner Lyons, the state prison commissioner, and sell him into your travelin' roadshow. Now, he will no doubt run it by the Governor, who by the way just happens to be the man who put Luciano where he belongs."

"So what you're tryin' to say is . . ."

"Good fucking luck, Commander." Haffenden tried not to flinch.

"So where do I find the name of one of the lawyers?"

"I'll have Gurfein reference it for you and give your office a buzz."

"That's all right. I'll wait," Haffenden said firmly.

Hogan had no idea how far he could push Haffenden. However, at this point he calculated that the officer was willing to go the whole way to call his bluff. Or, worse yet, he had all the backing he needed to accomplish his goal. The DA was finished playing political chicken.

"I think I remember a name. Polakoff, Moses Polakoff."

Haffenden continued to take notes. "How do we get a hold of him?" he enquired.

Hogan buzzed his secretary. A few minutes later Gurfein entered the office and handed a slip of paper to Hogan.

"If you want to save some time, we can call him now and try to set something up."

"Yes, that would be helpful, only don't tell him I'm here or what this is about."

Gurfein placed the call and it went through right away. However, after that it was an uphill battle. When Polakoff was told it involved Luciano, he declined right away. As far as he was concerned the case was closed. He complained about taking it all the way up through the Supreme Court and having lost. Finally, he fell back on the excuse that he really didn't know Lucky that well, that he only acted as his lawyer along with the others and that he really wasn't interested in approaching Lucky about anything.

Haffenden got the gist of the conversation and wrote a message to Gurfein while he was listening to Polakoff make his case to the DA's assistant. It suggested that Polakoff use an intermediary to contact Luciano. After five more minutes, Polakoff was persuaded. Round one to the Navy. However, Polakoff emphasised two points.

One, that the contact would remain nameless for now, and two, that he, Polakoff, would make no guarantees.

✦

Just before Lanza was about to embark on the first peaceful night's sleep he'd had in three weeks, the phone rang. It was Big Jimmy. Socks was quick to relay that he was no longer in business with the Feds.

"So Jimmy, are we okay or what?"

"Yeah, Socks. That's real good news."

"But are we okay?"

"You mean like okay okay?"

"Yeah, like okay okay!"

"Yeah Socks, we're okay. There's just one ding we gotta get straight between us though."

"What's that, Jimmy?" he asked with trepidation.

"You don't tell nobody I asked you fer diss! You got that?"

"No problem, I swear! Now what the hell is it you want at two-fuckin'-thirty in the a.m.?"

"I want you to go back ta that joint on Mott Street, Morrelli's, and get that recipe fer Cannolies. Ya know, the big ones wit the extra cream. Can you do that, Socks? I'll wack anybody ya want. No charge!"

"I'll see what I can do, Jimmy. Okay?"

"Okay."

Chapter Fifteen

Doc sat at the kitchen table while Mrs Birnbaum excused herself to get a fresh package of tissues. He explained to her what he had found out about the mysterious behaviour of her husband, but it didn't seem to sink in right away and the tears kept coming. Although he was happy at the way things turned out, he was very uncomfortable in the presence of a crying woman. Any woman.

"You mean to tell me my Ira isn't playing hoochie-coochie mit da bimbo?" she sobbed in between tears.

"No, Mrs Birnbaum, he's not. As a matter of fact, according to my notes . . . " Doc took his notepad out and made sure his client couldn't see the blank pages as he flipped through them. "He's working on something very special. Very hush-hush." Mrs. Birnbaum appeared more composed as she went to the stove and prepared some tea.

"Why he is suddenly doink this on Pearl Harbor?"

"That's when we had to mobilise the military, Norma. That's when the shi . . . that's when things started to get crazy." Suddenly she began to cry again. Christ! Doc thought to himself. You give them bad news, they cry, you give them good news, they cry! Doc had no idea what to do, so he stood up.

"Mrs Birnbaum . . . Norma, are you okay?"

"I'm sorry. I'm sorry, I'm so reliefted." She walked over to Doc and hugged him as she cried uncontrollably, allowing her two weeks of pent-up emotions to escape. "I'm so reliefted, yet I'm so ashamed dat I didn't trust him!"

Doc held her at arms length as if she were a baby with a loaded diaper as he floundered for words of comfort.

"I don't know vhat I vould do vithout my Ira."

Doc helped her back to her seat and squatted down in front of her. Holding her hand, he explained.

"Norma, it's all over. It was just a big misunderstanding. Talk to Ira tonight. Tell him what you told me, okay?"

"Tell him I didn't trust him? He vould die!"

"I don't think so, Norma. I think you'll be surprised at how he acts."

"Ya dink?" she reluctantly enquired.

"More than I dink! What? Ya dink I don't know from love?" They both laughed. "Maybe do something nice for him. Make you feel better, too."

Jesus! Doc the marriage councillor. Louie would die laughing! It was time to leave.

"I have to go, Norma."

Norma composed herself. "My Ira! A secret agent!" she said proudly.

"Well, I don't know if I would . . . "

She looked up at him. "Vat, Mr Macquen?"

"Nothing, Norma. You just have a big surprise for Ira tonight when he gets home, and enjoy the evening."

"Ven he gets home! Dare is no way to know when he is getting home!"

"Don't worry, I think I can help. He'll be home for supper tonight." Doc finally had an excuse to call Nikki.

"I haven't paid you, Mr Macquen! I'll get my cheque book."

"Norma, that's alright. Put it in the mail." Doc's protest was too late. Norma was back in a minute with the chequebook. She wrote and chatted like a schoolgirl talking about her first date. Doc fought back the smile.

"Supper! Dat's the perfect idea! Ve have some candles and I make him his favourite! Pigs' knuckles and black bread!"

"Norma! I thought you and Ira were Kosher?"

"Kosher smosher!" She bent forward as she handed Doc the cheque and whispered in his ear. "He dinks I don't know from him and his friends sneakik off to York Street to that goim delicatessen once a month! I know! But I don't say nuthink. Who he's hurtink?" As she stood up straight she issued a warning. "You don't say nuthik about pigs' knuckles!"

"Cross my heart and hope to die."

Once again he protested when she handed him the cheque, trying to explain that he really didn't do anything but follow her husband for a day. She persisted and Doc suddenly had a horrible premonition that she might start crying again, so he accepted the payment. Mrs Birnbaum thanked him three more times before he finally managed to get through the door.

Once outside in the midday sun, Doc decided to walk for awhile, and think about his future as a PI. With no new commissions on the horizon, things didn't look good. He reckoned that once he reached the south side of the park he'd call Nikki.

As he was thinking things over, he passed a garbage can, stopped and took Norma's cheque out of his pocket. He didn't feel good about taking so much money for this job in the first place, but when he thought about what he'd said to Louie, he had to do it. He tore it up.

Ira got a helluva a surprise when he got home.

Doc used to wonder why his father always took long walks when he was troubled. It had been a while since he had done it himself. By the time he walked to 58th and Third from the Birnbaum's, he not only felt completely relaxed, but comfortable enough to call Nikki and ask her to talk to Ira's boss about letting him get home early tonight – and maybe he just might accidentally let drop he had nowhere special to be on Saturday night.

However, the love gods were not smiling on Doc that morning. Shortly after entering the phone booth, while rummaging through his change in search of a nickel, his attention was caught by three men sitting at a side table in a small restaurant across the street. The guy on the left was unknown to Doc; however, the one sitting at the centre of the four top was the famous Meyer Lansky, Lucky

Luciano's best friend and partner since childhood. The figure which made the picture so curious was the man trying so desperately not to be seen.

"Doc, where you at, man?"

"Midtown, Redbone, on the East side."

Redbone was talking to Doc from his improvised office in the basement of 1929. Sitting in between the drainpipes of the utility room and sipping his mid-morning, regular coffee, Redbone spoke to his favorite tenant. His telephone was a discarded receiver wired to the primary telephone junction box on the wall.

"What's you need, Doc?" Redbone always spoke in a slow, comfortable rhythm.

"Doesn't your nephew work up here somewhere, Redbone?"

"What's the name'a the joint you at?"

Doc peered across the street. "Kitty's Koffee Kafé, all spelt with K's."

"Must be somebody don't know no English!"

"Must be, brother. Ya know it?"

"Never hoid of it, Doc. What's it near?"

"I'm right in the middle, between 58th and 59th, near the Queensboro. Ah . . . about a block from Bloomingdale's."

"Bloomingdale's, das it. Leon works at the lunch counter at Bloomingdale's. Da won downstairs."

"Great. Redbone, do me a favour, will ya? Go upstairs and tell Louie ta call me at this number, you ready?"

"Shoot, Cool Breeze."

"Murrayhill 7 2391, 2391. Got it?"

"Like fleas on a dog, brother. Hey Doc, you still want me get a hold'a that sign-painter fer ya new winda?"

"Nah. Little short'a green right now. Talk ta ya later."

Doc continued his improvised surveillance of Kitty's and noticed that Lansky was doing nearly all the talking. His curiosity was piqued. He looked around and found a matchbox on the ground. Breaking it up, he jammed a piece into the hook lever so it would still ring even though he was holding the receiver in his hand pretending to talk. The small café had only a single front door and the façade consisted of a large painted sign affixed to the wall above the picture window. He removed the matchbox on the second ring.

"Doc?"

"Yeah, Louie. Look, I'm at midtown at – "

"Redbone told me. You okay? What's up?"

"I'm fine. I'm watching some guys in a restaurant. I want you to come up here, I'll wait."

"You figure there's time, Doc?"

"Yeah, they don't look like they're in any hurry to order. Grab a cab. If I'm not here, stay glued to the booth across the street. I'll call ya there. Got it?"

"Roger, wilco, Doc! Captain Marvel to the rescue!" Louie hung up.

I swear that guy's only got one oar in the water, thought Doc.

Doc approached Bloomingdale's and entered through the 59th Street entrance. Leon wasn't hard to find. As soon as Doc saw him, he remembered the football scholarship Redbone talked about.

"Excuse me, you Leon?"

"Who wants ta know?"

"I'm a friend of your uncle, Redbone." Leon continued to sweep purposely towards Doc.

"So?" The six foot four, muscular athlete remained unimpressed.

"I'm a PI. I could use your help."

Leon stopped sweeping and stood upright to look down at Doc. *Jesus! My neck already aches from looking up,* Doc thought.

"Oh, so you that guy likes goin' around peepin' in ladies bedrooms at night?"

"No. That's the other guy, my ex-partner."

Leon continued to glare at Doc, remaining motionless, indicating that the clock was running.

"Look, I'm on to something. I need a closer look, but I can't get too close."

"Oh, so you want me ta do it 'cause nobody will notice me.

175

That it?"

This ain't gettin' any easier, thought Doc.

"Leon, how long are your breaks?"

"What?"

"Tell me, how long are your breaks?"

"Fifteen minutes, why?" Leon was suspicious but couldn't finger the scam.

"You make what, thirty-five cents an hour?"

"You figure I'm some sorta' chump? I make fifty!"

"Fifty cents, okay. All I need ya to do is go down the block ta Kitty's. Ya know it?"

Leon shot him a look as if to say, 'Did my mother drop me?' Leon knew all too well the pretty Puerto Rican waitress who floated around in Kitty's.

"There are three men sitting by the front door. The guy in the middle is the only one I know. I need the other two guys and anything else you can pick up." Doc reached into his trouser pocket and fished out a twenty. He offered it to Leon. "There's a week's pay for fifteen minutes work, and ya get to look at a cute waitress."

"Hey, Mr D!" Leon's voice boomed across the lunch counter to a small, middle-aged man working on books. "I'm going on break!" Leon took the twenty, undid his apron and set his broom near the corner.

"Go in through the back door," Doc offered.

"Som'a dem buildin's pretty old. How you know there's a back door?"

"That building was built after the Triangle factory fire, that means they had ta go by the new code. Gotta have one." Leon and Doc set off for the stairs.

An old man who was sitting next to Mr D and losing a fight with a BLT sandwich, commented about how there was no respect from the hired help any more. Not like in the old days. Mr D invited the old man to tell Leon that he couldn't go on break.

Upstairs on the south corner of 59th and Third, at Leon's request, Doc traded the twenty for two fives and a ten and then remained on the cold corner while Leon sought out the back entrance to Kitty's.

"Who the hell is that?" The three hundred pound man with the four day growth on his face, standing behind the counter, asked Rosie the waitress as he watched the tall, black athlete sweeping the floor. Rosie stuffed her newly earned five dollar bill into her left bra strap and answered the repulsive looking grill cook.

"He eez my brother. He on part-time for a leetle while." Rosie continued to draw coffee from the chrome-plated forty cup urn.

"Your brother?" he stated in disbelief. Rosie finished her chore and began to walk away.

"Yeah. My mother had a ding for de choofer."

As Leon swept closer to the table he found that the conversation was easily discernible owing to the sparse crowd in the café.

"Gurfein, quit worryin' about bein' seen! Nobody knows you up here!" Polakoff was annoyed at losing time from the office in the first place. Having to tolerate Gurfein complaining about being seen every five minutes only aggravated the situation.

"Lucky will do this thing, I'm tellin' ya without a doubt. He's very patriotic. He even tried enlisting, but got a medical rejection," Lansky reassured the Assistant DA.

"Whata you think?" Gurfein addressed Polatkoff without using his name. Leon could sweep for a long time in the same general area, but not forever.

"You heard it same as me. This is his school chum tellin' ya he'll do it. What more do ya want?"

"I want ta know I can trust him!" snapped the assistant DA.

"Trust him?" Lansky was irritated by a DA broaching the subject of trust but, as throughout the meeting, he maintained his composure and spoke in a level, controlled tone.

"If it weren't for this man sitting here, Mr Gurfein, this meeting never would have happened, because he is the only one we trust to deal with you."

"Don't pretend we're cut from the same cloth, Lansky! There's one important difference between people like you and people like us."

"If there's only one difference, Mr Gurfein, then we're more similar to one another than I thought."

Gurfein didn't respond. Instead, he looked over in Leon's direction. The time on Leon's meter ran out, and he swept around the room and made his way towards the back door. After thanking Rosie for the broom, Leon headed back to the corner where Doc was waiting.

"Well, the guy not doin' so good at tryin' ta look invisible's name is Gurfein. I couldn't get the other guy's name."

"What was the point of the conversation?" Doc was stamping his feet and had the fur collar of his bomber jacket up around his ears. The temperature had dropped considerably.

"They were talkin' about some guy named Lucky."

Doc stopped stomping his feet and got that dog-looking-in-the-mirror-for-the-first-time look. "Sounded like they was talkin' 'bout breakin' him outta jail or somethin'."

Doc peered around the corner to see Louie standing in the phone booth stomping his feet. "Anything else?"

"No, that's 'bout it. They was too busy arguin' about the difference between the two of them."

Doc laughed to himself. Toss up there.

"I owe ya one."

"No problem. Anytime you got a twenty you don't need, let me know."

Doc caught Louie's attention as he crossed Third Avenue to the pizza place catty-cornered from where he and Leon were standing.

Louie came inside with Doc to warm up, and they both stood watching the front door of Kitty's.

"Hey Doc. Nice day for a stake-out, huh?"

Doc held up two fingers to the guy behind the counter who prepped two slices. "Yeah, what were they doin' before you came over?"

"Well they still haven't eaten. Just sittin' there talkin'. Almost looked like they were fightin' over somethin'."

"They're not there ta eat."

"What're they doin' in a restaurant then?"

"Makin' some kinda deal."

"You know 'em?"

"Two of 'em. There's a DA and one of 'em's Lansky."

"Meyer Lansky? Shit! Looks like we're in the Majors."

As the implication slowly seeped through to Louie, a broad smile swept across his pudgy face.

"You look like Sylvester in the first reel of a Tweety Bird cartoon. What the hell you grinnin' at?" Doc asked.

"You tailin' these smucks wouldn't have anything to do with your father, would it?"

"This ain't about my father. Besides, who said anything about tailin'?"

The guy slid the two slices across the top of the glass display case. "I know you, Doc. This is gonna get more interesting."

"It's already more interesting. But first I need you to make a phone call."

"Phone call! Did you call Nikki yet?"

"No, not yet. I got distracted."

"C'mon, Doc! What's the problem? No guts, no air medals!"

"Good! Here's your chance to win an air medal, because you're about ta call her."

"*ME*? Doc, you ain't askin' me ta fix you up!"

"Fix me up? You got me in deep enough as it is. I don't need you fixin' me up."

"I don't want to call her, Doc! I'd be lost for words."

"Just make the call, Cupid. Tell her I need her to get Ira off . . ." Doc reached for the pizza.

"What . . .?"

". . . early! Tell her things are okay with Norma. She's waitin' on him for supper. Now go." Doc pointed to the phone booth in the back of the pizzaria. Louie moved away from the window. "And don't get creative!" Doc warned.

"Third District Headquarters. How may I direct your call?"

Louie talked as he ate. "Nikki? This is Doc McKeowen's partner, Louie Mancino. He asked me ta give you a call."

"Why didn't he call himself? No guts?"

"No, no. It ain't like that! We're on stake-out and he can't get to the phone just now, so . . ."

"But you could?" Louie was out of his league. The hell with etiquette.

"Look, I got a message. Tell Ira's boss that Ira needs ta be home tonight for dinnertime. Doc say's everything's okay with his wife. Got it?"

"Tell Doc that's fantastic news, and I don't know Ira's boss, but Shirley does, and I'm sure she'll help us out."

"That's great, Nikki."

"Anything else, Louie Mancino?"

"Yeah. I'm not supposed ta say nuthin', but he talks about ya all the time."

"Oh, he does, huh?" Nikki wasn't taken in for a second, but she was enjoying the ride.

"Honest, every day. He's been meanin' ta call, but we're on this really big case, see and he's such a sweet guy. He's so considerate of others. There's this old guy in our building . . ." Louie rattled on until he was hit in back of the head with a wadded-up coffee cup. He turned to see Doc signalling him to sign off. Doc pointed out the window and threw a dollar bill on the counter.

"You take the DA, he's the guy in the brown coat. I'll take the other two. And be careful, damn it!" Doc sensed Louie's apprehension. As they watched the threesome part company outside Kitty's, Doc patted Louie on the back. "Just relax and act natural, okay?" Louie nodded and they walked away from each other. "Hey Louie! See ya back at the Skull Cave!"

Louie smiled.

✦

Doris had the following day off, so she didn't object when Louie told her he'd be at Doc's late that night. Doris liked Doc and didn't think much of his wife for bailing out on him when things got rough. Louie was put through the wringer every night when he came home regarding Doc's progress in the romance department, and although he was annoyed by the constant questioning, Louie loved her all the more for her concern.

Doc had been in the office waiting for Louie for the better part of an hour and had been sipping the same drink while sketching out a flow chart. A half dozen crumpled pieces of paper littered the floor and Doc had just reached up for the bottle of Jameson when he heard a strange echo in the hall.

The Emerson had been playing the war news and as he turned down the volume, the echo grew louder. He smiled and sat back down, recognising the off-key voice instantly.

Seconds later, Mancino entered and stood in the doorway as he finished singing the last verse of, *Don't Sit Under the Apple Tree*.

"Evenin', Maxine," Doc said with a smirk. Louie struck a pose like a pin-up as he finished his number. Then he walked over and sat down at his new desk.

"Funny, you don't look drunk."

"Oh, I ain't drunk. Yet. I had a coupl'a beers on the way over. But I sure wouldn't mind a taste a the old Scottish."

"It's Irish, Louie. Not Scotch."

"Whatever it is, beats the hell outta getting' drunk on Amaretto!"

Doc poured Louie a drink and set the glass on the desk.

"If it's not too much trouble, you wanna tell me why you're on cloud nine?"

"Louie the almost PI did not lose his subject." He pointed at Doc as he spoke.

"Good man! Where'd he wind up?"

"You'll never guess!" Louie might as well have been in his cups. It was the post-revelation euphoria experienced by great men of science, philanthropists and explorers. Those who have not only discovered an extremely significant and vital piece of information, but realise that they have, by their discoveries and contributions, become destined to alter the course of human events.

"The DA's office?"

"Nope!"

"C'mon, Louie. I don't wanna play games. This thing's really got my curiosity up."

"I know. That's why when I tell you, you're gonna have a cow!" Louie's euphoria was contagious and Doc was starting to feel better than he had in a long time. Louie lifted his glass.

"When Mary had a little lamb the doctors were surprised. But when old McDonald had a farm, that really took the prize!"

"You sure you ain't drunk?"

"Alright, damn it. I'll give you a hint." Louie fell forward on his chair and leaned both arms on the desk as he began to sing. "*I had the craziest dream last night*."

"Ah . . . Helen Forrest, Forrest. He went upstate and into the forest!"

"Now who's drunk? Jesus, Doc! Where's the last place on earth you'd expect him ta go?"

"Okay, Louie. I give up. Where?"

"Number nine-zero Church Street!"

"A DA? You're shittin' me?" Doc sat forward in his chair.

"I wouldn't shit you, Doc. You're my favourite turd. Now, how about another drink before my fuckin' arm falls off?"

"Louie! Tell me you ain't been drinkin'!" Doc poured him another one.

"I'm not drunk Doc. But if I ain't drunk in about an hour, it ain't gonna be from lack'a tryin'." Louie shot the whiskey back.

"My little fat protégé found a connection between the DA, the US Navy and the Mob!"

"Yup!" Louie reached into his jacket pocket and produced a small notepad. "Subject entered building, see item thirteen." He flipped several pages. "Item thirteen, address number ninety Church Street. Shall I continue?"

"No, I believe you. But now we have to find out why."

"Well, first off, who was the guy with Lansky you were followin'?"

"Name's Polakoff. Lansky's lawyer apparently."

"So whatever they were doin', Lansky figured he had to have his lawyer there." Louie was being a PI.

"Right. But why?"

"Cuttin' a deal?" he suggested.

"Not in a million years. Besides, he's not in any trouble, at least none that's made the papers."

"I remember hearin' that he ain't legal. A Russian alien or somethin'. Maybe they're lookin' ta deport him?"

"Not likely. He's been here too long. Even so, he'd be dealin' with INS, not the DA."

"Squealin' on somebody?"

"Lansky? That'd be like you goin' on a diet and showin' up at a gym." Louie was not amused.

"Shit, Doc. I can't figure it! Give me another drink." Doc poured Louie and himself another one and then made a suggestion.

"Let's put it to bed for a while and talk about something else. Maybe it'll come to us."

"Good idea, Doc. Let's talk about why you ain't called Nikki yet."

"Jesus, Louie! What, is it your mission in life ta get me fixed up with somebody?"

"Doc, what the hell ya afraid of? She's smart, unattached, sounds sweet as apple pie, on the phone anyway. And I'll bet she's cute. Is she cute, Doc?'

"Yeah, she's cute." Doc smiled at the sudden image of Nikki's face that popped into his head. "As a matter of fact, she'd give Lauren Becall a run for her money."

"Okay, then!" Louie downed his drink. "Let's check the universal babe-o-meter. Brains, a ten. Availability, a ten. Personality, a ten." Doc was increasingly amused by Louie's floor show. "And looks? Makes your dick harder than Chinese arithmetic!"

"Does your mother know you talk like that?"

"Shit, Doc! My mom's Sicilian, she taught me to talk like this!"

"It ain't just about sex, ya know."

"I realise that it ain't just about sex, Doc! But it's mostly about sex! At least in the beginning. Hell, sex and love's the only real things men and women got in common. It's the only thing we really need each other for!"

"You ever thought about writin' a column?" Doc sensed the whiskey was kicking in and so egged Louie on by pouring him another one.

"Not really." Louie got up to pour himself another drink then realised his glass had already been charged. "But I used to give advice to farmers about breedin' chickens." He swallowed his whiskey then poured again. Doc took possession of the bottle.

"Oh, really?" *Where the hell is this going?*

"Yeah. Like this time this farmer over in Weehawken had a rooster. Guy was from Palermo, a friend of the family's. Problem was the rooster would try to screw everything in sight. The dog, the cat, the cows. All the chickens. He tried to get the rooster ta slow down or else he'd kill himself. Did that stupid bird quit? Hell no. Then one day, the inevitable happened. That's when he called me." Louie sipped his drink.

"You squared him away, huh?"

"No! Not much I could do under the circumstances! I went out in the barnyard with him, and there was that dumb rooster. Flat on his back, legs up in the air, head cocked over and tongue hangin' out. Dead as a doornail! Even had a big old buzzard flyin' around in circles over him."

"I'm waitin'."

"We both bent over that stupid bird and just looked at him. Then I guess that old farmer got overcome by grief, and he just let loose on that rooster. 'You stupid bird! Look what you done ta yerself! Now you're no good ta' me, yer no good ta' the chickens!'"

"So he lost a good rooster?"

"Oh hell, no! Just then the damn thing looked up at us, pointed up at the buzzard and said, 'Shut the hell up! She's gettin' closer!'"

"I think your elevator doesn't go to the top, Mancino, ya know that?"

"Could be. But I know I drink another need." Louie held his glass out unable to stand. It was only 10 p.m., but after Doc poured Louie his last drink, he prepared the cot in the back room and helped Louie to bed. Then he rang Doris to let her know Louie was okay. She thanked him and reminded him that if he needed anything to call her, and speaking of calling, he ought to call that nice girl downtown.

After he hung up, Doc sat back down at his desk, put his feet up and turned off the light.

Maybe Frank Capra was right.

Chapter Sixteen

"Lorraine, have our two doves flown the coop?"

"Yes, sir. I booked them on the 23:45 last night out of Grand Central. Their ETA is 07:50 this morning."

"Notify me if you hear from them. And have your pad ready. They may use code if they need to leave a message."

"Yes, sir."

"Also notify the mail room that the package is in their safe. Don't talk to some kid, either, tell that old supervisor, the one that was here when the Dutch landed."

A discretionary fund is like a secret lover. Everybody loves them, everybody would like to have one, but if its existence is made public, it gets extremely expensive.

So it was with the discretionary fund assigned to Third Naval District for the expansion of *Operation Underworld*. These types of discretionary funds were always in cash. This posed a problem for the Logistics Officer, who passed it onto the Disbursement Officer, who passed it onto the Communications officer because the mailroom fell under his domain. The mail room, which housed the only safe large enough to store $125,500 in small bills, the size of the discretionary fund The Boys in Washington decided The Boys in New York needed despite the fact they had only requested $62,250.

To keep the existence of said fund from leaking out to the public, or worse, to the auditors, there were no duplicates, triplicates or extra files anywhere in the system. The senator, who by United States Code was not supposed to issue such funds without the approval of Congress, knew about it, and the individual who received it also received the only receipt in the form of a memo in a sealed envelope.

"Sir, Ira Birnbaum is a very sweet old man. Just because he's old doesn't mean he doesn't contribute. I think it's wrong to insult him!" The senior civil servant was taken off guard by his secretary's defence of the mail room supervisor, and felt browbeaten into an apology.

Lorraine rang down to the mail room, but Ira wasn't there. It was close enough to coffee break so she decided a walk downstairs was in order. At the same time, she would try and locate Ira herself to deliver the message.

After ten minutes of searching the lower floors with no success, Lorraine wandered out to the reception desk, and asked Nikki if she would relay the message to Ira. Nikki informed the secretary that Ira had a special day off to be with Norma. As one comment gave way to another, Nikki, Lorraine and Shirley spent the next fifteen minutes telling each other what a sweet idea it was and how considerate this Doc guy must be. Ten minutes after their coffee break was supposed to be over, they all returned to work. In the course of the day Nikki came to realise that it might be okay if Doc called.

✢

The Naval officer dressing in front of the mirror in the cramped cabin of the Pullman car, finished putting on his dress blue jacket and made some last minute adjustments to the three ribbons on the left breast of his dark blue garment. He noticed the rolling landscape slowly drifting past the picture window of the small room in contrast to the whoosh of the telegraph poles as he checked his watch. He considered taking his gloves and cover with him to breakfast but decided against it.

"Arthur, you ready?" Lieutenant Commander Cowen banged on the door of the adjoining cabin and the much younger Ensign joined him en route to the dining car. Old eating habits from the Academy precluded conversation during the two to three minutes it took to eat the meal, and so the two officers only began to speak after they had finished their ham and eggs.

"Sir, is it SOP for the Nav to spend so much money on a two day trip just to play messenger boy?" The Ensign was only on his fourth month of active duty and so was keen to learn the ropes from the veteran Commander, whom he had come to respect.

"Some things can't be sent through regular channels. But it is a bit unusual to send a field grade with a message to a state employee." Reaching in his breast pocket, he produced the tiny, half-sized envelope the two were charged with delivering. Holding the envelope in both hands, he commented, "Sorta looks like a wedding invitation, doesn't it?"

"You suppose he'll come to the reception?"

"How do you mean?"

"Well, whoever in the Nav sent us to this politician must be askin' for some kind of favour. Are we to wait for a reply?"

"Ya know, Arty, that's the other strange thing. They said they didn't know if he would reply right away."

"ALBANY! TEN MINUTES! NEXT STOP, ALBANY!" The porter walked through the dining car with his announcement, and the Commander checked his watch.

"Fifteen minutes early! Very nice. Let's shove off."

The long line of Pullman cars cast a distorted shadow over the station platform as it pulled in, and the officers were not required to wait for baggage after they disembarked as they had been ordered to travel with overnight bags only.

An old man dressed in remarkably light clothing for the markedly cold temperatures in the northern upstate climate, sat on a bench smoking some sort of white clay pipe, overseeing the activity of the station. The Commander nodded to the Ensign and they approached him.

"Excuse me, sir. Can you tell us where to get a taxi?"

"Sure can." The old man enjoyed an uncomfortable silence from the two officers who looked at each other and then back at the old man. The Commander attempted to kick-start the conversation.

"Sir, are there taxis here, north to Albany?"

"Yup, sure are." Cowen looked at Lamberson, who shrugged and twirled his finger around his left temple and smiled out of sight of the man, so he thought. Being a glutton for punishment, the Commander sought to out-manoeuvre the old man.

"Sir, where is the taxi stand?"

"Right in front of the station, son, out on the street." He threw his thumb over his left shoulder.

"Thank you." The officers walked away.

"Welcome to Albany," the old man called after them. If nothing else, he was cordial.

After a fifteen minute wait in the cold, the two sailors discussed returning to the old man for further advice, but thought better of it. Instead, they made for the Station Master's office, and Cowen spoke through the small ticket window to the heavy-set man on the other side.

"Sir, we've got to get to the Prison Commissioner's office, can you call us a taxi, please?" The Ticket Master smiled.

"I will if you really want me to. But it won't do ya no good." Cowen turned to Lamberson.

"You're from this area, talk to these yokels!" he ordered the Ensign.

"I'm from Connecticut, sir."

"And I'm from Santa Barbara! Get us a damn ride!" The Ensign stepped back to the window.

"Sir, we're here on official business, and we need to get to the Commissioner's office. Can you please arrange for a cab to take us there?"

"I'm sorry, son. There's only one cab here anymore 'cause a the gas rationing and parts shortage, but if you can wait about ten minutes, Floyd'll be going out that way on delivery. I'll get him to take you out there."

Floyd's 1931 Ford pick-up was not only cramped with three men stuffed into the two man bench seat, but the heater didn't work and the god-awful smell of chicken shit was inescapable. On top of it, Floyd wasn't much of a conversationalist. Or a hygienist. However, twenty-five minutes later Cowen and

Lamberson were dropped off in front of the New York State Correctional Authority Headquarters, and were walking up the gravel path to the front door.

They walked through the cold, lifeless building and simultaneously came to the same conclusion. That if, after the war, they choose to remain in government service, the Penal System was the last branch they would ever choose to serve in.

At the end of a long hall, they were directed by a security guard to the Commissioner's office. They introduced themselves to the secretary and were told in no uncertain terms that no one saw the Commissioner without an appointment. After several failed attempts to explain to the secretary that the Commissioner had been notified by the Pentagon of their coming, Cowen had had all the Albany hospitality he could stand.

"Let's go." He signalled the Ensign and they by-passed the receptionist-secretary-aspiring bureaucrat and started for the Commissioner's door. The spindly, middle-aged brunette trailed behind them through the door and into the office, spewing protests. Once inside the room, they wasted no time and went straight for the Commissioner's desk.

Commissioner Lyons looked up from his work when he heard the commotion, and sat back in his chair. The officers were already standing in front of the Commissioner's desk by the time the fat guard seated to his right had time to drop the pen-knife he was using to clean his nails.

"Sir, we understand you were notified of our arrival?"

"Yes, I was. That's alright, Jane. Thank you." He dismissed the frustrated woman and turned his attention back towards the two officers.

"Do navy officers always barge into high government officials' offices, Captain?"

"The rank is Lieutenant Commander, Commissioner Lyons, and Washington would like to know if you are refusing to accept a Top Secret message sent to you?"

Lyons wasn't sure how to react. Whatever it was the two officers brought, he had been told through his grapevine that it was coming and that he probably wouldn't like it.

"What is it you want?"

Cowen reached into his jacket pocket and produced the small envelope and handed it to Lyons. The Commissioner accepted it, and without reading it placed it in his desk drawer.

"Sir, by order of the Department of the Navy you are to open it in our presence." In his short time in this billet, Ensign Lamberson had never heard the Commander speak in a more commanding tone of voice. "And then return it to us."

Lyons' face clearly registered his anger as he opened and read the classified document. He was incensed and wanted only to expedite the officers on their return journey as quickly as possible.

"I'm a god-damned former police inspector. I worked in New York City risking my life for half my career! I was appointed by the Governor himself! And now some god-damned Navy guy gets to tell me what to do with my prisoners? Son-of-a-bitch!"

Cowen and Lamberson fought back their smiles not out of any kind of respect, there was none, but out of the military discipline they had been taught by men whom they did respect.

Cowen held his hand out and Lyons threw the message on the desk. Lamberson moved a gilded ashtray from one corner of the Commissioner's desk and Cowen lit the piece of magnesium-impregnated paper with a match and dropped it into the ashtray.

"You bastard! That's my Governor's award for exemplary performance!"

"Sorry, sir. It looked like an ashtray to me," Lamberson said, with no trace of sincerity.

"Sir, you're required to answer to the Third Naval District Headquarters within twenty-four hours and you are cautioned against revealing the contents of this message to anyone. Thank you. Sir."

"Get the hell outta my office! I mean right now, god-damn it!" Lyons was on his feet, as was the guard with the clean nails. Cowen and Lamberson walked out the door and once in the hallway, clear of the secretary, Lamberson questioned Cowen.

"Suppose we should have asked him for a ride back to town?" Cowen snickered. "C'mon. Let's find Floyd."

✦

Doc was up an hour before Louie and so cleaned up, made coffee and went straight back to work on some diagrams. He'd been using the technique of flow charts ever since he happened to read about their application to any given problem in *Science Illustrated* magazine about five years ago. So why not, he reasoned, apply them to detective work? The thing that kept eating away at him was that he couldn't come up with any plausible theory as to why the DA would meet with someone as high up the chain as Meyer Lansky. There could be many reasons, theoretically, but the fact that he was trying so hard not to be seen could only mean one of two things. Either he didn't have Hogan's okay on the deal, or if he did, Hogan wanted it under wraps as well, which could only mean it wasn't legitimate. That was the part Doc was interested in.

Everyone on the DA's staff disliked, if not hated, men in Doc's profession. Partially because they were more trusted on the street than the DA's and their investigators. Of course it never occurred to the DA's that the PI's didn't have a corporate-styled political ladder to climb and so could go wherever the case took them. If they didn't perform, they didn't get paid. In addition, the DA's professional success was measured by how many convictions they have to their credit. Sorta like RBI's in baseball, Doc always figured.

However, to compound matters, beyond their dislike of PI's the DA's had nursed a special hatred for Doc McKeowen ever since the fatal incident involving his father. And Doc remained ever vigilant to any crack in their defences so that he might one day demonstrate the fact that the feelings were mutual.

Doc decided Louie had had enough time to sleep off his biannual dose of hard liquor and so woke him at about half past nine. Louie fought but lost the battle to remain in bed and a half hour later, they were in a mid-town restaurant finishing breakfast and preparing for the day's events.

"So what the hell's at the library, Doc? We gonna sit around reading all day?"

"Hopefully not all day, Louie. But I think if we look in the right place we could improve our battin' average a little."

"Well, the Silver Clipper ain't got nuthin' ta worry about, that's for sure. What the hell we lookin' for anyway, Doc?"

"Not a clue Louie. Not a clue."

Doc paid the waitress and they walked the four blocks to Bryant Park and entered the 42nd Street branch Public Library on the Fifth Avenue side. The two men were forced to detour into the street for a short way as there was a large crew of steel workers replacing a twenty-foot section of wrought-iron fencing.

"We'll check the records here first, then shoot over to the Times Building this afternoon," Doc explained as they climbed the granite stairs. Doc watched Louie rubber-necking as they entered the foyer.

"You've never been to a library, have you?"

"Yeah, sure. All the time."

"You ever check anything out other than the librarians?"

"You mean you can take these books home?" Louie knew Doc was angling to give him a lesson and he wasn't disappointed. After a fifteen minute introduction to the card catalogue, Louie learned about periodicals.

"The advantage of periodicals is they can supplement your research because they contain information that's not included in things that are on microfiche. Few other investigators use the library. If they don't find it in the newspapers or in the public records, they usually give up. That's where you can get a leg up. Got it?" Louie didn't respond. "Well, any questions?"

"Yeah! What the hell's a microfinch?"

"A very small bird. C'mon."

Five minutes later, Louie was an expert at locating, inserting and scanning microfiche film. Each of them took a booth and several canisters of film. Louie went to work on the *New York Daily News* and Doc took the *Times*. Doc instructed his partner to take notes on anything to do with the DA's office, starting back two months before Pearl Harbor. Two and a half hours later, he was snapped out of a mesmerising tedium when Louie suddenly yelled out.

"Incredible!"

"What? What'd ya find?"

"This lady, in Saskatchewan, not only gave birth to triplets that lived, but all three of them were breeched! That's amazing!"

"Am I gonna have ta go back over all your work and check for myself? What the hell good are you here, Louie?"

"Doc! I got all the DA shit! There just ain't that much of it. It's all shoved aside for the war news. The Japs doin' this and the Russians doin' that. Hell, all I came across was about ten articles havin' anything ta do with Hogan's office."

"Yeah, you got a point, I guess." Doc set his pencil down and rubbed his eyes. "Hell, most interesting thing I found was George M. Cohan's funeral and the Normandie thing."

"Yeah, I read that too." Louie sat back and yawned. "They sure stepped on that story."

Doc looked at Louie while digesting the offhand remark. "How do you mean?"

"Well, one day it's front page news all over the world, next day there's one paragraph on page two or three, and then, the story vanishes. Like it never happened. But she's still sittin' out there like a beached whale."

"Ya know what struck me funny? The API reports the eye-witness, Eddy Sullivan, saw the fire start from the welder's torch. But nobody ever mentions the welder, where he is, what he was doing, or who he is. And to top it off, the papers all said Eddy Sullivan's a carpenter. There's no wood anywhere near that part of the promenade deck. What the heck was a carpenter doin' there?"

"Doc, I'm startin' ta smell the same thing you are."

"What's that, Louie?"

"Not a clue, Doc, not a clue. But there had to be a reason for that DA goin' into Third Naval District Headquarters yesterday."

McKeowen sat back in his chair and gave a tilted nod to Mancino.

"Louie! I take back almost everything I ever said about you! Let's copy all the Normandie stuff, the rest of the DA stuff and get some lunch. I think you might have something!"

Chapter Seventeen

Murray Gurfein was not a happy DA as he stepped off the passenger train onto platform 12 at Penn Station. The cold, damp air was scant relief after two and a half days travel roundtrip to Albany. He had been sent there by Hogan in an attempt to avert a head-banging contest between the City and the State.

Hogan deduced Lyons was not over the moon about co-operating with the Navy and their little venture, and was attempting to force the issue back onto the New York City DA. Hogan was getting tired of being tangled up with the FBI, the USN and now the State Correctional Facilities Office and wanted out of the net.

To cover his own ass, Lyons sent a memo requesting "firm" backing from the NYC DA's office. So rather than post a letter, even a certified letter, Hogan thought it more prudent to send a representative and, since Gurfein was already in the middle of it, Hogan volunteered him for the mission.

Commissioner Lyons was none to happy about this counter strategy and, to show his deep appreciation, he sent Gurfein back with a laundry list of restrictions to be given to the Navy before he would consent to their little adventure. In this manner he was able to assure himself he hadn't lost any authority, and was able to keep the DA in the game for insurance against any future accusations of wrong-doing.

Gurfein cursed the cold. Then he cursed the baggage handlers for not being able to find his luggage. Then decided to go into the station and look for Hogan. The DA expected his arrival and cabled the hotel in Albany that he would meet Gurfein at the

Whistle Stop, a coffee shop in the main concourse of the station.

As Gurfein walked towards the café, weaving through the crowd with the intermittent blasts of the public address system echoing through the terminal, he wondered at the complexity of the civilian chain of command, and how much trouble it was to get anything done in the tangle of bureaucracy. At this level everyone had their own agendas, and before anything was allowed past them, they had to assess it in terms of its value to them.

In the military chain on the other hand, at least outside of DC, something was ordered done, and it was done. Next task, thank you very much.

"Murray!" It was Hogan. He was sitting at a table outside the café waving at Gurfein.

"How was the trip?"

"Complete shit! Next silly question."

"Speakin' of shit, you look terrible! You okay?"

"Thanks for the update, boss. Look, these clowns can't find my luggage, so let's get this over with. You can take off and I'll catch a cab back to the apartment."

"Yeah, sure. Look, don't bother coming in today. Take the rest of the day off."

Gurfein had no intention of coming back in anyway. On the other hand Hogan didn't give him the day off out of the kindness of his heart. Hogan did it because he wanted the rest of the day to assess the situation after he talked to his underling. Also, he knew Gurfein would be useless to him for the rest of the day, anyway.

"Talk to me about Lyons."

"Well, for starters – " Just as Gurfein began to speak, a waitress interrupted them. Hogan ordered two regular coffees and the girl disappeared through the maze of tables.

"For starters, Sing Sing's a no go."

"Why, for God's sake? It's maximum security and it's real close."

"That's probably the reason. He wants it perfectly understood we're on his turf."

"Is that the feeling you got from him?"

"No. That's the words I got from him."

"Did he say that?" Hogan was shocked.

"Verbatim. Next issue. It's probably going to be Great Meadows."

"Hell, that's ten to twelve hours from here!"

"For us. For him it's right up the road. Less than two hours from Albany. He wants us on a short leash." Gurfein had had hours to consider these possibilities while sitting alone on the way back to the City.

"You don't think it's just a matter of keeping a low profile up there?"

"C'mon! Which of the four high security prisons is less high profile than the rest? They're all the same. Besides, that ain't all."

"I can hardly wait for the rest."

"All visitors will be required to give twenty-four hours advance notice of arrival, and on arrival register with proper identification."

"That's standard for any prison."

"And all visitors will be required to be fingerprinted."

"That I'd like to see." Hogan rearranged his chair, crossed his legs and folded his hands behind his head. "I told Haffenden he was pissin' in the wind." Gurfein took a long drink of coffee.

"That ain't the whole shootin' match."

"There's more?"

"As I left, he called his secretary in. There was no one else in the hall, so . . . "

"So, like a good little DA, you eavesdropped."

"I took my time putting my coat on. Lyons calls the Warden at Great Meadows, fills him in and then tells him he's gonna get a memo. He's to keep track of everything and everybody, and send it all back to Lyons. The same day. They're gonna set up a special courier system. Nobody's to know about this except him and Childs."

"Who's Childs?"

"Warden at Great Meadows."

"Why the hell does he want all that the same day? It's all gonna be in the register, anyway?"

"Apparently he don't trust the register." Hogan finished his coffee, had a short think about what to do and came to a conclusion.

"Well Murray, ya done good, thank you. But I'll tell ya what we're gonna do. We're gonna dump this back in Haffenden's lap, and bow outta the spy business. We've wasted enough resources. Time, money and, worst of all, it's gonna be months before we get another phone tap on a suspected racketeering charge, unless we've got photographs of them committing the crime."

"What happened?"

"I got called into chambers yesterday. Judge Puzo is not amused that after two months we got nothing from Lanza's phone tap. He rescinded the order and lectured me about the basic right to privacy."

"Puzo lectured you on privacy? That's like a politician lecturing a hooker on ethics!" Gurfein finished his coffee and, after standing up, told Hogan he'd be in early tomorrow. They parted company and Hogan headed for the main exit.

Gurfein rode a cab back to his mid-town apartment cursing the baggage manager who had informed him it would be a day or so before they located his bags, which had inadvertently been put back on the train to Albany.

Gurfein vowed never again to curse a baggage handler. At least not out loud.

⊹

The weary, middle-aged warden slumped in his chair behind his desk and was annoyed that he had to yell twice before the senior guard responded and came into his office.

"Where the hell you been? You think I got nuthin' ta do but wait on messengers? Get this god-damned notice to 92168 now!" The senior guard of the Clinton State Penitentiary figured he'd had too many years in grade to run messages, especially to scumbags like 92168.

He took the piece of paper from the warden, said, "Yes, sir," in a smart, obedient tone and exited the office. It was only a matter of minutes before an unsuspecting younger prison guard crossed his path and was handed the message with the explanation, "I'm too old ta go lookin' fer this fuckin' bum. Go find him and see that he gets this!"

The young guard immediately recognised the well-known number and started off through the huge maze of halls and chambers. From the elevated structure which housed the warden's office down into the exercise yard, the guard made his way through the general population and into the wood shop. No one had seen the sought-after inmate, and if they had, they wouldn't have gone out of their way to tell the rookie screw. Down through cell block D into cell block B and across the north yard he searched for the prisoner he might one day tell his grandchildren about having met.

Twenty minutes after the guard's hunt began, it ended in the laundry. Amidst the noise and humidity of the huge tumble dryers, the messenger found the man he sought.

"*MR. LUCIANO! EXCUSE ME, MR. LUCIANO!*" He was compelled to yell over the loud thrashing of the laundry machines. The inmate turned slowly and the pock-marked face with the droopy right eye stared back at the errand boy. Removing his work gloves, Luciano took the message and read it.

"Well, whata ya know?" Despite the fact he was a native Sicilian, and spoke the lingo perfectly, his English was characterised by the dialect of the neighbourhoods of the Lower East Side where he grew up.

The next morning Lucky was packed two hours ahead of schedule.

"Hey, Lucky. What's the skinny?" His cell-mate was surprised to see him preparing to leave.

"My guys finally fixed it fer me ta get moved down state."

"Not bad, Charlie! Help ya get a handle back on the operations!"

"Dat's da general idea." Lucky cinched the ropes on the dark blue, canvas bag, threw it over his shoulder and reported to the cell block chief at nine on the nose.

He was escorted to the yard under armed guard, and rumours ran rabid throughout the prison. The stories ranged from expensive lawyers having paid a judge, to key witnesses having recanted their testimony.

Lucky was surprised to see six other inmates preparing to be transferred along with him. Surprised, but not suspicious.

"Okay scumbags, dump 'em!"

The prisoners were obliged to empty their bags into the dirt, and wait for a guard to rummage through their belongings. Weapons were the primary concern. Money or anything of value the guards thought they could get away with stealing, the prisoners hid on their bodies. This was a safe strategy as pat-downs were rare.

The guards conducting the search were the two who would make the trip with the prisoners. The younger one stood in front of Luciano, and looked down at his still full bag. He then stared nervously at the older guard making his way from the other end of the line.

"Lucky, ya gotta empty your bag!"

"I ain't dumpin' my stuff in the dirt, kid."

"But you'll get my ass in a sling!" the guard pleaded. Lucky looked at the kid and shook his head. He bent over lifted the bag and opened it wide.

"Here, stick ya hand in there and wiggle it around." The kid was reluctant, but the other guard was only two prisoners away.

"Go on, kid. I ain't got nuthin' in there, anyway. Anything I want I can get down state." The guard complied and then quickly ordered the men on his side of the line to repack their bags and mount the bus.

Roll was taken before they boarded, and again a half hour later as they went through the gate while the bottom of the bus was being searched. Finally, nearly an hour after the line-up, they were on the road.

The seven prisoners were huddled in the middle seats of the

vehicle, with one of the two guards brandishing a 12-gauge pump at each end of the bus. The only excitement for the first four hours was when the guards occasionally swapped positions.

Lucky figured the ride would be about eighteen hours which meant at least two stops for fuel and toilets. Food was stored in the back of the bus, and the fat, senior guard was already rooting through the packages liberating the cookies from the lunch boxes.

As there was no highway system, the roads were very rough and the trip wore on through a seemingly endless mass of mountainous terrain. The heater in the bus hadn't been serviced for years, and threw off just enough heat to remind the men they were cold.

At about six hours into the trip the fat guard stood and walked to the front of the bus. He pushed the young guard aside, and looked at the prisoners, shotgun on his hip, in his best Gary Cooper pose.

"We're coming up on halfway. We're gonna pull over, get gas and then one by one you pieces a shit can get out and take a leak. Don't nobody move till I say so."

They pulled over and he got off the bus, followed by the young guard who stationed himself next to the driver's seat at the door.

"Hey, Lucky!" It was the small guy across the aisle. "Thought you said 'bout eighteen hours?"

"Somethin's fishy," Lucky muttered, as he kept looking around through the windows.

The big guy in the last seat offered his contribution. "Lucky, I'll tell ya somethin' else. These hills ain't gettin' no smaller. If we was goin' down state, it'd be gettin' more flat like."

Lucky began to wonder what the plan was.

"Porky Pig ain't gonna tell us nuthin'," the small guy offered.

"I'll see what I can find out," Lucky assured the rest of the crew.

After twenty minutes of Porky playing footsie with the even fatter female cashier in the gas station, the men were allowed off the bus one at a time until it was Lucky's turn.

The kid stood facing Charlie with his shotgun at high port as

Charlie faced the woodline, back to the kid, and pretended to take a leak.

"Hey, kid. Where the hell we headed, anyway?"

"I'm not supposed to talk to you guys!" He looked around nervously as he spoke. Porky Pig was in the back again, stuffing his face with a Baby Ruth.

"C'mon, kid. Nobody's gonna lock ya up! We're gonna find out anyways. What's the deal?"

"For some reason the Warden's really pissed off!"

"I like it already! Keep goin'."

"These other guys are a cover. You were supposed to be the only guy transferred."

"What?" Lucky twisted around to look at the kid. The bus driver climbed back onto the bus and into his seat.

"C'mon, Mr. Luciano! Porky's gonna get pissed!"

"Youse call him that too?" The fat guard finished his second Baby Ruth and banged on the window.

"Everybody calls him that, even the Warden. Let's go." The kid moved away and Lucky took his time pretending to do up his trousers.

"So how long to Sing Sing?" Lucky asked as they mounted the bus.

"We ain't goin' ta Sing Sing." The kid followed him back to his seat and leaned forward. "This bus is goin' to Great Meadows at Comstock," the kid whispered back. Lucky hesitated a step, and then continued to sit.

Late that night, in the yard of his new home at Comstock, Lucky stood with the other six prisoners. Powerful floodlights allowed the new guards to search the prisoners' bags one more time. They stood in the cold for another twenty minutes until the head guard came out and gave them the usual welcoming speech.

Short guy said he could tell right away that it was the head guard, because the knees on his trousers were worn out. He must have whispered a little too loudly because his crack earned him a punch in the kidney with a rifle butt. Eventually, they were shown to their cells.

Lucky thought it unusual that the Warden hadn't asked to see him yet. The Warden's welcome speech was always good for a chuckle. It was pretty much the same spiel as the guard's, and although he had only been in two different prisons, both in the last twenty-four hours, Lucky had heard that all Wardens' speeches were identical. They must come down from the top. However, because of his notoriety, Luciano knew he would receive a special welcome.

A few days later Lucky's wait was over. He was summoned to the Warden's chambers. The guards escorted him to a room, but it wasn't the Warden's office. To add to his sense of curiosity, he was left alone in the room, without a guard. He had never heard of that before, anywhere. So he waited.

Luciano's claim to fame was that he is generally accredited with putting the 'organised' in organised crime. Prior to his arrival in the food chain, criminals were more or less congregated in large gangs, spread across the country, mostly east of the Mississippi. Luciano's younger, more Americanised gangsters replaced the 'Moustache Petes', as the old traditional Sicilianos were derogatorily known. These older types fought national syndication until Luciano, who fully understood the financial benefits of the American corporate structure, reorganised the 'Mob' into the Siciliano Unione. He accomplished this by downsizing the Mafia on September 11, 1931 in an organised simultaneous execution of approximately forty non-cooperating rival members. It would take nearly two decades before the FBI linked the murders.

After about fifteen minutes the door opened, and despite all the things he had been through, Luciano was awe-struck. Falling back into his chair, his mouth dropped open and for one of the few times in his life, Salvatore Lucania was speechless. Meyer Lansky, chaperoned by Moses Polakoff, entered the room.

Polakoff gave a cursory greeting and moved to a far corner. After a few minutes the boss regained his composure and stood with a smile on his face.

"What the hell are you two guys doin' here?"

"We got somethin' ta talk to ya about. Somethin' big." Lansky was there to do the talking. Polakoff was there as one of the concessions to Commissioner Lyons.

"Hold it! Why ain't there no guards wit you two?"

"You're gonna love this! Not allowed!" Lansky backhanded Lucky's shoulder as he gave him the unique news.

"What? Are you kiddin' me or what?" There were only two chairs in the room, so Meyer knocked on the door, and told the guard to bring another. A few minutes later the disgruntled guard returned with a chair.

"So what's the story?" Lucky pressed Meyer.

After catching up on current events in the City, Lansky explained to Lucky about the Navy's operation and Socks Lanza's involvement to date. Particularly the details about having limited influence and bringing suspicion on himself by working with the Navy. Haffenden was only mentioned as the Commander, and the operation was never mentioned outright.

Even though Meyer Lansky was a Russian Jew, his Sicilian was very good compliments of Lucky and their younger days east of the Bowery. They switched back and forth between languages, partially to talk about things in regard to the Unione operations and their current status, and partially to see how far they could push Polakoff.

After Lucky had been completely briefed about the Navy's request, he sat back and folded his arms.

"There's just one thing I gotta know."

"What's that?" Polakoff finally spoke.

"There's a deportation order out on me ta go back ta Sicily. If these clowns decide they don't want me here no more, and the Fascists win the war, that means I'll be executed. Especially if they find out I been helpin' youse guys!"

Polakoff didn't give a damn one way or the other. In fact, he didn't understand why Lucky used the phrase, "helping youse guys." He would only be helping the Navy. What Polokoff failed to understand, as did everyone on the DA's side of the case, was that Lucky had learned to think like them. There were no 'innocent bystanders' when it came to the government. Different circus, same clowns.

"Lucky, we were told absolutely no deals. You're still in for the full sentence. No parole, no help, that's it," Polokoff explained.

"I'm not askin' for a deal. I'll do it for my adopted country. I hate that shit hole I came from, you know that. All I'm askin' is that we keep dis ding strictly under wraps!"

"You think the United States Navy is in a hurry for the American public to find out they're workin' with organised crime? Don't worry about it," Polakoff reassured Lucky.

"Yeah, wouldn't look too good, the government dealin' with a crook, huh? Somebody might get the wrong idea," Meyer added. He and Lucky laughed, Polakoff didn't.

"Alright, look. Send Joey Socks up here, I'll tell him what needs doing. And Meyer, spread the word fer them to lay offa Joey. Tell them he was doin' it fer me in the first place."

"That'll mean a lot, Charlie." Luciano now switched back to Sicilian.

"And tell him don't worry. He ain't gonna get indicted. Anything else?"

Lansky smiled and nodded. He answered back in Lucky's native tongue. "Things went alright on Bank Street," he relayed to the Boss.

"*Primo*."

The first of many meetings was over.

Chapter Eighteen

Doc eventually called Nikki and after he beat around the bush for a while, she came out from behind her defences and they agreed to a date. It was arranged they would meet at Doc's office that evening around seven and go from there.

Nikki tipped the cab driver and, with a puzzled look on her face, entered Harry's. Doc had only given her an address, and so she didn't understand why she was now in a candy store, an unattended one at that.

"Excuse me . . . hello. Anyone here?" She called out a second time but only heard the muffled lyrics of *I Don't Get Around Much Anymore* emanating softly from a radio sitting camouflaged somewhere on a shelf. Other than that, there were no signs of life.

She ventured closer to the centre of the shop, just as Harry finished removing his wooden leg and sat up from behind the counter.

Nikki screamed when a grizzled old man suddenly appeared between the candy bars and potato chips and Harry, not having heard her come in, was obliged to return the greeting. After a few minutes, once calm prevailed and heart rates had returned to normal, they struck up a conversation.

"*YOU MUST BE NIKKI!*" Harry yelled loudly.

"*YOU MUST BE HARRY,*" she shouted back. "*NICE TO MEET YOU.*"

"*LIKEWISE.*" They shook hands over the Hershey bars. "*WHERE CAN I FIND DOC?*"

"*UPSTAIRS. THIRD FLOOR ON THE LEFT.*"

"*THANK YOU, HARRY. NICE TO HAVE MET YOU.*"

"*LIKEWISE, MA'AM.*" As she passed through the door to go upstairs, Harry shook his head. "Pretty girl. Shame about her hearing."

On the third floor, Nikki found the office door open, knocked gently and let herself in.

"Doc, you here?"

Louie came out from behind the partition. "Nikki Cole?" Louie was finishing off a quart of Breyer's cherry vanilla ice cream, on a break from his studies.

"Hi. Louie?" She extended her hand.

"Louie, Louie Mancino. Doc'll be right back. Have a seat."

She thanked Louie but declined the chair and looked with interest at the items scattered around the room. She began to form her first real impressions of Doc when her eyes fell on the bullet holes which marked the wall adjoining the front door.

"Termites, huh?"

"Ahh, yeah," Louie answered with false pride.

"What happened?" Nikki asked staring at Louie. He walked over to his table, sat back in his chair, and put his feet up. Louie soaked it for all it was worth.

"Just some guys, tryin' ta get tough. It happens."

"Anyone hurt?" Nikki couldn't help but wonder what she might be letting herself in for.

"Nah." Louie detected uneasiness and sought to change the subject. "So, you work for the Feds?"

"I'm a receptionist." She wandered over to the trophies on the shelf. The photo of the brunette was lying face down. Louie became nervous, and suddenly wished Doc would show up. He winced to himself as Nikki stood the picture upright.

"Who's this?"

A cascade of possible answers flooded Louie's mind. Doc's sister, his mother-in-law, his ex-business partner. "Janet. An old girlfriend named Janet," he blurted out. *Dodged the bullet on that one*, Louie thought.

"M-A-R-Y. Tell me. Where you come from, how do they spell bullshitter? L-O-U-I-E."

Louie winced again.

"She's his ex," he said resignedly. "Only don't tell him I told, huh? He needs ta tell ya himself. She kicked him in the head a pretty good one."

"What happened?"

Louie hesitated to answer. "I really don't feel too good talkin' about Doc's personal stuff an all."

She sensed his discomfort and didn't push it, but in the end womanly curiosity won out. "Word of honour, Louie. Won't breathe a word of it."

Louie adjusted his posture and decided to give Nikki the Reader's Digest version of Doc's marriage.

"No deep, dark secrets. It was a mixed marriage that didn't work out."

"Howd'a ya mean, 'mixed'?"

"Conflicting gods. Different religions. Hers were green with little pictures of presidents on them, his were non-tangereenneable." Nikki looked at him quizzically.

"Non-tangereeenable?"

"Yeah, you know. Things that can't be touched." Louie was proud of his five dollar word.

"Okay. What was it?

"Loyalty. He took that 'Till death do us part' stuff seriously."

"And she thought it was just words? I'm beginning ta get the picture." Nikki knew how hard it was to be forced apart. To not have any control over losing your spouse. Her attention turned to the photo of the man with the black ribbon taped to the upper right hand corner of the frame. She noted the names on the trophies were all the same, McKeowen.

"This Doc's father?"

Louie was determined not to discuss Doc's Dad with her. "Yeah, he was. Nuthin' personal. That's Doc's territory."

She noticed the memorial plaque and the black framed obituary column. As she began to read the article, footsteps echoed in the hall. Nikki turned to look over her shoulder as Doc came in. Louie shook his hand and gave the thumbs-up to Doc.

Nikki looked stunning. Doc had not realised how striking her natural good looks really were at the reception desk on Church Street. He had been too preoccupied with her sharp wit.

Although she wore a nondescript, dark green dress with shoulder pads, and her auburn hair in a Page Boy, Doc immediately realised she really could give Lauren Becall a run for her money. Her steel blue eyes sparkled when she smiled.

Doc changed out of his bomber jacket into a sports coat and when he emerged from behind the partition Louie smirked and Nikki shook her head back and forth. Doc conceded to the consensus of opinion and changed back into the jacket and his dark blue Negro League baseball cap.

Louie went up behind Doc as he and Nikki were leaving. "Compliment the dress!" Louie whispered in Doc's ear.

"Thanks, Mom," Doc whispered back.

Downstairs, Harry yelled goodnight to the couple and Nikki yelled back. Doc stared at the two of them as if they had a screw loose and as soon as they were outside he spoke to Nikki.

"What the hell was that?"

"Oh, Louie was nice enough to tip me off about Harry bein' in the war an' all."

"Harry lost his leg in the war?" Doc informed her, still confused.

"Yeah, I know. Louie told me. That and how working around the artillery made him lose his hearing. He should get benefits for that or something, ya know!"

"Harry was in the Signal Corps! Not artil . . ." He didn't finish his sentence. He didn't have to. He understood and then wondered what Louie had told Harry about Nikki. Little prick.

"What?" Nikki asked.

"Nuthin', ferget it. Where do you wanna eat?"

"I don't know. But I'm starvin'! I didn't have time for lunch."

"We could have something light, see a movie and then go to dinner?" Doc suggested. "*Casablanca* just broke at the Loew's."

"Took the words right outta my mouth! Where to?"

They began to walk across town towards the Loew's Theatre on 14th Street and planned on a sandwich before the show.

"Unusual weather we're havin', ain't it? So the paper said."
Nikki sought to break the ice and ease into the awkward part of the
date where the boy and girl feel compelled to talk about . . . nothing.

"The weather guy on NBC said we're due for a blizzard in the
next few days." Doc returned the volley.

"So, what are some of your favorite movies, Mr PI? I suppose
you go in fer those detective stories and whodunnits?" Nikki said
teasingly.

"I hate those things. Hats, trenchcoats. Always goin' around
hidin' in the shadows. Damn picture always crooked on the screen.
Looks like the camera guy is drunk or somethin'. And another thing
I don't get. Where do they get off shootin' all those guns off all over
the place like Randolph Scott or somethin'? I tell ya, wish I could
find a six shooter with ten shots!" Doc snickered at his last remark.

Nikki was amused at his passionate film review. "So how do you
really feel?"

"I don't carry a gun. They get people hurt."

Nikki stopped laughing and thought about the photo.

"How 'bout you? Whatta you like?"

"I just saw *Cat People* a little while back. Very different! I liked
it." Doc hadn't gone to see it because it sounded a little too artsy.
Not exactly off to a flyin' start, he thought.

"*Pride Of The Yankees*! There's a movie ta get yer blood up,
huh?" he tried again. Nikki hadn't seen that one. She thought it
looked a little too sappy. *Not off to a good start,* she thought.

"*Tortilla Flats*?" Nikki tried again.

"Steinbeck! The best." Doc's favourite writer.

"No, that was Spencer Tracy and Hedy Lamarr!"

"Oh! A comedian, huh?" They both relaxed a little more and the
subject came around to comedy and comic films. Doc was pleased
that Nikki liked the Marx Brothers and Nikki was pleased when
Doc said that he liked Chaplin. They laughed and relaxed even
more as they entered a pizza parlor on East Twelfth and both agreed
that *Now Voyager* was probably the worst film either had ever seen.

"*Buona sera*, Eddie. *Due slice e due coke, si prega di.*" Doc
spoke to the man behind the counter in the white tee-shirt and

apron, and they took a table in the back.

"I'm impressed!" Nikki told Doc as they waited for their order. "Have you been to Italy?"

"Hell, I hardly been outta New York. My mother was from Palermo. Came over before the last war."

"Maybe after the war you'll get ta take a trip over?"

"I'd like that." The slices came and after they had eaten, Nikki began to talk again.

"That was sweet what you did for the Birnbaums."

"They're good people. We should live so long."

"Do you think about how long you'll live?"

"I try not to. I don't think I wanna know the answer."

"What you do is dangerous, isn't it?"

"Not really." Nikki gave him that would-you-tell-me-even-if-it-were-look.

Doc reassured her. "No, really! It's rare someone pulls a gun or a knife. Mostly we tail people, find things out. I've only had one murder case."

"Did'ja solve it?" Nikki asked with genuine enthusiasm. Doc looked at her eyes and smiled.

"No. Not yet." There was a pause in the conversation and it became apparent to Doc that Nikki was mustering courage to broach a subject.

"Can I ask you something, Doc?"

"Sure what is it?"

"What happened to your Dad? I mean, what really happened?"

This was so completely unexpected that Doc had to adjust.

"I read about it in the papers last year, and when I saw the photo in your office I couldn't believe it was the same guy."

"You think my father sold drugs to prostitutes?" Doc asked in an irritated tone.

"I don't know . . . no!" Nikki was gripped with a sudden sensation of awkwardness. "Oh hell, Doc! When it was all over the papers no one could believe a senior cop could do somethin' like that, but there's some pretty crooked cops, ya know? And now that I've met you . . . hell, I don't know what I think." Nikki slid down in her seat with a sense of deep regret at having surrendered to her curiosity.

Doc tried to remain patient, and for some reason felt that maybe it was time to come clean. To finally talk about this thing and maybe get it off his chest.

"My father was a great cop. But a lousy politician. He could never understand how the DA and the higher-ups could know about the drug houses and the guys who ran them, and let them walk around in the open as if they were common, decent citizens. He'd been working on this idea for a bunch of cops who would train just to go after the drug guys. Ya know, talk to stoolies, stake out the houses, get all the info they could. Then start takin' them out one by one until it was too expensive for them to operate."

"That's a helluva idea, Doc. Did they do it?"

"He pushed like hell, and it got through the chief okay, but when it got to the D A's, they stepped on it. He fought back and the upshot was that if they could prove themselves, the DA would think about backing them. Well, it just so happened that they were planning a raid that week. Word leaked to the department that there was a house where they stored large quantities of heroin, and that except for one or two torpedoes standin' guard at a certain time, it was wide open."

"That was the place on East 34th?"

"Yeah. So they get there, everyone knew my dad would go in first. So it was him and a guy named Russo as back-up. Everyone else surrounded the house. And that was it. Like the papers said, over two hundred bullet holes, two cops killed and the drug guys got away."

"What about the heroin?"

"Wasn't any. Never was. It was a set-up ta show the city that the idea of flat-foot beat cops forming raiding squads was stupid and dangerous."

"What makes you think it was a set-up?"

"The word came down that the hide-out would only be lightly armed. Two hundred bullet holes ain't exactly lightly armed. The DA just happened to show on the scene. The DA has no business anywhere near a raid scene, ever. Unless he's got some kinda personal stake in it. Then the giveaway. No drugs anywhere. I went back in the next night. Spent the entire night searching for anything that might show there were drugs there at one time. Nuthin', clean as a whistle."

"They set that up just to kill your father?"

"No, not really. That was just an added bonus."

"So why the hell was the DA so against this drug fighting squad idea?"

"The fastest pipeline to the governor's office is the DA's office. But you need backing. Backing from the right people, and the right people's money. If this raid squad of my father's caught on, the profit margin would be drastically reduced and these 'right people' would only be able to drink champagne and eat caviar five times a week instead of seven. Know what I mean?"

Nikki reached across the table and took Doc's hand. "Jesus, Doc, That's a pretty deep hole. Sorry about bringing it up."

"It's okay. I'm glad ya did. I haven't really talked about it with anyone and it was kinda eatin' me up inside."

"Not even Louie?"

"No. But, that night when I asked him to break into the house with me, he didn't hesitate for a second."

"I like him. Kinda reminds me of Lou Costello." They both laughed. "Please don't tell him I said that!"

Doc glanced at his watch. "We'd better get over there."

The walk to the theatre was only five minutes but the wait was unsually long. They took their place in line, and as it slowly moved forward, Nikki held Doc's arm and spoke to him.

"So, it's our first date and we're going to church," she said.

"What?"

"Church, we're going to church. When I was a little girl we only went to the movies on Sunday afternoon. I always felt like going to the movies was a lot like going to church."

"How so?"

"The cinema is the new house of worship." She had Doc's attention as she suddenly assumed a documentarian's voice. "The congregation gathers. They pay to go in and hear the sermon, only they do it at the door instead of later. The holy Eucharist of popcorn, kept in its sacred pyx, is doled out to the faithful as they enter to hear the blessed words of the high priests and priestesses upon the pulpit of the silver screen."

Doc listened and realised that for the first time in two years, he was relaxed in the company of a woman. "You're wired to the moon, ya know that?" Doc wasn't sure if she was always prone to flights of fancy. He hoped she was. "And another thing. What's with the vocabulary? What the hell is a pyx?"

"It's the place where the Eucharist is kept. I used to be a librarian. Then I was a secretary for a lawyer. Did you know that there are over eighty thousand words in the English language? And did you further know that the average person only uses forty thousand of them?"

"I'll try to watch my language, Mrs Webster."

The couple in front of them were having an argument, and Nikki looked at the ticket booth and began to laugh. She pointed to the small shade pulled down in the window which read, *Sold Out*.

"The Lido on 8th Street?" Doc offered.

"Lead the way, benevolent bellwether."

"Remind me to never to do a crossword with you."

Ten minutes later, the couple had checked the movie times at the Lido and went into a nearby coffee shop to pass the twenty-five minutes till show time. Doc again placed the order and sat down.

"So, fair's fair," Nikki offered.

"How do you mean?"

"You told me about your dad and it was very polite of you not to ask who Bill was, so . . . "

"He's your ex-husband."

"You know?"

"I do now." Doc felt bad that he surprised her. "But you don't have to talk about it if you don't want to."

Nikki smled and sat back. "Bill saw the war coming as soon as the fighting started in China. He'd give me daily reports and predictions."

"Were they accurate?"

"Too accurate. That's when I started getting scared. I knew he was caught up in it. There was no way I'd pull him back. Finally, one day he sent me flowers at work and took me out to dinner. I don't remember a thing. The restaurant, what we ate. I felt like I was eating with a condemned man. It was all I could do to keep from running out of the room screaming. I didn't hear half of what he said that night, something about talking to some flying buddies."

She had to look away as she continued. "One of them started up a volunteer fighter wing and got it hired out to the Chinese government."

"The Flying Tigers?"

"Yeah. I knew I'd never see him again." Nikki was beginning to tell the story in short bursts, as if to get it over with as soon as possible. Doc reached across the table and took her by the hand.

"You should be proud, damn proud. Those guys are genuine heroes. Saved a lotta lives."

"They said he died a hero, whatever the hell that means. Doesn't make it any easier, ya know?"

"I'm sure you had some wonderful experiences together."

"Yeah, experience." Sarcasm tainted her voice. "That's what ya get when you don't get what you want." Tears welled in her eyes.

"We should change the subject," Doc suggested. There was an uncomfortable pause and Doc had nightmares of a Norma Birnbaum replay. Nikki saw her pain in his eyes and broke the silence.

"How 'bout that Stan 'The Man' musical, huh? Hitting a 315 so far!" Nikki tried to smile as a tear rolled down her cheek. Doc had to think of something fast.

"DiMaggio's gonna give him a run for his money," was the best he could do.

"*OH MY GAWD!*" The words booming from the front of the small eatery pierced Doc's ears like steel needles. The entire restaurant turned in unison to see the overweight middle-aged woman with the dress two sizes too small, dripping cheap costume jewellery like an over-decorated Christmas tree.

"*NIKKI! HOW AWE YOU?* It's so good ta see ya!" Shopping bags crumpled and plastic beads rattled as she waddled up the aisle. Despite the emotional poignancy of the last five minutes, Doc had to keep from laughing out loud.

Making a bee-line for the table, Blanch dropped the shopping bags without regard to blocking the aisle and smothered Nikki in over-animated hugs and kisses.

"I been worried about you, sweetheart! How ya been? And hoose dis guy?" Her over-painted lips smiled and looked like a bad Valentine's Day advertisement as she spoke in rapid bursts.

"Hello, Blanch. This is Doc McKeown, a friend of mine. Doc, this is Blanch, my mother-in . . . Bill's mom." *Jesus!* Doc thought. *This must be a test!*

"Hello, Blanch, nice to make your acquaintance." Doc was on his best behaviour.

"An Irish Doctor! Yaw doin' aw rite fer yaself!" Blanch said to Nikki via the entire restaurant. Doc sighed and showed better sense than to try and get a word in. "I been wonderin' what you been up to! When ya gonna come up fer dinner? Bring the Doctor!"

"I will, Blanch, I promise."

"We will, Blanch, promise, cross our hearts, hope ta die," Doc added. Nikki was feeling relief from her emotional anxiety. It felt good to be with Doc.

"Be sure you do! Don't make me come and find youse two!" Blanch threatened, with one of the sausages emanating from the palm of her hand.

"Night, Blanch."

Blanch started to waddle away. Nikki and Doc were exchanging smiles when Blanch once again appeared in front of them.

"And you tell me if you need me ta baby-sit! She's my grandchild too, ya know!"

"I will, Blanch. I promise." Doc made the Scout's honour sign and Nikki laughed into her hand as Blanch went off to argue with a man in a suit, tripping over shopping bags at the front door.

"That was Hurricane Blanch."

"She marked her territory." Doc pointed to her cheek and Nikki took out her compact, looked at the lipstick marks on her face in embarrassment and began to clean them off.

"Hadn't we better get to the show?" Nikki asked.

"No."

"No? No because you don't want to, no because it's not time, or no because you're havin' too much fun?"

"Yes."

"C'mon, quit horsin' around."

"Yes, because I don't want to. Yes, I'm having a good time and yes, because it's not time, it's past time."

"What do you mean, 'past time'?"

"Aside from Blanch, I've got some more bad news. It's twenty after. We missed the start of the show."

Nikki shook her head and smiled. "I guess we'll just have to keep talkin' then. Won't we?"

"I still owe you a dinner. We could go and eat."

"I'm full. Next time we'll go straight to dinner, then the movie." *Next time? That's encouraging.* The words involuntarily jumped into Doc's head.

"But I sure would enjoy an egg cream right about now," Nikki suggested.

Nearly an hour later, the couple were walking back towards Nikki's house on Mercer Street. The evening had turned cold but not intolerable. Neither of the two noticed the outside temperature, anyway.

"Was it always you and Louie?"

"No. Not always." Doc's reluctance to discuss details was emphasised by his silence.

"Well? Was there anybody else?"

"No baby, you're the first!"

"Hmm, doesn't want to talk about it. Must be a juicy story there!"

Thirty seconds earlier, Doc had been determined not to talk about his ex-partner. However, Nikki's infectious smile melted his barriers like a laser beam.

"Sammon. There was a fella named Sammon."

"Gut! Ve are makink progress, Herr McKeowen. But I zinc ve vill need to keep talkink and perrrhaps anozzer session."

"You're not saving anything for the second date, are you?" Doc became infected with her smile.

"Don't get over-optimistic, cowboy!"

"Sammon came in with me about three years ago. I didn't know it but he had a backer. Some joker from upstate who had money to invest. They came to an arrangement and about a month later he took off with all the top clients."

"Well, they couldn't have been very good clients if they all just up and left."

"Well, they didn't, not really. He told them I wasn't doing so good and that he did most of the work anyway so he was 'striking out on his own'. The few who were reluctant to leave he told I'd slept with a client's daughter and that it was only a matter of time before the lawsuit started up."

"Nice guy! Can you do anything about it?"

"Yeah, but I'd wind up in jail."

"I mean a lawsuit!"

"It's an option, but takes loads a dough. Five, maybe ten grand for a sure win. The more you have, the better your chances of coming out on top. Messed up the business pretty good."

"Jeez, Doc, I'm sorry I asked."

"No problem. No more questions about the past, okay?"

"Okay. What's Louie's story?"

"If you're not a cop, you missed a helluva an opportunity, you know that?"

"Sorry, Doc. Just naturally nosy, I guess. We don't have to talk about anything else."

After a short walk, they arrived at Nikki's apartment and Doc walked her to the front door. Neither one wanted the evening to end.

"I had a great time tonight. I can't remember when I enjoyed not having dinner and not seeing a movie so much." Nikki spoke first. Doc remained mesmerised by her crystal blue eyes.

"Do your eyes hurt?"

"No. Why?"

"Cause they're killin' me!"

Nikki leaned her head towards Doc and closed her eyes. Doc was on cue. He thought how sweet her lips tasted as he felt the heat of her body through her clothes.

Nikki was lost in the moment as well, but was suddenly snapped out of the thrill of the experience when she began to hiccup. First one, then two or three at a time. She was embarrassed and knew she had to make it a short goodbye.

"I'd like to see . . . hic . . . you again . . . hic . . . Doc." She spoke rapidly, trying to make her words dodge the hiccups.

"You would, huh?"

"Yes, if that's okay with you . . . hic . . . investigator." Doc turned without answering and walked down the stairs, ball cap cocked back, hands in his pockets.

"Don't get over-optimistic, cowgirl," he said over his shoulder. Nikki stood in the doorway and watched Doc walk down the sidewalk. Halfway down the block, without turning around, Doc called back to Nikki.

"I'll call you tomorrow."

"I know you will!" Nikki called back to Doc. She saw his shoulders shake as he laughed.

Nikki went through the door into the vestibule and Mrs Paluso opened her window to look down on the porch and investigate the racket.

Walking up Mercer Street, Doc was pleased by his change of fortune in the last few weeks. He felt like he could stand on his own two feet again and take on anything they could throw at him without wavering. Good thing too, because he was about to get his chance.

Turning the corner on Prince Street, he saw a man in a dress suit and a heavy overcoat approaching him head-on. In a co-ordinated movement, a second man, similarly dressed, moved towards Doc from between two parked cars. The second man obviously came from the other side of the street and was reaching into his breast pocket. Watching both men at the same time, Doc stopped where he was and adjusted his ball cap. Stopping just in front of him, both men produced bifold identity wallets with strange looking badges. Ones Doc had never seen before.

"You Doc McKeowen?" The one directly in front of him was the taller of the two and it was he who spoke first.

"My friends call me Doc. You can call me Mr McKeowen."

The two men gave no further clue as to who they were and it was much too dark to read the photo cards the men flashed.

"We'd like to talk to you, about an item that belongs to us."

"If you know who I am, then you know where I work. Office hours are nine to five. Call my secretary, she'll try'n squeeze you in."

Doc pushed past the tall one and was fully prepared for his clumsy attempt at restraint. As he put his hand on Doc's left shoulder, Doc grabbed his hand and spun towards his assailant, pushing his arm upwards to expose his back. By the time the man's knees hit the pavement, Doc had administered three or four kidney punches. When he released the former tough guy to engage his second assailant, the limp body fell forward and smashed face-first into the pavement, blood flowing from his nose and mouth.

Doc back-pedalled and pushed over a row of garbage cans to slow the second opponent. However, he was not prepared for the third man emerging from the shadows of the alley to his left.

"Oh good! Now we can play bridge." The words had no sooner left Doc's mouth when he saw the third man reaching into his breast pocket. Probably not for his ID, either, Doc figured.

Picking up a trash can lid, Doc was able to ward off several punches from the second man. As the man rubbed his sore fist, Doc connected with several square hits to the face, using the garbage can lid. The man slumped to the ground and McKeowen bear-hugged him in case the third man beat him to the draw and fired.

On the way down, Doc struggled with the second man's shoulder holster and managed to withdraw the .38 special. Rolling onto his right side, he emptied three rounds at the third man, deliberately missing him, but saving the last three rounds in case he didn't get the message. He did. Doc watched as the man ran serpentine up Prince Street, holding his hat down, and vanished onto West Broadway.

Doc lay there in between the two unconscious men, breathing heavily, eyes wide open and unaware that his face was bleeding from the cheek and forehead. After what felt like an eternity, he lowered the pistol and rolled onto his back, holding his head.

God-damned perfect ending to a perfect evening. Jesus! Nikki, tell me you don't have any brothers! As he rolled over and rose to his knees he realised he was in pain. He grabbed his right shoulder in agony and watched as blood dripped from his cheek and jaw onto the guy's overcoat.

Walking on his knees to mystery man number two, Doc emptied the guy's pockets. He did the same for the other would-be attacker and came up with a second .38 special, two Treasury agent ID's, two sets of house and car keys and over $1200 in cash.

Christ! I'm in the wrong racket! Doc was pleased with his night's wages. He stuffed his pockets with the items, then took a handkerchief from one of the unconscious men and held it to his bleeding cheek. Picking up his ball cap, Doc stood up and began to limp away, until he glanced into the alley and smiled at some discarded wine bottles on the ground.

A few minutes later, after crossing West Broadway, Doc ran into a cop walking the night beat.

"Excuse me, officer. I think there's something strange going on in the alley over on Prince Street, just before Wooster. You might wanna take a look."

"What happened to your face, pal?" the officer asked sympathetically.

"Cut myself shaving."

McKeowen continued towards Christopher Street, and when the cop found the two men a short time later, locked in a passionate embrace, smelling of cheap wine and both holding empty wine bottles, he immediately went to the police call box on the corner and rang for the Paddy Wagon.

By the time Doc reached Christopher Street, Harry was cleaning up and was surprised to see him come through the front door.

"Evenin', Doc. How was your . . . man, oh man! She musta said no!"

Doc still held the hanky to his cheek trying to stop the bleeding. With a wince, he reached into his pocket and produced the newly acquired bank roll. Peeling away a fifty and laying it on the counter, he asked Harry if Redbone was still around.

"Yeah, I think so. He was just locking up about ten minutes ago."

"Do me a favour, will ya? Have him run around to Jimmy's and get me a bottle of Jameson's. You guys split the change. Deal?"

Harry looked down at the fifty. "Hell, Doc! Deal!"

Doc went upstairs and fifteen minutes later Harry, Redbone and Doc were in the office having a late night baptism.

"Well, you gonna tell us what happened or do we have ta drink it outta ya?" Harry finally broached the subject of Doc's injuries. McKeowen didn't answer but reached into his pockets and emptied them onto the desk. Redbone and Harry stared in disbelief.

"Damn, Doc! I thought you was the muggee, not the mugger!" Redbone was the first to give his impression. Harry leaned forward and looked more closely. He looked at Doc, then picked a fifty out of the roll crumpled it up, tore it in half and then held it up to the light. As everyone watched, he pulled a cigarette lighter out of his pocket and lit the note on fire and watched it burn.

"Damn, Harry! That mustard gas shit finally gettin' ta you, man?" Redbone had only seen pictures of fifty dollar bills.

"Doc, that fifty you give me come outta this bank roll?" Harry asked.

"Yeah. Why?"

"I think your credit just ran out at Jimmy's."

"What the hell you talkin' about?"

"This dough is phoney."

Doc sat back and slowly smiled. Redbone downed his drink, sat back in his chair and offered his assessment of the situation.

"Sumbitch!"

Chapter Nineteen

There's little mystery about why authors such as James Fenimore Cooper and Washington Irving chose the mountainous terrain of upstate New York as the locale for their classic legends. The spectacular cliffs, magnificent waterfalls and plush forests combine to create a fairytale landscape.

The breath-taking scenery, however, was completely lost on the official messenger cautiously making his way by motorbike through the frozen mud of the winding mountain roads. Intermittent towns and villages offered the only relief from the unpaved roads, and the icy drizzle which began to gently fall greatly hampered the likelihood of his reaching his destination before dark.

An hour after dusk, mammoth courtyard spotlights reflected the mud-splattered 1939 Indian and its frozen rider as they pulled in through the twin steel doors guarding the main gate of Great Meadows Prison. A short time later, a sealed plain manilla envelope was pulled from one of the brown leather saddlebags and handed to Medford T. Childs.

Warden Childs was a third generation correctional facility employee, and Southern Baptist. In the unlikely event a prisoner assigned to his prison had any doubts about whose playground they were in, Childs considered it his 'God appointed' duty to take any and all remedial measures.

"Lawson!" Childs called out. One of Childs' many rules was that an armed guard would be posted to him twenty-four hours a day regardless of where he was. His wife wasn't very fond of this rule, but what the hell, they had been in separate beds for nearly twelve years.

Lawson entered the office. "Yes, sir?"

"I got us a couple new memos here from the Coo-missiona'. Says here one of 'em, dat we's no longa allowed ta give solitary for more than thuty days at a time. Take note."

"Yes, sir."

"From now on, solitary will be thuty days on, one day off, followed by thuty days on."

"Sounds fair to me, sir."

"Get me that Luciano fella up here, and close da doo. Don't let nobody in here 'til I's finished."

"Yes, sir." Lawson left to find Lucky and Childs had opened the red envelope which was also contained in the delivery. It was a follow-up memo to the one he had received only a few days prior instructing him that Luciano would be permitted visitors other than those usually allowed. However, this memo was more direct.

Dated: 6 March, 1942

To: Warden Medford T. Childs

From: Commissioner of Prisons, John A. Lyons

Warden Childs, you are hereby directed to obtain, in a discreet manner, the names of all persons who make contact with the prisoner known as Luciano. You will then, via special courier, send me said names, dates and times of visits. If you have any questions please contact my office.

Childs filed the memo in a locked filing cabinet drawer and sat back in an uneasy frame of mind to wait for Luciano.

It was suppertime so Lawson knew right where to find Lucky, and as he entered the large noisy dining hall, he headed for the front of the room, and made his way to the centre of one of the thirty-two seat dinner tables. Lawson spoke in a general manner, avoiding eye contact, despite the fact he stood directly in front of the head of the Unione.

"Luciano, you are requested to report to the Warden's office." Following his announcement, Lawson moved to the centre aisle to wait for his charge. Lucky took his time finishing his food, as several other inmates seized the moment.

"How the hell is a man gonna get his nutrition if you Screws keep on interuptin' us durin' mealtime?"

"Hey, errand boy, go tell Childs Mr Luciano is utterwise occupied dinin' wit his esteemed enterage." In a matter of seconds, everyone at the table was involved to one extent or another in the growing ruckus. Two shotgun-toting guards patrolling the overhead catwalk closed in towards the disturbance.

There was never any real threat of trouble. The inmates were simply practising the time-honoured tradition of harassing the guards.

Lucky moved as slow as he could and still be considered in motion, to give his crew maximum exposure time at the guard, and as he pushed away from the table he overheard a muffled conversation in progress, to his immediate right. A slightly built inmate was talking to another.

The man spoke softly, but in the lulls of the harangue party occurring around him, Luciano's ear picked up the words, "secret meeting".

By way of attracting his attention, Lucky made eye contact with a man at the end of the table whose nose pointed in several directions at once. Lucky nodded to the covert conversation, the nose nodded back and Lucky accompanied Lawson to the exit door.

Upstairs in the warden's office, Lucky sat in front of the desk listening to Childs while he was told, for the second time since his arrival, that his status in gangland meant absolutely nothing at Great Meadows, and Lucky had better get used to it.

Medford T. Childs was attempting the well-known intimidation tactic. He may as well have asked Adolf Hitler to attend synagogue.

Lucky got his name after being discovered by Staten Island police late one afternoon, staggering down a roadway severely beaten and bleeding. His nickname, as well as his droopy right eyelid, were a result of having been one of the few known individuals to have survived a gangland 'ride'. The authorities knew who he was when they found him and, after two days of grilling, he couldn't be intimidated by the police into telling them who had done it.

What chance did Childs have?

"And let's get one more thing perfectly clear, Mr Luckiano, I won't stand for any trouble in dis here prison! I don't want no problems!" Childs' melodramatic presentation was interrupted by a knock on his door.

"Come in!" It was Lawson. "What is it?"

"Sir, we have a problem." Childs glanced at Lucky.

"What kind of a problem?"

"There's a party here to visit the prisoner, but they won't comply with the visitor's regulations."

"You got any friends that don't make trouble, Luckiano?!"

Five minutes later, Childs was downstairs in the visitors' area consulting with his supervising guard while sporadically staring through the thick glass of the monitoring booth at the three would-be visitors. The guard explained the source of the problem. Staring back at the warden were Polakoff, Lansky and Lanza, all three with cigarettes hanging from their mouths.

"Send the lawyer up to my office," Childs instructed the guard.

Unfortunately for Medford, on inviting Polakoff to his office he failed to take into account how annoyed Polakoff was by the forty-five minute wait he had already endured, by the fact he was haunted by the late night drive back to the City, and that, to cap it all, he was now being told he had to go to the warden's office just to get permission to see his ex-client for which he was being paid absolutely nothing. When he was invited to sit down in front of the warden's desk, Polakoff refused and considered the mandatory invitation the last straw.

"Now look here, Childs! I been a lawyer a helluva lot longer than you been a prison warden, and I don't give a damn about your excuses!"

"Mr Pole-acoff, I am truly apologetic about your dee-lay. However, we have polocies in place foo your protection." Childs' response reflected a demeanour which was as transparent as it was comical.

"Bullshit! Understand one thing, Childs. I and my guests are gonna get in to see Luciano, and we're gonna do it tonight and we're gonna do it without you getting our fingerprints! And you can take that to the bank, god-damn it!" Polakoff surprised himself with his own outburst and walked across the room to sit down. Then watched as warden Childs placed a phone call on his private line.

Lansky and Lanza were still in the waiting area and working on their second pack of smokes. The two were increasingly uncomfortable with spending so much time in a prison and although neither one wanted to say it, both toyed with the idea that it might be a set-up.

Polakoff could not be sure of whom the call was to, but he listened attentively to the short conversation.

"Is he in your office now?" the voice on the other end of the line enquired.

"Yes sir, he is." Polakoff knew instantly, it was Childs' boss. The warden was talking to Commissioner Lyons.

Unknown to Polakoff, everything had been arranged. Or so Lyons led everyone to believe. Lyons calculated that if he were going to be strong-armed into playing this high stakes game of allowing high-profile criminals to visit the boss of the high-profile criminals, he had no intention of entering into it without a trump card. He wanted a name on which to hang blame when the day came. And Polakoff was as good as any.

"Tell him we'll waive the fingerprints but not the register. Tell him he has to sign in and out, and he will be required to accompany all visitors from now on. And he takes full responsibility for their actions. Any other questions?"

"No, sir. I'll make it all perfectly clear to him."

Childs terminated his conversation with Lyons and proceeded to top off Polakoff's evening by making "it" all perfectly clear. As he spoke in a regimented, bureaucratic tone, Polakoff resolved to make something perfectly clear to the New York City District

Attorney when he returned downstate, in the morning.

Around half past eleven that evening they finally got to talk to Lucky, but there wasn't much time before they had to leave, so a date was set for another visit in a few days.

Earlier that day Lyons had considered drawing up a list of organised crime members he would forbid from coming to see Lucky. Number one on that list was to have been Meyer Lansky. That's when the future founders of the international drug cartel got their next lucky break. Lyons abandoned the black list idea.

✦

Socks reached across his desk and picked up the phone on the second ring.

"Watchman's Protective."

"Hello, Socks. How's tricks?"

Lanza was unpleasantly surprised by the voice on the other end of the line. "Commander! What can I do for you?"

"Just wonderin' how ya been since our last meeting."

"Fer Chrissakes, Commander, keep it ta yerself, will ya? We got friends on the line!"

"Not anymore, Socks. We took care of that. But there is something you and I need to take care of." The Commander's voice was laced with an unnerving calm.

"Oh yeah? What's that?"

"I understand you had a little visit to Comstock?" The silent pause on Lanza's end confirmed Haffenden's intelligence.

"I was invited ta see the Boss. What the hell, I ain't seen him since he went up. Dat's six years ago. Don't bust my chops."

"I'm not bustin' ya, Socks. I just need ta know where ya stand. You told me you wanted out, next thing you're going upstate with Polakoff to see Lucky."

How the hell did Haffenden know I went upstate? Did the prison guys tell him? Or maybe it was Polakoff? Socks recalled that Lucky sent word that he was not going down for his impending indictment, and regained his confidence.

"Look, Commander, I said I was out and I am. Gimme a break

will, ya?"

"Just checking in, Socks. You will let me know if you hear anything. Won't ya?"

"Cross my heart and hope to die, Commander," Socks mockingly added.

"Nice talking to you, Socks. Say hi to the rest of the family."

✦

On this particular morning, people who would normally seek to avoid J. Edgar Hoover in the course of their daily routine sought him out. He gave a record number of project approvals that day, returned greetings and even spoke politely to Rollins. At least at first.

"Mr Rollins, would you please come into my office?" Hoover requested as he passed Rollins in the hallway. Rollins followed him into the office and Hoover closed the door and settled in behind his desk.

"Has the New York report arrived yet?"

"No sir, not yet. The courier won't be in until six o'clock this evening."

The report Hoover was referring to detailed the apprehension of two German spies. The arrest of the enemy agents was unrelated to Commander Haffenden's operation and so would give Hoover no break in that direction.

The element that was responsible for his chipper morning attitude, however, was the high profiled, high speed pursuit through Times Square by his agents prior to the arrest.

There were no shots fired, no private property damaged and no one was injured. The Germans simply surrendered when they saw they were surrounded.

The newspapers consumed the story with their predictable vim and vigour, and it was the impending positive press J. Edgar savoured. He wanted to thumbprint the report before forwarding it to Jackson or the Joint Chiefs, and he would award the agents a special commendation, personally.

"As soon as it arrives, find me, I'll be in the building. Sign for it yourself. Also prepare me a flight for day after tomorrow. I want a press conference at the award ceremony in New York. Make sure all the national dailies are there, too."

"I don't think that's gonna be a problem, sir."

"I'm gonna push those three commendations through the chain so – "

"Four, sir!"

"What?"

"There were four agents directly involved in the arrests. Not three."

"Better still! Anyway, take care of the details."

"Already started prepping the paperwork this morning, sir. The forms will be ready to fill out by eleven."

"Good. Now tell me what you found." Hoover prepared himself for more good news.

"Found, sir?" Rollins braced himself, as he tried to stall.

"Yes, found! On the Bridges affair!"

"Oh! The Bridges affair! Of course, sir. I didn't understand at first." Hoover gave Rollins that what-the-hell-are-you-waiting-for look. "From which agency, sir?"

Hoover stared at Rollins wondering if the man still understood the English language. "You didn't do it, didja? I told you to make some calls and you were afraid so you didn't do it!" The old J. Edgar slowly began to emerge.

"Well, I did do it, sir. But . . . there were some unexpected snags."

"What snags? Either you made the calls or you didn't! Either you found something or you didn't! This ain't the god-damned Shadow, Rollins! I don't know what evil lurks in the hearts of man! Did you find something, yes or no?"

"Well . . . yes . . . and no, sir." Rollins crossed his legs as if to protect himself.

"Your're PISSIN' ME OFF!" Several silhouettes could be seen in the hallway through the frosted glass of the office door, milling about as if there was another reason besides listening to Hoover unload on Rollins for being there. "If you people can't find work,

I'LL DAMN WELL FIND SOME FOR YOU!" The silhouettes vanished and J. Edgar turned back to Rollins. "Talk to me!"

"Sir. I contacted all the agencies you directed." Rollins sought desperately to maintain damage control. "Starting with the New York City District Attorney's office. They said they would not release any information to anyone in the Department Of Transportation except the director. Next, I found the representative for California and I called his office in the name of the FBI. They told me the representative was unavailable for comment. Then later, when I called back under a different auspice, the records clerk told me they had no record on file concerning a complaint from a Harry Bridges." Rollins could see the wheels turning in Hoover's head. "In desperation, I even called the American Communist Party headquarters in San Francisco to talk to Harry Bridges. Do you know what they told me, sir?"

"Pray tell me what, Ollie?"

"Sir, they told me that Mr Bridges had never been to New York. That his district was only in northern California. It's as if it never happened. Now how about that?"

Hoover fell back into his high-backed chair. "Shit!" There was somebody else in the game. After an uncomfortable pause, J. Edgar rested his folded elbows on the desk and brought his hands in front of his face. He spoke to Rollins in a calm, controlled voice.

"You did good, Rollins. You did real good. Sorry about jumping on you. You understand, sometimes I'm under a lot of pressure. What with the war on and all."

"Yes, sir." Rollins was shocked by the metamorphosis. "I understand. Is there anything else?" Rollins sought to exploit the window of opportunity, and escape.

"As a matter of fact, yes. Get me those numbers for the people you called before you go." In his mind, Rollins was already out the door. "I assume I don't have to tell you, this never happened."

"What never happened, sir?"

Two and a half minutes later Hoover's secretary came into his office and handed him a sheet of paper with the names, numbers and locations of the pertinent people involved in the covert investigation that half of Washington and most of Brooklyn knew about. He would place the calls himself to verify Rollins' information.

J. Edgar didn't know it, but he was about to have a bad phone day.

Chapter Twenty

"At this very moment, we have the most extensive network of anti-espionage agents ever assembled in the history of the bureau. They are combing the city to thwart any and all anti-American activity where ever it might arise." Hoover took an appropriate pause to allow a fresh wave of excited applause to erupt. He was speaking in a small auditorium of the New York Headquarters of the FBI to an audience of agents, civilian employees, press and a hodge-podge of local politicians who were riding the shirt-tails of the recent FBI success. The cadence of the delivery in his speech was well rehearsed.

"The efforts of these four heroic agents is only the tip of the FBI iceberg. There are untold numbers of agents working the streets round the clock so that you, your loved ones and the rest of America can sleep in peace." More frenzied applause.

It was March the ninth. Exactly one month to the day of the burning of the Normandie, and the numbers of operators on the streets were nowhere near what he wanted his newspaper and radio audiences to believe. Ironically though, the numbers were far greater than he knew.

"Before I present the awards to these brave men, I'd just like to say how great it is to be back in your great city." The applause was now wildly out of control and never really died down until J. Edgar concluded his remarks about New York.

"And I hope while I am here I'll get a chance to see if Central Park really has gone to the birds." Hoover smiled and the crowd looked puzzled, then slowly began to applaud.

"What the hell does that mean?" a reporter in the back of the room leaned over to a colleague and asked.

"The little guy's attempt at humour, I guess," came the bedazzled reply.

Hoover presented the commendations to the four agents, each got a chance to say how happy he was to be working with the FBI and fifteen minutes later, the mutual admiration continued in a small reception room across the hall from the auditorium.

The following hour and a half was an annoyance to Hoover, but not completely unsatisfying. He enjoyed the attention and the opportunity to espouse the untold merits of himself and his organisation. However, by the second hour, the gathering had deteriorated into a flesh-pressing session. After considering several reasons to excuse himself, he explained to his bodyguards that he wanted a breath of air and stepped out into the afternoon daylight.

It seemed colder than last month when he was in New York and he was compelled to do up his topcoat and raise his collar. Looking up into the grey afternoon sky, Hoover sensed a feeling of restlessness in the air.

After a few minutes, the bodyguards found him standing in the doorway of the building and asked if he was okay. Hoover replied that he felt like a little walk and would meet them back at the seventh floor suites in an hour or so. The agents left and headed back to the room at the Astor.

J. Edgar took a walk, for about two minutes. Or more precisely, the time it took him to walk around the corner to Second Avenue and hail a cab.

"Central Park. Near the zoo." Hoover had now transitioned to a clandestine frame of mind and so was brief and to the point when instructing the taxi driver.

"So whatta ya think 'bout Brooklyn?" Hoover had already opened his window part way to allow the cab driver's cigar smoke to filter out. As the unshaven middle-aged man attempted to make small talk, Hoover became irritated.

"I don't follow baseball." The driver missed the hint.

"Iz dat right? Myself, I couldn't make it tru da week witout da local scores. My wife . . . you married, Mac?"

"Central Park, and skip the chit-chat!"

"Okay! Don't get defensive, fella. Just tryin' ta make conversation!"

"Don't!" Hoover incensed the taxi driver who, for the next ten blocks, continually glanced in the rear view mirror attempting, in vane, to place the face staring back at him. Finally, after ten puzzled minutes, he realised who he had in his cab.

"Hey! I know you!" Hoover stared back at the mirror. "You're that writer guy with the column for the forlorn lovers in da *Times*!" Hoover made no response. "Ain't that right? C'mon! You can tell me! Jeez! Wait till Gladys hears about this!"

The Transverse Roads crossing Central Park from east to west are numbered. Transverse Road Number One is the most southerly drive and connects East and West 65th and 66th Streets. Hoover instructed the driver to drop him on the east side of TR One.

For a man just out for a morning stroll, J. Edgar moved with a definite sense of purpose. There was no urgency in his stride, however he seemed to know exactly where he wanted to go. After a short walk down the gravel path, he reached his destination, the most well known zoo on the eastern seaboard.

The Victorian design of the Central Park Zoo attracted many visitors, but was relatively quiet that morning. As he strode through the turnstile of the entrance gate, a retiree volunteer worker yelled after him. "Hey, mister! That'll be ten cents!"

Hoover ignored him. Checking his watch, he saw that he was ten minutes early for the twelve o'clock meet. Halfway down the path, a policeman approached him from the rear and tapped him on the shoulder with his billy club.

"What's a matter, Mac? You think you're better'n everybody else, or you just can't afford a dime?"

Hoover turned around, and the patrolman knitted his brow in a signal of vague familiarity. Remaining silent, but flashing his small gold badge, Hoover detected no signs of the shock he expected to see on the officer's face. The officer dutifully inspected the bifold identity, and decided it really was the head of the FBI, thanked him in a curt manner and walked away. Hoover thought again how much he hated this god-damned city.

Standing beneath the blue and gold umbrella of a hot dog cart, he paid the vendor for a hot dog and a soda and ate his early lunch as the Glockenspiel over the gate of the Children's Zoo chimed twelve o'clock. It was time and so he headed for the aviary.

The chief FBI agent's comment about Central Park having gone to the birds meant nothing to the assembled crowd in the auditorium that morning. However, it wasn't a throwaway line, either. It had meant something to an individual downtown listening to the radio broadcast of the awards. It offered the details of a meeting he had been waiting for all week long. At the conclusion of the broadcast, the individual switched off his radio and left to catch the subway north to the park. He had been listening to Hoover's awards ceremony from his office.

His office at No. 90 Church Street.

At half past eight that morning Shirley had received an urgent message via courier from the New York City DA's office. It was for the Commanding Officer of the Intelligence branch. Hogan didn't know about the Hotel Astor office and so sent the handwritten message to Church Street. It was short and to the point: *M. P. out of game. Row with Prison people. States he desires no further contact with either of our offices. Good luck. Hogan.*

"Office of Moses Polakoff, attorney-at-law. How may I help you?"

"Mr Polakoff, please."

"May I ask whose calling pa-lease?"

"Haffenden, Commander Haffenden, US Navy."

"One mo-oment pa-lease." Haffenden hated this politicking bullshit. He didn't give a damn if he ever made Captain, but the fact that the home defence front depended on his operation warranted him wooing Polakoff back into the game. After a short pause, the secretary came back on the line.

"I'm sorry. Mr Polakoff is not in at present. Would you like to call back at a later date?"

"Look, sister! Here's the skinny. You put your boss on the line pronto or in thirty minutes I'll have more agents over there than Chinamen on Mott Street, savvy?"

"Please hold, sir." A moment later Polakoff came on the line.

"Who the hell is this?" he demanded.

"Mr Polakoff, it's Commander Haffenden. Sir, it's urgent that we – "

"Urgent? I'll tell you what's urgent! It's urgent that you stop calling here, that's what's urgent! And it's even more urgent that you understand if you call me again or threaten me in any other way, I'll show you how I do business! We have nothing to discuss!" Polakoff slammed the receiver onto the hook

"Well, that didn't go as well as expected," Haffenden said out loud to himself, replacing the receiver. Typical Monday morning. He began to realise what Hogan had been talking about.

Accustomed to patriotic co-operation by others, Haffenden had difficulty accepting the fact that his keystone operator had just jumped ship. Worse yet, he realised that the entire operation was hanging by a slender thread, just as funding was renewed and an increase in personnel was authorised.

He rose from his desk and made his way out of his office suite at the Astor, to the balcony of the mezzanine. He walked to the rail overlooking the lobby and racked his brain for an angle, some way to get Polakoff back in. What the hell was he going to tell MacFall? What the hell was MacFall going to tell Washington? "Thanks for risking your political careers on a shaky operation, boys, but it fell apart."

Haffenden held the message in his hand as he looked down and watched the hotel guests mill around in the lobby going about their business. A small group of businessmen exited the elevator, hungover and wearing green paper hats, carrying small replicas of the Irish Flag. Eight days to Saint Patrick's Day, he thought to himself. Easy to lose track of time on this job.

He glanced at two of the Naval Intelligence agents stationed on sentry duty. Dressed in casual clothes, they sat at a table in the corner of the lobby discussing baseball. Haffenden checked his watch, nine forty-five, turned away from the balcony and went back into his office. Then a smile slowly made its way across his face as he remembered being told that Polakoff was a Navy veteran.

A few minutes later a bellhop informed the two agents that their room was ready, and they made their way to Haffenden's office.

"Gentlemen, we have something of a crisis." The two men stood in front of his desk as the Commander spoke in that calm but firm tone which had become the universal hallmark of a military leader addressing his troops in time of peril.

"You are to go to Church Street, they've been notified that you're coming, go to the reception desk. There'll be a manilla envelope for you. On a separate piece of paper will be an address. Moses Polakoff, a lawyer, it's his office. He leaves for lunch every day between half past eleven and one. Follow him, call me immediately with the name and location of the restaurant." The agents exchanged glances. "Do not open the folder. Do not let him see you and, if he hasn't left by two o'clock, call in to me."

"Here or Church Street, sir?"

"I'll be here until you call. Questions?"

Both agents shook their heads.

While J. Edgar Hoover was finishing his hot dog in the cold, surrounded by furry little animals, Moses Polakoff was finishing his prime rib lunch, in a warm, comfortable restaurant, surrounded by sharks.

Eddie's Steak House, next to Saint Benedict's on 53rd, was a popular place for mid-town lawyers to meet and bill their clients. Apparently, Eddie was the only one to notice the irony of so many lawyers congregating so close to a church on a regular basis.

Commander Haffenden's agents met him at a Greek fast food

stand a half a block west on Ninth Avenue. One agent huddled across from Eddie's in a doorway, shivering and swaying back and forth to keep warm, while the second agent took his turn in the Greek place, warming up with coffee.

"What's the story?" Haffenden asked by way of a greeting.

"He went in about an hour ago. Met with some other suits, probably lawyers. They had a drink, he ordered lunch and is eating alone. Goody is gonna give us the high sign when he's done eatin'."

"Good work."

"Sir, if you don't mind me askin', what's so special about an old lawyer?" The Commander looked at his agent and reasoned he would know about Polakoff's critical relevance to the operation one way or the other.

"He's the only way we can get into Great Meadows to contact Luciano. They want a lawyer with the visitors all the time."

"Can't we just get another lawyer?"

"It would take weeks to set up, the state people would fight us tooth and nail, and Luciano wouldn't trust anybody else at this stage. I don't think I would, either."

"I'll take that as a no."

Agent Goody waved from the doorway down the block. "You want us to go in with you, sir?"

Haffenden took the manilla envelope from the agent. "No. You two stay here and warm up. Eat your lunch and wait for me."

"Any idea how long it'll take?"

"If this morning is any indication, I'll be back before your souvlaki gets cold."

Polakoff had just flagged a waiter for the check when Haffenden approached him from behind and laid the sealed envelope on the table in front of him. It was obvious it contained some sort of folder or official record, but the lawyer was too experienced to be taken off-guard. He ignored the document.

"Looks like what we have here is a slow learner. I told the DA and I'm tellin' you for the second time today! Take a walk!"

"Mr Polakoff, all I want to do is talk."

"Oh yeah? Near fifty years on the bar and I've never heard that line. C'mon Commander. Dig deeper."

"I could have orders cut to reactivate you back into service."

"Good luck! I'm way past the age limit and you know it."

"They raised it for the duration of the war." Polakoff narrowed his eyes and stared at Haffenden, who had now taken a seat directly across the table from him.

"Yeah and by the time the court case comes up, the war'll be over." The waiter placed a small silver tray containing Polakoff's bill on the table as he passed by.

"Look here, Hafffenden. I'm a private citizen. You can't just go around threatin' people, hopin' ta get what you want by arm twistin'."

Haffenden readjusted his position and eyed the envelope to see if it elicited a reaction from the lawyer. Again, no joy.

"Reactivating you, even to fly a desk, wouldn't really be in the best interest of either one of us, Moses. Think of the good of the nation. The bad guys who are out there tryin' ta sabotage the war effort. Think of the lives we . . . you could be saving!"

"You really are a slow learner, aren't you? Apparently you forgot what I do for a living. Let me remind you. I argue. With some of the sharpest minds in the country. Your arguments are pathetic. There are a helluva lot more guys in Washington sabotaging the war effort than you're ever gonna catch in this town, Buster." Polakoff spoke like a man who wanted to get something off his chest. "All their bickering and self-serving interests, while patriotic young men are dying by the thousands. Don't wave the flag at me!"

"Moses, the human angle?" Haffenden was losing ground faster than he thought possible.

"More bullshit! Not one single life has been lost that can be attributed to domestic enemy sabotage. The Normandie is a perfect example. Contradictory statements by eyewitnesses, conflicting reports in the press, a mysterious welder. Reports from the Navy, the Department of Transportation, the City and the DA's office and what's the upshot? 'Still under investigation'!

You got no more idea what happened to her then you do Emilia Earhart, fer Christ's sake." As he finished delivering his last salvo, Polakoff rose and began to put on his coat.

"Aren't you curious about what's in the envelope?"

"I could care less." He picked up his briefcase, took the check and turned to leave. Haffenden played his desperation card.

"Hey, Moses!" Polakoff glanced over at Haffenden who remained sitting at the table. "Is it true?"

"Is what true?"

"All that stuff about saving that kid from getting executed during the last war?"

Polakoff hadn't thought about that case for nearly a quarter of a century. "What the hell's that got to do with anything?"

"At one time you gave a damn about something."

"You must've dug pretty deep to find out about that one, Commander." Polakoff ignored the cashier as she attempted to hand him the change from his twenty. Instead, he walked back over to the table, sat down and, without releasing his briefcase or removing his coat, began to speak to Haffenden.

"They were gonna put that kid to death for something they knew he didn't do. An eighteen-year-old boy, with a wife. A young man who volunteered to fight their war. But they needed a scapegoat to patch things up with some other clowns on the British side."

"Is that when you resigned your commission?"

"That's when I woke up."

"Woke up?"

Polakoff leaned forward, one elbow on the table and spoke to Haffenden with a renewed intensity.

"You don't remember the good old days, Haffenden. Murder, robbery, extortion. All the crimes that made this country great. Now it's drugs. In the arm, under the tongue, up the wazoo fer cryin' out loud! It's a fucking cancer! This country will never recover. It just means bigger, better and more heineous crimes. I'm glad I won't be around to see it."

"Are you suggesting that we're helping usher in this new super crime wave you foresee?"

"No, not suggesting it at all. I'm saying it outright! What the hell do you think is going on up at Great Meadows? You think for a New-York-City-second those bums give two shits about you and your top secret operation? Those bastards have forgotten more about working both sides of the fence than you and I will ever know!" He sat back to take a breath, then continued the lecture. Haffenden was enamoured with Polakoff's passion.

"They're not interested in helpin' you unless it's helpin' them. They're consolidating the Unione to strengthen and regain the control they lost when Lucky went up the river." Haffenden was no dunce, certainly he had thought about this angle of the operation. He just didn't think it was so obvious to those on the fringe.

"And as long as school's out, Satch, let me ask you this. You think there's not gonna be a public outcry when the truth comes out about this operation? Heads will roll! The first schmoe to stumble down the path who thinks it's politically expedient to expose anyone involved in your little spy ring, will be singin' like Bing Crosby at a War Bonds concert! And he won't give a rat's ass about the nation's best interest, whether it's now or after the war. Lucky knows it'll be your side to leak the news, and that means anybody with anything on him will be in trouble." Both of the men sat quietly for a moment. Polakoff was embarrassed he had cursed so much. "That's why I'm against this shit."

Haffenden sat in silence, considering his defeat. He needed final confirmation. "I hate to pose the question, Moses. But I have no choice. Does this mean you're not going to help us?" Haffenden became conscious that his hand rested on the envelope and quietly let it slide off. He took a deep breath. A blank look came over his face and he stared out of the window.

"Do you know that boy's mother wrote to me every month for the rest of her life. Cookies on my birthday, too. How the hell did she know it was my birthday?"

"The New York Bar register," Haffenden deduced.

"Huh! Son-of-a-bitch!" He released his briefcase, sat forward in his chair and looked Haffenden in the eyes.

"Alright, god-damn it! But there are some ground rules we're gonna get straight first."

"You have my undivided attention, Mr Polakoff."

"First and foremost, we get this visitor routine shit straightened out. Last time I was up there it was a freakin' fiasco! I seen better organised riots, fer cryin'out loud!"

"I'll call DC this afternoon."

"Lansky's responsible for everything, not me. I'm strictly window dressing. Dorothy Lamour in a *Road* movie, get it? Along for the ride, nothing more."

"Anything else?"

"I go up there once a week, no more. That trip is murder, especially in winter. That's non-negotiable, I don't care if the Nazis are landin' in Jersey! Are we in agreement?" Polakoff asked.

"Yes, Moses, we're in agreement."

Polakoff stood, shook Haffenden's hand and turned to walk away. Haffenden followed close behind and once out on the street, Polakoff turned to Haffenden.

"Would you really have tried to reactivate me?" In the distance, a siren sliced through the thin, crisp air, and quickly faded.

"I wouldn't have had a chance in hell. You're way over the age limit."

Moses smiled in appreciation of the tactic. "Prick!"

Owing to the drop in temperature the aviary was quieter than usual. Hoover was walking over to the trash basket to deposit his empty Coke bottle when he heard footsteps echoing through the bird house.

He looked at the man approaching him, and took a seat on a wooden bench facing a giant glass cage containing assorted birds of the great northwest. The man sat down next to him and removed his hat. It was treasury agent Johnson.

In an unusually subdued tone, Hoover opened the

conversation.

"What's going on?"

"The Navy's got some kind of operation going. Not sure about the whole thing, or all the details." Johnson was in league with Hoover, but only to an extent.

"What kind of operation? Information? Espionage stuff?"

"Like I said. None of our guys have the full dope."

"Well, is it local, national or what?"

"All we know at this point is they're havin' some kind of trouble, and the whole thing might collapse."

"There's gotta be some kinda paper trail. Records, something!"

"There's a book. A little black book."

"Tell me!"

"Apparently it has the names, dates and places of all the contacts associated with the operation."

"And chain of custody is followed to the letter?"

"With these clowns? Figure the odds!"

"Can you get it?"

"I think so, yeah." Johnson was hedging his bet. His men not only had the book, they had it hidden in a safe spot.

"I want that book!"

"Actually, I thought it would be safer to copy it and return it." Johnson was considering his retirement benefits.

"No. Get it, copy it and stash it somewhere. This way we have leverage against them if there's an investigation from another agency later on." Johnson liked the sound of that and nodded his consent.

"Won't they say something once it's missing?"

"To who? The Boy Scouts?" Hoover asked sarcastically.

"Who knows you're working for me?" Not knowing who in Washington knew about this mysterious operation, Hoover was exceptionally cautious.

"No one. There's only three treasury guys at the third district and they all report to me. They know about the book, but have orders to keep quiet to everyone downtown and to report to me if something looks fishy."

"What about money for outside help or miscellaneous expenses?"

"We're covered. We have our own sources."

A small group of school children paraded through the aviary, holding hands and chatting away excitedly. The teacher directed the giddy children to the display in front of the two men, and began to lecture. Hoover and Johnson stood up.

"I want that item. By Friday!" Hoover reiterated.

"Friday's not good," he said apprehensively.

"Why the hell not?"

"It's the thirteenth."

Chapter Twenty-One

It was just another Tuesday evening. In accordance with the new blackout rules, one by one the lights were switched off on all forty-seven floors and the offices and hallways fell into darkness as the workers gradually filtered out of the East Side skyscraper.

The Ludlow & Peabody Building in the Murray Hill District near the Public Library is at 10 East 40th St. Built in 1928, the last year of unbridled prosperity before the Crash, it housed mainly corporate offices. Its brown stonework is topped with a beautiful copper hip roof and rises 48 storeys to claim its place amongst the tightly packed chess pieces of the New York skyline.

As was his routine, the building superintendent stood in the lobby, locking and unlocking the door to accommodate the last of the sporadic flow of typists, secretaries and executives dribbling out of the building, ending another workday.

The head of maintenance strolled across the expansive marble floor towards the superintendent. He was accompanied by a young man in a dark blue uniform similar to the one worn by the two veteran employees. The red embroidery above his breast pocket identified him as belonging to housekeeping.

"Henry, this is Jimmy. The union sent him over this afternoon."

"What happened to Frank?"

"Beats me. They said he was transferred for personal reasons."

"Personal reasons? He empties garbage cans, fer fuck's sake! What happened? He have a disagreement with a mop?"

"All I know is this is Jimmy. Jimmy, this is Henry, the building Super, he'll help ya get your bearings. I'm outta here. The Yankee game starts in half an hour."

"So, Jimmy. You got a union card or what?"

"Yeah. I got a union card. You want I should show it ta ya?"

"Yeah. If you would be so gracious as to indulge my wishes."

Jimmy produced the bona fide yellow, Building Maintenance Union card and in an apologetic tone Henry explained.

"Nuthin' poisonal, you understand. It was just last week that a guy I used ta woik wit, who knows a guy that was married to a guy's cousin, seen dem FBI guys nab dem German spies. Ya know? So . . ."

"I get ya drift, Henry. No big deal. Just happy ta be workin', know what I mean?"

"I know what ya mean! Cleanin' gear's in that closet over there, start on 45 and work ya way down."

Jimmy collected his cleaning gear from the mop closet and headed for the elevators. Henry sat down at the reception desk, tuned in the radio and waited for the Yankees game to start. He put his feet up on the desk and then, out of idle curiosity, watched the brass plated indicator point to the successive floor levels as Jimmy's elevator car gradually climbed to the top floor.

Jimmy got off on 45 and immediately stashed his cleaning equipment in the store room down the hall. Returning to the elevator, he stared at the indicator for several minutes. It didn't move, and so he was satisfied that Henry was not on his way up. He checked his watch.

The young man dashed for the stairwell and bounded down the staircase to the forty-first floor. Once there, he walked quickly while consulting a piece of paper he removed from his pocket and began to systematically pan the office doors up and down the hallway.

He stopped in front of suite number 4109, knelt on one knee and produced a small lock-picking kit from his hip pocket. His expertise allowed him entry to the suite in a matter of seconds, and once inside, he referred to a small floorplan of the office taped to the back of the lock pick kit.

It was seven o'clock. He had three more offices to do before Henry began his nightly rounds. Jimmy moved swiftly through his work. Filing cabinets, desks, storage units and cupboards of any size were all carefully searched, and all items replaced exactly as they were found so as to leave no trace of intrusion.

Suddenly, heavy footsteps echoed in the hall, and Jimmy nervously looked at his watch. Eight ten! He had lost track of time on his last office. Henry was ten minutes late.

Jimmy froze as the sound of rattling doorknobs grew louder, and realised that Henry was checking that the officers were locked. Jimmy had not locked the door behind him when he entered the last suite.

The knob rattled, the door opened and there was the flick of a switch. Blinding light flooded the room.

"Jimmy!" Henry scanned the small office. "Jimmy!" he called out again. "Where the hell are you? God-damn it! First day on the freakin' job and ya freakin' disappear on me!" Henry switched off the light, closed and locked the door, and moved down the hall in search of the new janitor.

After he was sure that Henry had had enough time to move onto another level, Jimmy slithered out from underneath the over-stuffed couch in the middle of the room, and breathed a sigh of relief.

The next morning Jimmy reported to Commander Haffenden that, with the exception of a few porno magazines, nothing of any significance was found in the suspected office suites he was assigned to search. Similar reports filtered in throughout the day from other agents around the city.

In spite of the fact it was only one day after Polakoff had rejoined the group, the operation was now in high gear. In contrast to its meagre beginnings with Socks Lanza and the Fulton Street Fish Market, *Operation Underworld* now generated a frenzy of round-the-clock activity. So much so that Haffenden was hard pressed to keep pace with the influx of information flooding into the command centre his office suite had now transitioned into.

If the Commander was contented with his handling of the previous crop of problems which had sprouted up in the planting of the operation, he was certainly dismayed at the new bumper harvest of headaches caused by the explosive expansion of this new phase of activity.

The increase in manpower and operational capital were accompanied by a disproportionate increase in paperwork. Captain MacFall issued a second memo requiring Haffenden to forward daily status reports to his office on the progress of the operation. That was three weeks ago. The Commander had yet to forward one status report, and as a consequence HQ had nothing to give DC, which made some people PO'd. All were getting nervous. Rumours began to circulate that Haffenden was in over his head on what increasingly appeared to be a very expensive snipe hunt.

✦

Labour pipelines, such as factories, piers, warehouses and trucking companies, were considered to be the primary targets of enemy agents, ergo much attention was initially directed at these areas by the government operatives. Counter-espionage assignments were determined by potential importance of a given facility to the war effort. However, ammunition storage facilities and shipping firms in support of those installations were poorly monitored or ignored altogether in the early phases of the operation.

"Meyer, we gotta talk right now!" The voice on the other end of the telephone line expressed a sense of urgency Lansky was unable to ignore.

"Johnny! Where the hell you at? What's wrong?"

"How soon can you be at Carlucci's, the one on the West Side?"

"'bout an hour. Why?" Lansky was puzzled, but knew Johnny Dunn, whose father had fought in the Easter Rising in Dublin, was not one prone to panic.

That afternoon in the back room of the Italian American Club on Mott Street, Lansky himself met with Haffenden.

"One of our people from the West Side says that your security at the receiving station for the Piccatinny Arsenal is terrible."

"Bullshit! We got armed guards all over the place." Haffenden was incensed.

"You do, huh?" Lansky reached into a burlap bag he had under the table and produced a detonator for a 2,000 lb blockbuster.

He threw it across the table and Haffenden jumped up, his chair tumbling to the floor. Several of the clubs regulars took mild notice.

"Don't worry. It's been deactivated. We got it from the main stores bunker in Area Seven." Lansky made his pronouncement in a matter-of-fact fashion in order to emphasise his point. The Commander righted his chair and eyed the detonator.

"Some asshole could waltz right in there and plant a bomb on one of your outgoing supply ships. I ain't no sailor, but I think if New York Harbor got blocked up by a sunk boat . . . ferget about it!"

"We'll . . . rectify the situation." Haffenden was pleasantly surprised by Lansky's initiative and enthusiasm as he stared at the detonator.

The food service, housekeeping and entertainment industries were no less affected by the increased anti-spy effort. Restaurants, hotels and nightclubs were descended upon by eager, dedicated agents posing as waiters, porters and hat check girls.

For a brief period in New York history, there was no way to tell if your fedora was being babysat by a kid working part time waiting for her next audition, or guarded with all the might of the US Government.

However, the success of these infiltration measures was not due to the far-reaching power of the Federal Government. It was due, instead, to the far-reaching power of its purported sworn enemy and latest business partner, organised crime.

With orchestration from Lucky Luciano, the lieutenants swiftly formed an intricate network of co-operating union factions. Factions who previously were hostile to one another.

The establishment of this network, which reached from the Canadian boarder to Florida and as far west as Ohio, allowed union credentials, papers, ID cards and financial records, to flow freely across interstate boundaries, oblivious to local, state and federal restrictions.

The Unione Siciliano was not one to look a gift horse in the mouth and with their new-found, interstate freedom, many other commodities flowed freely across the boarders as well. Booze, cigarettes and clothing topped the list, and within a week, all were flowing in record scale.

The boys were back in town.

✦

Lucky, accompanied by two guards, walked past the trustee mopping the floor on his way to the warden's office. Lansky and Polakoff were already there and the warden had received strict instructions to leave when their meeting began.

The trustee averted his bruised face as Luciano walked by. It was the slightly-built prisoner who had passed the comment at the dinner table.

"You get the problems straightened out about comin' up here?" Lucky asked, after the warden closed the door behind him.

"Yeah. Polakoff worked somethin' out." The conversation was casual and unhurried. Polakoff sat in the corner with a newspaper, doing a crossword puzzle.

"How's Albert A. doin?"

"He went under."

"He's hidin' out? Where?"

"You ready for this? The Army. He joined up."

"Good place ta hide." Lucky smiled and shook his head. "All the shipments come in?"

"Everything right on time."

"Any problems I need to know about?"

"You'd be proud, boss. Unprecedented co-operation. It's like they're all pulling in the same direction."

"Dat's good news." Lucky leaned in and spoke a little lower to Lansky, despite the fact that they continued in Sicilian.

"I been doin' some thinkin'. This is a pretty convenient

252

arrangement. But it ain't gonna last forever."

"How'dya mean?" Meyer asked.

"No matter if they catch spies or not, sooner or later some politician is gonna figure it don't look too good youse guys comin' up here all the time."

"I follow. You sayin' we should look for spies all the time?"

"Nah, dat ain't important. We can always come up wit a few spies if they need 'em. What I'm sayin' is, we need to come up with a plan to reconsolidate and rebuild soon."

"Things are comin' back together pretty good right now. Whata ya wanna do different?"

"I mean a big plan, fer after the war."

"Who the hell knows when this thing is gonna blow over?"

"Who cares? But it will, and when it does we gotta be ready. No matter who wins, things ain't never gonna be da same again. Da old markets are gonna shift or dry up and new markets are gonna hav'ta be opened up."

"You already got some'a those 'new markets' in mind, don't ya?" Lansky studied Lucky's face.

"Yeah, I do. But what I'm woikin' on is way too big fer just one family."

"We need a council," Meyer said as he began to cop on.

"Exactly. Contact all the heads. Don't tell 'em why until they show. The Camardos'll get ya a warehouse on the Brooklyn side. Then get a hold of our friends in Naples. Tell them to contact me. Only me! Got it?"

"I'm with ya."

"Set it up fer tomorrow or Thursday and then get back up here and I'll give ya an agenda and tell ya what to say," Lucky instructed.

"That won't work out."

"Why not?"

"Part of Polakoff's deal is he can only come here once a week."

"Shit!"

"Look, with the word from you, we know they're gonna show up." Lucky listened and nodded as Lansky suggested an alternate course of action.

"Tell me what you got in mind. Tell me what you want them to know. I'll call the meet this week, we'll give them a couple days ta think about it and I'll be back up next week."

"Sounds okay, but dat don't give us much time ta contact Naples. And I'm worried some'a de utter heads may not go fer it."

"I'll get a wire off to the guys on the other side today, and phone them tonight. As far as the other heads, does it involve makin' money?" Lansky asked.

Lucky smiled and sat upright before he answered. "It'll be the rebirth of the Family. They'll be enough dough ta keep your gran'kids going," Lucky assured Meyer.

"Then they'll go fer it. Anything else?"

"Yeah. I got a parole hearing next week. If the board knows I'm helpin' da country, it might carry some weight. De're no doubt keepin' records of dees visits, but dat prick DA will move ta keep dem from bein' introduced. Just in case dey get cute an try sayin' day lost 'em or somethin', you keep detailed records of dees visits and how we talked about catchin' spies 'n stuff."

"Piece a cake." Lansky stood and shook hands with Lucky. Polakoff picked up on the signal and called for the guard. A few minutes later the warden, who had been in the room next door, appeared and escorted the visitors back downstairs.

✦

Doc leaned against the flat wall of The Castle Memorial and watched the morning visitors as they strolled by, read newspapers or lined up for the boat ride out to Liberty Island.

He adjusted his position and continued to scan the crowd. A smile gradually came across his face and he walked away from the memorial, north across Battery Park towards the fire boat house.

Louie, who was sitting on a bench reading a newspaper, saw Doc approaching, and smiled when Doc sat down next to him.

"So? Pretty good, huh? Took ya almost ten minutes ta pick me out! What gave it away?"

Doc casually took the paper, folded it up and handed it back to him. "When you pretend to read a paper, do it like this. Nobody reads a paper full open like that." Louie said nothing. "And don't use yesterday's paper."

"Anything else?"

"You did good. But think real hard next time you want to blend in somewhere. Be careful of the details. What day is your test next week?"

"Friday morning."

"Maybe we should lay off some of these street skills. Ya know, give ya more time at the books?"

"I'm sick a them books, Doc! Besides, I got 'em mesmerised. They're all up here." Louie tapped his head. "I like this blendin' in stuff, it's fun. By the way, how's it going with Nikki?"

"Tell Doris it's going good with Nikki, thanks for askin'. We're gettin' together this weekend."

"I like her, she reminds me of Maxine Andrews. Don't tell her I said that!"

"Alright, let's talk about what's on your test."

Doc and Louie sat on the bench for half an hour looking out over the harbour, discussing details of the material Louie would be tested on to get his New York State Private Investigator's licence.

"Good job," Doc complimented Louie as he stood up. "C'mon, we gotta get back before lunch. We got a call yesterday from a potential client. We're meetin' her at noon."

"Hey, Doc! I got an idea!"

"How come all of a sudden I don't feel so good?"

"No, really. Instead of catchin' the subway back, let's walk over to State Street and up Broadway. You stay behind me, I'll pick a guy out, you watch me tail 'em? How 'bout it?"

"Louie, how old are you?"

"Why?"

"What does Doris say when you act like a little kid?" Doc smiled.

"C'mon! It's only half past ten, we got plenty of time."

"Okay Dashiell, let's go." The two walked north and after about five minutes, when in front of the Cunard Building on lower Broadway, Doc slowed his pace.

"What's up, Doc? Jeez, I've always wanted ta say that!"

"Yeah, and you're the first one ever to say it, too!" Doc had now stopped walking altogether and was looking up in the air. "Louie, we're gonna do this one a little different."

"Great!" Louie watched Doc peering up at the Renaissance-inspired building as if looking for something.

"Okay, this place'll do.'' Doc nodded at Louie and led him into the vaulted, ornate lobby of the building.

"Doc! Where we goin'?" Louie was gaping at the elaborate murals of mythical sea creatures and wooden masted ships.

"We're gonna punch a ticket. C'mon."

"You flipped or what?" Despite his protests Louie went along with Doc. Once inside the building, Louie became more persistent.

"Doc, what the hell we doin'? I thought we was havin' a tailin' lesson?"

Doc ignored Louie as someone exited the lobby and he watched a reflection in a glass pane in one of the doors which opened out onto the avenue. He saw the image he was looking for.

"We are, Louie." Doc quickly removed his jacket. "Give me your coat. Hurry!" Doc stuck his cap on Louie's head and climbed into the overcoat. Louie looked at Doc.

"Doesn't work without the bowlin' shoes, Doc. What the hell are we doin'?"

"You said you wanted to be more like me someday. Here's your chance."

"Yeah, but I was drunk."

Doc ushered Louie over to the second set of double doors which led to the inner building. "Stand here, face that way. Don't move."

Doc hurried back over to the main doors, faced into the corner and pretended to be searching his pockets. Just as Doc assumed his position, a tall man came through the doors and stopped next to him. He was unsure what to do next as he stared at the painting of the beautiful woman on the back of the bomber jacket. Just then Louie turned around.

"Doc, what the hell . . ."

The stranger turned nearly at the same time as Louie but it wasn't fast enough. Doc's right hit him hard enough to send the tall man crashing against the opposite wall of the vestibule and crumpling to the floor.

"Ow!" Doc put his fist under his arm. "God-damn, that hurts!"

"That's why they use brass knuckles, Doc," Louie said in a cocky tone.

Doc held his hand up for Louie to see. "Thanks for the update!" He was wearing brass knuckles.

"Did you just want to show me how to use those things, or you know this guy?" Louie asked.

Doc looked around to see if there were any witnesses. There were none.

"We're old buddies, Louie. This is one of the assholes that jumped me coming back from Nikki's house." Doc did a fast frisk and produced a wallet from the man's breast pocket. He then reached into his own pocket and produced an identical bifold. He held them side by side. Both credentials were the same, treasury agent ID's.

"Bingo!" Doc declared.

"You owe back taxes or something?"

"I don't know, Louie. I can't figure what they hell they want." Removing a second set of brass knuckles from the man, he tossed them to Louie.

"Happy birthday."

Trying them on, Louie commented, "Hey I never seen these things up close. They're pretty neat." He pretended to swing at someone. "Maybe they're pissed off 'cause you keep takin' all their stuff?"

"Well, now they got something ta really get pissed off about. This guy's gonna be eatin' through a straw for a coupl'a months. Looks like I broke his jaw. They're not gonna have any sense of humour about that. We better make ourselves scarce."

Louie started for the front door but Doc grabbed him by the arm.

"Through the building. We'll come out on Trinity."

Both of them were already through the lobby doors when Doc had an afterthought. He ducked back into the vestibule and quickly dug into the hip pocket of the unconscious man. Doc found what he was looking for. Money. He returned to Louie with a small wad of fifties and twenties. A lobby guard noticed them and slowly made his way over to the vestibule. They made it through the building to Trinity Street and back to Christopher Street without incident.

Once safely inside Harry's, Doc went over to the counter to talk to Harry.

"Well, if it ain't the Dynamic Duo," Harry greeted them.

"We had any visitors today, Harry?"

"Yeah, early this morning. Big tall fella. Looked like a Fed."

Doc showed Harry the photo ID.

"That's him."

"Did he say what he wanted?"

"Said ta tell ya he wanted 'it' back."

"Wanted what back?"

"Beats me. Said you knew what he was talking about."

"Thanks, Harry." Doc and Louie went upstairs to put their heads together. Louie emptied the letter box and Doc took out the whiskey bottle and sat at his desk.

"Hey, Doc, looks like ya got yerself a fan club. This one's a real letter. You wanna look at it?"

"Is it from an Irish society?"

"Don't look like it."

"Alright, gimme." Louie threw it across the desk and Doc opened it. As he unfolded the handwritten letter a hundred dollar bill fell out onto the floor.

"Nice fan club! How do I join?!" Louie exclaimed. "What's it say?"

Doc handed the letter to Louie.

"I need your opinion on this bill. Please contact soonest. Except Saturday. A grateful client," he read out. "Who the hell is – "

"It's Ira," Doc declared.

"How do you know? He didn't sign it."

"That's because he's afraid of these clowns."

"How do you know it's Ira?"

"How many grateful clients we had in the last month? Plus he's Jewish, that's why he mentioned Saturday. He must think he's onto something." Doc thought for a moment. "Louie, run this down to Harry." He handed Louie the hundred and then reached into his pocket. Peeling away a twenty and a fifty from the wad he had recently confiscated, he added them for Louie to take to Harry and then threw the remainder of the wad into a cigar box with the other bills.

In ten minutes Louie was back upstairs, out of breath.

"You're gonna love this one," Louie panted.

"Talk to me." Doc abandoned the diagram he had been sketching and took the bills from Louie.

"The hundred's phoney. Harry says he'd bet it came out of that original batch you brought in."

"No big surprise."

"The twenty and the fifty are real."

"Real?" Doc was surprised. "This wad'd choke a horse! There's over six hundred bucks here! You sure he said they were real?"

"Coin o' da realm." The phone rang and Doc picked it up.

"Hey, Doc, it's me."

"Hey, Harry. What's cooking?"

"I can't see too good, but I think maybe you got a visitor."

"Who and how many?"

"Just one. I think it's your girlfriend."

"Well, tell her come up."

"That's the thing, Doc. She's just sittin' on the other side of Christopher. She don't look too good. You bust up wit her or somethin'?"

Doc stood up from behind his desk and looked out the window. There was Nikki, sitting on the curb crying. She appeared uninjured and clutched part of a newspaper. The pages were blowing away one at a time in the breeze. Scanning up and down the street, he saw no one else.

"What are you, my mother? You don't bust up after one date. Keep an eye on her. I'll be right down." Doc hung up and made for the door. "Louie, watch out the window, when I look up give me the all-clear. If you see somethin', point at it. Got it?" Doc was out of the door before Louie could answer.

Moments later, Nikki was safely up in the office, sipping hot tea. She had stopped crying and was settled enough for Doc to talk to her.

"I didn't know where else to go." She fought back the urge to sob again.

"Sweetheart, what happened?" Doc asked as Louie handed her another tissue.

"He didn't show up for work the last two days, so I called his house. No answer. That's not like him."

"Like who?"

"He's dead. Ira's dead."

Doc and Louie exchanged glances. "How do you know?"

She held up the last torn piece of newsprint she had been clutching in her hand. Doc and Louie shared the same thought. Even before Doc checked the tattered page, Louie was moving for the door.

"It's the *Daily News*." Louie nodded at Doc.

"Got it!"

"I don't know what to say." Doc tried to console her. He was unsure what to do and so walked over to the hot plate to make some more tea.

"Doc I . . . I don't think it was natural causes."

"Why not? What'd the article say?"

"It didn't. But there was somethin' about an autopsy. They wouldn't do an autopsy if it was natural causes, would they?"

"Not usually, no. Where'd he die?"

"I . . . don't know. I couldn't get past the first paragraph."

Doc was digesting events when he heard Louie coming back down the hall.

"Doc, there's somethin' else," Nikki said.

He came back over and sat down next to her. "Tell me."

Louie came in the door with a copy of the *News* folded over to the appropriate page. Doc took it from him and began to read.

"Shirley's gone."

Doc looked up from the paper. "She quit?"

"No. Gone gone. Like missing gone."

"How do you know she's missing?"

"Because she wasn't at work today, or yesterday either, and she doesn't answer the phone at her apartment." Tears began to well in her eyes. Doc signalled Louie behind her back to make her a drink. He handed Doc a short measure which he poured it into her tea. He motioned to Louie a second time to sit at his desk and take notes on what Nikki was telling them.

"Maybe she's sick and went over to St. Vincent's?"

"She's healthy as a horse! Shirley doesn't get sick damn it! Listen to me!" Nikki turned and saw Louie writing at the desk. "And don't waste your time calling the hospital. I already did." Louie crossed out the note he just made on the pad.

"Look, Doc, you gotta believe me. She doesn't miss work, ya know? The day after Pearl Harbor, she was in that building for seventy-two hours straight. One of the officers had to order her to be escorted home. After thirteen years, that place is her whole life."

"Okay, let's assume she's missing. Was she out with anybody in the last few weeks?"

"No. The last guy she was out with never showed for their second date. That was eight months ago."

"Do we know anything about him?" Louie interjected.

"Plenty! He made up with his old girlfriend and now they're married with a kid in Atlanta. The dopey son-of-a-bitch even sent her a wedding invitation!" Nikki succumbed to her frustration.

"Does she have any relatives in New York?" Doc asked.

"Her mother's in Jersey."

"You got her number?"

"No, but it's probably on record somewhere down at the Third District. But I don't think I can get it."

"Why not?"

"I'm afraid to go around askin' questions. I think maybe that's what happened to Shirley. She started gettin' these weird messages through her switchboard, and started askin' questions."

"Weird messages?"

"Yeah. Real cryptic stuff. The kinda thing you'd think would be classified. Only she told me the guys on the other end of the line didn't sound like they were Navy."

"How'd they sound?"

"She used the word 'rough'."

"She ever say anything, or you ever hear anything, about money going through that place?"

Nikki thought for a moment. The whiskey was kicking in. "No, not that I ever heard of. All the financial stuff is handled through the Bursar's Department."

Doc opened the desk drawer and took out the over-stuffed cigar box. He showed it to Nikki. "The night we went out three guys jumped me coming back from your place. They were treasury agents. They had all this dough on them."

"Jeez! Nice work if ya can get it, huh?" Nikki had never seen so much money. "We got a couple of treasury agents working down at the district. I don't know what they do, but they're with the Naval Intel department."

Doc laid the cigar box on the desk and showed Nikki the four wallets. "Recognise any of these guys?"

"Yeah, these two. They're both assigned to the district. That one's the creep who's always hittin' on us." She pointed to Johnson.

"Is it him?" Louie asked.

"No, another one." Doc answered.

"Him who?" Nikki spoke to Doc.

"We met another one earlier today. This one." He showed her

the duplicate ID, one she didn't recognise. Doc put everything away then thought better of it. He retrieved a cloth money bag from the bottom drawer of the desk and put the money from the cigar box and the identification cards in it. Holding back two twenties, he held them out to Louie.

"Louie'll take you back downtown. I'll meet you at five and take you home. Okay?"

"I'm not going back to work! I already told them. They brought in a temp. I'm gonna go home. Kate has a half day today. She's probably already at Mrs. Paluso's."

Doc picked up the phone and rang downstairs. "Harry, get Nikki a cab, will ya? Tell him ta honk twice when he shows up."

"Where to, Doc?"

"Tell him we'll let him know when he gets here." Doc turned to Louie. "Call Doris. Tell her ta call Mrs Birnbaum, see if she needs anything. I'll take Nikki down to the cab."

"Roger, Doc."

On their way through Harry's, Doc put the cloth bag on the counter. "Put this somewhere safe, will ya?"

Harry waited until the couple were outside to stash the bag.

Downstairs, Doc held the taxi door open for Nikki. He got a nice surprise. After she kissed him, she told him how good it felt to know she could rely on him. The cab pulled away and Doc went back upstairs, unsure of how to take Nikki's compliment.

"Hey, Doc. I been meaning ta ask ya. How the hell does Harry know so much about rubber money?"

"Harry has a past. Let me see that article." Louie continued to speak as Doc perused the article.

"Says they found him in Bushwick Creek. That's up in Greenpoint. Whata ya suppose he was doin' over there?"

"He probably wasn't in Brooklyn. They iced him somewhere else and dropped him over there. The Mob uses the East River all the time for their private cemetery."

"You think it was the Mob?!"

"No. If they did it, he wouldn't have been found so soon, if at all. I think they wanted it to look like the Mob. Looks like we're gonna meet the Kings County Coroner."

"You know somebody over there?"

Doc reached into his pocket and began to count the bills he had on him. "No, but I got a feelin' somebody in the Coroner's office and myself have some mutual friends."

"You're not gonna give him that phoney dough, are ya?"

"Only if I have to. Besides, look at it as doin' him a favour."

"What?"

Doc continued to talk as they headed for the door. "The law says a bribe is takin' money for doin' somethin' illegal. This ain't really money now, is it? So he really won't be breakin' the law now, will he?"

"Yeah, that'll hold up in court!"

It was a quarter to twelve when they left the office to head over to Brooklyn.

Thirty minutes later, there was one pissed off potential client storming back down the stairs and out through Harry's onto Christopher Street.

✦

As Nikki climbed the stairs to Mrs Paluso's apartment, she experienced an overwhelming sensation of relief from the familiarity of her surroundings. The extra time in the taxi had allowed her to compose herself prior to Mrs Paluso's routine culinary onslaught. Predictably armed with potatoes and sausage, the Polish neighbour was only satisfied with no for an answer after Nikki relented and told her a friend had died. She finally accepted a cup of tea as a compromise.

"Is Kate in the front room?" Nikki asked, sitting at the kitchen table.

"Yes. You vant I call her?"

"No, no. I'll surprise her." Kate did not hear her mother approach and for a brief moment Nikki's heart was once again filled with the special kind of joy as she watched her daughter content at play. From behind the door jamb Nikki could see Kate had lined up several play chairs and boxes and had dolls sitting on them to form a mock classroom. Teacher Kate was reading the class an imaginary story from a small book. As Kate turned to ask the pupils if they were enjoying the story, she spotted Nikki.

"Mommy!" She ran to Nikki with open arms.

"Hi, sweetie! Reading a story, huh? What's it about?"

Katie took Nikki aside and shielded her answer from the class by whispering to her mom. "I'm not exactly sure. This is a weird book. So I'm telling them about the beautiful princess and the evil sheriff. But they don't know what's really in the book." Nikki took the little black book from Kate and glanced through the pages. Her mouth involuntarily dropped open and her knees weakened. She knelt down and held Kate by the hands.

"Honey, where'd you find this book?" Nikki was fighting back a tidal wave of panic as she spoke.

"In the porch."

"You mean *on* the porch, sweetie."

"No, in the porch. There was a loose brick. We were playing there the other day and Stachie found the brick. It fell out and the book was there."

"Do Stachie and Lydia know about this book?"

"Lydia doesn't. But you know Stachie, he's a boy. He probably forgot about it already."

"Honey, listen to me. This will be our little secret. You musn't tell *anyone*. Understand?"

Katie didn't understand, but nodded to her mom in agreement.

At half past two in the morning ,Nikki was still sitting at her kitchen table, a half cup of cold tea at her elbow next to a full ashtray, staring at the little black book lying in front of her, trying desperately to decide what to do.

Chapter Twenty-Two

The Daily News sports page gives the track attendance for Belmont every day, and this number is always in the five or six figures. The last three numbers of the attendance are the most important numbers in many a New Yorker's life. These numbers are known, in the vernacular as, 'The Number'.

A leading economic indicator of how good things are in the waterfront neighbourhoods, is how busy the bookies are. Jimmy Erickson, who fixed the bets at the track for Hoover, so he'd laid off the New York families, couldn't keep up with the workload. Even though his wife had thrown him out of the house twice already for roping her younger brother into running the numbers for him, he risked it again. He had no choice. He even took in two more runners just to keep up.

By order of Luciano, and by virtue of the all-round increased profit margins, the Mob were directed to back off on petty crime, in order to lower their profile in the media. The decreased profile placated the public, which thereby placated the politicians and allowed the Unione to consolidate more efficiently and preserve resources to make inroads into bigger and more profitable enterprises. A primary building block of how Lucky thought an organisation should be run.

Additionally, the inter-union co-operation was breaking all records. The cloak of secrecy provided by the US Naval Intelligence service allowed the boys to run circles around anyone they felt should be restricted from sharing future dividends in the new world order of organised crime.

Slack about crime stories in the press was taken up by war

news and political rhetoric telling everyone how it was only a matter of time before the Allies struck back, and when the headlines heralded the meeting of Roosevelt and Churchill at Casablanca following the taking of Africa, it became common knowledge that Italy was not far behind.

Lansky was successful in making the Sicilian connection and that Thursday night, within yards of John Roebling's Brooklyn Bridge, a meeting of unprecedented magnitude took place on Front Street.

Meyer Lansky, in his last major act with the Unione before going legit after the war, laid out Lucky's plan to traffic heroin into Sicily from Turkey following the Allied invasion. Lucky would provide the Navy strategic intelligence about the island in exchange for reinstatement of as many of the local politicians as he could wrangle. The OSS would be only too happy to co-operate.

These 'politicians' would in turn help export the 'slow death' to the United States after the war. Only one of the five family heads was against the plan to shift from prostitution, extortion and robbery to the drug trade. He objected on moral grounds. In time he would be persuaded to reconsider. The others were tripping over themselves to get involved.

The next day a trustee passed the word to Lucky that "the Dodgers were a shoo-in". Lucky immediately ordered Lansky to donate fifty large to the campaign fund of the Honorable Judge McVay. The judge who, coincidentally, would preside over Lucky's bid for parole in less than two weeks.

✦

"Whatch'a readin'?" Doc talked to Louie over the screeching of steel wheels as they passed into the East River tunnel. They were on the F train to Brooklyn. Doc wanted to snoop around Bushwick Creek before approaching the Brooklyn DA. Louie carried the copy of the *New York Daily News* with the report of Ira's death.

"Winchell's new column. He's slammin' Luciano again."

"Luciano? He's been up the river for half a dozen years. Must be hard-up for material."

"Winchell says they outta hang 'em."

"Ever notice how much braver Winchell got after Luciano got tagged?"

"He says here he has sources that say Luciano's people gave Roosevelt nearly seven thousand for his '32 campaign. That's how he beat Smith."

"Ya mean Walter's tryin' ta say the Presidency can be bought? Say it so, Joe!"

"Says here further, that that's why FDR let all them drug dealers go while he was still Governor. All them ones that went back to Sicily."

"Walter's braver than I thought." The train slowed to a halt. "This is us."

A taxi from the station dropped them at 14th and Kent. Doc and Louie stared in disbelief as they exited the cab. A giant iron gate patrolled by a pair of Marine sentries greeted them.

"Son-of-a-gun!" Louie expressed their surprise. "It's a god-damned Navy base. It didn't used to be a Navy base."

"Yeah, but now it is and we got a snowball's chance in hell of gettin' in there."

"Unless we enlist," Louie jokingly suggested.

"Been there, done that. I need a drink."

"Jeez, Doc, where we gonna find a bar in Brooklyn?"

✦

Brooklyn, although only one of the five boroughs, was the third largest city in the country and so was large enough to its own police department, fire department and District Attorney's office.

Even during the war, the Brooklyn District Attorney's office was habitually swamped with murder cases of every mode and description. However, at a special session of the senior investigators and prosecutors with the borough DA himself, Ira Birnbaum's homicide was stamped a priority. The fact that he was a federal employee weighed heavy, and part of his motivation for moving as swiftly as possible was to avoid a federal investigation by solving the crime quickly.

"Justin, what have we got for sure?" the DA addressed the head investigator at the special afternoon meeting. The investigator read from a hastily composed file lying in front of him on the large conference table.

"White male, late seventies, early eighties, found face down in the reeds at Bushwick Creek. Cause of death asphyxiation secondary to strangulation. Manhattan resident, federal employee. Survived by wife."

"Who found the body?"

"Coupl'a guys fishin' in the river."

"Where'd he work?"

"Third Naval District. Mail clerk."

"Mail clerk? What happen, somebody's relief cheque come late? Who the hell'd wanna take out a mail clerk? Any priors?"

"Not this guy. Paragon citizen."

"Possible motives?"

"He was close to retirement. He and the wife hadn't saved much. We think maybe he was in over his head. Sharks, ponies. Who knows?"

"You think it's Mob related?"

"Virtually certain of it. Has all the earmarks. Strangulation, dumped in the East River. Probably met the perpetrator, or perpetrators at Greenpoint on one false premise or another and that's where they gave it to him." The investigator, who spoke with confidence, finished his remarks and sat down.

"Gentlemen, for years the Mob has been using Brooklyn for all its dirty work. Meanwhile, whenever there's some kind of breakthrough on the crime front Manhattan gets all the credit." The assembled group nodded and commented to each other in agreement. "I intend to change all that. I spoke to the mayor this morning and he's agreed to allow us to carry the ball on this one. As of right now, I'm open for suggestions."

One of the junior investigators spoke up in the back. "Sir, I understand this may not be what you want to hear, but . . .

realistically, we may never catch the guys that did this." Loud objections flooded the room as the young man continued to make his case.

"In a way, it's not all that critical that we do. But if we can parley this murder, this heinous act of violence, arrogantly perpetrated against the people of this fair city, in flagrant defiance of all that is right and just, then . . ."

The objections began to subside as the group began to realise where he was going. "We can dominate the headlines of all the major dailies for at least two to three days. Be a helluva boost for the campaign image."

"I like the high profile angle." The DA nodded his support. "John, get a hold of Patricia. Draw up a press strategy and get it out to the API and UPI for tomorrow. What else. People? C'mon, talk to me."

"History of similar crimes in the last six months and how we have to move to curb the ever growing menace?" someone else chimed in.

"Go with it but change it to the last year. What else?" The DA was anxious to maintain the momentum.

"A special joint presentation to the widow by the mayor and the DA. Great photo op!" someone else suggested.

"I hope you mean the Brooklyn DA, Samuelson?"

"You mean there's another DA?" Laughter circulated the room. Suggestions flowed for the better part of an hour and by late afternoon there was nearly enough material to launch a presidential campaign.

Ira Birnbaum's murderer may never be brought to justice, but it was sure as hell gonna look like he was.

✦

"I can't for the life of me figure out why the hell anyone would want to kill Ira." Doc twirled his shot glass idly as he spoke.

"The universal motive, Doc. You taught me that." The only problem Doc and Louie had with finding a bar was which one to choose. They settled on O'Casey's on 14th and Nassau. Webs of shiny cardboard shamrocks and green crêpe paper loomed everywhere.

"Yeah, greed. But what the hell could he possibly have that anyone would want?"

The middle aged barmaid wearing a green paper hat floated over to the duo. "You boys wanna go again?" Doc looked up at her.

"Yeah one more." Doc pushed some of the coins forward which he had laying on the bar.

"Well, he sure as hell wasn't into anything illegal," Louie said authoritatively.

"You sound like you know that for a fact." Doc was surprised at Louie's statement. Louie took one last pull on his beer.

"I do. I had Doris ask around the neighbourhood when we first got the case. Any cleaner, the guy would squeak."

"Son-of-a-bitch! That gossip circle is good for somethin', ain't it?"

"Doc, there's gotta be a connect with the money."

"I agree, Louie. But he wasn't killed for money."

"What then?"

"I don't know. Maybe information."

"Somthin' he found out about the money?"

The barmaid brought the drinks, took a few coins from Doc's pile and began to walk away. "Hey, doll!" Doc called after her.

"Yeah?" She came back over.

"You familiar with the Coroner's office?"

"You that desperate for a date, honey?"

"Never knew a waitress could resist a bad joke, Louie," Doc fired back. "I need ta know if there's a bar or restaurant nearby."

"There's Botticelli's on Temple. Great food, good service," she informed him.

"You got a phone?"

"In the back, near the john."

Doc glanced over his pile of coins and picked up a dime. "Ya got a couple'a nickels?" He handed her a dime.

"You want me ta dial the phone and drink ya drink for ya while

I'm at it?" she asked.

"We goin' bar-hoppin'?" Louie threw in.

"Nah. Just had another brainstorm. Be right back."

"You guys cops or somethin'?" the barmaid asked. Louie slid right into the role.

"Yeah. Workin' a murder case." He leaned forward to emphasise the secrecy of the case. "Very hush-hush. Guy worked for the Feds."

The barmaid had been around the block. "You mean that old guy they fished out of Bushwick, the mail clerk? Amateur job. It wasn't the Mob. That DA's just lookin' ta get himself re-elected."

Doc returned from his phone call and the barmaid walked away. "You want another one? We got a little while yet," he asked Louie.

"Nah, let's walk a little. Talk about the case." They headed for the door and once over on Nassau Street, flagged a cab. As they got in, Louie offered a theory.

"Doc, I been thinkin'. That was an amateur job. It probably wasn't the Mob. I'd say that DA's probably just sayin' that ta get re-elected."

✦

Doc and Louie were now accompanied by Harry. Doc had phoned him from O'Casey's, and they met at Botticelli's.

The three entered the police headquarters building which housed the Coroner's main office and approached the watch commander's desk.

"Coroner's office?" Doc was brief, but authoritative. They had no business sniffing around this murder case, and if they got caught it would be very expensive. Especially with the phoney twenties and fifties Doc was carrying.

"Downstairs, turn right." The burly Sergeant never looked up from his paperwork until they had walked away. He puzzled at Harry's limp and smiled at Louie's shoes.

"Doc, how come we were waitin' till six-thirty ta show up over here?"

"Change a shift. Night guy's more likely ta go for a bribe. Besides, less of crowd after hours."

As they turned right, they could see the Coroner's office was about fifty yards ahead. However, that was as far as they were going.

The hall was jammed with reporters. Thirty or forty of them. The DA was taking the high profile angle seriously. In just over twenty-four hours, Ira's murder had become national news.

Wading through the press corps was the little headache. The big headache was the two policemen standing in front of the office door. Not rookie kids, either. If these guys owned dark suits they could have worked for Luciano.

Halfway through the reporters, Doc diverted the trio into the men's room. Once inside, he cocked back his ball cap and put on his game face.

"This ain't gonna be easy, guys. If we get nailed, it's all over but the cryin'. Harry, give me the sack." Doc brandished the government bifold wallets.

"These ID's will likely get us by. But neither of you has to do this."

Harry and Louie reached for the wallets simultaneously.

"I wanna be Johnson," Louie declared.

"What is this, *What's My Line*?"

"We gonna stand around jabber-jawin' all night or we gonna do this thing?" Harry asked as he limped towards the door. A moment later, they were in front of the two cops guarding the door.

Doc did the talking. "We're here to see the Coroner." He flashed his Treasury Department ID, thumb partially obscuring the photo.

"Is it about the Birnbaum case?"

"Yeah, why?"

"His personal possessions are still at the DA's. They didn't bring them over here," the officer explained. Harry was quiet, but Louie did his best to look like a mean treasury agent.

"Why would we want his personal possessions?"

"Ain't you guys here to see if his money was phoney?" This is where Doc pulled ahead of the pack in the PI business. When he was pitched a curve ball, he could swing low and inside.

"No, we work with him, down at Third Naval District. His boss, Admiral Mancino, asked us ta look in on how it's going." The officers looked at each other. "The Admiral's flying out to DC tomorrow. He wants ta know the score before he leaves."

The cops looked at each other a second time in a challenge to see if either one was willing to assume responsibility. Doc picked up on their reluctance. "The Admiral has to report whether or not your people are doing all you can. If not, the FBI'll be brought in."

They slowly stepped aside to let the trio pass.

As they went through the door, both cops noticed Louie's bowling shoes.

"Talk about dedicated. You'd never get me in off the alleys to go back to work," the older policeman commented.

As soon as they got inside, Louie and Harry realised right away that Coroner's 'Office' was a misnomer. Through the dim light of the large, open room, they saw what was in fact a large medical lab. Glassware covered black, marble-topped tables, a large beaker boiling, discharging some sort of distillate into a stainless steel receptacle and the whole place appeared abandoned.

"Igor, send up the kites!" Louie commented in a bad accent. Harry shook his head.

Doc disappeared off to the right and Louie went poking around like a kid in a toy store. Harry heard Doc and some young guy talking in the back. Although the voices were subdued, they were clearly audible.

"Look, I appreciate your orders from the DA, but they dragged this guy out of retirement and flew him all the way up here," Doc explained.

Harry saw the kid poke his head around the corner to look at him. He waved and Doc continued. "Now, I know it's highly unlikely, but if you guys miss somethin', especially on the forensics of the money, it's gonna look pretty bad for the department." Harry heard Doc pause to let it sink in. "Now, you may not get fired, but you'll sure as hell be buyin' your own coffee and donuts till you retire."

A moment later Doc and the kid emerged from the back

"Doctor Kravitz, this is Special Agent Harry . . . Patton."

"No relation," Harry quickly added.

"And that . . . that's agent Johnson." Doc pointed over to where Louie was trying to see how fast he could get the centrifuge to spin without his pen falling off. "Doctor Kravitz, Harry is one of the world's leading experts on currency forensics." They shook hands and Doctor Kravitz displayed a guarded admiration for Harry.

"Harry, the good Doctor has agreed to let us examine a sample of a twenty they have from the money which was found on the deceased." Kravitz showed Harry to a table and helped him get situated.

While Harry looked through the microscope, Doc quizzed Kravitz.

"Was the victim killed in Brooklyn?"

"No, somewhere else. Probably across the river."

"How'd they do it?"

"Strangulation. Yesterday, between eleven and one, rough guess."

"It's phoney," Harry announced.

"We haven't determined that yet," Kravitz explained.

"Why not?" Harry asked in genuine disbelief.

"We've been concentrating on the body. We haven't gotten around to the sample and the experts from Albany haven't arrived."

"Have you done a simple smug test or a litmus?"

"Well . . .no." Kravitz was puzzled. Harry sat back from the scope and went into action.

"I need two strips of litmus paper, five drams of hydrochloric acid, two drams of sulphuric acid, some bicarbonate of soda, sucrose, two droppers, and three pipettes. Oh, and some phenophathelene, if you have it." Harry looked at Kravitz, who was motionless.

"And a partridge in a pear tree," Louie chimed in.

"You guys are the strangest treasury agents I've ever seen," Kravitz commented, looking around the room at his guests. He turned to Harry. "You want that SO4 concentrated or diluted?"

Harry worked for about ten minutes, Kravitz asked questions and finally a page of notes was handed to Doc, which he read aloud.

"Hand engraved, soft metal plates. Three to six months old. Manufactured south-eastern US. All same batch."

"What does that mean, all same batch?" Kravitz inquired.

"We had a similar case last year," Doc countered as he continued to read. "That mean anything to you, Harry? Soft plates?"

"Yeah. Limits your run 'cause the plates wear down. If you're runnin' twenties, best you can do is twenty, twenty-five grand. Upside is you can carve your plates faster."

"Then whatta you do?" Kravitz asked.

"You melt the plates down so they can't be traced. Whoever did this wasn't in it for the long run. Sounds like they just needed spendin' money."

"What about this south-eastern US. How can you tell that?"

Doc knew Harry was good, but he had never seen him shine like this. The only time Doc remembered Harry discussing money was when he used to complain about the government reneging on the Expeditionary Force Bonus promised to the First War veterans. That and the fact that he would clam up if anyone asked where he got the dough to open the news stand.

"There's a distinct style. I recognise the workmanship."

Kravitz and Doc looked at each other in amazement. Harry made it clearer.

"I think I know who made these notes."

"Who?" Kravitz was astonished.

"I'm sorry, but that's classified by the Department of the Treasury," he answered authoritatively. Doc was proud of Harry.

"Doctor Kravitz, have you done the autopsy yet?" he asked, to divert attention from Harry.

"Isn't gonna be one. Not unless we get an exhumation order."

"It's a homicide, why wasn't there an autopsy?"

"Two reasons. His religion, which says he has to be in the ground, intact, before sundown the next day. And the fight."

"What fight?"

"The one that's going on between the Mayor's office and the DA right now about spendin' two to three million on the court battle, along with the ensuing press war."

"What court battle?"

"The one it's gonna take to get him outta the ground and on the table. You know how many lawyers that guy had? Plus, we just found out he's got a five and a half million dollar estate bequeathed to orphaned Jewish children, providin' the money doesn't get used for legal battles. You wanna be the shit who forces a bunch of Jewish orphans to miss out on five million so it can go to lawyers?"

"Can't fight City Hall, huh?" Doc smiled as he remembered Ira's passive demeanor.

"Guess you won't need those guys from Albany after all, eh, Perfesser?" Louie added, tapping Kravitz on the back as they left.

Chapter Twenty-Three

The taxi ride from Brooklyn back to the Village was a frenzied debate of murder theories and potential motives and enroute there were three stopovers. Two for drinks and one for Chinese take-out. By the second drink stop, the cab driver turned off the meter, and joined the trio for a beer. Intrigued and drawn into the deliberations, Murray, the taxi driver, reasoned that it was okay to turn off the meter because he was helping to solve a crime. Besides, he was due to go off duty in a mere four and a half hours anyway.

After dropping Louie home, Doc, Harry and Murray proceeded to Christopher Street. Murray was naturally invited up to continue the debate, but explained he had to get home to his wife and seven kids, so Doc tipped him a twenty.

"Harry, do you really know who made these bills or were you just yankin' his leash?" Doc asked the next morning, lying on his desk where he had spent the night. He held one of the fifties up and was examining it.

"Scheinfeld. Ernie Scheinfeld." Harry was in the cot.

"How do you know him?" Doc prepared himself for a captivating story which never materialised.

"Reputation. Never really met him. But anybody who can say the word 'counterfeit' knows about him." Harry could see that Doc was wondering if he was being strung along. "Honest ta God, Doc! Never met him, he was way outtta my league. Never did business with anyone he didn't know. So they say."

"That's how you knew the southeast?" Doc had walked across the room to man the hot plate.

"Yeah. He used to operate outta Hot Springs a lot. Mob jobs, mostly."

"Is he still around?"

"Depends on what ya mean."

"I mean like, you know where he is? Can we talk to him?"

Doc's excitement was building, but Harry maintained an even keel. "Sure. Everybody knows where he is. And I guess anybody can talk to him. Long as you're there during visitin' hours."

"You're enjoyin' this, ain't ya? Ya old bastard!"

"Louisiana State pen, ten to twenty."

"What happen? He spell 'In God We Trust' wrong?"

"Back alimony. Said he'd rather go ta jail then give her a penny."

"Man of principle, huh?"

"Hey Doc, was all them bills crumpled up the same?" Harry propped himself up on one elbow and assumed a quizzical look.

"Jeez, Harry, no idea. What does it mean if they were?"

"When you do a run, ya want the new bills ta look old before ya pass 'em, like they was used. So there's a variety a ways to do it. Basically, they should look crumpled. Like they been handled."

"So whatta we do?"

"Get a few of 'em out." Doc and Harry began to compare the real notes with the home-made brand. Soon, the desk, table and any other available flat surface was occupied with money, neatly laid out in rows, by denomination.

"Harry, this ain't workin' too good. Let's move the furniture away and use the floor."

After ten minutes of crawling around the floor, Harry found something.

"Well, whatta ya know!!" Doc looked up at Harry as he made his exclamation. Then the inevitable happened. Laying the bills out on the floor had seemed like a good idea at the time, until Hurricane Louie barged through the door.

"Hey guys! What'd I miss?"

The bills flew in every direction.

"God-damn it, Louie!!" Doc jumped up but Harry stayed down

279

on the floor staring at two of the twenties he had pinned to the floor with his fingers.

"Louie, sit at the table," Harry instructed while his eyes continued to scan the rows of notes.

"What for, Harry?"

"I want ya to do somethin' for me. Sit at the table."

Louie complied while Doc started laying out the bills again. Harry went over to Louie's table and handed him a single twenty, and then a separate stack of twenties. "Look through all these notes and put them in numerical order. But keep this one separate."

Harry walked over to Doc, who was trying to arrange the bills.

"Ferget that, Doc, look at this." He handed Doc the two twenties. Doc saw it right away.

"Son-of-a-bitch! Why would they do that?"

"Come on, Doc, that's the easy part! They switched the fake dough for the real stuff. Even Louie could figure that out!"

"Hey, guys some a these numbers are the same!"

"Keep lookin', you'll see a lot of em's the same. Each real bill will have an identical serial number on a counterfeit bill," Harry explained. "Doc, run downstairs, get me a couple of bags. We'll weed out all the Monopoly money, and see what we have left."

Doc returned with the cash bags a few minutes later and, as he came back in something else occurred to him.

"Harry, when did Sheinfeld go up the river?"

"Before the war started. Thirty-five or six, I think."

"And you said last night you thought these bills were how old?"

"Six months to a year, max."

Doc and Harry looked at each other.

"If Scheinfeld made these, he did it while he was still on the inside."

Harry nodded in agreement.

"I found one!" Louie yelled excitedly.

Knowing that Harry was secretive about having done time, Doc was hesitant about posing his next question. But he couldn't let it go.

"Harry, is it possible? I mean, are there art studios or something in the joint?"

"I only done two years, Doc."

Louie looked up from the table and then glanced at Doc, but remained silent.

"But it was in a federal pen. And there ain't no possibility that I know of ta have the time and materials you need ta carve plates on the inside." Harry was emphatic.

"Couldn't they have been made before he went in?"

"No way! They're soft metal. They wouldn't have kept for five or six years. Heat, humidity, general abuse. They would'a been ruined. Any little defect, a bump, a chip, would'a rendered 'em useless. Easy to trace. Besides, who the hell would you trust with a pair of plates of that quality?"

Doc sat at his desk. "They were definitely made on the inside?"

"He had backin'. I'd stake my leg on it! Someone with a helluva lotta pull. Like in the Mob, or in the government."

Doc involuntarily turned towards the window as his thoughts raced ahead of him. "Or in the department of the Treasury?" he half whispered.

Silence shrouded the room. Doc continued in a subdued voice.

"Those pricks murdered an old man because he found out they switched the money."

"Doris is right. All the rats aren't 'over there'." added Louie.

Doc continued to stare out of the window, thinking about his wife leaving him for money, his business partner's tactics for money and the motivation of the DA to stop his father at all costs as they collided in a blinding light in his mind. There it was again. That feeling in the pit of his stomach like falling off a tall building and waiting for the impact, only it never comes. But the feeling stays.

"Doc. Hey Doc!" It was Louie. "*DOC*! The phone!"

The ringing of the phone suddenly snapped him out of his trance. He reached down and picked up the receiver.

"Hello?" He spoke in a mechanical voice as the residue of the disturbing thoughts lingered in his mind.

"Doc, it's me." The soothing sound of Nikki's voice cleared the air.

"Doc . . . I just called to see . . . if we're still on for the parade." Doc was instantly alerted by the forced composure he detected in Nikki's voice. "Kate's here and she asked me to call." That was her signal to Doc that she was upset about something, but didn't want Kate to know.

"Put her on." Doc had to know if someone was in the house with them. Kate's voice would tell for sure.

"Hi, Doc! This is Katie! I'm really excited for you to take us to the parade! Mommy says there's music, clowns. All kinds a neat stuff!"

Doc sat down, relieved. "You count on it, sweetheart! I'm excited too! Put your mommy back on, okay?"

"Doc?"

"Are you alright?" he asked.

"Remember those men you mentioned? I think they were here."

"Why? Why do you think they were there?"

"I found something they might have left."

"Bring it in the morning. I'll have a look at it."

"But Doc! It's a book. A strange book, with – "

"Nikki! Bring it tomorrow! I'm sure it's nothing. See you at noon. At Woolworth's." He hung up.

Nikki had no idea what the hell the comment about Woolworth's was or why Doc down-played the importance of the black book. Not knowing about the developments of the last twenty-four hours, she also couldn't understand that Doc was just being cautious. It was a good thing, too.

+

Huddled in the cramped space of Redbone's makeshift basement office, were three of the very men Doc and Nikki sought to avoid. Mistakenly believing that Doc probably had the book, they listened in on the phone call. At least one in their company was shocked to hear that Nikki actually possessed the secret document.

"Just outta curiosity, where did you morons stash that book?" Johnson pushed away from Redbone's desk and addressed the two men who stood before him, heads bent to one side to avoid the steam pipes criss crossing the ceiling.

"We thought it'd be a good idea ta have someone ta blame it on . . . case they start a investigation."

"Case they start a investigation." Johonson mocked the agent's reply. "Your mother have any kids that lived? Case they start an investigation! So you picked *A GOD-DAMNED SECRETARY*! What the *HELL* would her *MOTIVATION* be for stealing a top secret *CODE BOOK*? Keep people from copyin' her *JELLO RECIPES*?"

"We were just try'n ta cover our asses!" The agent who had been doing all the talking sought unsuccessfully to extinguish the fuse he ignited. "Besides, how the hell did she get it?" he asked, seeking to change the subject.

"*WHO GIVES A FUCK! SHE GOT IT!*"

Redbone arrived in the basement to check the pressure in the number two boiler. He had no idea he had visitors until Johnson's little temper tantrum attracted his attention, and drew him back towards his office.

"If we don't get that book back and she goes to anybody with this, there'll be a hundred investigations. Every agency, newspaper and freakin' aspiring politician in the country will want a piece of this! There won't be a hole deep enough to hide in! Worse yet, we got two more outsiders dragged into this thing that we gotta contend with." Johnson's voice was tainted with desperation as he tried to make his cohorts understand the ramifications of their mistake.

The old metal door creaked open to reveal Redbone's frail, bent frame standing in the doorway.

"Who da hell are you people and why's you in my office?"

The dumbfounded look on the agents' faces only lasted until Johnson gave the order. "Take care of him!"

One of the lackeys grabbed the defenceless old man and pinned his arms behind his back. The other had seen one too many movies, and hit Redbone in back of the head with a pistol butt, causing him to yell out and kick wildly with his feet. His heavy work boot found a mark in the shin of the agent, who disengaged, howling and hopping around the room, both hands holding his leg.

The second agent remained occupied with restraining Redbone's arms, and that's when Johnson intervened. A punch to the jaw, followed by two vicious blows to the back of the head with his brass knuckles rendered the frail man unconscious.

The agent, who had not uttered a word until now, released Redbone, allowing him to fall to the floor and looked at Johnson.

"Looks like now we got three, huh?"

"Three what?" Johnson enquired with a puzzled look.

"Three ta contend with."

"Less than a year to retire," Johnson said to himself.

"Should we go to Woolworth's?" enquired the agent with the bruised shin.

"Yeah, good idea. We'll just split up so we can cover all hundred and twenty-nine of them in the greater New York area quicker! Fuckin' morons!"

"You wanna go after the book?"

"No. We'll wait until tomorrow. Use the parade as cover," Johnson replied.

"What about him? He ain't breathin' too good!" the agent with the bruised shin asked, pointing to Redbone. Johnson eyed Redbone's brutalised body before answering.

"Fuck him. By the time they find him we'll be back in DC with a cover story."

"And McKeowen?"

Johnson thought before answering. A smile crept across his face as he stared through the agent. "Déjà-fuckin'-vu." He uttered under his breath. The two agents exchanged glances.

"That guy's father was a prick, and his kid's a prick."

"You knew his father?"

"Yeah. I helped the DA on an operation one time to control some rogue cops. Now I get to take this prick out."

✦

Although winter appeared to have lost her way to New York City, tell-tale signs of the season encroached. The defoliated trees in front of Gracie Mansion in Carl Schultz Park waved in the late afternoon breeze.

The Mansion is normally reserved for charitable, humanitarian and social functions as opposed to hardcore, political head-banging sessions. Those are done downtown. However, the afternoon of Friday the thirteenth was a notable exception.

A single patch of brown, windswept grass was the first thing that caught Captain MacFall's eye as he stepped out of the marbled entrance into the blustery afternoon, donning his white dress gloves. Despite the fact it was the informal request of Fiorrello LaGuardia which brought him to the Mansion, he thought it prudent to wear his dress blues. Out of more than courtesy, LaGuardia accompanied him to the door.

"So can I tell the council we're on the same sheet of music?" LaGuardia sought one last confirmation.

"I understand your position, Mayor, but I must repeat myself. I'm not at liberty to discuss anything relating to any classified operations in the Third Naval District."

"Roscoe, I have to tell the city council members something! There are serious privacy issues here! I thought we . . ."

"Tell them what you like, sir. All I can say, off the record," MacFall looked LaGuardia straight in the eye, "is that I promise you there won't be a problem."

"That's all the city can ask, Captain." The mayor extended his hand. MacFall reciprocated.

"Thank you for your hospitality. Look forward to the parade tomorrow."

Captain MacFall's black 1938 Chrysler staff car pulled around to meet him and as he got in, he instructed the driver to take him back to Church Street.

To the staff driver, who had been with MacFall over three years now, the Captain seemed unusually quiet.

"Ya think the Pin Stripes'll do it on Sunday, sir?"

MacFall continued to gaze out at the bluish-grey East River. He watched a pair of river tugs as they effortlessly cut through the current, heading up river and memories of the DE's he served on and the sea-going tugs which serviced them at each liberty port flowed through his mind.

"Sorry, Eddie. I was somewhere else."

"The ball game. The papers are sayin' we could wind up with a second Murder's Row!"

"I don't know if I'd go that far. But if Gherig has a good day, there could be a lotta bookies with smiles on their faces come Sunday night." Sunday night, he realised. One day before Monday. Monday, which would be seven days since he had been in Washington and been given the seven-day deadline for the operation.

He remembered Charlie Haffenden's words: "Like pulling a Band-Aid off." MacFall made a decision.

"Eddie, what time is it?"

"Sixteen-thirty, sir"

"Belay Church Street, head for the Astoria."

"All ahead full for Hotel Astoria, aye sir." MacFall smiled at Eddie, pretending to man a ship's helm while at the steering wheel.

Traffic was accumulating, but not yet jammed, and fifteen minutes later they were cross town and pulling into the hotel car port at the front entrance.

"Put the priority tag in the windshield, Eddie and wait over there. I have no idea how long I'll be."

Eddie eyed the hot dog cart across the street. "Sir! I missed lunch. Any chance me runnin' over for a coupl'a tube steaks?"

MacFall eyed the cart as well. "Stand by. I'll take care of it."

Walking past the doorman, the Captain handed him a five dollar bill and asked him to run across the street. The doorman at first refused until he was told to keep the change. MacFall gave him Eddie's usual lunch order. Four dogs, heavy mustard and sauerkraut and two Yoohoos.

The last time Captain MacFall had seen the mezzanine suite, it was devoid of anything except some furniture and Commander Haffenden. As he opened the door this time, he was greeted by a scene which appeared to be nothing short of mayhem.

There were at least four people busy dashing back and forth across the rooms, two more at desks, busy writing away, and a line of what MacFall guessed to be operatives, waiting to see the Commander. One of the uniformed personnel sighted the Captain and immediately called out. "Attention on deck!"

Everyone momentarily stopped in their tracks, stood at attention and awaited MacFall's counter order.

"As you were!"

The room slid back into a noisy buzz. Proceeding straight to the Commander's back room, the Captain let himself in and was greeted with a picture which made his mission even more difficult then it already was.

Camouflaged by mounds of paperwork, Commander Haffenden sat at his desk, head down, all but oblivious to his surroundings. He could not see who had entered the room without permission, and assumed it was the next operative, there to give his report.

"You're supposed to wait until . . . Captain! Out slummin', sir?" Haffenden stood to greet his commanding officer.

"Quite an op you got going here, Commander. Well done."

"Thank you, sir. Things are finally on track. We're flowing pretty good. This time next week, we'll have the last of the rotating schedules worked out for the Bronx and Queens, and that'll be all five boroughs."

Haffenden was surprised to see the Captain on his home turf. This was only the second visit from his boss since the operation began. He was, however, prepared for the rough seas he was about to face. The delinquent reports he assumed the Captain was there to complain about were nearly finished, and Haffenden was confident he could fend off any attack MacFall was about to launch.

"Sir, I have the back status reports and I apologise if you got any flak from the higher-ups." Haffenden began digging through the paper mountains.

"Haff, let's take a walk," the Captain suggested.

Haffenden looked up and stopped rummaging. "Sir, it's near seventeen-hundred. I have to get the next shift of operatives out before eighteen-hundred. There are others coming in, we've got . . ." Haffenden had a bad feeling as he watched the Captain stand, signalling they were going to have a heart-to-heart, regardless of the Commander's busy schedule.

He decided that if he were to accept what ever form of bad news the Captain couriered, he would do it at his desk, in his office. "We can talk here, sir."

"Why didn't you set this up downtown? I'm not tryin' to second guess, mind you. Just curious."

"Space, prying eyes. Besides, I can get food here, got a bed in the back and a rain locker in the head. No real reason to leave."

Macfall chose his words carefully, without being condescending. "That's what I explained to the people downtown. It's that level of dedication that drove me to pick you for this project."

As the Captain began to talk in terms of 'The Project', Haffenden began to experience serious concern. "Pull the Band Aid, sir."

MacFall sat up straight in his chair. "I just came from LaGuardia's place. They've received some complaints from some influential business types concerning privacy issues."

"What the hell does that mean?"

"These guys are no dummies. They have connections, too. They know you're snooping around their places of business."

"We're snooping around wherever the trail takes us. Besides, most of the leads on that target list come straight from DC! The FBI, the Pentagon. The President's own advisory committee, fer cryin' out loud! On top of it, they all want separate reports of the findings, and they're tellin' us they don't want each other to know about it!"

"I understand your dilemma."

"Since when do local officials influence Navy policy, anyway?"

"That's not the only issue." Haffenden waited for the Captain to continue.

"This murder case is bringing unwanted focus on our existence right here in the middle of Manhattan. They feel things like little old men being dumped in the East River scare people and increase their feelings of paranoia."

"They damn well should! There's a war on, god-damn it!"

"Look!" MacFall took a breath. "It's not just him."

"What are you tellin' me?"

"Chuck, it's outta my hands." Now Haffenden sat back in his chair. A strong sense of betrayal crept over him.

"You're shuttin' us down because we're not producing?"

"I told you it's outta my hands!" The Captain was becoming increasingly irritated at the difficulty of his task.

"Why? Because a bunch of money-hungry merchants in the downtown area are scared to go out at night? This is the murder capital of the world, for fuck's sake! They'll catch the guy!"

MacFall, as an experienced executive, understood the dynamic of allowing a colleague time to adjust to bad news, and so permitted Haffenden to continue. The Commander readjusted his sights.

"We're just gettin' on track here, sir. The increase in manpower was exactly what we needed. Hell, I wouldn't be surprised if some of these contacts lasted until after the war! Some of these guys are really playin' ball here."

"How many spies ya catch, Chuck?" MacFall reluctantly reduced the argument to the numbers game.

"We're buildin', you know that. Just gatherin' momentum. It's barely been six weeks, fer Christ's sake!"

"How many?"

Haffenden sat in silence. Now MacFall entered into the convalescent stage of the mission.

"Look, Haff. You're not really being shut down. It's more like a conversion."

"Conversion? Conversion to what?"

"The Casablanca summit was an important turning point in the war. Now that we have Africa, we can turn our sights to the continent. It's not official yet, but most of the DC boys are bettin' it's gonna be Italy by way of Sicily. Some sources have already agreed to work with us to gather intel on potential landing sights."

"Where do I fit in?" Haffenden asked cautiously.

"They're calling it 'F' Section. They want you to head it up."

"Am I officially being relieved of command?" Every officer's worst nightmare. A sure dead end to a career. MacFall laughed at the suggestion.

"Relieved? Don't be stupid!" He leaned into the desk. "I'm not supposed to tell you, but you're to receive a special commendation."

"For what? Not catchin' spies?"

"Don't lose your military bearing, Commander. Not at this late stage in the game." At that exact moment Commander Haffenden made a vow to himself. Immediate retirement the day the war ended.

"Anything else I need to know?

"One more thing. I need you down at Church Street, zero seven hundred tomorrow. Report to the mail room. The new clerk will issue the remainder of the op fund. Arrange an escort, take the money to the Federal reserve on Wall Street. Find a guy named Paladin. Your contact code is 'You can't take it with you'. Go with him."

Haffenden was puzzled. "What for?"

"Accompany him to the incinerator vault and observe him burn the remainder of the fund."

Haffenden was completely lost. "Am I at liberty to ask why? There's just over twenty thousand dollars left in that op fund!"

"You're not at liberty to ask, you don't have a need to know. However, I am at liberty to tell you. DC is worried about accountability. About the possibility that if the money is sent back, somebody might start sniffing around."

"Well, why not just leave it where it is and use it for 'F' Section?"

"No need. They've already allotted funds for the new op. They're worried about how to explain the money if it went back up the chain. People would find out that the Op was . . . converted. It's an unnecessary security risk."

"When do we have the fire sale?" MacFall was pleased to hear Haffenden maintained a sense of humour.

"Cease and desist not later than midnight tomorrow. See you in my office zero eight hundred, Monday morning."

Faster than it was begun, *Operation Underworld* was laid to rest.

MacFall never told Commander Haffenden about the deadline for *Operation Underworld* he had been given the previous week in Washington.

In addition, Haffenden never received his copy of the top secret message, informing him that his op fund was suspected of having been tampered with and that an investigation was underway in connection with the disappearance of $45,000 in counterfeit bills from the US Treasury.

✦

Nikki sat bolt upright in bed. Had she dreamt the sound or was it real? The clock on the night stand read one-thirty.

There it was again. A knock on the door. Who the hell was at the door at this hour? Her mind raced. Kate! The knock came again, this time a little louder.

Her fear mounting, Nikki jumped out of bed, threw on her night gown and raced down the hallway. Passing by the front door, en route to the kitchen, she gasped as the intruder knocked again.

Frantically rummaging through the silverware drawer, Nikki found the Thanksgiving carving knife.

Standing to one side, she spoke through the door. "Who is it?" Her throat was dry and the words were difficult to form and came out as a whisper.

"It's me!" Doc's voice whispered back.

Nikki unlocked the door and opened it slowly. Still brandishing the knife, she greeted Doc. "Jesus Christ on a cross!! You scared the hell outta me!"

Doc peeked his head through the door. "I'm sorry, ma'am. We were just in the neighborhood conducting a survey, and were wondering if you happened to have any highly classified, government documents lying around the house?"

Nikki let him in. "So now I'm dating Emmet Kelly? How the hell did you get past the vestibule? I didn't ring you in!"

"Trade secret, sweetheart. You alright?"

"Nothing one of those magic teas of yours wouldn't cure! Come into the kitchen so we don't wake Kate."

She locked the door behind him and followed him into the kitchen.

"Get the book," Doc instructed and after Nikki set the kettle, she reached into the cupboard and removed the sugar bowl. Removing the lid, she held it over the sink and fished out the small black book. Handing it to Doc, he flipped through it, shaking sugar crystals out onto the table.

Nikki set the tea tray and motioned to be quiet as she led Doc into the front room. She took a seat in the bay window and clutched her tea with both hands.

"Well? Whatta you think?"

"Looks like an ordinary address book. Some sort of non-standard, internal code. Names, places, dates."

"So, whatta we do ?"

"We make a deal."

"But . . ."

"But nuthin'! We make a deal. The book for our lives back. They get it, they agree to leave us alone."

"And if they don't, we go to the press or somethin'?"

"I don't think that's gonna be an option."

"So how do we get it to them? Cops?"

"Definitely not the cops! These guys are Feds. They control the cops."

"You were a cop. Don't you have any friends left on the force?"

"Not so's you'd notice."

"What then? The mail?"

"A meet, face to face. It's the only way."

"Doc, that's risky!" As Nikki spoke, Doc realised that she was ignorant of Johnson's involvement in Ira's murder.

"I'll call one of the Treasury guys you work with. What's the name of the head guy? The creep?"

"Johnson, Robert Johnson. Doc, that guy's bad news!"

"How do I get a hold of him?"

"I don't know. He wouldn't be downtown at this hour."

"Is there a way to get him a message?"

"Call the OOD."

They went back out to the kitchen, Nikki dialled the phone and handed it to Doc.

"Third Naval District, Chief Petty Officer Badowski."

"Chief, I need to contact Treasury Agent Johnson, Robert Johnson."

"You'll have to call back at the main number, tomorrow after zero nine hundred, sir."

"It's sort of an emergency, Chief. I have some information for him."

Nikki leaned over and whispered into Doc's ear. "Tell him it's a Micky Mouse priority!"

Doc displayed a puzzled look, covered the receiver and mouthed "What?"

Nikki nudged him in the ribs and whispered loudly, "Tell him!"

"Chief Badowski, this message is a Micky Mouse Priority!" Doc spoke with the authority of the Joint Chief himself.

"Sir, Agent Johnson can be reached at Murray Hill-7-9232. That's his home phone sir. Please treat it with discretion."

"Rest assured, Chief, I will."

Doc replaced the receiver and smiled at Nikki.

"None'a your shit, you! I don't make them up! They come down from DC."

"Wanna have some fun?"

"Whatta you gonna do?"

"What time is it?"

"Nearly two. Whatta you gonna do? Tell me!"

Doc dialled the number the Chief gave him, listened as someone picked up, and Doc quickly hung up.

"What the hell was that?" Nikki asked.

"Musta been the wrong number. A woman answered."

"Probably his wife. Or than again, maybe not."

Doc redialled and this time it was an angry male voice that answered.

"Who the hell is this?"

"Agent Johnson?"

There was a brief pause on the other end. "McKeown." Johnson recognised the voice from the wire taps as well as the street encounter.

"Actually it's the Eve Arden Lady! I understand your supply of roll-on asshole is running low. Time to reorder!"

"Figured I'd hear from you. You're a real wise-ass, aren't you, McKeown?" Johnson understood the advantage of not letting on he was caught off-guard. "I hear your old man was a wise-ass, too!"

Doc suddenly felt a surge of anger roll over him as Johnson turned it back on him.

"Sounds like you lost your sense of humour, McKeowen."

"You want your book, quisling?"

"I'm listening." Johnson drew satisfaction from hitting a nerve.

"This book is like penicillin. We meet tomorrow, I give you the book then, like a venereal disease, you go away."

"Your place or mine, hero?"

"Somewhere public, just the two of us." Doc looked at Nikki.

"A museum?" she whispered.

"Hayden Planetarium. There's a one o'clock show."

"I'll be there, hero."

"And Johnson, don't waste your time wreckin' my office. It ain't there."

"Aw, gee, McKeowen! You shoulda told me earlier. Now I feel bad!"

It was worth a try, thought Doc.

Johnson continued: "By the way, that Federal agent you assaulted? He has a wife and kid to feed."

"Well, that's good news. 'cause now he has somebody ta feed him. I guess that puts you a little short a players, don't it, Bob?"

"We'll manage! You just show up, Doc."

"You'll know me. I'll be down front wearin' – "

"Yeah, I know. A skirt! It's your day tomorrow, isn't it? The day when you Irish wear skirts?"

"I'm not Irish," Doc said in a calm voice.

"Scotts, Irish, all the same to me. Buncha worthless drunks! Same as your old man."

Doc hung up, slightly pissed off at letting Johnson get to him.

"What'd he say?" Nikki asked. Doc realised for the first time that he was compelled to smile whenever he looked at her.

"He said, 'Happy St. Patrick's Day'."

Nikki took Doc's hand and led him back out to the bay window. As they sat down and looked down onto Mercer Street, sporadic snow flurries sparkled in the lamplight.

"Should I tell Kate we're not gonna make the parade?"

"Don't even think about it! The parade doesn't start until two. I'll drop the book off at one and still have plenty of time to meet you, Kate and Louie's family by two."

"Louie's family?"

"Sure. You'll like them. They're great people."

"I like Louie, and I suppose it would be nice for Kate to be around some new people."

Nikki never saw it coming, but once Doc sprang it on her, she was angry and flattered all at once. "His wife is real nice, too. As a matter of fact, I was thinking . . . maybe to save some time in the morning, you and Kate could spend the night at Louie's."

"To save some time? You're crazy! It's two a.m.! Kate's sound asleep!"

"Look, these guys are not pulling any punches. It would be

better if you and Kate were some place else for a day or so. By tomorrow afternoon, this'll all be over and we can have our lives back."

"Doc, I don't know. Stayin' in a stranger's house, Kate in a strange bed . . ." Nikki was startled when the downstairs buzzer rang. "Who the hell is that?"

Doc peered out the window. "Well, whatta ya know? It's Louie."

"You son-of-a-bitch!" She raised her hand. Doc caught her by the wrist and gave her a quick kiss on the lips.

"That's five cents in the swear jar!"

The buzzer rang again.

Chapter Twenty-Four

"Winthrop Pinchnell of Pinchnell Real Estate is doing his patriotic duty. Winth . . . Mr Pinchnell has agreed to allow the use of his empty lot at the corner of Hudson and West 12th Street for tomorrow afternoon's rubber drive. So get those old tyres, tubes and garden hoses down to West 12th and Hudson, tomorrow afternoon from noon until six, and 'Help stun the Hun!' And remember, if you're looking for a store, a home or even an apartment, Pinchnell's will help you 'pinch' the most real estate for your dollar!"

Doc rolled over and averted his eyes from the bright winter sun flooding the room. For the second time that week he'd spent the night sleeping on his desk. His radio case was broken, and the speaker hung by a wire, but the black, enamelled Emerson still operated.

He had considered renting a room uptown the night before, but reasoned that they would have searched his office and that they knew he wouldn't be stupid enough to carry the book with him. So, being sure that Nikki and Kate were safely tucked away at Louie's, Doc decided it was okay to return to Christopher Street.

". . . And finally, this update from the Provincial Chinese capital of Canton. The Chinese Ministry reports that Chan Khai Shek's Liberation Army has halted the Japanese Imperial forces . . ." Doc glanced around the room.

Whether or not Johnson and his goon squad actually searched the office for the book was questionable. What was clear, however, was that they left their mark. Not a single stick of furniture remained intact. Files littered the room, all the trophies

297

were broken and Doc's cot had been slashed apart.

It wasn't until he finished his futile search for Ira's file, that Doc saw the piece that didn't fit the pattern.

There, speared onto the wooden partition with a pearl handled stiletto, was the picture of his father. The knife was carefully stuck between the eyes. He pulled it out of the wall, laid the picture on his desk and put the knife in his pocket. Johnson mentioned his father during their phone conversation: why? What could he possibly know about his father? Doc decided it was probably through the publicity of the case that Johnson knew, and was only using the information to scutch him.

Kicking a path through the debris, Doc made his way to the sink.

As he began to shave, he felt uncomfortable at the thought that his friends had been sucked into this mess. He then wondered what Johnson's next move would be. One thing was for sure, there was no chance he was going to let anyone walk away from this. However, with Nikki out of sight, Doc bought himself some time to form a plan. He had three hours.

Halfway through his shave, the phone rang, and Doc immediately wondered who the hell could be calling. Louie knew not to call until he heard from Doc and Nikki was with Louie. The options narrowed. It must have been Johnson. Maybe he wanted to change the meet or buy time to set his trap. Doc let it go for five rings before he decided to pick up.

"Calling to gloat about your handiwork, asshole?" Doc asked as he surveyed the damage.

"No! Calling to warn you about this treasury character, dumbshit!"

"Sullivan! What the hell do you want?"

"It's Detective Sergeant Sullivan and I already told you what I want! I don't know what kinda shit you got yourself into, but it's pretty god-damned deep, boy-o!"

"What the hell you talking about?"

"A patrolman from the thirty-fifth saw J. Edgar Hoover himself in Central Park with this treasury clown last week and now I catch wind you're goin' ta meet him up at the planetarium!"

"And here I thought they jumped me, wrecked my office and murdered my client by mistake."

"Sounds like they were on the right track wreckin' your office and kickin' your ass. Who was this client ya got murdered?"

Did Sullivan know, or was he fishing? "Fuck you, Sullivan! Why are you callin'? And make it the Reader's Digest version, I got a date!"

"I'm callin' 'cause I promised your father I'd keep an eye on you. But I didn't promise him I'd lose my job for you. So now you come clean, or I'll send a squad car over and we'll talk about this dead client down here! If you have knowledge about a murder you're required by law to come forward. By the way, your licences up to date?" Doc was too tired and irritated to care about Sullivan's threat. "You got no friends in this department, McKeowen. And most of 'em would throw a ceilidh if you got dusted. So I shouldn't even be talkin' to you!"

"Stop it, will ya? I'm gettin' all misty eyed!"

"You're a regular wise-ass, you know that?"

"Yeah. Apparently word's out."

"I don't know what the connection is, McKeowen, but you're running with the big dogs now. This ain't no divorce case!"

"Thanks for the update, Sully. I'll be in touch." Sullivan continued to rant as Doc replaced the receiver on the hook. "This just keeps gettin' better!"

Sullivan took himself off the drug raid detail the day Doc's father was killed. So much for the 'promised your father' spiel. If Sullivan didn't know about Ira, why did he call? Whatever it was he called to tell Doc, he was torn between telling him and the consequences to himself if he did set Doc wise.

Doc finished washing up, put on his bomber jacket and ball cap and left, not bothering to turn off the radio.

"Here's a tip for you parade-goers out there. If you're packing up the family to go watch the big event, dress warm! That beautiful white stuff you see outside your window right now is going to pick up by parade time, and the Central Park

Meteorological Center says there might be a little accumulation." The hourly NBC chimes sounded, signalling it was ten o'clock.

The *Front Page* was closed and Doc had to use his key to let himself out through Harry's. He thought that unusual as Harry didn't normally celebrate holidays.

"Doc! I been waitin' for your call! What's the plan? Where do we meet?"

Louie's excitement made it more difficult for Doc to give his rookie partner the bad news. Doc had ducked into Feinstein's Druggists for a hamburger and egg cream breakfast before the big game, and was calling from a phone booth in the back.

"Sorry, Mancino. You're not in on this one."

"Doc! You gotta be shittin' me!" Louie was devastated.

"Look, Louie." Doc chose his words. "This is not what you signed on for. Not your run-of-the-mill PI stuff. This is serious, nasty, the 'we'll put your kids and grandmother in prison, drain you dry and make sure you can't ever earn a living again' type shit! The kinda stuff that makes Tojo and Tokyo Rose look like Roy Rogers and Dale Evans, ya follow?"

"Gimme a break, Doc! If you're tryin' ta scare me outta this, it ain't workin'!"

"Louie! Listen-to-my-words! You have a wife and kids! There are licensing issues here!'"

"Like what licensing issues?"

"Like you ain't got one! Look, I need you to watch out for Nikki and Kate. You have no reason to do this Am I gettin' through to you?"

"Jesus, Doc! What better OJT? As for my wife and kids, Doris told me that no matter what happens I have to stay with you until this thing is over. And if I gotta choose ta risk my life or argue with Doris, no fuckin' contest! This is my chance of a lifetime. And if you're so worried about loved ones, why are you doing it? Why not let the cops handle it?"

The question about loved ones had never occurred to Doc.

"Because, they killed a client. They killed a client and someone I care about might be next. It's gettin' personal."

"Care about, or love?"

"Don't push it, asshole! I need you in the back field in case I blow it."

"Aw, c'mon, Doc! If we don't come out on top of this, it's back to garbage trucks for me. Besides, I already got my own brass knuckles!"

"You're not gonna listen to me no matter what I say, are you, Bonehead?"

"Not a chance in hell. Doc!" There was a long pause on Doc's end of the line as he realised it was safer to know where Louie was and what he was doing than to risk him meandering about when things got thick.

"Make sure Doris stays in the house with the girls, and doesn't even think about leaving until she hears from us! You got that?" The 'us' part was all Louie needed to hear.

"Roger that, Green Hornet!"

"Don't start that shit. This is serious."

"Doc, don't lose your sense of humour on me, huh?"

"Get over to the office, and don't move until you hear from me! I'm meetin' this Bozo at one."

"I know, at the Hayden."

Doc thought about Sullivan's call earlier. "What, did somebody take out an ad in *The Times*, fer Christ's sake?"

"Nikki told me."

"All right, get over to the office. I'll call and give you an update as soon as I made the drop. And Louie . . ." Doc hated to say it, but given Louie's propensity for not being in the right place at the right time, he felt obligated. "I might get myself up the creek on this one, savvy? You need to be there! Got it? Kato."

"Roger that, Doc! Count on me. And Doc?"

Doc sensed Louie was going to say something sentimental. "What?"

"If you die, can I have your desk?"

"You're a sick son-of-a-bitch, Mancino. You know that?"

✦

"Hey, Al. Get a load'a this!" The gate guard perched in his armoured tower high above the fence-line called over to his partner as a black, chrome-plated Chrysler limousine pulled up outside the steel gates of Great Meadows.

"Three guesses who that's for, and the first two don't count," the second guard replied.

From their vantage points, the guards continued to watch as the limo pulled up next to the granite wall beside the gate and Meyer Lansky got out, followed by Socks Lanza.

Both were dressed in silk suits and Lanza carried a clothes bag and a pair of brown wingtips. The two made their way through the gates with no resistance from the sentries, who knew why they were there. In fact, by way of every newspaper in the country the entire New York penal system knew why they were there.

Lucky Luciano had made parole.

An hour later, dressed in his new, charcoal grey suit and shoes, Lucky, escorted by Lansky and Lanza, walked through the gate a free man, sort of.

Even though the parole board granted him parole, they were ever mindful of their political careers. The board, the judge and the Governor attached severe restrictions. Actually, only one restriction. Get the hell out of the country.

Ironically, it was DA Hogan, the Third Naval District and Commissioner Lyons who were directly responsible for Lucky's favourable parole decision. Despite the fact that he had up to forty years remaining on his greatly inflated sentence, he was out of prison because of the aforementioned bureaucrat's refusal to co-operate with the parole board when questioned about Lucky's contribution to the war effort. Instead of being told that Lucky had or had not made a contribution to his adopted land, the parole board investigators were essentially told it was none of their business. So, by way of showing their authority, and the fact that they had no sense of humour about being told to piss off, they set Lucky free.

"Do you, Charles Luciano, understand and concur with all the conditions of your parole as set forth by the New York State

Parole Commission?" The tall, lanky administrator, one of the two who would accompany Lucky to New York City and keep him under close eye until Monday morning, spoke mechanically as he filled out yet another document for Lucky to sign.

"Sure, I understand. You want me to take my boys and go home."

"Sign here, please."

Lucky signed and without waiting for his copy of the papers, walked out of prison. The two administrators followed the new limousine in their state issued, 1934 Ford.

"So how long you got?" Lanza asked Lucky as they made their way down the mountain road.

"Forty-eight hours. Then they get ta watch me leave."

"These rat bastards gonna be with us until Monday morning?"

"They might hang around, but sometime tomorrow they'll take a powder and some INS guys'll show up. They're the ones gotta put me on the boat."

"The boat? Why don't you fly, Boss? You could go first class! We could a bought you a ticket!" Socks asked.

"They're the ones kicking me out. Let them pay for the ticket!" Lucky looked out the window at the world he hadn't seen for six years. Smiling, he added, "I'll take a plane when I come back."

✦

The parade route was scheduled to start south of the American Museum of Natural History, a structure which dwarfed the adjacent Hayden Planetarium situated next door to the museum. The early afternoon crowd were dressed in heavy, winter clothing, and snow continued to lightly coat the pavement as wind sporadically made its way up the avenue.

McKeowen cautiously approached from the 78th Street side and slowly walked up Columbus Avenue, to the back of the museum complex. At 81st Street, across from the park, he took full advantage of the steady stream of spectators making their way down Central Park West by peering around the corner. He noticed that there were an inordinate number of police in the area, but put it down to crowd control. To play it safe, he decided to enter the Hayden through the museum, via the annex hallway.

"Excuse me, miss?" Doc was at the coat check just inside the door, and a young girl came to the counter.

"Yes, sir?" Over her shoulder Doc could see the nearly full Lost and Found bin. He shifted to a thick Jersey dialect.

"Miss, I was here last month, on a field trip with some of my students, and . . . well, I'm embarrassed to say it, but I was so tired, I think I left my overcoat here."

A few minutes later, Doc strolled through the museum annex wearing a grey tweed overcoat on top of his leather jacket, and approached the lobby of the planetarium. He stood there for a few minutes, glancing around the room as he pretended to read the programme until he picked out two of Johnson's stooges. One he recognised and the other was new. Johnson had brought reinforcements. It was five minutes to one, and after assessing his situation, he proceeded directly into the planetarium theatre where the crowd were taking their seats.

Doc took a seat in the front row and removed the overcoat, letting it fall back onto his seat. No sooner did he have his arms free when two men sat down, one on either side of him. The one on his right was Johnson, the other was another new face.

Doc looked at all four of the exits of the circular room and saw that each was manned by an agent accompanied by a policeman.

"Jeez, Bob, how many assholes does one guy need?"

"Hi McKeowen, how's the bedroom peepin' business? I hear Sammon is doin' real well uptown. Even lives in a penthouse now."

"I really want you to know how flattered I am that you take such an interest in my personal life. But let me ask you something. How does it feel to murder a defenceless mail clerk in his eighties?"

"I don't know, Mac. You tell me."

Johnson reached into his breast pocket and dropped a piece of paper into Doc's lap. As he read it, Doc realised what Sullivan was too cowardly to tell him. It was an arrest warrant with Doc's name on it, for the murder of Ira Birnbaum. It was hard to contain himself, but Doc focused on knocking Johnson off balance as soon as possible.

"And just in case you're thinkin' about any local connections, you'll notice it's a Federal warrant."

A middle-aged couple holding tickets approached the seats where Doc and the two agents were sitting. The man double-checked the ticket numbers and then looked to Johnson. The tourist adjusted his glasses as he spoke in a mid-western dialect.

"Excuse me, I believe you're in our seats."

Johnson looked up at the man and smiled. "Hit the bricks, Mortimer. These seats are taken." The couple exchanged glances.

"Excuse me, sir but we paid for those seats!" the man insisted. Johnson flashed his badge.

"Tough shit, Henry! Looks like you either stand or go look at the dinosaurs! Now, get the hell outta here before I run you and the misses in for loitering!"

The wife tugged at her husband's arm and they walked away. Doc called after them, smiled and waved. "Welcome to New York!"

The house lights began to dim and an older man stood at the podium which was off-centre of the amphitheatre.

"Guess this means the deal is off?" Doc held up the warrant.

"Oh no, we still got a deal. You give me my book and I'll think about speakin' to the judge so you don't get the chair. But I can't make any promises. That young DA over in Brooklyn is makin' a pretty big deal over this murder." Johnson leaned in to Doc in mock emphasis of his point. "Rumour has it he's talkin' about goin' for governor."

In the centre of the room, two trap doors opened up and a large, black object began to rise above floor level. It gave the appearance of a six foot metal ant, freckled all over with white dots as it slowly came to life. It was the Zeiss projector. Doc saw his cue.

"This little black book must be pretty important, huh?"

"Where is it?" Johnson didn't want to play any more.

"You get the book, you leave everyone alone!"

"Otherwise what? You're gonna give it to the press? The papers have been notified that a top secret document has been stolen by a murder suspect, and if anything surfaces, they're to notify me personally. Any other clever moves, rookie?"

"Always one step ahead, huh, Bob?"

"I get my book, and you don't face espionage charges along with premeditated murder. Last chance, hero, where is it?"

The smile Doc had been wearing evaporated from his face as he hung his head. Putting his hand over his mouth, he nodded at the projector, just as the show's presenter began his lecture about the wonders of the nighttime winter sky.

"Taped underneath," he said to Johnson. Johnson looked at McKeowen and then at the projector.

"C'mon, I'll show you," Doc offered. Johnson slapped his hand on Doc's chest and pushed him back into the seat.

"No! You sit there, and don't even think about moving!" He turned to the other agent. "He's under arrest. If he moves, shoot him!"

Brandishing his badge, Johnson walked over to the astronomer presenting the lecture and ordered him to stop the show, while the back-up cops and agents closed ranks in front of the exits. By now, it was obvious to everyone in the house that there was some kind of disturbance down front and Johnson was being showered with assorted cat-calls and abuse which temporarily distracted him, until he yelled back at the crowd to be quiet, this was a police matter.

At the same time, the other agent produced a pair of handcuffs and ordered McKeowen to put his hands behind his back. Doc complied while judging the distance to the Zeiss projector to be about ten yards. The presenter's podium looked to be about twice that, and when Johnson momentarily turned his back while giving orders to the speaker, Doc stood, hands still behind his back, gripping the overcoat off the seat back.

One moment the agent was looking at his handcuffs, opening them, the next moment everything was black. Doc had him covered in the heavy garment, punching furiously until the agent offered no more resistance, and fell to the floor. The crowd whistled and began to clap. This caught the attention of Johnson who was so affronted by McKeowen's audacity that he saw red.

Charging at Doc, who was scanning the room after finishing punch-bag practise on the agent, he ran at full speed, his hat flying off and his open coat flapping behind him. Johnson couldn't have done Doc a bigger favour.

Doc stood perfectly motionless, poised as if to catch Johnson as he attacked. Instead, at the last second, Doc side-stepped the charging bull and grabbed hold of him as he flew past, pushing Johnson as hard as he could, headfirst into the steps leading up the aisle.

The crowd let out a tremendous cheer, and Doc made his break for the base of the projector, between the trap doors. As the cops and agents scurried down the aisles to converge on the centre of the theatre, Johnson rolled over, rubbing his head to tumultuous applause, while looking around, trying to focus on the room.

Running at full speed, Doc dived to the marble floor and slid through the open trap doors into the darkness below. After getting to his feet, Johnson regained his focus and started shouting orders.

"You two, down the hole, now! Berryman! Take a cop and search the projector!" Then he turned to the presenter. "You, perfessor! Where does that hole lead to?"

Doc was learning the answer to that question as they spoke. The hall beneath the lifting device for the projector was barely wide enough for one man to walk through, bent over. Originally designed for repair access only, it was unlit and showed no signs of ending. Doc could hear the two men following him stumbling around in the dark, trying to light a cigarette lighter.

He guessed he was under the annex passageway and assumed there must be an access panel somewhere. Suddenly, Doc felt a wall in front of him with his foot. He systematically felt right and left. More walls. It was a dead end. The sounds behind him grew louder as he quickly ran his hands up and down all three walls, while above he could hear the other agents and policemen running through the annex.

Finally, he felt an iron latch. Lifting it as slowly as he could to avoid unnecessary noise, he pushed open the narrow steel hatch and peered through to the other side. A short iron ladder, embedded in the wall, led up to a grating in the museum floor.

"I see light!" The voice behind him signalled he was spotted. Slamming the door hard, he braced his foot against the adjoining wall and pulled out as hard as he could on the latch of the handle. The latch bent, not much, but enough to keep the handle from being able to slide open. The men behind the door rattled it furiously but couldn't open it.

Back inside the planetarium, a very annoyed crowd were being told that the show had been cancelled, and refunds would be afforded. The Zeiss projector revealed no little black book, and so was lowered and the trap doors were closed and locked.

Up on the lobby level, the men's toilet door slowly opened and Doc stuck his head out, looking up and down the hall. He saw a welcome sight – a bank of phone booths just outside the ladies' toilets only yards from the main exit. Time to call for back-up.

Once inside a booth, he unscrewed the overhead light and dialled the office. He could get out and lie low until Louie showed up with a cab. The phone continued to ring. And ring, and ring.

"God-damn it, Mancino! You better be dead or dying!"

"He's in here!" Through the glass of the double folding doors, Doc could see a cop's uniform, and an arm pointing into the phone booth.

The cop grabbed at the door handles and Doc followed suit. He resisted letting the officer open the doors just long enough to establish a rhythm, and as the cop gave one determined mighty pull, Doc released the handles, trapping the officer's right hand between the doors as they folded open. The cop yelled. Doc punched him twice in the stomach, and closed the doors so he could collapse onto the floor, gasping for breath.

With no hope of back-up, and the lobby crowd now swollen with the ranks of the planetarium people, Doc reckoned the main exit was a good bet. The parade was due to start in less than half an hour, so the streets should be equally as mobbed.

Once again, Doc donned his Negro League baseball cap and tried to blend in. The crowd ebbed and flowed around the twin Brontosaurii mounted on their bronze replicated landscape, displayed in the center of the massive lobby. Doc could see the sunlight peering through the large brass doors as he approached them. He cautiously looked around; no cops, no agents.

Then Doc hit the floor, hands sprawled in front of him. Shit! He'd been tackled from behind. He was able to roll over and see the cop who tackled him removing his billy club from its holster. Things switched to fast-forward.

The cop swung and Doc rolled left and the hardwood club struck the marble floor. Doc pinned the arm holding the club to the floor and climbed onto the cop's back. Holding the officer by the hair, Doc slammed his face into the floor and the fight was over. Out of breath, soaked in sweat, he looked up. The exit was only ten feet away.

As he rose to his feet and looked around, he was struck in the back of the head and fell to the floor. Doc kept waiting for unconsciousness to overtake him, but it didn't. Instead, he rolled over onto his back and looked up. He recognised the agent who was swinging down hard with the cop's billy club towards his face. Doc instinctively moved to block the blow, and the full force was taken by his right forearm. He knew instantly that his arm was broken.

Strange how you notice insignificant details of your surroundings when you're scared, thought Doc. He focused on the polished marble floor. Then turned to the walls and ceiling. He thought about the great times he'd spent here as a kid and how for the longest time he'd vowed to be an archaeologist in a far away place, and dig for dinosaur bones. Then things slammed into focus.

Amazingly, the agent wasn't swinging any more. He was standing upright calling to other police and agents. Doc seized the moment. Kicking the agent's feet out from under him, he watched as feet flew in one direction and the Billy club in another. The bone-crunching thud when his head hit the floor, and the agent writhing in agony holding his lower back, told Doc he had bought more time.

Doc struggled to his feet, one knee at a time, cradling his arm, and continued to make his way to the door. The pain surged up his back and into his head as he made his way through the crowd. His brain on high alert, he pushed the door open with his left shoulder and stepped out into the sunlight. The cold, fresh air helped to clear his head and he was compelled to take the stairs one at a time, holding his broken arm close to his chest.

Leaving the danger of the museum and entering the carnival atmosphere of the street was surrealistic. In contrast to the relative dark and quiet of the museum, everything outside was colourful and busy, like a Dali painting. A clown across the street stood against the Central Park wall selling balloons, dozens of men in kilts made their way south to the parade route, and women in varied costumes accompanied them as kids scurried in all directions. Doc tried to focus on making it into the park to hail a cab.

Crossing Central Park West was easy as traffic was blocked off further north to accommodate the parade. Weaving between a marching band who were just forming ranks and some shivering baton twirlers, Doc heard a voice from behind.

"Hey, asshole!"

As he stood in the middle of the sidewalk, across the street, Doc slowly turned and saw a treasury agent standing on the sidewalk behind him. Something was wrong. This fat, slobby guy didn't look like Johnson or any of the other agents. As the agent slowly removed his top coat, Doc stared in disbelief.

The guy's chest rose to touch his jaw, and he had no discernible neck. His biceps nearly exploded out of his sleeves and Doc thought that he looked like an Aryan genetic experiment gone amok. It was one of the few times McKeowen regretted not carrying a gun.

Doc decided that, under the circumstances, there was only one reasonable course of action. He took a deep breath, held his broken arm, looked around . . . and ran like hell.

Through the crowd and up the sidewalk, trying desperately to make it to the park wall, he scurried on the icy walk. *Maybe I could lose him in the undergrowth. Yeah, the bare, winter, defoliated undergrowth! Shit!* As he reached the wall, Doc heard a sound like raw meat slapping the pavement.

Just as he got one leg over the low granite wall, a woman screamed and he looked to his left in time to see a couple of dozen balloons floating into the air and the balloon-selling clown frantically administering non-stop punches to no-neck. The agent was on his knees, but the clown, now with a stranglehold on the agent's necktie, kept punching. Blood spurted from his face, and on the fifth or sixth punch, the unconscious agent fell face first onto the pavement with a sickening thwack. Blood pooled around his face.

The clown was out of breath, propped against the park wall for support when a panicky woman made her way through the onlookers and ushered her kid away from the scene.

"It's okay, lady. He just tried to steal the kid's balloon." Doc squinted, stared and made his way over to the clown. In between gasps, he spoke to Doc. "I have got to get another set of these!" He held up his right hand covered in blood and brass knuckles. "Hey Doc! How's it hangin'?"

"Louie! What the . . . ?" Louie's big clown feet flopped over to Doc.

"I tailed you all the way from downtown! Never even seen me, didja?" Doc smiled and fell back against a soot-stained bench, holding his arm. "Doc! You okay?"

"I think I got a busted arm, Louie." Doc looked very pale. "We gotta get outta here before the rest of the goons show up."

Louie helped his friend over the short perimeter wall into the park and they kept to the narrow footpaths snaking through the shrubs and trees. By the time they reached Belvedere Lake ten minutes later, Louie noticed Doc was slowing down.

"Here, Doc, sit here." Louie brushed the light, powdery snow from a bench and sat Doc down facing the frozen lake. He walked over to a garbage basket and removed the rest of his clown outfit, stuffing it in the receptacle. He put the collar up on his coat and returned to Doc.

"Louie . . ." Doc inquired in between pants, "why'd ya keep hittin' that guy so many times?"

"He wouldn't go down!" Louie put Doc's collar up as well, then adjusted his ball cap. "Besides, it's jocks like him that are always yacking about how bowling ain't a real sport. They piss me off." Louie rubbed his hands together. It was getting colder, with a slight wind and the snow was now falling in big, wet flakes and starting to stick.

"Hey, Doc, you want some coffee, or you want to push on to the hospital? Lenox Hill is only about six or eight blocks away."

"Sure thing, Kato," came Doc's weak reply. Louie smiled and looked over at his friend. He did his best to conceal his horror as he saw the back of the bomber jacket was covered in blood that was oozing from the back of Doc's head. Doc slowly closed his eyes and slipped into unconsciousness.

Chapter Twenty-Five

Treasury agent Berryman dashed out of the taxi even before it came to a full stop in front of number 90 Church Street. Flashing the night sentry his credentials, he went directly upstairs to the Department of the Treasury office, where Johnson and two other agents were packing up.

"They found him!" Berryman announced as he burst through the door.

Johnson was taking a framed certificate off the wall and turned towards Berryman with a smile. "Where?"

"They think he was taken to Lenox Hill Hospital!"

"Huh, Park Avenue. He didn't make it very far, must be hurt pretty bad. That's a good thing." Johnson nonchalantly turned back to packing and placed the framed DA's special commendation into a box. The other agents resumed their tasks as well.

Berryman had a puzzled look on his face. "Well? Aren't we gonna go get him?" he asked.

Johnson didn't turn, just kept working. "What for? Cops know where he is. He's hospitalised, where the hell's he goin'? Besides, our job is done. They'll arrest him, he'll spend one to two years tied up in court, that's if he can afford a good lawyer, then the rest of his life in jail."

"But there's no evidence he did it. What if he walks?"

"Walks? Come back to Kansas, Dorothy! Guilty until proven innocent. Plus the publicity around this thing. The cops know he did it, the DA will take it from the cops, make sure he gets the right judge, the rest is history. Even if he gets a good lawyer, he can't fight the system from inside a cell. End of story."

"Hey Boss, what about the money?" One of the other agents was holding a small leather carrying case as he spoke to Johnson.

"How much is left?"

"Little over eighteen grand."

"Divvy it up five ways. Give me Robbie's cut, I'll take care of it. The rest of you. . ." The agents stopped what they were doing and paid attention. "Every man is responsible for himself. That not only means the money, but your alibis, and everything else. From the time you walk out of this office, you're on your own. Questions?"

Their silence signalled they were in agreement. Johnson turned back to Berryman.

"You reschedule the travel arrangements?"

"Yeah, here." He reached into his breast pocket, took out a thick envelope and opened it.

"This is your plane ticket. Your wheels are up at eight-thirty. You guys are goin' out by train, nine forty-five. All separate cars." He dealt out train tickets to the other agents as he spoke. "I'll follow tomorrow by car. We meet back on F Street Monday morning, and go back to work."

"Last chance. Questions, comments, snide remarks?" No one spoke. "Gentlemen, it's been a slice." Johnson headed for the door.

        +

As evening settled in, the glitter of the falling snow caused the trees, greens and lake to take on a magical, winter wonderland ambience. The view across Central Park East from the tall office buildings and apartment houses revealed a fairytale quality not often seen in a wartime metropolis. The serenity was momentarily interrupted by the flashing red light of a Cadillac ambulance and the shrill echo of its siren resonated throughout the neighbourhood as it made its way down the avenue.

The side doors of the vehicle were lettered in gold leaf and red enamel, *Lenox Hill Hospital, NYC, NY*.

"When the hell you think you're gonna see a machine ta monitor the human heart inside a ambulance? And besides standin' on it to reach high places, what we gonna do with it?" The ambulance driver spoke with the courage of his convictions. His partner, slumped down in his seat gazing out the window, answered with the same amount of intensity.

"If we vote at the union meeting to take the pay cut, and let them institute their new training programme, we'll know how to use the machine!"

"You're dreamin', Carlos! We ain't doctors! We drive a meat wagon, dat's it! Pick 'em up and drop 'em off. Period! It's simple. All you gotta do is think about it. We ain't paid, trained or supposed to save nobody's lives!"

"I got somethin' for you to think about! Think about all them medics and Navy corpsmen coming back after the war. All that shit they seen and done! Watcha you think? They're gonna go back to deliverin' milk and bread?" The driver signalled his rejection with a smirk.

The ambulance pulled up to the emergency department and unloaded the patient. The blood-soaked blanket which covered the patient's face horrified several people in the waiting room as the gurney was wheeled down the hall to the morgue's holding area. Two people in the waiting area took no notice at all.

Nikki and Louie stood in the back corner of the room, pretending to drink their coffee. After what seemed to be an eternity, a doctor, who appeared older than his years, found the duo and told them Doc was awake and asking to see them.

"Which one of you two checked me in here? The cops are searchin' every hospital from the Bronx to Coney Island!" was Doc's way of saying hello as they entered the room. Nikki was embarrassed and started to answer until Louie put his hand on her arm and stepped forward.

"You got seven stitches in your head, your arm is broke in two places and they gave you two pints of blood. You passed out, fer Christ's sake! What were you gonna do? Go home and take an aspirin with a whiskey chaser, Doctor Mayo?"

Doc closed his eyes and put his head back on the pillow. "Shit, Louie! I'm sorry! I'm a little pissed off about that son-of a-bitch gettin' one over on me."

"We used a fake name," Louie reassured Doc.

"*We*? Do I want to hear this one?"

Louie launched into the story with a smirk of pride. "We told them you guys were married. You got in fight over her, with your brother-in-law. He's a Jar Head and he's pissd off 'cause you ain't in uniform. Ya bum!" Doc fought back an agonised smile. "Your name's O'Malley. Should be ashamed of yourself, not doin' your bit!"

Nikki felt obligated to interject. "If you don't like it, we can fly to Vegas and have it annulled, Mr O'Malley."

"So it's a conspiracy!"

"How ya feelin', cowboy?" Nikki put on her brave face. What she really wanted to know was, if Doc was going to be stupid enough to go after Johnson.

Doc pointed to his head with his right arm wrapped in a thick cast. "Except for these little guys inside my head pounding away with sledgehammers, I don't feel too bad."

"Just pretend it's another hangover," Louie consoled Doc as he helped himself to Doc's Jello-o. Nikki moved over and sat on the side of the bed and Doc sensed the impending tone of the conversation and told Louie to go look for a nurse.

"But Doc, I'm married! Besides, you got a buzzer hanging right there next to – "

"Louie! Why don't you . . ."

Louie copped on when he realised Nikki was no longer sitting, but lying on the bed. "I'll go find a nurse."

"Thank you, Louie," Doc said as he turned back towards Nikki.

"Doc, I know you want to go after him . . ." Nikki spoke hesitantly for fear of how Doc might interpret her words. "But this guy is worse than bad news, he's evil incarnate. There's no way they can prove you killed Ira, 'cause you didn't do it. Plus, we know about the phoney money scam, we can peg him on that!

Doc, what I'm tryin' to say is . . ."

"I know what you're tryin' ta say, baby, and it means a lot. But if I don't find him, he sure as hell will find me. He'll duck down ta DC for awhile, but he ain't gonna let me walk away. And that means he has to deal with you, too. I can't let that happen. That's what I'm tryin' ta say. In my own pathetic, clumsy way."

Doc smiled and put a hand on Nikki's face. She leaned forward and kissed him. He forgot about the pain in his head as he held her with his good arm. Just as they were about to kiss again Louie burst into the room and ran around the bed to peer out of the window.

"What's the matter, you piss the nurses off, too?" Doc asked.

Louie continued to look out the window. "Doc, I got good news and bad news. The good news is we still got two or three minutes." Louie did a good job of concealing his excitement.

"Till what?" Doc slid off the bed and stood there.

"Till a whole shit load'a cops comes bustin' in through the door." Doc reached for Nikki with his good arm and took her hand. "They don't know about Louie, where he lives," he told her urgently. "Go there, stay there. Wait for me to call. If I call you from any place other than jail, you'll know I'm okay! Got it?"

Louie threw Doc his clothes and Doc began to dress quickly.

"But Doc, what if . . ."

"We're outta time, baby. Get outta here now, go down to the waiting room, sit there, read a magazine like you're waitin' on somebody and wait till it blows over, then just walk out through the back door."

"You ready, Doc? It's all clear." Louie had the door partially open, peering down the hallway and as Doc approached the door Nikki grabbed his arm.

"They're flying outta LaGuardia tonight, back to Washington."

"How do you know?"

"I talked to Agnes, the secretary who made the arrangements for them."

"I owe ya one, sweetheart!" Doc smiled and stroked her cheek.

"There's just one thing I want you to do for me," she added.

"Name it."

"Get that prick son-of-a-bitch!"

"If you're tryin' ta get me to love you, you're doin' a helluva job!"

Louie was getting nervous. "Any time this week, Romeo!"

Doc kissed Nikki and followed Louie through the door.

At street level, over a dozen uniformed officers accompanied by two detectives poured out of five squad cars and stormed into the hospital lobby. They assembled at the reception desk and looked to their chief detective for instructions.

"Remember, this guy's not just a cop gone bad, he's a murderer! Be careful!" With that, the police moved to infiltrate the building.

At the elevators, the officers were directed to split up and cover all four elevators and both stair wells.

Doc and Louie were descending the stairs as fast as possible.

"They'll have to find out what room you were in. That'll buy us some time." To his credit, Louie was thinking strategically; however, no sooner had the words left his mouth than they heard the police rushing up from one floor below.

"Looks like they already know," Doc suggested. "Quick! In here!" He grabbed Louie's arm, and led him from the landing into the third floor ward.

As the door closed behind them, they instantly realised that if they were looking to blend in, they were definitely in the wrong place. Female nurses and pregnant women were everywhere. They were in Maternity.

Back on the stair well, a senior officer shouted orders to his minions. "Last man in line, check each floor as we go then catch up! Do it!"

"Yes, sir!"

As the detail passed by the third floor, the last officer in line stopped on the landing and pulled the door open. Stepping onto the Maternity Ward, he saw nothing suspicious about a few pregnant women standing around chatting and two new fathers standing in front of the newborns' window, congratulating each other and tapping on the glass. He moved on.

A few minutes later, McKeowen and Mancino were in the lobby. The main entrance was covered so they diverted down the hall to try and get out through Emergency.

Reckoning that they weren't looking for Louie, and so wouldn't recognise him, Mancino went through the exit first. He made it safely and standing outside in the falling snow, signalled Doc that the coast was clear. Doc carried his bomber jacket over his arm to conceal the bloodstains on the collar and his cast as he walked to the exit.

Outside on Park Avenue, there was no trouble hailing a taxi and in a moment they were heading south.

"Airport, on the double!" Doc instructed even before they were in the cab.

"What for? Airport's been closed for two hours." The cabbie reminded Doc of Spike Jones with glasses on relaxation tablets. "Blizzard's movin' in."

"What if we wanted to go to DC?"

"Washington DC?" Dollar signs flashed before the cabbie's eyes. "How much money you got?"

"Not by cab. Public transport!"

"Well, ya got your storm movin' up from the south, specifically Pennsylvania. All your secondary roads were closed an hour ago. That means . . ." Doc and Louie looked at each other. ". . . that all your primary roads will be closed in about an hour. That eliminates your cars and buses. So . . ."

"Hey pal! How 'bout we skip the meteorology lesson and you tell us the best way to DC. Tonight!"

"Best bet, if you gotta travel tonight, is by train."

"Penn Station?"

"Only place to get a train to DC from the City."

"How long to get there?"

The cabbie gestured with open hand to his windshield. "You tell me!"

Through the wet glass and the rhythmic slapping of the wipers, Doc and Louie saw red tail lights the entire length of Park Avenue fading into the darkness.

"Shit!" Faced with the possibility of losing Johnson, Doc realised that confrontation was becoming an obsession.

On the long cab ride from 77th Street to 29th, McKeowen had adequate time to consider the ramifications of not intercepting Johnson in time. Not only would Johnson be able to solidify his position and reinforce his alibi if he made it back to Washington, but Doc would be faced with evading the police for an indefinite period of time. Johnson had to be stopped and made to show Doc's innocence, but how?

"I wouldn't worry about it if I wuz you," suggested the cabbie.

"Oh yeah, why not?"

"If your planes are down, your trains are gonna be delayed. Penn Station is gonna be a mess!"

Describing Penn Station as a mess was like saying Fred Astair and Ginger Rogers could dance a little. It was pandemonium. The foot and a half of fluffy white stuff which had fallen since that afternoon had turned into thick, black slush as a result of the non-stop traffic. Worse yet, it showed no signs of letting up, and even seemed to be getting worse with wind adding to the discomfort, forcing more people inside.

Commuters had been converging on the unsuspecting station staff since midday, bound for all points up and down the Eastern Seaboard and, for the most part, were concerned with getting back to their jobs and homes by Monday morning.

Entering through the East Portico, the two were overwhelmed by the scene which greeted them. Thousands of stranded commuters were jammed into the expansive Grand Concourse.

"Doc! There must be ten thousand people in this place! How are we gonna find him?"

"He's here, we'll find him."

"Hell, he may not even be here."

"He's here, Louie. I can smell him."

"Jesus! Talk about a needle in a haystack."

"This must be what the train stations in Europe looked like when the Nazis went on the rampage." Doc's analogy was a good one.

Penn Station is large enough to be considered a small town, and this city within a city was packed with people. People sleeping on benches, sleeping on their luggage and sleeping on café tables and chairs. Some were even sleeping standing up. In the midst of the undulating crowd, Doc and Louie found a porter who directed them to the lower level platforms. Downstairs, they found an engineer, sitting on a bench, eating a sandwich and reading a newspaper, oblivious to the chaos.

"Hey, Buddy. Where would we get the train to DC?"

"Best place tonight'd be Carolina or Florida." The engineer took a swig of his orange Nehi soda and continued to read. Doc was maintaining his patience, but only by a thread.

"How about from here?"

"Everything is shut down from here to Pittsburgh south to Altoona. I don't see anything leaving this station tonight."

"What tracks do the DC trains leave from?"

"Twenty-five, twenty-six, twenty-seven and sometimes twenty-eight. End of the platform," he added through a mouthful of bologna on rye.

At the same time as Doc was getting a lesson on the station plan on track fourteen, Johnson was waving his Treasury Department badge in the face of the platform manager, down on track twenty-five, attempting to beg, borrow or steal three seats on a train south. He neglected to take into account New Yorkers' attitudes toward emergencies, national disasters and catastrophes.

"Look, Mac. I don't care if you're J. Edgar Hoover, the Attorney General or Amelia Earhart, all the trains that are leaving this station tonight, are gone. Read my lips. No more trains!"

As Doc and Louie moved up the platform, dodging commuters, Mancino sought to organize their plan of attack.

"Okay, Doc. How we gonna do this? You want me to distract him? Sneak up from behind?"

Doc stared straight ahead, perusing the crowd, and kept walking towards the southbound tracks, weaving between commuters with surprising dexterity.

"Or maybe you could sneak up from behind?"

Doc didn't answer but increased his pace.

"Look, Doc, I know you're pissed off to beat the band, but . . ."

Doc stopped, opened his jacket, and continued to glare forward.

"Told ya he was here, Louie."

Louie looked at Doc's evil grin and transfixed eyes. Then, following Doc's line of sight, he saw Johnson, off to one side of the crowd about fifty feet ahead, standing in front of a railroad employee, arguing.

"Doc, we gotta talk about how we're gonna do this! We can't just go up and get this guy!" Louie's voice which previously registered excitement, now began to register apprehension.

"Why not, Louie?" Doc maintained the look of a man possessed as he began to walk. His pace quickened and he soon pulled ahead of Louie as he broke into a run, still dodging commuters. Louie ran, two steps behind Doc, not so successfully negotiating the crowd.

"Doc, there might be more than one!" Doc ignored the pleas. "They got guns!"

Without breaking stride, Doc reached into his jacket and produced a strange-looking pistol that Louie had never seen before.

"Shit! Shit, shit, shit! Now *we* got guns! Why didn't I listen to you on the phone!" Louie gasped as he tried to run faster. "What the hell is that thing, anyway?!"

"Marakov 7.65."

"Fuckin' great! Now we're huntin' elephants in Grand Central Station!"

Johnson was at the peak of his frustration and thought he was having a bad night until he glanced around through the crowd and saw that the night was about to get a lot worse.

At first, he wasn't sure it was McKeowen, but as the aberration drew closer, the bruised face, blood-stained jacket and cast poking out of the jacket sleeve confirmed his worst fears. For the first time since he knew McKeowen existed, Johnson realised what he was dealing with. Beaten, bruised and broken, this bastard kept on coming. He didn't give a shit, it only seemed to piss him off worse. Now, with nothing left to lose, he was ready to cross the line.

"Do you understand what I'm trying to tell you about the train situation, Agent Johnson?" the manager asked for a second time.

"Never mind that! Where's the nearest transit police?"

"What?"

"*TRANSIT POLICE*! *WHERE ARE THEY*?"

"Ground level, upstairs, why?"

Johnson was already moving. "Call them! Tell them they've got a convicted murderer on the premises!"

Doc was only twenty feet away by now and picking up speed. Johnson saw the gun, and broke into a run.

"A *what*?"

"Do it! *NOW*! Tell them he's armed and dangerous! Shoot on sight!" Johnson abandoned his luggage, taking only a black leather satchel, and darted into the crowd. The station manager stood and watched as Doc and Louie flew past the small booth.

As no trains were arriving or departing, there was eight or ten feet of space, closest to the rail heads on the platform, which for the most part was clear. Doc saw it first and, moving to his right, was able to close the distance between himself and Johnson.

By the time Johnson realised where he was it was too late. He had already passed the last flight of stairs to the upper level and Doc was only two tracks behind, and closing fast. Johnson looked around at the people and then at a porter driving a luggage tractor. Reaching the end wall of the lower level, with the tracks to his right, he waited until the tractor, with its train of empty carts, turned to head onto the last platform. As it passed in front of him he could see Doc over on track twenty-nine, standing on a bench waving hello at him.

Doc was surprised when he heard the two shots. He didn't expect even Johnson to fire in a crowd. As he ducked behind a post, Doc understood what Johnson was doing. He wasn't being shot at, Johnson fired into the air. The shots had the desired effect. Even jaded New Yorkers knew when to duck.

In seconds, everyone was on their hands and knees, there was screaming and commuters on their way down the stairs were now quickly on their way back up.

Doc peeked carefully around the post. Johnson had vanished. Where the hell did he go? Doc quickly hopped back on the bench, weapon at the ready, and scanned the crowd. No sign of him! Fuckin' Houdini!

"*DROP YOUR WEAPONS, AND PUT YOUR HANDS ON YOUR HEAD! THIS IS THE NEW YORK CITY TRANSIT POLICE! DO IT NOW!*"

Doc turned around and saw three Transit cops, about forty to fifty yards away, drawing a bead on him. There was no way it was going to end here! Putting his hands up slowly to buy time, he realised they had snub-nosed .38's. They were at the outside limit of their accurate range. He made a decision.

He fell to the floor, rolled under the bench and off the platform and onto the track. Once there, he ran. Shots rang out behind him, but from the ricochets he knew he was out of range.

Through the shadowy tunnels, Doc couldn't see where the tracks exited up onto the streets, even though he now judged himself to be about four hundred yards from the passenger platforms. A hundred yards ahead the track disappeared into a warren of tunnels, and he hoped Johnson hadn't made it that far and lost himself in the labyrinth. Then McKeowen got a break.

Two more shots echoed through the tunnel, and the bullets hit the wall behind him high and to the left. It was too soon for the Transits to be this close. He had found Johnson.

"Why don't you give it up, McKeowen? The cops'll get you sooner or later."

Doc was crouched behind a metal tool bin, against the far wall and smiled as he thought to himself, *That's supposed to be my line*. He didn't call back, gambling that Johnson wasn't sure where he was. After about five minutes the gamble paid off.

Footsteps echoed through the tunnel, and Doc peered over the tool bin to see Johnson's dark figure running along the tracks to the farthest branch of the railway. Doc stood, felt a little dizzy and steadied himself on the metal bin as he felt behind his head. His hand came back with blood on it. His head wound had reopened.

As he took off after Johnson, he heard three gunshots from Johnson's tunnel. Louie!

Doc realised that, in his blind fury, he had lost his unarmed friend back on the platforms. *This is his neighbourhood and he musta known where the tunnels came out! Stupid bastard!* Doc shook off the dizziness and ran for all he was worth. Reaching the tunnel, he didn't like what he saw.

There was a man, in coveralls and a work hat, bent over another man who was lying on the ground. Doc looked at the chest and head wounds as he approached the scene. It was a Transit cop. The older man in coveralls looked up at Doc while stooping to hold the head of the dead policeman.

"He just popped outta the wall and shot. Nuthin' I could do. Never said nothin'. I thought I was next!" The old man was in shock. Doc put a hand on his shoulder and crouched down next to him.

"It's okay, Pop," Doc consoled in between breaths. "Take it easy. There'll be some more cops along in a minute. You just tell them what you saw, okay?" The old man nodded in agreement. "Where does this tunnel come out?"

Johnson had run as far as he could and slowed to a walk. A sign on the tunnel wall told him he was no longer under Madison Square Garden but nearing the back of the General Post Office, so he figured he must be past Eighth Avenue. He picked up his pace again, and soon saw the lights of Ninth Avenue, about two hundred yards ahead, peering back at him. He walked swiftly, smelling freedom, adjusted his clothing and smoothed his hair to shake off the dishevelled appearance, then reloaded his weapon.

As Johnson emerged from the south bound tunnel, adjacent to 31st Street, he stopped, dropped his satchel and stood motionless.

There, about a hundred yards ahead on the track, flanked by four Transit police, guns drawn, with his arms folded across his chest, was former garbage man, US Treasury agent and almost PI, Louie Mancino.

Johnson instinctively looked behind him, and Louie called out. "Never look back, Johnson. Somethin' might be gainin' on ya!"

Johnson swung back around, blasting. Louie and the cops dived for cover with bits of ice-covered rock and timber flying around them and, once on the ground, Louie yelled out, "It's okay guys! Treasury agents only carry wheel guns. He's only got six shots!"

There was a lull in the gunfire and Louie and one of the cops rose up and brushed the snow from their clothes. Two of the others tentativly followed.

"Let me show ya why Satchel Paige never made it to the majors!" a composed Johnson called back. He reached into his overcoat and removed a pair of chrome-plated .45's.

Dirt and rock exploded around their feet as the .45 rounds shattered the stone and ricocheted off the steel rails. Louie's group spread out, ran for cover and burrowed deeper into the gravel and frozen dirt with their hands. When the shooting stopped and they looked up, Johnson was gone. The cops looked at Louie, who smiled back.

"Must be new issue!"

As Doc emerged from the tunnel, the nervous cops drew a bead on him. Doc stopped where he was and raised his hands.

"*NO, NO, NO*! He's one of us!" Louie jumped in front of the police with his hands in the air until they relaxed their guard.

"Mancino! You okay?" Doc called out, running on the loose gravel.

"Bastard's got an arsenal!"

The men were forced to talk loudly to one another, as the wind surrounding them raised the level of ambient noise in the rail yard. Doc began giving instructions to the police.

"He killed a cop, body's back there. Be careful tramping around the crime scene. You've got a witness so get a hold of the NYPD right away so they can talk to him. There's a good chance there's a couple more of them back there posing as treasury agents, here's their ID's." He gave the transit cop two of the bifolds. "Be careful, they're armed! Which way'd this one go?"

The officer he was addressing, responded, "He headed off towards 31st. But if he stays on foot he won't get far. This stuff is supposed to get worse. He'll have to find shelter."

"Or transportation," Louie added.

"Exactly where the hell are we?" Doc asked, still talking in a hurried tempo.

The cop used his gloved hand to indicate directions. "10th, 9th, 33rd and 31st."

"So West Side Drive's that way?"

"Coupl'a blocks, but ta get on it ya gotta hit Eleventh Avenue and head south."

Doc and Louie began to climb the granite embankment to the street level and Doc called back, "Let your Captain know there's two men in pursuit. We'll call in on the nearest police phone when we make contact! Got it?"

"Yes, sir. Nice working with you, Agent Mancino!"

Louie waved back from halfway up the embankment, and Doc looked at him. Once on street level, the two were unsure of which way to go. Any direction would have been a guess. The question was answered when a loud scream, followed by cries for the police, emanated from Ninth Avenue.

"Let's go, *Agent* Mancino!"

At the corner of Ninth they were in time to see a vehicle speeding away, down West 31st, and a woman violently beating a mailbox with her purse.

"Louie, find us something to drive, fast!" Doc ran over to the women. "Ma'am, what happened?"

"Dickless bastard stole my cawr! Ran up, pulled me out and stole my gowd-damned cawr! I find out who he is, I'll cut his bawls off wit a butta' knife! *A RUSTY ONE*! So help me, *GAWD*!" She hit the mailbox once again.

Doc took the irate women by the shoulders and looked her in the eye. "Describe your car to me. It's very important!"

"Dark Green Mercury, tan interior, Wendal Wilkie bumper sticker, why? Youse guys cops?"

"No, but we know the man who did this. We'll take care of

your car."

Doc heard a horn beep and looked to his right. Louie sat in a mother-of-pearl white '32 Ford coupé hot-rod with a dark-haired stranger, barely out of his teens, in the driver's seat.

Doc shouted instructions to the confused women as he ran to the car.

"Find the nearest police box. Call the station house, tell them what happened. Tell them the guys in pursuit think he's headed towards the Battery."

"What's the number?" she called back.

"Just pick it up and talk!" Doc got in and gave the order. The hot-rodder spun a 180 on the snow-covered street and they were in pursuit. Louie noticed the radio was on.

"Hey! Gene Krupa! Mind if I turn this up?"

"Be my guest, Cool Breeze!" The young driver answered, as they sped down West Side Drive, *Drum Boogie* blasting away.

Due to the deteriorating weather conditions, traffic was sparse on the WSD. Ice hadn't yet formed, but the wet snow made it impossible for the cars to do over fifty and not spin out of control.

Just south of Canal Street, around Pier 29, Louie spotted him.

"Doc! There he is! A few blocks ahead, step on it!" Louie instructed.

"No! Don't! Drop back," countered Doc.

The driver was confused. "Doc, why?"

"He's not speeding. He doesn't know we're back here. Drive slow, keep about ten car lengths back. After Chamber's Street, there's only a coupl'a places he can get off."

"Say, Daddyo, how'd you know this cat was makin' fer the Battery?"

"He wants outta here and south as soon as possible. The GW is either jammed or closed, and without going all the way round through Brooklyn, Jersey's the best bet. Maybe tryin' get out in the morning at the Newark rail yard."

"That's far out! You should be like a private investigator dude or somethin'!"

"Naw! Pay's lousy and the conditions are shit," Doc answered, just as Johnson spotted them. He sped up and weaved in and out of the few cars and trucks on the drive.

"Don't lose him!"

"Not to worry, Big D!" The young hot-rodder's driving was impressive. He brought them to within eight or ten car lengths in no time. "You want me ta get next to him?"

"No, hold it here. He'll have to slow down at Battery Place to turn onto State." Johnson again surprised them. He had no intention of slowing down, or turning.

All three watched, stunned, as Johnson picked up speed and headed straight for the wooden barricades bordering Battery Park. His car flew off the exit ramp, became airborne and his chassis ploughed through the top half of the red brick wall.

"Sorry, Doc!" The driver slammed on his brakes, and executed two perfect donuts in order to lose momentum and stop before the broken barricades. "That cat does not have both oars in the water!" The Mercury slammed hard onto the park lawn, and sped off around the Castle Clinton Monument.

"Go around to State Street! Go, GO!"

They fish-tailed out and rounded State Street in time to see Johnson tearing through the lower end of the park. Two late-night lovers scattered as he sped towards them, knocking over trash baskets and taking out a couple of signs.

From their cold seats in the hot-rod they could see Johnson continuing to drive down the footpath through the south barricade and on past Pier One.

"Shit!"

"What's wrong, Doc?"

"I was wrong about Jersey. It's Pier Two!"

"So?"

"Governor's Island! It's a federal reservation! He gets out there, we can't touch him. We go anywhere near that place, they'll shoot us then arrest us!"

"Whatta we do?"

"Step on it!"

In less than a minute they came to a screeching halt in front of

Pier Two, next to the dark green Mercury sitting on the pier, its door open, engine still running. Doc was the first one to reach the waist-high accordian gates of the loading ramp. A sign posted the hours of the ferry and showed that the last run of the day to the island was an hour ago. But Johnson was nowhere in sight. A foghorn sounded over on Pier One and Doc vanished around the corner.

Louie and the driver caught up and saw Doc standing on the edge of the ramp, staring at the growing wake of foam as the Staten Island Ferry lumbered out of the slip. Johnson was waving good-bye from the fantail.

Doc wasted no time and ran past the two. Looking at the slowly widening gap, Louie thought Doc ran back to get a running start.

"Doc, what the hell you doin'? You can't jump that . . ."

Mancino was only partially right. He turned just in time, and was forced to push the bewildered hot-rodder out of the way in mid-dive to avoid being hit by the oncoming Mercury.

Doc hit the ramp at nearly forty miles an hour, but the wet snow reduced traction significantly. Taking off wasn't a problem, but the gap to the fantail of the ferry was now twenty feet wide and growing. The car leaned to the left once airborne, due to the weight of the driver, and Doc squeezed the steering wheel, sat back with his elbows locked and held his breath.

The last thing he saw was Johnson running for all he was worth and the horrified faces of the two crew members as they dived away from the path of the incoming car and slid into the fantail bulkheads. The undercarriage jack-knifed from the impact as it hit the deck just forward of the rear wheels. The front axle broke on impact and dug into the timber decking, as the vehicle began to slide backwards towards the water.

Doc pushed desperately at the door, but the impact had jammed it closed. He looked through the rear window to see the foam wake generated by the rhythmic churning of the ship's screws growing slowly larger. The low rumble of her engines grew louder as the slow but steady backwards sliding of the vehicle threatened to end the chase. He banged and kicked harder at the door.

Suddenly, the windshield exploded with gunfire and Doc ducked under the dash. Three more rounds ripped through the seat upholstery in rapid succession, before he was able to return fire by sticking his hand over the dash and shooting in the direction of the upper deck. The suppressive return fire seemed to work and Doc took advantage of the lull.

Bleeding from the forehead after hitting the steering wheel on impact, and covered in broken glass, his cast cracked open, he scrambled to climb through the windshield. Once outside the vehicle, clinging to the hood ornament, he was about to make one last thrust to the deck, when the car slid out from under him.

Doc hit the deck hard, lost his .45 and most of the air in his lungs. Rolling over and gasping in an attempt to regain his breath, he peered over the edge of the deck and watched the Mercury slip backwards through the iridescent green foam of the wake and vanish silently into the cold darkness. *Hope you had insurance, lady*, he thought as the water closed over the car.

His coffee break didn't last long. A double ping and sparks from the deck cleat near his head gave him the incentive to scramble for cover behind a large steel chest full of life preservers.

He heard screaming with the last volley of shots and looked across into the car deck, where some passengers and a crew member were huddled against the interior bulkhead of the superstructure.

"How many passengers on board?" Doc yelled at the crew member. The crewman yelled over his shoulder to someone behind him. Another shot reminded Doc to keep his head down.

"Yo! Donnie! How many tickets?"

"Fifteen!"

"Fifteen passengers, five crew."

"How many in the pilot house?"

"Two!" Doc knew the engineer was below, so it was likely to be the Captain and mate above.

"You two and the passengers get down to the engine room. Dog the hatch! Stay there till I come for ya! You understand?"

The crewman signalled okay and began to herd everyone through the narrow hatch and onto the ladder. A single shot ricocheted off the chest to Doc's right and he reckoned Johnson was bracketing his target.

Waiting till a second shot sounded, Doc exposed himself to the shooter's blind side of the steel box and took careful aim with the Marakov through the heavy snowfall. As he focused on the overcoat moving across the upper railing, the chest came into perfect view.

Squeezing off a single round, he saw blood spatter on the bulkhead behind his target and the man's stomach area quickly became a mass of red. The limp body tipped over the rail and fell two decks in a broken heap about ten yards in front of him. Doc breathed a sigh of relief.

Rising up slowly with his back against the port-side bulkhead, he had an irresistible urge, probably out of morbid curiosity he thought to himself, to look at the man who he didn't even know, who was willing to put him in prison or take his life. Holding his arm wrapped in the remnants of his soaking wet cast, his hair matted to his head with freezing water, he approached the body, and kicked it over. There was a sudden burning sensation running through his leg and he heard a shot.

Falling to his knees, Doc struggled to understand what was happening as he stared at the face of the body lying on the deck. It was one of the unknown agents from the planetarium.

Crawling into the car deck out of the line of fire, a voice called after him while he stared at his Marakov lying in the open, next to the body.

"Hey McKeowen! Happy St. Patrick's Day! How come you didn't wear your skirt to the party?"

Doc frantically tore a piece of his shirt and tightly wrapped it around his leg wound. "Johnson? Isn't that a slang term for penis?" Doc yelled back.

"Listen, I'd love ta chat all night, Mac, but I gotta get over to Governor's Island, you understand. So I got a friend comin' down to help ya outta your misery."

"Still subcontracting your dirty work, Bob?" While he spoke Doc looked at the body of the dead agent and then at the five foot long steel fog nozzle clipped to the bulkhead. The sign above the apparatus read, *For Emergency Use Only*.

A minute later, a second agent came down through the hatchway from above to the main deck level and instantly fired three rounds through Doc's brown leather bomber jacket into the slumped-over form lying on the deck. Before the last round was discharged, the agent was struck across the back of the head with the hose nozzle repeatedly until he was unresponsive.

"Asshole! You're supposed to say 'hands in the air' first!" Doc threw one in for good measure. "I had that jacket for twelve years!" Picking up the agent's gun and looking for any other visitors, Doc spoke to the unconscious agent as he frisked him. "That's the second time I pulled that on you dumbshits!"

The passengers in the engine room were not faring well. Between the choppy wintry waters and the unexpected, prolonged length of the ferry ride, speculation erupted into arguments about hijacking, kidnapping and pirating the ferry to some faraway place like Atlantic City. All they'd wanted when they boarded was to get back to a nice warm house and a quiet meal. Instead, the noise of the hot, smelly engine room began to grate on their nerves as they apprehensively awaited their fate.

A scared, middle-aged bakery clerk clung to her husband as they stood beneath a hot noisy bilge pump.

"Jesus, Phil! What if dey're Nazi saboteurs, sent ta take over the ship?"

"I think there are more important ships then the Staten Island Ferry, Edna!" The man held his wife to reassure her. "Besides, if it is something big, not to worry, there's probably government agents on board right now!"

Doc frisked the unconscious agent for extra rounds while he tried to formulate a plan. He was feeling a little light-headed and knew he would have to move fast. He couldn't tell if it was getting colder or it was the loss of blood, as he struggled with frozen hands to retrieve his damaged jacket.

Doc struggled up the iron ladderway to the pilot house and as he pushed open the door, he was forced to blink his eyes several times to clear his vision. He didn't like what he saw.

The Captain was sitting in the corner with his hand on his chest, trying to stem the bleeding, and Johnson stood behind the Mate who was at the helm, a gun to his head.

"I gotta give you credit, Mac. You don't quit! You'd a made a good treasury agent!"

Doc stood, propped up against the doorway of the pilot house, arms outstretched in front of him, the .45 pointed at Johnson. Doc reached into his hip pocket and produced the little black book. The rocking motion of the boat aggravated Doc's ability to maintain a bead on Johnson as he held the book up for Johnson to see.

"Thank you. Throw it here."

"Take the gun away from his head."

"Book! Now!" To emphasise his point, Johnson fired his weapon just above the head of the crew member, who cringed.

"You must be pretty scared of whoever this belongs to." Doc tossed the book across the centre-board console, away from Johnson and the Mate, purposely throwing it hard enough to land on the deck on the opposite side of the pilot house.

Johnson reacted instantly and fired two rounds at Doc from around the left side of the Mate's head. The sailor fell to the deck, holding his left ear, deafened by the report of the weapon.

Doc's attempted dive to cover behind the console was more a fall and crawl manoeuvre. Johnson spoke as he fired two more rounds through the console.

"Just outta curiosity, why didn't you bring the book to the Planetarium?"

He then took time to kick the Mate out of his way as he came around the center-board, firing ahead of him. On the other side, all he saw was a circular trail of blood, and quickly surmised that Doc was coming at him from behind. Instead, Doc dived for the Telegraph and was just able to signal the engine room for full aft before Johnson emptied his weapon into the signalling device. Despite an heroic effort, the Mate was unable to remain at the helm, and was forced back onto his knees, covering his head as the pieces of the shattered Telegraph flew around him.

Realising his weapon was empty, and now possessing the two things he wanted, the book and his leather satchel, Johnson abandoned his desire to fight. Making for the port-side hatch, he scooped up the book and scurried down the ladderway. Doc forced himself onto his good leg and lifted a fire extinguisher off the bulkhead, near the hatch. Without looking, he flung it with everything he had so that it ricocheted off the companionway bulkheads and down the ladder. Hearing it hit its target, Doc said to himself, "Spare in the ninth."

Making his way down the ladder, and across the deck, he watched as Johnson, blood covering his face, tried to get to his feet without success. As he attempted to crawl towards the fantail, Doc grabbed him and punched down hard at his face.

"You should a used your secret decoder ring, dickhead!" Doc bent down and took the book from Johnson's hand. "You were ready to kill people for this. You think I was gonna let you get your hands on it?"

Johnson's face wore a puzzled look as he stared up first at McKeowen, then at the little black book.

"Yeah, that's right. This is *my* little black book. The one with Charlene Meeny's phone number in it. The real one's been mailed back to Third Naval District."

Police boat sirens sounded in the distance.

"Uh-oh, Bob! Sounds like the fat's about to sing!" Doc looked over the starboard fantail and saw the blue flashing lights of two NYPD Harbor Patrol boats quickly closing in on the ferry. However, the smile melted from his face when he looked out over the bow.

With an unmanned helm, the rudder had swept the vessel into a wide arc to port. They had completely missed Governor's Island, which was now off the starboard rail, and were heading directly into the piers of Brooklyn Heights.

Doc immediately thought of the passengers and crew below

as he watched the waterfront lights grow rapidly larger. Johnson took advantage of the distractions when McKeowen stepped forward to limp around the felled agent to get to the pilot house. Grabbing him by the ankles, Johnson brought Doc to the deck, and immediately began to punch his leg wound, opening the clot and causing it to bleed vigorously. Doc yelled in pain, but refused to release his grip on Johnson collar. He punched him repeatedly with the tattered remnants of his cast, ignoring the pain in a blind fury. Doc spoke as he intensified the beating, speaking his words in between punches.

"I was gonna be a treasury agent . . . but they wouldn't let me! Found out my parents were married."

In the pilot house, the Mate struggled furiously to avert what seemed to be an inevitable collision with the oversized freight docks on the Brooklyn waterfront. Unable to communicate with the engine room due to the smashed Telegraph, he could only pull back full on the throttle, and fight the helm hard to port. The Fairbanks-Morse motors vibrated the entire vessel in protest and began to overheat, which spooked the passengers and caused them to run for the ladderway.

Johnson kicked his way free and made it to his feet. Doc was running out of gas fast. Lying on the deck, he noticed Johnson desperately clinging to the black leather satchel. Both men were far too engrossed in their struggle to notice that the police boats had caught up to the ferry and were now attempting to put men aboard.

Using everything he had left, Doc made a desperate dive for the bag as Johnson intensified his grip.

"What's in the purse, Gladys?" Doc managed only a partial grip, tore the bag open, and turned it upside down. The stormy wind scattered money across the fantail of the ship, and out into the harbour. Notes of varying denominations swirled into the nght air and clung to fixtures and bulkheads.

Johnson screamed like a wounded animal, clutching the near empty satchel, wet notes stuck to his face and chest. Rage consumed his mind as he bent over, grabbed Doc by the collar and lifted him to his feet. Doc hung like a wet rag, smiling, exhausted and soaked in frozen snow and blood. Johnson dragged him to the edge of the fantail, and looked at Doc and then at the churning wake.

"Say hello to your father, you Irish prick!" Now, with their faces only inches apart, the wind and snow whipping between them, Johnson was puzzled by Doc's smile. Suddenly, he understood.

A painful burning sensation in his ribs made him look down to see Doc's left fist covered in blood, tightly clutching the stiletto which was buried to the hilt. Doc moved his face closer to Johnson's, and spoke in a loud whisper.

"I'm Scottish, not Irish." Doc twisted the knife deeper into the agent and Johnson opened his mouth as if to yell in agony, but nothing came out. "And it's called a kilt."

Releasing his grip on Doc, who crumpled to the deck in a painful heap, Johnson stumbled backwards, struggling to remove the long, slender knife from his ribs. Glancing up, mouth still open in disbelief, the last thing he saw was the surrealistic sight of Mancino and two policemen, moving across the slippery deck, back-lit by a police boat spotlight.

He stumbled back, still fumbling for the knife, tripped over the mangled fantail safety gate, rolled off the fantail and disappeared into the white foam of the wake. The wake instantly turned pink, and tatters of shredded clothing churned to the surface, mixing with the remnants of the money floating off the deck.

Louie ran over to Doc and surveyed his wounds.

"Doc! You okay?"

"Call Lennox Hill, will ya? See if they still got my room." Louie looked back at the jetsom in the wake.

"I'll have the mixed green salad with extra tomatoes!"

"You're a sick son-of-a-bitch, Louie." Doc's eyes slid closed and his head dropped back onto the wet deck.

The large white wake continued to arc across the harbour back towards Manhattan and back to Pier One, as the first snowfall of the season, which came in the form of a blizzard, began to show signs of letting up.

Chapter Twenty-Six

Doc didn't mind Monday mornings, especially this Monday. It was nine-thirty, a lovely young nurse who'd give Veronica Lake a run for her money had served him breakfast, he was still in bed and he was offered pain medicine on request. To top it all off, his favorite switchboard operator was en route to pick him up.

Rumours floated through the nurses' station that Doc was to have a press conference with LaGuardia, as soon as he was well enough. In addition, he had the pleasure of telling the head nurse that he was too tired to take the long distance call from Tampa which had come in an hour before.

"Well! Look at you! Mr. High and Mighty!" Doc was sitting up in bed reading the newspaper, amused by the much embellished accounts of the 'Staten Island Ferry Hero'. He looked up to see Nikki standing in the doorway. She was dressed to the nines and had turned heads from the lobby all the way to Doc's room.

"I'm sorry, did you make an appointment with my secretary?" Doc asked in a mock executive voice. Nikki slowly sashayed over to the bedside, one hand on hip the other holding her black clutch.

"You have a secretary? What a coincidence. I'm currently unemployed and dropped by to talk to you about a possible position!"

"What position would you prefer, Ma'am?"

"Well, naturally I would be looking to work my way to the top as soon as possible."

"So, you want to be on top? In an executive sense, I mean."

Nikki pretended to ponder the question. "That would depend on who's under me. You understand?"

Doc lost his composure, laughed out loud and grabbed Nikki, pulling her into the clean, crisp sheets of the hospital bed.

"Ow! God . . . darn it! This fu . . .freakin' arm!"

"Getting old, cowboy?"

"It ain't the years, sweetheart, it's the mileage."

Hugging him, Nikki looked into his eyes. "You sure it's okay to leave here? The doctor told me at least a week," she asked suspiciously.

"That head nurse makes Boss Tweed look like the Pope, and I'd rather watch a Singing Randy movie than eat hospital food for one more day!"

"You have lost weight. Mrs Paluso is gonna have a field day with you!"

"Can't wait to meet the lovely lady!"

"So what are you tryin' ta say?"

"It's the end of the third reel. Point me towards the sunset!"

Nikki got up off the bed and crossed the room to help him pack.

"You fit all your stuff in this little bag?" she asked, holding up Doc's YMCA bag.

"Yeah, what about it?"

"We need to go shopping!"

"God help me." Doc closed his eyes and dropped his head.

"What?"

"I forgot about that part of it."

"Very funny. Get your ass up!" She began to put his toiletries into the bag.

"I got a phone call from Shirley this morning."

"Shirley? Where the hell is she?"

"Connecticut. She eloped."

"Eloped? Jesus! And we've been worried sick about her all this time! Did she have anything to say?" Doc asked as he struggled into his trousers.

"Yeah. Wanted to know if she'd missed anything."

Twenty minutes later, Doc McKeowen and Nikki Cole were riding up the West Side Drive in the back of a Yellow Sunshine cab, headed for Mercer Street, and an indeterminate period of rest and relaxation.

+

Louie was in his glory. For the first time in the six months he'd been with Doc, he was in charge of the office.

He occupied himself with menial tasks, basking in the comfort of actually belonging to the small firm, and thinking how proud Doris was that morning as she packed him an extra package of Yankee Doodles cup cakes in his lunch.

"McKeweon and Mancino, Private Detective Agency?" the postman enquired as the sign painter was putting the finishing touches on the big eyeball in the middle of the glass panel.

The sign painter gave him a 'What's the matter, you illiterate?' look and continued to paint.

As Louie was cleaning up the files from Johnson and his goons' redecorating party, there was a knock at the door. Louie walked over, opened it and was confronted by the elderly man in a US Post Office uniform. He was holding a carton in one hand and a slip of paper in the other.

"Doc McKeowen?"

Louie smiled to himself, reached into the breast pocket of his new three piece suit and produced one of the treasury department leather bifolds. He held it up and let it flop open in front of the postman. It contained a photo ID and a brand new Private Investigator's licence personally issued earlier that morning by the Deputy Mayor. Louie Mancino, Licensed Private Investigator.

"Louie Mancino, Private Dick. What can I do for you?"

"I'm not supposed to give this ta nobody but a guy named McKeowen."

"It's okay. I'm his partner. I'll sign for it if ya want. Doc's in the hospital, he got shot up. Maybe you seen it in the papers?"

"Yeah. That's how I knew it was time to deliver this package."

"What is it?"

"Beats me. Ira give me the ticket a few weeks back. Says if somethin' should happen ta him, I was ta get it outta classified storage and get it ta some Mickey named McKeowen."

"I promise ya, he'll get it." The mail man was unsure of what to do. "Look, you can call Norma if ya like. She'll vouch for me." He was reassured by Norma's name, gave the box to Louie and left.

Louie set the box on Doc's desk, trying not to succumb to the temptation of opening it. He signed reports, sorted files and swept some more, all the while glancing at the carton. He dusted, dreamt and finally decided.

Carefully opening the mysterious package, Louie knitted his brow, then held his breath as he looked inside. His mouth dropped open and he fell back into the chair.

Neatly stacked in denominational order, was twenty-two thousand dollars in cash.

Harry would later verify that the notes were real, and that the serial numbers were the originals for the counterfeit bills they discovered last week.

+

For the last forty-five minutes, methods of transport of every shape and description had been arriving in front of the main gate, depositing pressmen, police and memebers of the public onto the planks of Pier 88 along Luxury Liner Row, just off 49th Street. It was utter chaos.

Normandie's charred hull had long since been removed and moored in her berth and scheduled to depart for Naples in two hours and forty minutes, was the eloquent but ageing luxury liner, Laura Keene.

From stem to stern she was surrounded by longshoremen brandishing various tools of the trade such as bailing hooks, 'J' bars and skiff hooks. They stood shoulder to shoulder behind a rank of US Coast Guard sailors armed with white billy clubs. As an added precaution, LaGuardia had ordered the pier to be canvassed with city cops. Lucky would have more protection than any United States president.

The only people, without exception, who were permitted to board the beautiful vessel via her single gangplank, were those who the Chief Stevedore decided were legitimate ticket holders. For fear of trouble, the crew members had been ordered to report the night before.

"Fuckin' Sicily! Whatta shit hole! I'll be back here before the end of the year. Have everything ready." Lucky directed his comments to Socks Lanza, who was sitting directly across from him in the black Chrysler limousine as they pulled off Bank Street onto the pier.

"Whatever happened with that treasury agent, wanted to get in on the ground floor with us?" he asked.

"Was gonna come up from DC so we could see what he had. Never showed for the meet."

"Fuck him. There's plenty'a others where he came from. Keep things ready, you'll hear from me in a coupl'a months."

As the limousine turned off Bank Street and drove onto the dock, past the *No Vehicles Beyond This Point* sign, the longshoremen forcibly parted the mob of reporters and rubber-neckers.

Lanza was compelled to yell over the din of the crowd as they got out of the car.

"Hey, Charlie!"

"Yeah?"

"How does it feel to be a star?"

With his topcoat draped over his shoulders, he made his way to the gangplank escorted by six of Lanza's union men, while ten federal officials, representatives of various agencies, rushed to meet him but were not allowed to come in contact. As soon as his foot touched the deck of the Laura Keene, the Feds considered their duty done, and disapeared. Despite the fact his deportation was ordered by the US government, Lucky was determined to disallow them to play a part in the actual execution of the order.

Although he had no idea what he would have done had trouble broken out, the Captain of the liner considered it his duty to be there when his famous guest came aboard, and so stood by symbolically at the top of the gangplank.

The reporters were unable to accept the fact that they were not going to get to grill Lucky and so pushed forward and shouted questions at him, even after he was out of sight. When this tactic failed, they turned back on the government bureaucrat standing to the side of the ramp, on the inside of the human cordon.

"We were told by Immigration there was gonna be a press conference with Lucky!" one reporter yelled out, receiving jeers of support from his colleagues crowded around the entrance, unable to cross the triple picket line. Formal notices had been sent to the press by INS that Lucky would give a press conference. Unfortunately, no one at INS had told Lucky.

The lanky INS officer now stood erect on the gangplank, behind the army of longshoremen, and adjusted his glasses as he responded to the agitated demands of the press corps.

"I'll see what I can do," he said, in an attempt to placate the angry mob. He made his way up the ramp and vanished into the passageways of the ship, only to return a few minutes later, physically escorted by two of Lucky's torpedoes back to the top of the gangplank.

"Ahh . . . Mr Luciano has changed his mind and declines to speak to the press at this time."

"Give us a break! Your office released an official memo yesterday saying he would talk to us if we showed up!"

"This wouldn't be a political ploy to show us what a good job you're doin' after we criticised you for lack of criminal deportations during the war, would it, Francis?" one reporter shouted out.

"Well? How 'bout it, ya schmuck!"

The government official made a lame attempt at self-defence. "Mr Luciano just wants to relax in his modest accommodation and is looking forward to seeing his homeland."

The reporters had little alternative but to mill around the dock and speculate.

"What the hell is all the mystery? It ain't like his deportation wasn't in the papers for the last two weeks!" one of the frustrated pressmen said to a colleague.

Being pushed aside to make way for a second, third and fourth limousine, the second reporter responded as they watched a New York District Court judge, a well-known former police official and several prominent businessmen get out of the cars, "There's your answer!"

Impeccably dressed and bearing fruit baskets, boxes of expensive clothes and other gifts, the newly arrived entourage approached the gangplank brandishing Longshoreman's Union identity cards.

"Dock workers musta gotta raise!" the second reporter commented as the officials were admitted to the ship.

"Yeah, looks like they're payin' pretty good these days!"

The first reporter, determined not to accept the chain of events, made his way to the gangplank entrance, only to be stopped with a hand to the chest by a pugnacious stevedore. "Sorry, dock woirkers and union members only. Dis here's a dangerous place. You could axsa'dentally trip over a deck fixcha or somethin'. Next ding ya know, dar's lawsuits!"

The reporter looked to the New York City policemen who were standing a short distance away, watching the scene.

"Well? How 'bout it?" he addressed them, in a frustrated tone. The two cops smiled at each other, and shrugged to the reporter before resuming their conversation about the Yankees' victory over the Brooklyn Dodgers.

Lucky's deportation was in reality a *bon voyage* party in the grandest sense. Anyone entering the first class cabin was greeted with visions of elaborate, oversized fruit baskets, a room full of dignitaries, canapés and a glass of Dom Perignon served by a ship's steward who was standing behind the four foot long, chocolate layer cake in the shape of Luxury Liner.

There was no name on the hull.

No one showed up without an envelope, a small package, or, in Frankie Costelloe's case, a valise full of cash to pay homage to the god of organised crime who, in 1907, arrived at this very same port, riding in steerage on a freighter which was one step above a garbage scow. Now, with his abject poverty and squalor a distant memory, Lucky Luciano was being sent off with the honours of a prince.

A prince of thieves.

EPILOGUE

The ineffectiveness of *Operation*, or *Project*, *Underworld*, will probably never be officially acknowledged. No case of sabotage in the operational area of the New York City waterfront was ever discovered or claimed. Twelve would-be German saboteurs did land out in Long Island but, apparently underestimating the requirement for a local dialect, were quickly apprehended when one of them stopped to ask directions. The last of them were captured in a high-speed pursuit through Times Square. Apparently they underestimated the Midtown traffic, too.

For more than thirty years, officials denied the existence of the operation, in all probability motivated by their apparent poor judgement in employing high profile, organised crime figures in a top secret operation, whom they had earlier touted as the scum of the earth. However, in fairness to its originators, spurred on by desperation and panic, it must have seemed like a good idea at the time.

Coincidentally, on the morning of the 9th of February, 1942, as Normandie was meeting her demise, Roosevelt vetoed HR 6269, a bill which sought to require all aliens to register with official authorities. Roosevelt believed the bill would impede the spirit of co-operation between allied nations as it was worded specifically to include foreign dignitaries.

As regards the players, D. A. Thomas Dewey made two attempts at Governor based on his prosecution record, and won in '42. Attempting to follow the Yellow Brick Road, he ran for presidential nominee for the Republicans and lost to Wendall Willkie, who lost the election to FDR. He was re-elected

Governor, got the Republican candidacy in '44 and lost himself to FDR. He gave up in 1952 and went into private practice in upstate New York where he could frequently be seen in organised crime establishments gambling and socialising in his off hours.

The Kefvauer investigators noted this, called him as a witness during their infamous 'hearings', and he told them he was too busy to testify. In 1964, over the high-profiled and energetic protests of the Italian-American community, they named the New York State Thruway after him.

Speculation continues as to why he agreed to approve parole for Luciano. He turned white and his mouth dropped open in 1940 when he found out from a fellow prosecutor how close he came to being assassinated by Dutch Schultz and that it was Lucky who saved his life. He also knew Lucky had done something for the war effort. However, at least two sources, Luciano and Lansky, admit he received up to $90,000 from the Unione for his 1946 governor campaign. He was later heavily implicated and then connected in dealings with Meyer Lansky, specifically with Mary Carter Paints' national conglomerate and Resorts International.

Thomas Dewey died in 1971.

Frank Hogan, former Chief-of-Staff to Dewey, retired from public office after gaining notoriety by prosecuting the perpetrators of the quiz show scandals, comedian Lenny Bruce for obscenity and several college basketball teams for rigging games and later assisted Senator 'Tail Gunner Joe' McCarthy in his infamous witch hunts. He was re-elected nine times, retired in 1973 and died in April of 1974.

Murray Gurfein joined the OSS, served with distinction in France and was a assistant prosecutor in the Nuremberg Trials. He was later appointed by Nixon to be a US District Court Judge and went against the government in the famous Pentagon Papers Trials. He died in 1979.

Fiorello LaGuardia, elected in 1933, was sworn in, walked to his office, phoned DA Dewey and told him to arrest Luciano. From that point on, he spent his life cleaning up and rebuilding

New York City. Bennet Field on Long Island was eventually renamed several times, but to this day remains LaGuardia Airport. He retired after three terms and died in 1947.

Charles Heffenden, the unsuspecting lynchpin of Anastasia's original plan to get Lucky released, retired after the war and became very sick in the early fifties. He was the key figure who refused to help Luciano later in his bid for freedom after the war. However, with some reticence, Heffenden testified before the circus-like freak show which became known as the Kefvauer Hearings in the early fifties, stating that Lucky did help the government. Sort of. He died in 1952.

J. Edgar Hoover, who started his dubious career in 1919, was permitted to remain in power until his death in May of 1972. Both Johnson and Nixon waived mandatory retirement rules to allow him to linger on the thrown. He remained "the best Director organised crime ever had", until the Kefvauer Hearings focused the spotlight on organised crime after the famous Apalachain bust occurred. Up to forty members of the various families were arrested when their meeting was accidentally discovered, as somebody drove by a remote house in upstate New York and saw all the flashy cars and well-dressed people wearing expensive Italian shoes. It was then that the American public realised that, aside from the government, crime was also organised in the US. These events made it no longer profitable or politically advantageous for Hoover to ignore the now unsolvable problem.

Only weeks after the sinking of the Normandie, Albert Anastasia, born Umberto Anastasio, President and CEO of Murder Inc., became Private Anastasio US Army, enlisting presumably to disappear for a while. The photo of his death, which appeared on the front page of the *New York Times*, is world-renowned as he lies covered in blood, his bullet-riddled body sprawled out on the floor of a New York City barber shop where, in a fit of confusion after being shot several times, he attacked the mirror thinking it was his assassins. His murder on October 25th, 1957 in the barber shop of the Park Sheridan on 56th Street and Seventh Avenue in Manhattan, gave rise to a barber shop tradition still adhered today, at least in New York City. While getting your hair cut, the chairs face away from the mirror.

As regards the Normandie, after she was launched on October 29, 1932 with the entire world following the events, she embarked on a non-stop ten year career of notoriety. The largest object ever set in motion by man at the time, Normandie was the centre of international attention the day she took to the sea. Naturally, the world's largest bottle of champage was used to christen her, with VIP's and dignitaries in attendance including Madame Lebrun, wife of President Albert Lebrun, who officiated the launch and set the behemoth in motion. As the enormous hull entered the waters of the Loire, a tremendous backwash swept ashore, dousing spectators and washing workers into the river. The floating work of art would go on to set several speed and passenger records until confiscated by the US Navy at the outset WW II, when she would be stripped of her luxurious trappings and plush furnishings to be renamed USS Lafayette and be entered into the registry of the US Navy. Although captured in 1939, and not officially seized by the Navy until December 7, 1941, debates raged for the better part of a year as to whether her ultimate function should be as a troop ship or an aircraft carrier. The argument was settled at about 2:15 p.m. on February 9, 1942. Just as Titanic and Lusitania were never recovered, neither was Normandie ever salvaged. Despite the Third Naval District's claims that she would be salvaged, she humiliatingly lay on her side, beside the 49th Street pier, (Pier 88), for nearly a year.

She was righted in 1943 and towed to the Brooklyn shipyards where, for the duration of the war, she remained a sideline spectator. In 1946 she made her final voyage, under tow, the short distance across the harbour to the Port Newark shipyards. Just as she was launched in October and Albert A. met his demise in October, it was in October they started to cut her up for scrap and, thanks to her massive size it took until the following October to complete the job. I was once shown what I was told was a piece of her superstructure at the home of friend in Jersey City, New Jersey.

To this day, most contemporaries of Normandie know it was a fire. Many people I interviewed still believe the initial, incorrect reports, of a U-Boat in the harbour. The quote below, credited to Charles T. Collins, an 18-year-old USN ironworker, was taken from a Normandie website quoting *The Journal of Applied Fire Science*, Volume 8, #4, 1998-1999. The fact that there are a number of dedicated sites about the Normandie implies there is somewhat of a cult following of her short but interesting history.

"I was working on a chain gang. We had chains around some pillars and eased them down when they were cut through. Two men were operating an acetylene torch. About 30 or 40 men were working in the room, and there were bales and bales of mattresses. A spark hit one of the bales, and the fire began. We yelled for the fire watch and Leroy Rose, who was in our chain, and I tried to beat out the fire with our hands. Rose's clothes caught fire, and I carried him out. The smoke and heat were terrific."

As a graduate of the US Navy Damage Control/Fire Fighting course in San Diego, I can state that the above actions given in this statement, if accurate, violate no less than three, possibly as many as five of the Navy's standard fire safety procedures at the time. However, there was no reported action taken against any worker or supervisor. There would have been no point.

The report given by Admiral Andrews to the press is taken verbatim in this manuscript from newspaper accounts. He is quoted as saying it was Mae Wests, (a type of life preserver), which acted as the initial fuel for the blaze. Other reports blamed fresh paint, a worker named Sullivan, (who is listed as a carpenter not a welder), and various other circumstances and materials.

Admiral Adolphus Andrews' statement in answer to the question of a possible breach by a saboteur, also gives confusing details regarding security: *"I'm not telling you that couldn't happen. However under the circumstances I'm telling you that it would have been impossible due to our unbreachable security."*

Most mainstream papers in New York reported that the fire originated on the promenade deck, but show a ball room or dining room space of some sort in their accompanying photos, despite the fact that photos of every part of the ship including the engine room were available. However, the case is not so open and shut as some may like it to be.

Thomas Dewey's high profiled proscecution of Luciano is well documented. The ties and relationship between Luciano and Albert Anastasia are well documented, as is Anastasia's loyalty to Charlie. The following statement is from Wikipedia:

During WWII Anastasia appeared to have been the originator of a plan to free Luciano from prison by winning him a pardon for "helping the war effort." (Well documented by FBI files and independent historical research).

With America needing allies in Sicily to advance the invasion of Italy and the desire of the Navy to dedicate its resources to the war, Anastasia orchestrated a deal to obtain lighter treatment for Luciano while he was in prison, and after the war, a parole in trade for the mafia protecting the waterfront and Luciano's assistance with his associates in Sicily.

To accomplish this goal, Anastasia set out to create problems on the New York waterfront so that the United States Navy would agree to any kind of deal to stop the sabotage. The French luxury liner SS Normandie, [sic], which was in the process of being converted into a troopship, mysteriously burned and capsized in New York Harbor. While newspaper accounts suggested it was the act of German agents who had infiltrated the United States, it has been suggested that Anastasia ordered his brother, Anthony 'Tough Tony' Anastasia, to carry out the sabotage.

Meyer Lansky, in his memoirs/autobiography, states he had a chat with Anastasia after he was discharged from the Army and had returned to New York. "*I told him face to face he mustn't burn any more ships. He was sorry. Not sorry because he'd burned the Normandie. Sorry because he couldn't get at the Navy again. He hated them.*"

Joachim Joesten, author, along with Sid Feder, of *The Lucky Story*, the only complete biography of Luciano, was granted an interview in 1953 at the Hotel Turistico in Naples. The question was put to Luciano as to whether or not it was Albert Anastasia, of Murder Inc. fame, who set the fire aboard the Normandie, presumably to dupe the Navy into believing there were saboteurs and using the Mob to protect the waterfront and thus return Lucky's control of the vast territory. Lucky's retort, accompanied by a shrug, was, "I guess he got a little carried away."

Years before this interview, it was well documented that soldiers, sailors and Marines, when in Naples, sought him out or asked about him, often seeking autographs. Curiously, firemen had a special propensity to meet Lucky and get his signature on a menu or whatever was at hand. Some papers did suggest German saboteurs, which would have been all that Anastasia and Luciano would have needed. Whatever happened, it worked like a charm. Lucky was down-state and out of 'Siberia' in less than 48 hours. He did regain control, Albert A. disappeared and J. Edgar got a bloody nose. Once again the New York docks were back in the hands of the Unione.

Prior to the invasion of Sicily, Luciano also helped with information urging the entire Italian-American community to cooperate with Haffenden's people. Once again, his efforts were rewarded as organised crime members were installed as mayors and officials across the island country in the wake of the successful Allied invasion. The missing link between the Far Eastern poppy farmers and the American drug importers was established as planned. Salvatore Lucasia, (Lucky Luciano), was deported in 1946 after an extensive, essentially unproductive investigation by the New York State Parole Board concerning his involvement in *Operation*, or *Project*, *Underworld*, a title it was unlikely they even knew. It was out of sheer frustration, due to lack of co-operation by the Navy and the NYCDA's office with the parole board investigation, that the Board gave Lucky his walking papers. The father of organised crime spent the rest of his life attempting to re-enter the US and made it as far Cuba, where he was asked his blessing to eliminate Benny Siegel, the founder of the Las Vegas empire, for skimming Vegas receipts, primarily from the Flamingo.

He died in Naples airport awaiting a flight to leave Sicily on January 26th, 1962. He was flown back to New York and interned in St. John's cemetery with one of the largest funeral processions in New York history. For the remainder of his life, Lucky had harboured nothing but disdain for the poverty of his homeland, and sought to escape it and return to the New World.

He died trying.

Historical Background

"Never ever trust what your government tells you."
Bruce Springsteen, *Born In The U.S.A.* tour, 1984

As a scientist and historian, it's sometimes hard to reconcile the concept of fate. To be objective and thus well rounded, you try to see history as a simultaneously occurring series of separate events, on countless different planes, all unfolding in different places at various tempos. But when you come across a single event which took minutes to initiate but would inextricably bind the US Navy, the FBI and the Mafia and eventually tens of thousands of lives for the duration of WWII and then some years after, it's hard not to lay down the pen, close the texts, pour a drink and go down to the beach to watch the sunset.

Even more captivating is that the plethora of historical ironies peppering this story were brought together by Albert Anastasia, a man who didn't finish primary school, possessed barely a modicum of intelligence and whose claim to fame was that he murdered over 500 people as CEO of Murder Incorporated.

By way of setting the stage for the story, it should be understood that the period between the two world wars saw the birth and growth of several organisations in America, the developments of which initiated a dynamic that would spawn a plethora of major historical events, any one of which would not only supply material for a dozen novels and several films, but are still revealing stories today.

Three of the most significant of these were the establishment of organised crime, the FBI and Naval Intelligence. They all grew up, went to school and came of age in the late 1920s as separate entities; however, like predators prowling an ever shrinking savanna, their collisions were inevitable.

As is the case with most great stories, the story of how and why the US Navy came to hire Lucky Luciano and the Unione Siciliano in what was known as *Operation Underworld* unfolds in a great place, New York City, and involves several central figures aspiring to greatness but only one of which sought notoriety, J. Edgar Hoover.

As an added attraction, the New York City District Attorney's office, headed by the infamous Thomas E. Dewey, unwittingly acted as catalyst.

In February of 1942, one of the key players was in his sixth year of what was essentially two and a half life sentences, convicted of a crime for which the law allowed ten. To exacerbate the situation Salvatore Lucania, 'Lucky' Luciano had, by technical legal guidelines, been framed by the testimony of others obtained under, in some cases, the threat of violence and rather thin circumstantial evidence.

The real life, dramatic irony extends even further when one considers that the man who engineered his trial and had him convicted and imprisoned was the very man whose life Luciano had saved less than a year before, New York DA Thomas Dewey.

There's little doubt that Luciano was guilty of multiple violations under the White Slavery Act, (a dramatic term for prostitution), but the entire United States legal machine was not enough to actually catch him with his hand in the till and so, in order not to look too stupid, they had to 'bend' their own laws.

Lucky Luciano was a classic American rags-to-riches success story. He was not only co-founder of the Unione Siciliano, or National Crime Syndicate, or the Commission, as it was known by its members, but he also organised and established what became the International Drug Cartel, built a casino-based empire in Havana and Las Vegas and then, at a council in Cuba, gave the nod to kill the man who built it for him, Ben 'Buggsy'

Siegal. All of which, with the exception of organising the Unione, he did while in prison or in exile. Not bad for a kid from the slums of a fourth rate town in a third world country.

As if to show he had a sense of humour, Dewey made sure Luciano's indictment came at a time when he truly believed himself sufficiently insulated from the law to have any worries. The multiple count indictment was handed down on April Fool's Day.

It also came at a time when the position of New York City District Attorney bore no small legacy. The next step up was Governor, after which, if you had a), an adequate popularity quotation and b), adequate financial backing – which was virtually guaranteed if you had a) – the salutations on your mail thereafter would read: *Dear Mr. President*. All compliments of the New York City-based Tammany Hall leadership. Such was the Yellow Brick Road of the times.

There can be little doubt about Thomas Dewey's politically driven actions against the likes of Waxey Gordon, Louie Lepke and Dutch Schultz. After all, if a man wants to be President of the United States, essentially the head lawyer of the country, starting out as a prosecutor is a good place to be. Starting out in New York in the 1930s is a better place and getting the big name gangsters, whatever it takes, is a shoo-in. Almost. Dewey's political ambitions were assured if he could convict Schultz and just as he was about to pounce, the Dutchman decided enough was enough and set up a hit on DA Dewey, the 'Gang Buster'.

Unfortunately for Shultz, Lucky Luciano and Meyer Lansky, founders of the Siciliano Unione, were adamant about the 'keeping a low profile' clause in their corporate agreement.

So, a day before Dutch gave the okay to kill Dewey, Lucky gave the okay to kill Dutch. Schultz was hit in a New York chop house, eating a steak, and it is widely held that this is where the myth of a condemned man's last meal, commonly steak, originated.

Following this hit, in 1936 New York City DA Dewey decided that Luciano, despite having been arrested about twenty-five times and only jailed twice for short periods, was going down regardless of what was required to do it. Bear in mind that Luciano was a hoodlum, but also bear in mind that his statement, "We never killed no one that didn't deserve it," is, so far as anyone can determine, true. This includes not only ordering the death of Dutch Schultz but sanctioning the assassination of one of his most ardently loyal followers and supporters, Albert Anastasia, after he needlessly ordered the death of an innocent bakery apprentice for insulting him.

Like the Unione, Naval Intelligence had recently been dealt its worse blow since its inception, namely Pearl Harbor. It had been only two months since the bombing and, in a long laundry list of parallels with the Twin Towers attack, politicians were asking, "How did we not know this was coming?", and flinging such helpful suggestions as, "Somebody has to swing!"

Interestingly, in 2004 documents were released to the news agencies by some historians in Britain showing that as a result of efforts by the British intelligence agencies, code breakers who had cracked the JN code were able to inform Churchill about plans for the attack as early as November of '41, over a month before it happened. In turn, it was reported Churchill waited two weeks before informing FDR who, American historical documents adequately testify to, never informed the two commanders of the full extent of the probability of the attack. In all likelihood, some speculate, this was motivated by America's failed economy being mired down for over a decade in the Great Depression.

The second central player, Lieutenant Commander Haffenden, (coincidentally carrying the same first name as Luciano), appears to have fallen into the *Operation Underworld* scenario by being in the right place at the right time. As the officer in charge of the ports of New York, he wasn't really privy to Washington DC's decisions but by all accounts was certainly the right man for the job. With an outstanding record of past intelligence exploits, a good sense of command and a 'can do' attitude, he threw himself into an operation which had little chance of any real success from the start, that is catching German spies. To his credit, he so impressed and maintained the respect of Meyer Lansky, that Lansky not only kept his son away from racketeering but sent him to West Point. Although we are not sure of the extent of Haffenden's influence, Lansky himself went straight not long after the war.

Rather than the serious game of spy, counter spy originally envisioned with the inception of *Operation Underworld*, it turned into more of an expensive game of cops and robbers, mostly without the robbers.

German war records clearly indicate that generals had no intention of launching any serious attempts at espionage or sabotage in the Continental US and pretty much viewed it as a waste of resources. Records also indicate that the group of twelve German operatives sent over and landed by submarine on the shores of Long Island, were a write-off and seen to be an experiment, forgive the pun, to test the waters.

In contrast, it wasn't as bad a time for J. Edgar Hoover's FBI. Finally, they would be given a chance to show what they could do, as long as it wasn't going toe to toe with the Commission, which according to them didn't exist. Their resource allocation was drastically increased, as were their jurisdictional guidelines, and they were going to be allowed to catch spies. Problem was, they had a lot of catching up to do themselves and Hoover fantasised that it fell to him alone to see it done.

Much like Luciano, Hoover was able to exploit the emergency situation the war created to his advantage; however, he did it by greatly increasing his public persona, while Lucky did it by further receding into the shadows of secrecy. Commander Haffenden saw it strictly as a matter of duty. Interestingly, all three utilised government agencies, large amounts of cash and lots and lots of unwitting civilians.

Keep in mind that this is only one small part of the historical picture of the time, but it's a damned interesting one by any standard. There were other organisations with other spheres of influence, and Luciano's direct influence in America was only from 1931 to 1946. Although he was imprisoned in 1936, this merely caused him to restructure the way he did business. Lt. Cmdr. Haffenden was directly involved for less than a year and Hoover was never really allowed to be involved at all.

These are but a few of the primary elements contributing to the atmosphere in early February of 1942. After the Armistice, each player left the table, cashed in his chips and went looking for the next game. It's another story as to who won, who lost or who drew, but for that brief period in the Spring of '42, the paths of all concerned were unexpectedly and inextricably interwoven into a unified operation: *Operation Underworld*.

✦

If you lived through these times, I apologise if the details are not related the way you remember them. If you were not around in 1942, then I apologise for all the characters not wearing trench coats, Fedoras, living in black and white and leaning at Dutch angles. The characters in this story are representative of the Government, Organised Crime, and The People of the times, the three corners of our narrative triangle.

This story, the story of how the most critical arm of the US Government at the time, Naval Intelligence (whose New York branch curiously seemed to be comprised largely of lawyers), during wartime gave the highest priority to, and actively recruited, the man who established organised crime, (a fact they were likely not sure of but at least strongly suspected), to work for them.

A man who the left hand of the government, Politics, had, just a few years earlier, enthusiastically touted as their Number One poster child on crime and incarcerated on questionable testimony for a period five times in excess of what the law proscribed.

Anyone familiar with the upper echelons of US Government shouldn't have been too surprised by this, I suppose, as any relationship with them is comparable to a bad marriage. What's mine is mine and what's yours is mine.

The waterfront is essentially a fifth character in the story and was the most interesting perspective from which to tell it. It was where I got my first real job in 1967 and the first place I actually watched, (from a safe distance), two men out to kill each other. Thus the incident on the loading dock is true, although reset in '42.

The true parts are essentially everything to do with the government characters.

The incidents concerning the naval officers are all taken from newspaper accounts, such as Admiral Adolphus Andrews' comments when meeting with the press, and incidents in the briefing room office, and interaction with the New York City District Attorney's office, which is taken from period documents as well as post-war interviews.

The business between the New York City DA's office, the Navy and the prison system is all factual, although, especially in '45 and '46, the events surrounding Lucky's release from prison would make an interesting study in American politics on their own.

All of the dialogue in the White House is historically accurate, taken from Oval Office transcripts, although the 'shocking' discovery of Italian frogmen and mini-submarines, (a notion like jumping out of airplanes with silk sheets strapped to your back was one that the US military leaders initially rejected out of hand and then had to play catch-up with when the Nazis jumped into Crete), did not reach FDR at the same time as Enrico Fermi's telegram announcing that he had cracked the code of atomic power in Soldier's Field, Chicago. The incidents were more than a year apart but nevertheless are accurate.

I could find no documented evidence that FDR knew about *Operation Underworld*; however, it is hard to imagine that an operation that high up the naval chain of command occurred without his knowledge or consent, particularly when he kept a Navy captain as his official Adjutant, personal advisor and confidant.

Additionally, much to his credit, FDR was quick to pick up on unconventional approaches to operations such as tactics from the departments of 'dirty tricks' of other nations, as evidenced by the response telegram he dictates in Chapter Thirteen, taken from his personal collection at the National Archives.

The initial contact with Socks Lanza by the DA is accurate, save the actual wording of the conversation that night in the park along the Hudson, and is documented by individuals who had later contact with parties on both sides.

Although based on real people, Doc, Louie, Nikki and Treasury Agent Johnson, (who, along with the 'the little black book', connect the reality of the story with the fictional elements), are fictional. The 'Little Black Book', containing the most intimate details of the operation, actually existed but vanished sometime just near the end of, or just after the war, when everybody from Truman to a Department of Corrections' secretary wanted to know who exactly was involved. It was never traced or found.

Hoover was never fully briefed about what went on and did chase his tail trying to find out. However, he had already established himself as a collector of information to be used to blackmail or exert leverage on people and so, despite what was said in public, he was never fully trusted in political circles, particularly by those not given to maniacal paranoias based on race, colour, creed or national origin.

The incident concerning a young JFK being secretly taped in a hotel room making love to Inge Arvad, the Danish journalist, is all true and leaves little doubt about the bad blood that existed between the Kennedys and J. Edgar. One can only wonder how the little cop felt when FDR ordered JFK to be transferred to PT boats in the Pacific, and Kennedy returned home a highly decorated war hero thanks to the PT109 incident.

This, in conjunction with a second unforeseen event, the death of JFK's older brother Joseph while on a secret mission to bomb a Nazi U2 base, would put him as the front runner of the Kennedys to move into 1600 Pennsylvania Avenue. Thus the significance of Hoover's vindictiveness can possibly be seen as helping Kennedy get elected. Speculation will probably linger for generations as to whether or not he helped him out of office.

The primary influence for telling this story is William Manchester, a consummate historian who understands, and has taught me, the significance of the inter-relation of historical facts, meaning that nothing stands alone. For example, our fathers were taught and learned important points in history such as the USS Maine being blown up by saboteurs, Teddy Roosevelt charging up San Juan Hill to win the battle and the war, about the sneak attack on Pearl Harbor and how important it was to get the Communists out of Hollywood before they brainwashed the country.

The USS Maine was not blown up by Spanish or Cuban saboteurs, Teddy never charged up San Juan Hill, there is recently released documented evidence that FDR knew about Pearl Harbor at least two weeks beforehand, and the Thomas-Rankin and Truman-McCarthy witch hunts and HUAC were about stopping the Writer's Guild of America from gaining inroads into screen credit and decent pay, and had nothing to do with communists taking over Hollywood.

So, because these and hundreds, if not thousands, of other events are still taught in the American school systems as fact, to some extent the victor does get to write the history, but sooner or later some nosy, educated writers like William Manchester and Gore Vidal, or journalists like Woodward and Bernstein will happen along and piss off a bunch of people by finding out and telling the truth.

It is from the narration of the burning of the Hindenburg and the story of the Normandie that I came to understand the significance of knowing about those who came before us. I came to understand that you are what you are because of Genetics. You are where you are because of Geo-Politics. However, you are who you are because of the Genetics of Geo-Politics, which is History.

Glossary

Automat – A self-serve eating establishment whereby the customer is required to insert coins into slots adjoining small compartments with glass doors which contain the desired food item. Horn and Hardart's were the pioneers in this food service technique and popularised it throughout the greater New York area for more that twenty years.

Beeline – To move in a straight line towards something; interpreted to mean move swiftly towards a given location or person.

Bozo – A popular American clown figure.

DE's – Destroyer Escorts. Smaller than a Destroyer.

Flipped – "Flipped Your Wig", to have gone crazy.

Goim – One who is not Jewish; not of the faith. Usually Christians.

Grapevine, The – A source of unfounded gossip; rumours. In naval terminology, "The Scuttlebutt".

G.W. – Short for The George Washington Bridge.

INS – Immigration and Naturalisation Service.

Lead pipe cinch – An absolute sure thing. An event whose outcome is 100% certain.

Maxine, Patty and Leverne – The three Andrews Sisters.

OJT – On the Job Training.

Regular Coffee – The most common way to take your coffee in New York City at the time, with milk and sugar.

Savvy – To understand or comprehend.

Schmoe – A looser.

Schmuck – A sucker.

"School's out, Satch!" – Wise-up. In the *Bowery Boys* films, Satch was the reflective/comic relief character who always had to be told the score.

Scutch – Short for Scucheem, American mispronounciation of Sfaccimme. Sicilian for son of an unmarried, pregnant woman in heat. A son-of-a-bitch or bastard. To annoy, aggravate or purposely irritate.

Shadow Box – To compete against oneself; interpreted to mean to a waste of time.

The Silver Clipper – Joe DiMaggio, famous New York Yankee team member who in 1942 earned 96 hits in 56 consecutive games. Second husband of Marilyn Monroe.

Singing Randy Movie – Merriam Morrisson's, (John Wayne), attempt to break into cowboy movies. Randy was a singing cowboy who gave the audience a number before, and sometimes after, killing the bad guy, and winning the girl. It was an effort to compete with Gene Autrey and Roy Rogers.

"The skinny" – The story, the lowdown, the dope, what's going on.

Yoohoo – A popular chocolate soda/drink

Legend Press
Independent Book Publisher

This book has been published by vibrant publishing company Legend Press. If you enjoyed reading it then you can help make it a major hit. Just follow these three easy steps:

1. Recommend it
Pass it onto a friend to spread word-of-mouth or, if now you've got your hands on this copy you don't want to let it go, just tell your friend to buy their own or maybe get it for them as a gift. Copies are available with special deals and discounts from our own website and from all good bookshops and online outlets.

2. Review it
It's never been easier to write an online review of a book you love and can be done on Amazon, Waterstones.com, WHSmith.co.uk and many more. You could also talk about it or link to it on your own blog or social networking site.

3. Read another of our great titles
We've got a wide range of diverse modern fiction and it's all waiting to be read by fresh-thinking readers like you! Come to us direct at www.legendpress.co.uk to take advantage of our superb discounts. (Plus, if you email info@legend-paperbooks.co.uk just after placing your order and quote 'WORD OF MOUTH', we will send another book with your order absolutely free!)
Thank you for being part of our word of mouth campaign.

info@legend-paperbooks.co.uk
www.legendpress.co.uk